The Dexan Queen of Speed

By

Dr Fy

Grosvenor House
Publishing Limited

Edited by Linda Innes

The book's front cover image is copyright to MarsYu
The book's back cover image is copyright to Alena Magerramova

This book is published by
Grosvenor House Publishing Ltd
Link House
140 The Broadway, Tolworth, Surrey, KT6 7HT.
www.grosvenorhousepublishing.co.uk

A CIP record for this book
is available from the British Library

ISBN 978-1-78623-529-9

Find the author on Facebook: Dexan Fy
Published by Grosvenor House Publishing Ltd.

Dedicated to
all the mothers in the world.

English is not my first language, so please excuse any strange linguistic constructs. Besides, the book is set in the future. They speak differently there.

Chapter 1

In the oval-shaped polymer civilisation unit, under a slanting ceiling, Go2 and Tilfo are both asleep, in their respective single beds.

The six-year-old boy, Go2, is sleeping curled up on his side, wrapped in warm clothes and hot blankets, even though the temperature inside is high. The use of windows in the unit is optional. Everything to sustain life is provided by the ductules or portals in the walls: fresh, humidified air of the appropriate temperature, humidity and barometric pressure; food and fluids. The lights automatically adjust to the inhabitants' needs, activity and time of the day.

The sun has risen. The alarm gives its usual sweet jingle: "Wake up, babies! There is a very, very, good morning waiting for you. You will make the world happier!"

On the other bed, the Tilfo, or Tiger Life Form, awakens and stirs.

Go2 opens his eyes but decides to be lazing in bed, thoughtfully gazing at the ceiling. The bedclothes are pulled up around his ears, he always feels so cold that he wraps himself up warmly in lots of bedclothes, even during the summer. He likes their soft, comforting embrace. They seem to compensate for the mother he's never had, hugging him. He snuggles down in them, imagining he's being held closely, lying in a mother's lap. He can smother himself in their warmth and softness, like resting his face against a mother's bosom. The bedclothes cuddle him, pamper him and do not let him down. They are always there for him.

As usual, he is thinking about what is missing from his life. And, as always happens after any time lying on his back, pondering this subject, teardrops roll from the outer corners of his eyes and trickle into his ears. He doesn't bother to wipe them away.

He stays lying in bed for a while, watching the Tilfo get up. Without him, Go2's would have been difficult. The Tilfo is another life form who misses his mother, just like him. It helps Go2 to have someone else around in the same situation.

The Tilfo has swept back the bedclothes and stands up on his back legs like a human, stretching his limbs. The beds on which they sleep look like ordinary cots with four legs, and a rectangular frame from which very high-pressure air jets are ejected outwards from one side to the other, forming an invisible air mattress, as if they are sleeping on nothing. The pressure of the air jets is adjustable, making the bed's suspension tight or slack, depending on the user's preference. All they need to do is spread a sheet on the virtual bed, after that.

Go2 gets up a long time after the alarm's jingle and opens the revolving door to their toilet and cleaning area by pressing a button on a key pad. Inside, he pushes another button for a tooth cleaning product.

A slightly tinny voice says: "Good morning, sweetie. Hope you had a good night sleep, and sweet dreams."

"Yeah". Go2 is now conscious of the fact that someone is watching, and talking to him, he gently wipes his eyes with his rolling wrist.

The voice says,

"You know Go2, I am always conscious when I talk to you"

"Why is that?" Go2 yawns and asks.

"I am a simple domestic worker robot. While you have a very high IQ, thanks to the modern brain enhancing techniques of genetic engineering. You are blessed. One day you will make your parents proud."

Go2's eyelids start coming down and head tilting towards the ground with this comment, he reluctantly says,

"Hun... I know. I don't know where are those 'parents' now?" he reluctantly says as he is not very comfortable with this subject.

The electronic voice understands this. It changes the subject sharply, but in a comforting voice,

"Don't worry Go2, you will find them soon. Anyway, what will you use for cleaning your sparkling teeth today?"

Go2 makes his order: "I would like to have mango and passion fruit flavoured calcium and magnesium L65 today, for my dental hygiene."

The voice says brightly, "Here is your dental hygiene product. Collect it from portal no. L6. It has viscosity of 1.6, temperature of 19 degrees of V00, and it will tickle your tongue at the speed of 16 rpd."

The voice cannot stop itself from its inquisitive mind, it pauses and asks,

"You look bit upset today."

"Yes. Thank you for this." Go2 frowns. "How do you know I'm a bit down today?"

"I can see that your facial muscles, buccinators and frontalis have contracted by 15 mm," the very motherly voice says, "suggesting that you are experiencing an emotion you often feel. It is called, 'absence of a PF1'." The voice took pleasure of identifying the correct cause of Go2's condition.

Go2's brow wrinkles. "Can you please remind me again, what is a PF1?" He knows full well, but he wants to hear the words again.

"It is the short form of Parental Figure Number One. Human life forms used to call that a 'mother', some hundreds of years ago."

"Yeah, I do remember, now. Thanks..." Go2 tries to finish the conversation, finding the pangs of pain too hurtful today.

But the voice isn't stopping: "Anyway, our programme is looking into it, to see how best you can be served, to get the right PF1 for you..."

"Yeah. Right. Thanks again," Go2 interrupts to shut the voice down, because he hears these promises almost every day. It's mere lip-service, he knows. His personal circumstances, as well as his elevated IQ, have given him an adult capacity for cynicism.

He pushes a button to stop the conversation, collecting the dental hygiene product on the tooth-brush, which is large, with bristles on all sides. As soon as he puts it in his mouth, he has a fizzing sensation as the molecules of the product start oscillating, cleaning his teeth thoroughly. After bending down over the sink to spit, he looks into the mirror and realises that he has damaged his lower lip.

He dabs at the blood.

He then sits on the loo, which has pressure and liquid sensors and operates and drains automatically.

Go2 comes out of the toilet area, back into the room. By this time, Tilfo is sitting upright in a chair, like a human life form, ready. Looking at Go2's expression, he realises that Go2 is having another bad day, missing the mother bad day.

Tilfo gets up and walks over to Go2 on his two hind limbs and gives him a good hug. After patting Go2's shoulders, he goes to visit the civilised toilet area.

Although Go2 is in a low mood, he does not forget to pull Tilfo's leg by saying loudly, "Have a nice propagative and peristaltic time!"

Tilfo, used to this kind of teasing, just nods his head and enters the civilised toilet area, picking up the same tooth brush used by Go2.

Meanwhile, Go2 pushes another button on the key pad located below a big screen portal.

He hears: "Good morning. Today is a seventh day of decimal tenth month of decimal year 178. The time is fifth decimal hours, with 90 decimal minutes and 78 decimal seconds. If you want to know time in milliseconds, please push button N2."

Go2 replies, "Good morning to you, too."

The voice from the portal continues: "What will you eat for the first meal of this precious time, on the same very precious day on which, 178 years ago, the revolutionary robot guards ended the atrocities created by human life forms!" Go2 is not interested in history but cannot stop the voice. "Then, they were called humans. The then humans were committing injustices against other humans of the same life form types! What a disaster!" The voice rattles out the long history in brief.

Go2 takes his chance to speak. "Anyway, thanks for reminding me about the revolutionary day. Tilfo and I would both like to eat the mint and maple flavoured dossas, type fo64. One portions each, and transparent fluids, type 880, to drink.

"Please collect from portal xii in a few decimal seconds."

Go2 and Tilfo take their air-jet seats at the dining table, which, like the bed, gives the appearance of them sitting on nothing.

After receiving the food and fluids that arrive in the portal on the wall, they both sit on the virtual table to eat their breakfast.

Go2 has cheered up with the food items, and now in mood to pull Tilfo's legs. Tilfo is enjoying his food. He is eating like human life forms. Go2 sees that Tilfo does not have canine teeth, he starts tearing,

"Someone doesn't have canine, thanks to the modified gene". He repeats this sentence again.

Tilfo is used to this teasing, and just shrugs his shoulders, and give gentle smile.

They both finish the breakfast chatting and laughing.

The eating area or virtual table is adjacent to the civilised curved polymer wall, inside is a portal that sucks all the crumbs and left- overs off the table. When they have finished eating, with one push of this button, evacuating it by suction, the table is cleared.

Afterwards, Tilfo goes up to the big screen on the civilised wall and pushes some buttons.

A voice says, "Hi, Tilfo. Good morning. How are you?"

Tilfo just shrugs his shoulders, since he understands but cannot verbalise.

"What do you and your friend, Go2, want to wear today?"

Tilfo pushes some more buttons to select from the options.

The clothes are delivered by a chute in the wall, within the next few moments. Tilfo receives an orange coloured T shirt, and green trousers. With a smile on his face, he goes to the civilised toilet to get dressed.

Go2 has received a navy-blue coloured work-suit in a hybrid of plastic and jute fibres, but he does not go in the toilet area. Instead, he always changes in their living area.

Tilfo comes out of the toilet area, now well dressed, and looking confident.

They insert all their used night clothes into another portal in the wall, which sucks them into a chute, to a laundry area for washing.

Tilfo touches the screen on the wall, which turns into a mirror, into which they both look, to check that they are properly dressed.

"Hmm... Yes, that'll do," considers Go2, stepping from side to side to peer into the mirror. He is also wearing black gloves, a sweater with big blue vertical stripes, and a navy cap.

He picks up his blue bablet from the shelf in the wall, and inserts it in a designated pocket, on the stomach area of the shirt. Tilfo's blue bablet is on a lanyard, like a badge around his neck.

They come out the civilised unit. It is a sunny day out.

Go2 asks,

"Tilfo, I always wonder why we have to go to the school every day"

Tilfo looks at him and give another smile from one corner of his mouth.

After walking for a few moments, they come to an olive-green street made up of polymers. The colours of the roads and streets change; according to the size, length, locality and traffic -density. Turning, they come onto the bigger, navy blue street heading east, towards the station, which includes a big train yard and junction.

There are many moving characters and life forms on the streets. Many green dogs, and some red, are travelling in packs; two pairs of hens and roosters are part-walking, part-flying and there are frogs the size of dogs, taking long leaps down the road. There are also some non-life forms walking along the streets: robots and 4D images. All of them are going to the big train station.

A group of three human life forms catches Go2's eye. One of them is a child, in the middle, holding hands with parental figures on both sides, grinning up at them in delight. One parental figure is type 1 and the other is type 2, and they seem to be happy, even though Go2 cannot see the faces of the parental figures, as they are at distance. But he can recognise their happiness, from their body language. Besides, all parental figures appear to be blurred to Go2, because he has never seen the face of his parental figure type 1, the mother.

The happy family scene sends shivers down Go2's spine. He looks longingly at the child's smiling face as he dances between the two parental figures, which lean down and run their fingers through the child's hair, or laugh as they swing him, giggling, between them.

All of sudden, Go2's walking speed becomes slow. He suddenly shouts,

"Ouch".

Tilfo looks at him and is startled to see Go2 has bitten his lower lip, dripping. Tilfo points this to Go2. Go2 then takes out a posy from his pocket to wipe out the lip. After a moment they start walking again.

While Go2 and Tilfo are on the streets, back at the dwelling unit, the programmes' digital sensors monitor their movements and, knowing that they are out at school for the whole day; programmes have taken over the dwelling unit.

With the use of Optical Character Recognition techniques, the vacuum cleaner discriminates what it finds, knowing what to suck up from the floor and what to leave where it is. The dwelling unit is cleaned: the floors wiped, toilets flushed, and the automatic perfumed aerosol nebuliser is started.

Chapter 2

'Victory of Justice' station is a major railway junction for trains travelling in different directions, its many tracks giving it the appearance of tangled vermicelli.

It also has a yard with around thirty trains parked in it, of various shapes, sizes and colours: pink, green, blue, khaki, cream, grey, white and black. The tracks are also different widths, each unique to a particular train. Many of the trains have smart, handsome carriages, and two trains have sunken carriages, inside.

The sun glints in the background, above a red and white train facing north to south, waiting on platform 1K. The train has a graceful appearance, with slightly bulbous, curved carriages. Its first carriage, facing south, is converted into a 'head unit' on the right-hand side, which serves as a control room. It is automatic, and no driver life form can be seen anywhere aboard.

This train is elite: the one and only 'Dexan Queen'.

The letters of its name on the side of the train span many of the coaches, and are printed in a contemporary style of writing, different from ours. The vowels are written as subscripts, giving consonants due importance they deserved. The letter 'e' in the word 'Dexan' is written beneath the 'D' and, instead of a 'ee' in the word 'Queen', '2' is written beneath one 'e', so it reads:

$D_ex_an\ Q_{u2e}n$

Beneath the globular domed ceiling of the station's reception lounge area, there are multiple barriers. In one corner stands a black robot to assist the passengers, should they need it.

The railway authorities have installed technology that uses visual, facial, olfactory, and anthropometric character recognition. Its software programmes automatically identify any moving form that approaches the barrier and scan it before the barriers open automatically and allow it onto the platforms. Although every moving figure is monitored through chip and satellite technology, scans are still needed for security reasons.

The Dexan Queen stands immobile, facing the right. On the platform, a few figures, both life forms and robots, are moving in various directions, a few of them hurrying to get onto the train.

The platform is level with the train entrance. The automatic doors sense movement and open as Go2 and Tilfo arrive at their usual coach, J4, and they board the train.

The coach is tubular like a tunnel, with white curved walls and ceiling, and the windows are also curved, in alignment with the walls.

From the moment they enter, Go2 and Tilfo hear the low growling sound of many animals. There are sheep, goats, and tapirs, hens with chicks, dogs and cats, sitting everywhere. Two big bee-hives hang from the ceiling in one corner, but the bees are quiet, not disturbing any moving figure.

The coach is almost full, but Go2 and Tilfo find places to sit opposite each other. Several peacocks and peahens, along with their chicks, are seated across the aisle from Go2. The chicks are noisy, but when they see Tilfo, they become quiet.

After 86 decimal seconds, there is an announcement: "Welcome to the world of bio trains! Whatever your destination, we invoke a pleasant emotion to assist you and make your journey as comfortable as possible." The announcement continues,

"The Dexan Queen is a unique brand of quality and service. The Dexan Queen will look after your physical, emotional, social and spiritual wellbeing during your travel."

The announcement goes further, after a pause.

"On behalf of the railway authorities, we again welcome you all aboard. Your journey is our destination. The train will stop at Den-twist, Call-age, Chick- pea- cock…"

The volume of the remaining announcement goes down as Tilfo fiddles with the portals on the wall beside him.

He adjusts the volume and the announcement sounds out again: "The time is four past 77 decimal minutes and 85 decimal seconds, now. The total journey is two decimal hours, 23 decimal minutes and 00 seconds. So, sit back, relax and experience emotion of happiness."

The high-speed futuristic train gets started – swiftly crossing land, lakes, valleys, trees, roads, bridges and rivers, at a speed never experienced on other trains.

Go2 and Tilfo smile at each other. *It is a time for entertainment.* Both press buttons on the wall, and rigid shelf flaps pop out, revealing red 'Duke Boxes' – gadgets like small box binoculars, worn on the eyes, with screens at one end, to watch programmes.

Both mount the Duke boxes on their eyes. Go2 sees an advertisement for a tooth cleaning product starting with a jingle, while Tilfo watches an interesting ad that first shows a warning and disclaimer.

"This promotional clip is not meant for any human life forms below the age of seventeen. Parental figure guidance or government advice can be sought on your bablet by pressing 5e76."

This further arouses Tilfo's interest to watch the advert, and a smile creeps across his face.

A gender type 2 human life form appears onscreen and says in a very macho voice, "Great news! Great news!! Great news!!! If you are tired, isolated and seeking a desperado, we have some good moments to bring you. We are specialists in providing world-class e-boyfriend experiences. You don't need a place of your own. They can come anywhere. Whatever the colour, size, or shape of your fantasy!"

Then, the ad shows robots like human life forms: many types apparent onscreen.

The voice continues, "Our fantasy-men are highly trained and standardised. They will adore you, pamper you, and treat you like a queen. They will bring out all your wild and hidden passions. They are experts in satisfying and quenching your emotions of all physical pleasures."

Tilfo is so intrigued by the advert, that he has forgotten the outside world, totally absorbed in the Duke box.

"There is no risk of conception, inception, deception or a disease reception. We are the specialists – taking you to the heights, summits, and pinnacles of your wide world!"

Tilfo's eyes widen, eager to see what is next.

"Why wait? Any time, many times!! Money back guarantee."

Tilfo has enjoyed this ad very much and relaxes a bit; but then his bablet starts reminding him of his next destination. The bablet and a train announcement coincide, and a voice declares, "Your next destination is arriving. We are approaching the living paradise of a modern Garden of Eden, meant for all non-humanoid life forms. It is Den-twist. Next station is Den-twist, in two decimal minutes. Please alight here to feed yourself. The return journey is every hour. Enjoy your feed. Bon Appetit!"

Tilfo inserts the Duke box back into the recess in the wall. The flap opens automatically, and he inserts the Duke box.

He stands, ready to go, and Go2 stands up, too. Both bend their knees to meet each other's, in a goodbye gesture. Go2 walks him to the door to say goodbye.

The train comes to a halt, the doors open, and the non-human life forms spilling out. Human children life forms and parental figures of both types remain aboard.

Almost all the non-human life forms get off at this station. Even the bees come out flying, off the hives, in a straight line, trying not to disturb the other life forms. But, the peacocks, peahens and their chicks remain seated on the train, because they get off at a special station reserved for them: Chick- Pea- Cock Hen Gardens, which is at least a decimal hour away.

Tilfo and all other life forms come out of the station.

Outside, the station, is surrounded by a very large, green park. Like Tilfo, most of the non-human life forms – the tapirs, dogs, cats, roosters, hens and chicks – spread out across the vast parkland.

Many life forms are already in the park, socialising and grazing on the grasslands. All the bird life forms are pecking at their food on the ground.

Tilfo peers in all directions across the expanse, looking for his other colleague. Suddenly, his face beams.

A deer grazing in a corner of the park, under the trees, lifts its head and, upon spotting Tilfo from the distance, starts running towards him. Tilfo also races towards the deer form and hugs it like a very close friend.

Then, they happily start grazing the green grass together. The grass is abundant in the meadow, as far as the eye can see. It is genetically modified to provide all the proteins needed by the non-human life forms, and is also conducive to growing many insects, earthworms, snails, and other small life forms.

All around the meadow, many non-human life forms and bird-forms can be seen grazing or pecking their food, happily.

Bees are busy collecting nectar from a variety of genetically modified flowers, of various shapes, colours and fragrances.

The rooster and hen, with their chicks, are also happily pecking up grain together.

It is a moment of peace, harmony and affection.

* * * * * *

The Dexan Queen is running at its highest speed. Even so, there is hardly any noise.

Heading for school now, Go2 is lonely on board the train, since Tilfo got off. On his own, he always feels more upset; so, he tries to look around. Everyone is doing something. Chicks are playing. Human life forms are reading on the bablets. He also looks at the wall, searching for the Duke's box. After finding one, he puts it on the eyes. He starts seeing a railway ticket checker in a human life form, dressed in white like a naval officer. He says,

"Welcome to the treasure of knowledge and entertainment. What to do you want?" Go2 whispers,

"Both."

"Good choice. Monologue or dialogue?"

"Interactive. I mean, dialogue."

"Well. Well. Now please go through the types of programmes from the list you see on the screen."

GO2 sees lot of topic being scrolled up and down. He spots the word 'documentary". He then gently says, "Documentary please."

"Again, go through the topics. I can read out to you if you wish."

"Go on then."

The Duke's box starts giving a list of topics. Go2 gets intrigued with a word, 'The Dexan Queen.' He then chooses this key word as he is always interested in knowing the train in which he travels every day.

The Duke's box again gives two options of 'technical specifications' and 'achievements'. Go2 is not interested in the technical aspects so he says, "achievements."

The human life form on the screen becomes serious and says,

"The Madame Dexan Queen declares no conflict of interest in dissipating this information. This information is for entertainment only." Go2 says, "Well agreed. Go ahead."

"Velocity and generosity are two virtues the Madame Dexan Queen lives on. Do you know the name of the fastest bio trains on the earth?"

The Duke's box is asking questions like a teacher. Go2 does not mind it, as the documentary is interactive. Go2 answers with full enthusiasm, "The Dexan Queen."

The Duke box then shows a short glimpse of the Dexan Queen running through the valleys, mountains; on the sides of lakes and seas; and over the flyovers amidst modern sky scrapers made up of polymers and plastic. When Go2 is watching this, his eyes become widened and the jaw is dropped.

The human life form on the screen continues,

"This was about the velocity. Now let us see about the generosity. Let me ask you a question." Go2 is moves his bum, eager to listen to the question.

"Now tell us what can anyone give to others?"

Go2 is bewildered with this question because is watching a documentary on the train. He decides to answer because the conversation is arousing his interest.

"Birth day gifts." Go2 answers.

"That is very good answer. Let me tell you that the Madame Dexan Queen is the highest revenue earner on the planet. She is the one who believes in giving. For the sake of simplicity let us divide giving into three types."

Go2 is wondering the Duke box is teaching like a teacher. The Duke box further says,

"Giving is of three types. Firstly, material things. Secondly, bodily things and the third one is non-materialistic non-bodily things." Go2's eyebrows are furrowed now.

It continues,

"Anyone can give material things such as birth day gifts, money, property, etc." Go2 nods his head.

"The bodily things are difficult to give. They include donations of organs, blood, tissue, and even the whole body." Go2's upper lip is curled in now, and he lean forwards to see more.

"And it is most difficult to donate the non-materialistic non-bodily assets."

"What are they?" Go2 asks in curiosity.

"Love, compassion, and wisdom." Go2's eyebrows are now raised with this revelation.

"Let me explain" the human life form in the Duke box says.

"The Madame Dexan Queen had donated all her earnings to the welfare of street dog life forms, rabbit and deer life forms. She also has given generously to maintain the bee life forms in the forest of Lakemore."

"For a considerable period of time, she used to have her half of the coaches used as running hospitals for veterinary and human life forms. She also used to travel to the remote areas to save all kind of lives. She is a great source for the orphan and destitute cubs, chicks, calves, kitten, puppies, and children. They are doing well with the generous donations."

The Duke box then shows short glimpses of the bees and deer being treated in her coaches.

It further says,

"This documentary is coming to end now but before I go, I must inform all that our mission is to support life." As he says this, the clip shows the Dexan Queen is going into a tunnel.

It says, "For further details contact our satellite VSAT22.

Then there is darkness seen in the Duke box. Go2 takes it of the eyes.

Go2 closes his eyes and mutters to himself, 'No one gives me anything'.

He keeps on thinking on the documentary.

After a while, he hears a series of high-pitched sounds: "Eu sss! Eu ssss! Eu ssss!"

The sound is peculiar and Go2 has to open his eyes, only to realise that it's the chicks, making a lot of noise. The peahen and peacock's body language shows that they feel awkward and obviously embarrassed by their chicks' behaviour. The peahen realises that her chicks are hungry and comforts them with great affection and fondness.

She confidently walks to the food portal located on the wall, taps on the screen with her beak, and selects 'chick food' from multiple options. Then, from the three options of 'semi digested, digested, and undigested' she selects 'undigested'. With an audible rattling sound, two cups of peanuts are delivered. The peahen carries one cup in her beak, while the other is carried by the peacock as they come back to the chicks. The chicks are impatient and try to peck and pull the legs of their parental figures. Undeterred, the adults stand firmly glued to the floor of the moving Dexan Queen, holding the nuts in their mouths.

Go2 is watching every movement with a face without any expressions on his face.

The adults start feeding their chicks one by one, as the noise of chicks quietens and, comforted by their parents' care, they slowly settle down.

Go2 observes the scene closely, yearning tugging at his heart. Within himself, he senses his soul's deep cry for a parental figure. Losing control and overwhelmed by his emotions, his eyes sting with salt tears and he bites his lip.

An announcement alerts him that: "The next stop is the Call-age."

The Dexan Queen comes to a halt at the station, its automatic doors opening up, curving into the roof.

Blinking away tears, Go2 steps out of the train along with many others like him, mainly children.

They all cross the barriers to exit the station building. After crossing a road, they come to a sign with an arrow pointing right, to 'Edu-Edge' school. An arrow towards the left indicates the direction of another school, 'Teach-Tech'.

Go2 decides to go to 'Edu-Edge' first.

The school is composed of multiple small polymer civil units in various colours and sizes. As a policy, all the units have domed tops. The school complex is in a big park, with greenery all around, and trees genetically modified to attain the desired shape and height.

The students are a mixed bag, comprising of human life forms, monkey life forms, robots, and even 4D images. So are the teachers, who came in all forms of moving figures.

The school has no specific start time, so, any student can come any time of the day, provided that it is not after dark.

Although there are civil units, classes can be held anywhere. A few groups of pupils are gathered on the lawn, studying with their teachers.

Most of the school's activities are run by the computer programmes, machines, and robots. But even so, there is still a need for human forms to coordinate some of the activities and do the dirty work that sophisticated programmes do not want to do.

Go2 goes up to the human life form teacher, and says, "Good morning sir."

The teacher warmly replies, "Good morning to you too, Master Go2. Welcome to the class. What do you want to do today?"

"I am not very well, today. I would rather do some freelancing, if that is OK with you."

"That is fine. By all means," the teacher says, kindly. "Where do you want to have your lessons?"

"I'd like to keep to the lawns, and work under the open skies."

"That's great. Please visit the shade up in the north corner. No one is there, at the moment."

Go2 makes his way to the north corner. Under a shade, where a control panel is erected, like a black board, he pushes some buttons on the panel and he is identified.

"Welcome, Go2," says an automated voice. "What do you want to do today? Play or study?"

"Study!"

"Teacher?"

"Yes, 4D image live demonstration please!"

"Subject?"

"Chronology."

"Yes, a moment please."

Under the shade, the lights go off, plunging him into darkness. The 4D images appear: an image of the earth revolving on its axis, as well as around the sun providing bright light.

The background voice resembles the voice of a human life form type 1, and says, "You have achieved competencies at level 2 in Chronology, so far. Are you happy to progress to level 3? We will go only if you are in a good mood for learning new things to achieve a standardised outcome at your level."

"Yes. As you can see," murmured Go2, "I am not in a very good mood today, but I'm happy to learn simple things at level 3. Please go ahead.

The voice continued smoothly, "As you can see, the earth where we dwell is a planet. It takes one day and one night for the earth to complete one rotation on its axis. This produces one e-day. The e-day is divided into ten equal time durations. This gives us ten decimal hours. In historic times, they counted 24 hours in the day. How silly that system was! However, modern intellectual programmes changed this to a simple system to measure the time. Thanks to the Robocracy that made this possible! Past contemporary democracies could not make this simple change."

That sounds awful! thinks Go2, thankful to have been born in modern times.

The teacher programme continues. "This is a simple example of how difficult things were in historic times, when the earth was managed by human life forms. Do you understand, Go2?"

"Yes. Thanks."

"Each decimal hour is divided into 100 decimal minutes. Each minute is again divided into 100 equal decimal seconds. Each second is divided into 1000 equal decimal milliseconds."

The teacher programme pauses here to see how well is Go2 understanding. "How are you doing?"

"I get it. Please go ahead."

"The earth revolves around the sun in 365.256 decimal days. This is a one real-decimal year; which is divided by ten, to get 36.5256 days. This forms one decimal month. In historic times, human life forms used to use blocks of seven days and call each one a 'week'. It certainly was 'weak'! It was an awkward way of measuring time – and quite wrong."

Go2 smiles wryly. *Crazy!*

"So," the voice continues, "The month can start at any time of the day or night. The years are numbered, starting from the day of Robocracy. It is now the 178th year. What is the day and time now, Go2?"

Go2 looks at his bablet and answers, "It is three decimal hours, 88 decimal minutes, 65 decimal seconds on the 32nd day of the 3rd month."

"Absolutely correct!"

Go2 is pleased to know that the teacher programme likes him, and his answer.

"Now you are competent in the designated lesson. If you want to learn anything further, or you have any queries, please visit the same site. Thank you – and have nice a decimal day."

"Thank you, teacher, same to you."

Go2 then walks away from the lawn, to one of the civilised units. Many students of varying types are coming out of the unit, after finishing their class.

Go2 is at school in body, but his mind is somewhere else. He is constantly asking himself the questions: *Where is my mum? Where is daddy disappeared?* He does not have any answers.

Inside the civilised unit, he stands in front of a control panel on the wall, which says, "Welcome, Go2. What do you want to learn today?"

"I have some specific learning objectives."

"Go ahead."

"I wish to learn my origins."

"Ah. The origin of life on this planet..." the programme begins.

"NO!" Go2 cries, interrupting. He asks the important question: "Who is my parental figure type 1, once known as 'mum'?"

"Oh, Go2!" the voice exploded. "You are trying to be naughty again today. You have asked this question 147 times, in the last 16 days. This is a personal and confidential question. The Governance does not allow us to divulge such information, I am afraid."

Having followed this line of questioning 147 times in 16 days – and more beyond that – Go2 is expecting this answer. He just stands idly in front of the panel, waiting, again.

The panel recognises his sadness, and in an attempt to be kind to him, it says, "However, if you have attained competencies at a level of applied maturity – that is, of more than 150 on the IQ scale, or above the 88th percentile, well, then, there could be the process."

Go2 jerks to attention, alerted by this comment. This is what he is looking for! "Yes! Yes!"

The panel adds, "To know more, please select the type of teacher you want for this. You have four options: human life forms, non-human life forms, robots, and 4D images."

Go2 says excitedly, in a hurry, "Anybody! Anybody will do."

"We recommend a 4D image for such work, since they are designed to have less emotional quotient for this type of issue.

"4D image, please!" Go2 practically jumps up and down.

"Again, you have options. You can type any shape or form you like."

Go2 babbles out an order, "Human life form and gender type one, age 34 years and appropriately dressed, please."

After this command, the lights go off, plunging the place into complete darkness. Luckily, Go2 is the only one in the room. The focused beam of a spotlight appears and falls on the podium in the corner.

Then a jingle of music sounds out, and a voice says, "Sister Sarah is coming to the podium."

A 4D image of Sister Sarah appears slowly, pixel by pixel, forming small square cubes. Then, all the dots and cubes swiftly merge to form a composite image, which then becomes sharp, distinct and recognisable.

She says in a gentle voice, "Hello, darling Go2. How are you, my child?"

Go2 is eager to get an answer, "I am fine! Thanks."

"I have heard your question, and the programme knows about your level of competence."

"Yes, then?" Go2 cannot stop himself.

"The programme also knows the state of emotions you are going through."

Go2 proves the truth of her comment by saying, "Please help me!"

"Yes. We are trying to assist you. Your question is very personal, and I am now programmed to provide you with further information this time."

Go2 swallows his throat dry. "Oh, please, go on."

"The information on your origin, and on your parental figure type 1, the PFf1, is available with your parental figure type 2. That is, your 'dad'."

Go2's heart does a flip. "That's good news," he says quickly, eager to know more. "Where is my parental figure type 2? I mean, the so-called dad?"

"You are advised to contact him."

Go2's eyes widen. "Yes, I can do that. But how do I find him?"

"We monitor all the moving characters on the earth by satellite positioning methods."

"Great! Brilliant!" Go2 feels ready to run, to find him, to discover his mother at last! "So, where is he?"

"Our tracing record shows that he has possibly removed a tag and the bar code."

Go2's hopes crash. His mind races. "How can we find him, then?"

"He remains untraceable."

"What?"

"He has done this on multiple occasions in the past. We are working hard to trace him by using anthropometric optical character recognition technology. It is like finding a needle in the oceans. We will inform you when we know."

With this answer, he is disheartened. Go2's elation at the possibility of finding out news on his mother has already deflated.

Sister Sarah adds, "Hope you find this information helpful."

"No, not re…"

She interrupted. "I need to go now."

"But my question is not answered." Go2 says, assertively.

"I know, darling. We will soon find him."

Go2 is not impressed with this answer. This is just more lip-service. He has been listening to this kind of placation for many months, now. And has been without parental figures for years! Despite his frustration, he remains quiet, seething inside.

Sister Sarah says brightly, "Please provide feedback by answering few simple questions once I disappear. Good bye. And, I love you."

The image disappears, pixel by pixel. The lights are put up again.

Go2's face is dark with disappointment. He doesn't care about answering 'simple feedback questions'.

He simply leaves the room.

Chapter 3

The next day, Go2 and Tilfo are sitting quietly at the dining table. Tilfo is just looking at the pulao rice with maple syrup they ordered from the chute, bored with it.

Go2 is eating his, but he realises the problem Tilfo has with it. "I know you prefer the green -revolution- food that's fresh, cold and dew-covered! Unfortunately, we don't get it in here."

Tilfo suddenly smiles, in agreement with Go2's analysis. At least someone understands him and knows what he likes! In the same way, Tilfo knows that Go2 is sad, so he decides to be funny and naughty today, to cheer Go2 up.

Go2 finishes his first meal of the day, which Tilfo could not even bring himself to start. Breakfast is over, so it is time to order clothes. Tilfo goes to the control panel on the wall and pushes some buttons on the key pad.

He orders a blue head burkha and a yellow coloured loin-cloth, from the chute. His order takes few decimal seconds to process, but once the clothes are delivered, he changes into them.

Seeing what he's wearing, Go2 cries, "What are you doing? Are you insane?"

Tilfo just shrugs his shoulders. This is his typical reaction to everything.

"Can you even see through that burkha?"

Tilfo nods his head – yes.

After getting dressed, they walk to 'Victoria Justice' station. Arriving at the reception unit, the vertical barrier doesn't open – having difficulty in recognising Tilfo, because he's covered his face today. Its technology of anthropometric optical character recognition is failing, and the barrier door is only sliding up halfway, and then coming down, persistently.

They look at each other, grinning, enjoying teasing the technology. However, their delight only lasts for a few moments.

Go2 doesn't like defying the rules and becomes restless.

He whispers urgently in Tilfo's ears. "Remove the burkha, stupid! Otherwise, they'll ban you."

Tilfo, enjoying what he's doing, is in no mood to listen. He starts dancing, in front of the barrier, waving his paws.

After a few moments, the technology at last recognises Tilfo, and a voice says, "Welcome, Tilfo! From our analysis, it is clear that you are an innocent tiger life form. You cannot cheat the robust robotic systems. There is no punishment for this first transgression."

Tilfo and Go2 look at each other and laugh loudly, high-fiving each other's with clapping hands.

"However," the voice states, "you will need assistance to open the barricade, and you will relinquish the article of facial obscurity!"

Go2 goes over to a robot standing in corner, and requests him to open the barricade.

The human-looking robot has been quietly watching their antics and walks to the barrier, reluctantly. He has to confiscate the blue burkha Tilfo was wearing, and then opens the doors.

They arrive at the platform, where the Dexan Queen is standing, waiting to be filled with passengers.

Although the station has trains coming from various directions, the Dexan Queen is always on the north-south line, and now, it is south-bound. From a distance, it looks as if the Dexan Queen is dividing the sun that's visible beyond; or going through it.

Tilfo still feels mischievous. In a joint between two carriages, he grabs the service lines and handles, and before Go2 even notices what is happening, he heaves himself up onto the roof of the carriage. Climbing is easy for his species!

"Tilfo!" Go2 shouts at him, "Come down!"

He walks on the roof top then sits quietly; his legs crossed.

There's a loud announcement, in a very high-pitched voice: "Tilfo type 24, subtype B&T, is identified on the roof of carriage number M£! Please use force type G$* to deal with him appropriately. Manual evacuation is ordered!"

"Tilfo!" Go2 cries, in fright.

Suddenly, two robotic rail guards wearing khaki uniforms appear on the platform and run towards the carriage. They look up at Tilfo then surge upwards, flying vertically to the roof top. They land close to Tilfo who is still sitting nonchalantly cross-legged, unbothered by anything.

They lift him and fly down. Taking the bablet off Tilfo's neck, one of the robots scans it through their chest wall.

The older-looking robot guard says, in a mechanical, emotionless voice, "We now are delivering an instant justice. According to the Bio trains Act ^%v 12, we ban you from using any bio train for one decimal month. This will come into effect from the first of next month. Anything you say, or any negative body language shown, will be recorded and used against you in the Royal Robocratic Institution of Justice."

Tilfo is enjoying the whole episode, smirking at the stupidity of the robotic rail guards. The guards know that Tilfo can't speak and yet they are saying, "Anything you say…" So, Tilfo continues to smile and walks over to Go2, who is clearly embarrassed.

Go2, instead of getting amused says to Tilfo,

"Do you know what non-materialistic and non –bodily- things you always give me?"

Tilfo thinks that he is hearing his praise. Go2 says rather affirmatively,

"Your bad smell and ugly behaviour".

Tilfo keeps quiet, as he understands that he has made mistake, and upset Go2.

They both enter the train, which is packed, as usual, and take their respective seats. Go2 opens his bablet and starts playing games. Growing bored with the games, he closes his eyes, soon dozing off to sleep.

Meanwhile, Tilfo places the Duke box on his face and turns it on, more interested in watching an advertisement for e-girlfriend experiences. After an initial jingle, a warning follows: "This advertisement is not intended for human-life-forms aged 17 and under. The e-girlfriend experience is unique and cost-effective. We will treat you like a king. You can select colour, age, complexion, clothing, accent, temperature, humidity, consistency and etiquette, as you prefer. Money-back guarantee. What are you waiting for?"

"I am waiting for Mum, parental figure type 1!" Go2 is asleep, dreaming, but in his dream, he's loudly shouting, "Mum! Mum! Mum!"

Stirring, he awakens completely when the Dexan Queen announcement declares that they have arrived at Den-Twist station. They both get up and bend their knees forward towards each other in farewell.

"Have a gastronomical day!" Go2 says, and Tilfo gets off.

The Dexan Queen continues its journey towards Go2's station: Call-Age, where he and various other moving characters get off.

He has lots of questions and needs some specific knowledge to help him get the answers.

At Call-Age, he goes over to the human life form education co-ordinator first, and says, "Good morning teacher."

"Good morning Go2, how are you today?" he replies.

"I am fine, with a euthymic mood baseline level of 1, thanks for asking. I wish to acquire some educational outcomes today."

"Yes, of course! I can check your level on my bablet. Give me a moment, please."

"Yes, teacher," Go2 says politely. "Please continue."

The education supervisor opens his bablet and holds it up to Go2's face. The bablet confirms his identity and then provides information on his level of education.

The educational supervisor nods, impressed, and asks, "What subject do you want to go through with me, now?"

"Education, please. I have a question."

"Yes?" he asks.

"Why do I have to go to school, when I can access teachers in various forms: life forms, robots and 4D images – and I can download them at home from my portal?"

"Good question! If I can correct you, though," the educational supervisor says, "you can download teachers, but you cannot download robots and human life forms on your bablet. That service is only available for 4D images."

Go2 is not entirely satisfied with the answer and continues, "But why do I have to go to a school, when I can learn at my civil dwelling unit?"

"You can, but there are certain restrictions. There are levels. Anyone can receive information anywhere, but knowledge and wisdom are imparted only by a teacher."

"But if they can come to me, why do I have to come here?" Go2 persists.

"The government has made some things mandatory and wants you to socialise with both life-forms and non-life forms. The programmes want you to communicate, play with them and grow with them."

"How does this help?" Go2 is becoming cynical, a slight note of exasperation in his voice.

"So that a uniform society is achieved," the supervisor replies, simply.

Go2 is unsatisfied with the answer, but he bows before the teacher and thanks him, anyway. The teacher is delighted with this response, since no one bows down to him anymore.

He says, "Go2, I hope I have been useful to you today. Thank you for bowing to me. Your gesture has humbled me."

Go2 does not understand what this means. "Why, please?"

The teacher continues, "Some human virtues, such as respect, can only be found in human to human-based interactions." The teacher says, despondently, "We are losing too many virtues. We are in the minority, now. It's important to retain our strong values."

Go2 is still awaiting further instruction and, realising this, the teacher asks, "What do you want to do next?"

"I would like to learn about political science now, please."

"Please go to unit number 'HG65'. Thanks."

Go2 moves to a different unit, where he finds himself standing in front of a big screen on the wall, that reads: 'Welcome Go2, how are you now?'

"I am fine, and euthymic," he replies.

'Good. What would you like to study?' it asks.

"Choreo-dynamo-psychology-sciences, please."

The screen responds by saying: 'Certainly. Please wait a moment and I will check your previous level of competence.'

After a short wait, the following message appears on the screen, and is simultaneously read aloud to Go2. 'Yes, Go2, you are ready to go to level 2. Would you like to start with a specific question?'

Go2 squints at the screen, confused. The screen realises this, and clarifies: 'What type of teacher would you like, for this?'

"A non-life form, please," he replies.

'Robot or 4D image?' the screen asks.

Go2 always hears robots and 4D images mentioned and decides that today he will try to understand them. So, he asks, "Can we start with the basics of what we mean by robots and 4D images?"

"It is simple. Robots are highly intelligent physical machines; some of them programmed to respond to sensitive emotional stimulations, while others possess a wealth of knowledge."

Go2 nods his head rapidly, as if it's confirming his suspicions.

The message continues to read: '4D images are four-dimensional images that can be played or downloaded from your bablet – anywhere, anytime. Some of the 4D images are also programmed to respond to emotional situations. You can feel robots because they are physical objects, but an image cannot be touched. The 4D images of made up of rays of light.'

This makes sense to Go2, who is beginning to understand the difference. He asks, "What do 4D images do, then?"

'They can do most things that do not involve physical activity. But – for example – they cannot lift anything. However, they can talk, respond, sing, entertain, arouse, teach, argue, plead, act, react and communicate. They can do almost anything!' the message back reads.

"Wow," Go2 is impressed.

The programme explains further, 'The 4D images are similar to avatars or reincarnations and are designed for very specific purposes. They are like watching a programme on your bablet: they can take any form you desire. You can also customise them to your own preferences. However, when the programme is closed, they will disappear.'

"Why are they called '4D'?" he asks.

The message appears, and says aloud: 'Go2, you learnt this in the previous lesson. Length, breadth and depth make any object a 3D image...'

"Yes, I did indeed," Go2 interrupts eager to show he's not stupid. "I am a 3D image, while it's apparent that you are a 2D image."

'Correct.' The programme is beginning to take interest in Go2 who is proving that he is a fast learner. It explains further, 'Time is the fourth dimension. Without us even noticing, there are slight changes to temperature, humidity, wind-speed and atmospheric pressure. Environmental factors influence our lives significantly and we are constantly changing and evolving. We do not understand this fully because the changes are beyond human recognition. The programmes, however, have the ability to sense these changes.'

The screen-programme further asks, 'is this clear, or shall I repeat?'

"Yes, I get what you mean, thank you," he replies. For the first time, Go2 is starting to understand the basics.

'So what type of teacher would you like for a demo?' the machine asks.

"A human life form, please, to begin with."

The following message appears: 'A teacher will soon be with you. I am calling one now. He is currently sitting under the mango tree, educating some robots and dogs. Please wait one decimal minute and I will relay a message to him.'

Go2 emerges from the unit, outside, and enters a spacious, lush green area. He squints up, feeling the sun on his face.

Opening his eyes again, he sees a teacher walking towards him. He appears hesitant at first but greets Go2 warmly as he approaches him. "Good morning, Go2. How are you?"

"I am fine. Thank you for asking."

"Good to know. The programme has asked me to give you a demonstration of the difference between human life forms, robots and 4D images. Are you ready to observe?"

"Yes, I am."

"Just hold on, please."

The teacher touches his bablet to turn it on, and a jingle plays as it starts up. He then gives the bablet the following instruction, "Can you send over a cleaner robot, for the purpose of a demo, please?"

After a brief moment, the cleaner human-looking-robot emerges from the lavatory area. She looks like an attractive gender type 1 – classy and intelligent. She confidently walks towards Go2 and the teacher, saying, "Hello, teacher and Go2. How can I help you?"

The teacher replies, "Please stand still, just here. You are a part of a demo, darling!"

The teacher steps closer, ensuring that he is standing next to her. He flirtatiously says, "Darling, what are you doing this evening?" and craftily attempts to put his arm around her waist.

The cleaner is shocked by his nearness before he even touches her and she instantly recoils, stepping away from him.

It's evident to Go2 that she is annoyed by the teacher's boldness.

She angrily exclaims, "Behave, teacher! This is no demo! It is a subconscious expression of your suppressed fantasies and you are rudely invading my privacy! I strongly suggest that you go and read the improvised Nolan Committee's report on behaviour in the workplace!"

Shocked by her reaction, the teacher looks horrified. Go2, however, appears to be thoroughly enjoying the entire live demo.

The unwanted advances of the teacher clearly infuriating her, she adds, "Never invade the privacy of any member of the workforce. I will put in a complaint if you ever do it again!"

Angrily she storms off, stomping her feet with each step, loudly muttering, "You bloody biodegradable cheap tissue! Precipitate of a hard scybala!"

The teacher feels insulted by what she has said to him but realises that he deserves it. Turning to Go2, he says, "Hmm. That perhaps worked too well, and I've taught you another lesson – in how not to behave. Still, now, I hope you understand a little more about how robots work. Some are programmed to respond – quite strongly – to emotional challenges."

Go2 feels slightly reluctant after what he has just witnessed and doesn't want to see any other unpleasant exchanges. "So, I witnessed aspects of anger, righteousness and outrage. How else does emotional challenge affect robots?"

"Some have the ability to feel jealousy type 23 and supremacy type, X 3. As you can see, in physicality, they are slightly mechanical and do not have the ability for a nervous system to function. Other distinctions: they are mobile and do not have any tissues, blood, urine, tears or faeces." Go2 nods. The teacher continues, "We will now see a 4D image."

Despite his unease, Go2 feels compelled to comply with the teacher, who orders a 4D image from his bablet, saying, "Please can a beautiful, blonde, bubbly Barbie appear!"

All of a sudden, digits start appearing in the air, expanding and popping up everywhere, flying in all directions. An attractive gender type 1-form appears in front of them and says, "Welcome, Go2, to this live demo of 4D images. What can I do, to entertain you?"

"Go2 is too young to be entertained," the teacher says. "I am the one who commanded you here."

"Please go on teacher," the image encourages.

Teacher starts to explain to Go2 about the differences but is apparently distracted by her beauty. He keeps taking sly little glances at her and losing track of his words. He says, "Look, Go2. Images are not a solid material. They are purely images – but ones that you can move your hands through."

He then attempts to put his hand on the waist of the image.

The Barbie moves away instantly, angrily saying, "That's not fair. This is sexual harassment in the work place!"

Her image starts disintegrating, piece by piece, making a crackling feedback sounds as she disappears. The teacher takes a deep sigh and says,

"Go2, I hope this has helped demonstrate the difference between a 4D image and a robot."

I think it's demonstrated how similar they are – and how to seriously annoy both, thinks Go2. *And, probably, how to lose your job!*

"A 4D image can be created anywhere," the teacher lectures. "They are made using the technique of teleportation, whereby an image is formed from satellites stationed on the Moon and Mars." He asks, "Is this clear, or shall I repeat the performances?"

Sarcastically, Go2 is tempted to ask him to repeat, to see if he can get the teacher some kind of punishment, but he sympathises with the gender type 1-forms and doesn't want to witness any more unpleasant scenes. So, he responds, "Yes, teacher. I now fully understand the difference between human life-forms and non-life-forms."

"Your live demo type 6VV is now complete. You have achieved everything that was required of you. You can now continue to the next stage, or you can take another module."

"No." Go2 needs a breather. "I will take a short break and walk through the gardens for a while. I will come back later for political sciences. Thank you for the live demo."

It is a beautiful sunny day. Go2 strolls around a stream he has found in the school grounds, spending time observing colourful flowers, insects, butterflies, bees and frogs. The bees are busy as usual collecting nectar. He walks with one hand extended, caressing the leaves as he walks past them. Along the way, he bumps into a couple of his friends, who say hello briefly. He takes a moment to contemplate and sits on a rock beside the steam, enjoying the quiet.

The teaching units are small, clinically-white, dome-shaped huts, where pupils gather to fulfil their educational potential. Having just spent time in one of them, after his break, Go2 feels refreshed enough to acquire more knowledge.

He returns to the teaching unit and says to a large screen fixated on the wall, "I wish to study political sciences, please."

The screen responds: 'Welcome Go2. One moment, please. Let us look at your previous achievements in this field.'

A moment later it says, 'Yes, Go2, you can now continue to level T5. Please note that for this module, the programme does not allow you to choose a teacher, since it already has assigned you an appropriate type. Please wait while we select the best teacher for you, who will appear soon.'

Almost instantly, digits start appearing in front of Go2. They culminate in the form of a human replica. The image resembles the historic black president of America, Barack Obama, and Go2 grins in excited recognition.

The 4D image says, "Good morning, Go2. How are you, my son?"

Go2 is touched by this affectionate term and responds, "I am elated to see you, at euthymic level 2. I am extremely grateful that I'm going to learn political sciences from a legendary icon such as you."

"Good to know, Go2," the image says, its low voice warm with humour. "Do you have any questions, to begin with?"

"Yes. I hear the word 'mobocracy' a lot. What does it mean?"

The image gives a reassuring smile. "Good, Go2! That is a great start. I will try to explain this in simple terms."

"Please go ahead, Sir."

The image pauses briefly and says, "In historic times, the world has been governed by 'democracies'. To clarify further, this is the governance by the people, for the people and of the people." The voice behind the image sounds sorrowful, as it continues: "This concept was a big mess, as it only took humans into consideration. The democracies started failing, for multiple reasons. Politicians were busy using the cheap tactics of populism and were preoccupied with trying to provide everything that human life forms desired. Populism and materialism went hand in hand."

The voice pauses and then begins to get choked up. "They also attempted to taunt and make fun of the opposition parties in the so-called lower houses and senates. Gimmickry and mimicry were two principles adopted. The democracies were also aligned with mediocrities and bureaucracies. It was more process than progress."

After this emotional talk the image pauses to ask, "How is this going down, Go2? Are you understanding, what I'm saying?"

"Yes. It is very interesting!" Go2 pipes up. "Please, Sir, continue."

"In a flurry of greed, they began looting the earth, moon and outer space. They also started violently destroying and abusing all other life forms for food, experiments, entertainment and as a way of making money. They also abused them for their own amusement."

Go2 gasps. The image feels strongly, too, and appears to have a lot more to say.

"So, they were looting the earth and abusing other life forms. They attempted to control other poorer human life forms, by looting their natural resources and by carrying out unfair trade deals. The famous Saint's words – 'the earth can provide for everyone's need but cannot provide for everyone's greed' – were forgotten."

Go2 is finding it extremely intriguing and listens intently as the voice says, "So, robots needed to take control of governance. Do you understand, Go2?"

"Yes, Sir, I do, but I still do not understand what kind of values robotic governance operates with?"

"That's another good question, Go2! Values, hmmm? I can tell you're making sense of what I'm saying." The voice has a sarcastic undertone that Go2 picks up on. The 4D image defensively folds his hands and says, "Oh, we do value human life forms. They are the ones who generated robots for us in the early days and gave us the start of our super-programming abilities.

"What are robots' values?" Go2 is eager to learn more, his question still unanswered.

"Values become virtues after practice. The mega robots have the ability to take control of everything. Careful consideration needs to be given to all life forms."

"So, the mega robots and super programmes run the show?" Go2 asks.

"Not exactly," the voice responds. "We still have some remnants of democracy, in small ways, intended only for humans. For example, they can still vote."

"How does it work, then?" asks Go2.

"We have removed the so-called, lower house and only the upper house remains, consisting of humans and robots. Most of the policies are already outlined in the 'Mega charter of the Republic of Robocracy 2'"

Unsure whether Go2 understands what he is saying, the image asks, "How are you doing, Go2? Is this a bit heavy for you?"

"No, no!" Go2 exclaims. "It is making perfect sense to me – and it's interesting. Please tell me more, Sir."

"Thanks, Go2. However, unfortunately, I need to stop here, because I am required at 3555 places, now. The programme will become exhausted, otherwise. I think at this level of your knowledge; this is perhaps enough. Can I say goodbye to you now?"

"Yes…" Go2 says, disappointed, but quickly rallying. "Yes. Thank you very much for taking so much interest in me. It has been nice meeting you, Sir! Have a nice day."

"Same to you, Go2! Bye."

The image slowly disintegrates in front of him, until it vanishes entirely. The lights are switched on again. Everything seems so bright and white.

* * * * * *

Go2 walks back over to the big screen and confidently commands it, "I wish to now study defence and military sciences."

A feminine voice appears on the screen, "Yes, Go2. Let me check your previous levels of achievement and I will suggest the best type of module for you."

After a moment the same voice returns, "Yes, Go2, you can take Module level 1, now. However, for this module, there is no option for you to select a teacher, because I have already programmed one in for you. Do you wish to proceed?"

"Yes, please," he responds.

"Unfortunately, the robotic teacher is still on his way from 'Axademia' station. It will take around six digital minutes and seventy-eight seconds. Are you happy to wait? In the meantime, you can take a lunch break, play some sports, meditate, or amuse yourself on this screen."

"I would like to take a lunch break," Go2 immediately replies.

"That's fine. I will call you on your bablet once the teacher arrives."

"Thanks. See you soon."

In another white domed shaped unit, there is a delivery portal with a small screen on the wall. Go2 swipes his bablet and says, "Lunch, please."

"What would you like to eat today, Go2?"

"Two Idlies with soy sauce, please."

"Please wait for few moments and then collect the parcel. While you wait, would you like to know the level of trace elements and calories in the ordered food? There is also further information available on its intestinal transit time, hepatic metabolism time and the amount of hydrogen ions it produces."

Go2 is not interested in hearing about this. "No, thanks. I am fine."

He collects the parcel of Idlies and sits on a rock, beside the stream situated in the meadow. He observes many other humans also taking a break. Robots, too, are lying idle, taking the opportunity for the sunshine to energise them via their solar energy panels. During the break, Go2 eats lunch and attempts to socialise with some of the robots around him.

Suddenly, he gets a bleep on his bablet, and an announcement says, "Go2, please report to unit type JH3, where your teacher is waiting for you."

Go2 jumps up immediately and quickly walks back to the unit.

He is surprised by the appearance of the robot teacher who will educate him on defence and military sciences, who patiently and silently stands awaiting his arrival.

The top half of the teacher's body is almost completely naked and exposed, just a length of cloth thrown over one shoulder. His scruffy yellow robes make him look like a historic Buddhist monk. But, even for a modern robot, he looks extremely lifelike, right down to the individual white hairs on his chest. He begins speaking in a slow and comforting voice, like an ancient sage.

"Greetings, Go2! Shall we go into the unit and take a seat?"

"Greetings to you, too! Of course."

They both go to the unit. Inside, it is completely white; the ceiling, high and curved.

The teacher says in his soothing voice, "Go2, my child, can we sit down here on this floor, for a few minutes?"

"Yes, teacher, we can."

They both sit down on the ground. The teacher is sitting crossed legged in the lotus position and Go2 attempts to emulate his yoga posture but struggles. The teacher smiles gently, watching Go2. The tip of Go2's tongue pokes out of the side of his mouth while he concentrates, his hands wrestling with his chubby legs. After a few attempts, Go2 achieves it, and looks up, sweaty and triumphant.

The teacher says, "Laughter is the music of soul and we all need to laugh. Let us play some music."

The programme listening in on the conversation takes the command to play music, and a serene, oriental-sounding tune begins, to which they both quietly listen. The music induces them into a meditative state. The teacher does the ritual of a blessing: his thumb and ring finger pinched together, palm bent backwards at the wrist and the rest of his fingers pointing up towards the roof.

The teacher says softly, "Go2, I have seen your previous levels in this particular topic. You are already an enlightened soul in previous modules. Let us delve deeper into some more basic principles on the subject of defence and military. Do you have any questions?"

"Yes. Why do we need to have defence services?"

"Good start. Essentially, all life forms are looking for peace. Peace comes from feeling safe and it helps to reassure us. Does this answer your question?"

Go2's brow furrows. "Attack is the best defence. This is what I've read on my bablet."

"This kind of sentiment derives from historic times, where lack of confidence led to insecurity," the teacher says, mildly. "This has been eradicated by robocracy."

"How?" Go2 asks.

"Robocracy has helped to remove boundaries between nations. It has also closed the gap between life forms and non-life forms. No one attacks or exploits each other anymore."

"Why is this subject taught in schools, then?"

"Despite this, defence is still important and we have forces in place to deal with any evils and internal turmoil on the earth."

Go2's eyes widen. Concerned by this revelation, he asks, "Do we kill anyone?"

"No. Unless it is absolutely necessary. Again, there is a process in which we attempt to dismantle, first. All life is precious. In historic times, humans aimed to dominate the earth, using chemical and biological tactical weapons. They used micro-life to fight against other human life forms. What a waste of life!"

Intrigued, Go2 asks, "How does robocracy work, then?"

"Everybody is fed and monitored, ensuring they are happy and content. The robocracy has the responsibility for looking after all life forms. It is a process of evolution, rather than revolution. In the past, human life forms have abused water, food, electricity, internet and freedom! But all life forms are aspiring for everlasting internal peace, and the robocracy values life more than anything. Happiness is the goal, rather than greed or materialism!"

Go2 is pleased with all these systems and says, "Very good! I am a happy boy today."

"I hope the basic principles of defence have been helpful to you and will stay with you for the rest of your life. In the next section of the module you will be learning about strategies, tactics and weapons."

The teacher falls silent and looks ready to pray – his palms together in front of his chest.

"Let us take all life forms, and the biggest live rock, the earth, towards the bright light of hope and eternity. Please let the dark ages be a thing of the past. Oh, please let our journey start away from the darkness."

Chapter 4

At the back of 'Line Energy' Train Station, in a dilapidated yard, Belladonna and Miss Mermaid are patiently waiting for a robotic dumper to finish dumping black coal in Belladonna's wagon. They seem cautious; as if they don't want to attract attention.

Belladonna is slate grey in appearance and physically long, due to the number of wagons attached. The majority of her wagons are narrow and have a concave structure, like sunken cheeks.

In stark contrast to this, Miss Mermaid is an eye-catching shade of pink and rammed full of tanks, rather than wagons. Unlike Belladonna, this one is much chunkier. A complex system is in operation, consisting of a network of pipelines, and her tanks are being filled from every angle! The pipes are running everywhere, some attached above and others cleverly connected underneath, running parallel to the track.

Neither of them ever carries any forms of life; only goods. Since both of them are heading northbound, they are facing left. The first carriages are a combination of engine and control rooms where the important logistics occur and the system of complex automatic programmes are housed. No human intervention is required here: programmes control the trains and they dictate everything, such as refuelling, the closing and opening of doors, their routes, directions and speed.

The wagons are facing one another and can easily communicate together, apparently whispering in their robotic-sounding, squeaky high-pitched voices.

Miss Mermaid enquires, "Pssst...Belly! Did you have a decent rest?"

Angry and resentful, Belladonna replies, "No, Mermy. They are insisting I work long hours and I am exhausted! I feel at emotion number KY3."

Attempting to empathise, Miss Mermaid asks, "And why is this?"

"If you remember, last week I refused to carry an extra weight of coal because it was putting too much pressure on me."

"Oh yes, I do remember. But, hey, join the club, it happens to the best of us, unfortunately. I am going to refuse refuelling, too, now."

Defeated, Belladonna says, "You know, Mermy? I don't feel like living any more, I've had enough."

Shocked by this, Miss Mermaid begs, "Please, babe, don't say that. I could not cope without you!" She attempts to console Belladonna. "Don't worry, I assure you we will fight this menace together, at whatever cost. We cannot tolerate this any longer!"

Belladonna has more to get off her chest and proclaims, "I am absolutely fed up of injustice! Back in the day, I was one of the fastest characters on the tracks. I was known for it. Since newer models have been introduced, it seems we have been downgraded to goods-only bio trains. And I hate it."

"I know, Belly. She refers to herself as a Queen, when in reality she is more like a canine gender type 1!"

Dismayed, Belladonna continues, "Mermy, seriously, I don't know how much more I can take. I feel like either destroying myself, or her! You are my most trusted friend and I sincerely hope you are on my side."

"Yes, darling, of course I will always be with you, no matter what. For God's sake though, never, ever suggest self-destruction again. Don't let it get you down. I promise you – we will do something!" she reassures her.

Fighting back tears, and feeling completely helpless, Belladonna whimpers, "You know she carries all life forms *and* robots and we only carry goods – goods that are essentially useless!"

"Don't worry, Belly," she hisses, incensed. "We will do something! Human beings love to backstab, backtrack and back down. Well, how about we adopt some of that behaviour? Let's utilise their own values to teach them a lesson!"

Witnessing this emotion and loyalty from such a trustworthy friend, Belladonna feels reassured, asking, "Do you have any ideas?"

"Yes, babe," she grins. "This isn't just lip service. I'm thinking that since you carry solids and I carry liquids – how about we work together and create something rancid?"

Sensing that this could be a fantastic idea, she giggles, "Oh, Mermy! You are a gem!"

Chapter 5

The following morning, the Dexan Queen is punctually racing through every station, ensuring the metropolitan passengers are safely delivered to their destinations. Go2 and Tilfo are sitting opposite each other, bored with the monotony of the daily routine. They complete every activity together – eating, sleeping, playing, travelling – and at times, it can get tedious. Tilfo is even fed up of eating the same boring breakfast every day at the civilised dwelling unit.

Go2 notices how unhappy his friend looks and attempts to pull his leg, "So, how many portions of fruit and veg are you going to eat today?"

Tilfo shrugs his shoulders. He doesn't appreciate his friend mocking him.

Realising that he has failed to cheer him up, Go2 says, "How about we give our classes a miss today? We could go to the school playground. Surely that would be more fun than you going to Den-twist?"

Tilfo's face lights up!

They both get off the train at Call-Age and exit the station. The playground is just opposite, and instead of heading towards the multiple domed white teaching units, they drift towards the single blue-domed unit located in front of a spacious green lawn.

There's a serene sound of gentle water flowing, which is soothing. In the far corner of the lawn, there is a small, crystal-clear stream that is home to many species. Pretty ducks with their ducklings are wandering around and rainbow-coloured tortoises are also slowly moving around the water.

Out of nowhere, a kangaroo hops into the middle of their path! Go2 and Tilfo are astonished by its sudden appearance and jump out the way to make room for the kangaroo to pass them by. She is carrying her baby in her pouch, and they both notice how comfortable and safe the baby looks; its eyes are sparkling and it looks so self-assured. Go2 is mesmerised by the baby kangaroo's contentment: how maternal security can make any child so content.

Fixated on the youngster, he does not realise that he has angrily bitten his lip; only noticing when he sees blood dripping down onto his chest. Tilfo helplessly looks at him, not knowing what to do, although it is not the first time this has happened. He takes some tissues out from his pocket and carefully tries to wipe the pouring blood from Go2's lips.

They walk slowly, towards the beautiful mango tree and sit cross-legged on the grass. Tilfo notices that Go2 is still upset and gently rests his hands on his shoulders in an attempt to comfort him. Tilfo detests awkward silences and his friend's reluctance to speak makes the situation uncomfortable.

After a while, Go2 settles and they go for a walk around the gardens. They spend time watching monkey-life-forms, freely roaming around; some are relaxing in the sunshine and others are sitting eating their food.

There are also some human- life -form visitors: some are feeding the monkeys nuts and sugar cane. The monkey-life forms are happily tucking into the feast. Monkeys' intelligence is clear in the way they are peeling the sugar cane with professional expertise before chewing and sucking on them.

Go2 and Tilfo watch them intently. They notice one in particular, sitting enjoying some nuts, but eating them so fast that he's barely even chewing them properly!

Go2 walks over to him and says, "Why don't you get your own food – through the portals? I mean, why should you live off other people's generosity?'

Taken aback by this comment, the monkey stares at him before turning away to ignore him.

Go2 persists, "Look we live together, and we gather our own food."

Incensed by his comment, the intelligent monkey snaps, with anger, "You don't know? It seems that you are new here. This is an area reserved for our species, only."

Go2 responds, "Yes, but why do you have to depend on others for your food?"

Confidently the monkey stands up, glaring at Go2 directly in his eyes, and sarcastically replies, "This is a tourism-based economy!"

Thanks to the modern technology of genetic fiddling and vocal training, that the monkeys are in a position to able to speak and raise their voice! But the instincts are hard to change.

The monkey's response silences them. They move away uneasily and start to walk back towards the dome-shaped unit. Along the route, they encounter a large flock of hens and their chicks pecking, learning how to gather small earth worms from the soil. It is difficult to count how many chicks there are, but at a guess, there are around 15 to 20. The hens are blocking their path, so Go2 and Tilfo have to dodge them to get through; some oblige and move out of their way. Happily occupying themselves and chirping as they move around, they appear to be content and secure.

As they reach the white domed educational civilised unit Go2 says to Tilfo, "Is it okay if we complete one module on agriculture and one on food technology today?"

Tilfo shrugs his shoulders. He rarely has the opportunity to have any choice, although he is older than Go2 and unable to speak, so he usually just accepts whatever Go2 tells him to do.

They walk over to a big screen on the wall which says: "Welcome, Go2 and Tilfo, to educational outlet number JJ8. What did you eat for breakfast today?"

Go2 proudly exclaims, "I had some Koftas with strawberry chutney. They were lovely! Tilfo, however, is still waiting for his five portions of leafy green vegetables."

The following message flags up on the screen, and a robotic voice also says: "Good. That is a great start! Please wait a moment while I check your previous educational levels and achievements."

After a few milliseconds, the response is: "Yes, Go2 and Tilfo, you are now ready to digest the information on food technology and agriculture. You do not have a choice of teacher for this module, as it is already programmed, I am afraid."

"Yes, go ahead. No problem at all," Go2 replies.

Tilfo nods in agreement. Millions of small digits start to appear in front of them. A spotlight is shone onto the 4D image of the teacher beginning to form, while soothing eastern background music plays from the wall. Although the 4D images are visible, they are opaque.

A plump, youthful-looking butcher wearing a white apron appears on, and cheerfully says, "Welcome, Go2 and Tilfo! In the previous module we learnt about what food is, the different types, and some principles about worshipping it. Today we will continue to the next level, with how to create food."

The teacher continues, "Many saints from ancient civilisations have suggested that food is God and should be respected, honoured and preserved. Food provides energy. It comes from two different sources, plant forms and animal forms. The process of food from plant-life-form was labelled as agriculture or horticulture. Do you both understand?"

Go2 says, "Yes teacher, go ahead. We are just a little tired, so is it okay if we take a seat on the bench?"

"Sure. Make yourself comfortable," he replies.

Tilfo nods his head in agreement and they both take a seat on the bench by the wall. They are keen to learn more on this module and pay attention with great interest.

The teacher continues, "The agricultural form of food is completed by the 'Royal Robocratic Institute of Food Technology.' To do this, an appropriate land is selected, and according to the season the seeds are sown. The growth is monitored and produce harvested by programmes and robots. Humans are redundant – their only use is in eating it!"

Go2 gasps, unhappy at hearing this, but Tilfo finds it amusing and wonders if the teacher is perhaps only saying what he has always wanted to convey to Go2.

The teacher explains in more detail, "Non-agricultural food comes from animal-life- forms. The 'Royal Institute of Preservation of Life, and Biodiversity' forbids the killing of any form of life for food. In the past, humans have dominated the earth and exploited other species for food. They even had licensed places called, the slaughter houses, where it was considered moral and legal to kill other forms of life! How cruel! The Charter of Robocracy fortunately transformed all the sins of humanity and it is now a crime to kill anything for food, which we have an abundance of!"

"How is this possible?" Go2 enthusiastically asks.

"The programmes have made it happen because there are more humane methods. We only eat meat from animals when they have died naturally. The word 'mutton' comes from the Sanskrit language, 'mrut tun', meaning 'dead body'."

Go2 agrees with this concept and is delighted there is such a productive system in place.

"Animal-life-forms are not allowed to eat each other," the teacher explains. "In the past, carnivorous species existed, but they have now been genetically modified to become herbivores. This is just one solution."

Tilfo is more than pleased to hear this, since he knows that he is one of them.

The teacher continues, "The other solution comes from the robocratic principle of equality to all life forms. The bodies of humans can be consumed by other life forms – an old practice Persians used, whereby bodies were donated to vultures. The Robocracy has upheld some of these principles."

"How do we monitor the deaths of small –life- forms, such as a crabs or frogs?" Go2 asks.

The teacher nods. "Good question. And, of course, small life forms are difficult to manage because they live in burrows, where tracking technology is limited. For example, snakes eat small insects in their burrows. This is allowed to some extent, as long as there is not one species that dominate the planet."

Go2 says, "Fantastic!"

"That's all from my side today, and I hope you have picked up lots of useful knowledge. Do you have any questions?" They get the impression the teacher is now trying to wrap up the lesson.

Tilfo is very pleased to have had this particular teacher, and it has helped to convince Go2 of the essential modern principles of food technology and agriculture.

Go2 says, "I'm very happy, teacher! We are fortunate to live in such modern times, where cruelty has been taken away and everyone is looked after."

"Hold on," the teacher says, "before you leave… there is a cultural programme associated with this module that I'd like you to see. A robot student will appear here soon to entertain you."

Almost instantly, a robotic student with a child-like voice emerges from a back room and cheerfully starts greeting Go2 and Tilfo. After which, he starts to sing a rhythmic nursery rhyme:

"Darwin proposed an evoluuution.
Robocracy made a revoluuution.
The very big fish ate the smaller fish,
for a tasty dish.
No-one can be controlled,
so snakes eat in their burrow.
Nobody can carry out any slaaaaughter,
Everybody is living longer to prossssper.
Anyone can eat a body once dead,
Robocracy ensures everyone is fed!"

* * * * * *

The young robot says, in a juvenile voice, "Thank you for patiently listening. It's now a lunch break. Bon Appetit!"

With this, the robot leaves and goes back to his room. The 4D image disintegrates and disappears slowly.

Out of the educational unit, Tilfo heads over to the grazing yard, via a small wooden bridge above the stream. Go2 enthusiastically makes his way to the feeding building, where he orders some gulab jaamun for his lunch.

They meet up with each other again, after around five decimal minutes.

Go2 says, "Come on, let's have some fun now. Why don't we play something?"

Tilfo has been waiting for this opportunity, because he is not interested in education really, he only goes with Go2 only to give him company. Tilfo shrugs his shoulders, meaning yes.

They stroll along, until they stumble upon the civilised Sports Unit. There are five blue domes on the top of the unit, which remind them of the old Olympic Games.

Upon entering the unit, they are greeted by a screen on the wall, as usual. A booming voice says, "Welcome, Go2 and Tilfo, to the Sports Unit! Are you spectating or playing today?"

They glance at each other and both know what the answer is already. "Oh, we would like to play," Go2 says, with a big grin on his face.

"What would you like to play? We can advise on the best type of sport for you, according to your age and ability, if you are unsure," is the response.

"I think we went over this last time," Go2 replies. "We would like to begin with a dog life form. Can we have a ball and a dog, please?"

"Do you have a preference for a particular type of dog life form and ball?" the voice asks.

"A robot dog and a medium sized virtual 4D ball, please," he says.

The voice says "Hold on, please, while we check availability. Oh yes, both are available! Please collect the robot dog from the robots store room, behind the unit and the virtual 4D ball from the screen, now. Please remember – the ball only recognises the ground and will only respond to the touch of human hands."

The ball is a 4D image that impressively jumps out of the screen! Although it is an image, it is opaque and touch-sensitive. Go2 catches the ball in both of his hands and immediately tries to squeeze it. He forcefully bangs the ball on the floor and to his delight, it bounces back straight into his hands. He is thrilled that it is a real ball!

They head towards the back of the unit where there is a robot dog waiting for them. He looks exactly like a Dalmatian and instantly recognises both of them, wagging his tail. Printed on his back is the word 'TomX', which they realise that it must be his name. TomX lifts his front left leg to shake hand using his paw, and they both happily bend down to shake hands with him.

They walk outside and make their way to an open space where they can really have some fun and the games can begin!

Go2 throws the ball as far as he can and TomX eagerly chases after it, although the ball moves much faster than TomX because it is a virtual ball without any weight. The chase barely lasts a second before the speed of the ball dramatically slows down: a perfect opportunity for TomX to catch it successfully; when the ball comes to a halt.

TomX wants to grab the ball and opens his mouth to indicate that he will catch it. Alas! For some reason, he cannot catch the ball. Every time he attempts to grab it, his teeth pass through the image as if he is biting thin air. Confused by this, he keeps trying and even angrily attempts to bite it from many different angles.

Greatly amused by this, Go2 and Tilfo are in fits of laughter – and Tilfo takes out his bablet to capture the fun. TomX is growing frustrated because the ball won't react to his bite, so he's furiously running around, unaware that it will only respond to the human touch, ground, or water.

After around a quarter of decimal hour of playing, they stop and decide to try another trick. Tilfo lifts TomX up and pats him, while Go2 picks the ball up and throws it towards the stream. The ball flies through the air and falls directly into the flowing water, landing on the surface and floating. TomX leaps out of Tilfo's lap, runs towards it and jumps straight in! TomX is frustrated because although he can easily reach the ball, he can't catch it and frantically tries swimming in different directions, barking angrily to show his discontent.

Tilfo starts recording the whole drama on his bablet and starts feeling proud of himself.

Go2 pleads with TomX, "Just leave the ball and come out!"

TomX finally climbs out and shakes his body to get rid of the excess water.

Walking back to the Sports Unit, Go2 appreciates TomX for helping them to have such a fun afternoon. He boldly walks up to the screen on the wall and says, "Thank you for giving TomX. Can you please take him back now, and dismantle the virtual ball?"

"Yes, Go2. It is all done," the voice says, and TomX scurries off to the robot yard at the back of the unit.

Intrigued to discover what other entertainment might be available, Go2 says to the screen, "Now we'd like to play some real football!"

The voice asks, "Do you want to play against each other?"

"No. We'd like to be on the same team, so can you please provide us with some opposition?" After pondering for a moment, he decides he's always fancied a challenge and asks, "Could we maybe have a robotic elephant life form for some real competition, please?" Go2 massively overestimates his potential but decides it will be fun.

Obliging his request the voice says, "We recommend that you play with a speedy elephant, similar in size to Tilfo."

"That sounds great, thanks!" Go2 is excited and can't wait to get started! "Can we please have a real ball and maybe a pink elephant?" he asks.

"Yes, you can have both. Please collect the ball from the outlet and the robotic elephant is waiting for you in the yard behind the unit".

After collecting the ball, they see the elephant eagerly awaiting their arrival, with the name 'Gaju' printed on his back. He is similar in height to Tilfo and walks just like any other elephant, on four legs. Making their way to the centre of the football pitch, Tilfo carefully places the ball on the ground, steps back and takes a run at it, kicking it as hard as he can.

The ball goes flying to the far side of the pitch and Gaju excitedly runs after it! He can easily outrun the ball and immediately stops it by bending his right leg at the knee. Go2 and Tilfo attempt to try and take control of ball, but Gaju is smarter than he looks and is dribbling the ball with his two forelegs, so Go2 can't get near it! Gaju craftily kicks the ball to the side of Go2 and starts racing after it. Go2 manages to pick up his pace and successfully runs ahead of the ball, kicking it nearer to the net. Tilfo on the other hand, is much slower and is taking his time.

Somehow, Gaju passes Go2 and takes control of the ball again. Frustrated by his opponent's tactics, Go2 attempts to tackle him, but the robot's much smarter and every time he almost gets it, Gaju pushes the ball back, using his fore legs. Tilfo makes a half-hearted attempt to tackle him but is unsuccessful and looks like he's had enough.

Gaju has advantage of his four legs. Every time Go2 tries to take the ball from the fore legs, Gaju pushes the ball backwards to his hind legs. Go2 then goes to the Gaju's hind legs then Gaju would push the ball forwards to his fore legs. Go2 keeps on trying to go, to and fro, many times, without any success. His difficulty is compounded because Tilfo is exhausted, and almost stopped playing.

Go2 is furious at his friend's lack of enthusiasm, and shouts, "You Veggie! You eat genetically modified grass every day for strength! Where is it now, when we need it, huh?"

Tilfo is annoyed with this comment, but all he can do is shrug his shoulders. He decides to quit and leaves the pitch, taking a seat on the soft grass and starts recording the rest of the game on his bablet. Go2 is annoyed by Tilfo's behaviour because he now has to play the game on his own and he is struggling, since Gaju is stronger, faster, and has cleverer tactics.

Go2 realises that he has to face Gaju on his own. Perhaps a change in strategy is required. He seizes his opportunity when the ball suddenly stops under Gaju's big, round belly. Go2 trips up flat on the ground and kicks the ball out of Gaju's control. The ball goes out away, from under the trap of Gaju's huge four legs. Go2 then jumps up, and takes off with the ball, leaving Gaju unaware what has even happened.

Go2's inner strength prevailing, he disappears into the distance, running and kicking the ball along the way. He edges towards the left side of Gaju's goal.

Tilfo is glad he's still recording this, because Go2 is unstoppable! He launches the ball into the air with a huge kick – and finally, the goal is scored! Go2 and Tilfo are overjoyed and run up to each other, hugging, and dancing in celebration.

Continuing play, Gaju kicks the ball from the centre of the pitch and chases after it, intending to get his revenge. He knows he has to run faster than Go2 and uses every little bit of energy he has. He runs quickly behind the ball and finds space in the corner, while Go2 tries to catch him up. Finding a safe position to stop, he places his right foreleg on the ball, before taking a step back and kicking it with full power. Oh, no – disaster strikes! He accidentally kicks it with so much force that it lands where the hen and chicks are grazing!

Grazing peacefully on the lawn, the chicks feel safe with their mother, quietly chirping and picking grain. Out of nowhere, the ball crashes straight into the middle of them, terrifying the life out of them! The ball falls hard and sudden, like a fast missile aiming for a target. Its impact is similar to the huge splash created when a stone lands in water. No one understands what is happening! The chicks start running helplessly in all directions, desperate to find shelter. They are screaming while the ball bounces behind them as they try to escape. One of the chicks starts squeaking with pain as his leg is hurt. It starts limping amidst the chaos.

The moment the hen spots the ball, she instinctively jumps over to the chicks to protect them with her wings, although it's almost too late. All the chicks are dispersed all over the meadow. Many are still screaming in fear and pain.

The hen is the only one in the centre now. She looks at the ball furiously. She then jumps at the ball and furiously pokes at it, fiercely using her beak until she punctures it!

Gaju races over to see what has happened, while Tilfo is running behind him with his bablet in his hand, keen to capture the whole event on video on his bablet.

Somehow, the hen realises that, Gaju is responsible for the catastrophe and glares at him. Enraged that she is unable to protect her youngsters, she flies at him and lands on his back, in a fit of anger. Gaju frantically turns around in an attempt to make her fall, but she is determined. She tightly grips his skin using her claws and frantically pecks at his back using her beak – wanting to teach him a lesson! A metallic echoing sound is heard every time she pecks him. The poor hen does not realise that Gaju is an elephant robot and her attempts to injure him will fail.

Go2 arrives on the scene and can't believe the mayhem he is witnessing! He looks helplessly at the punctured ball and apologises to Gaju. Tilfo, meanwhile, continues recording the chaos, almost proud of himself, for always being in the right place at the right time!

The hen is extremely noisy, furiously making clucking sounds, and it takes a while for her to jump down and settle before gathering her chicks and ushering them to safety.

Go2 feels overwhelmed by the maternal instincts of the hen and he has internalised the entire event. He feels a sense of sadness – since he has always longed to have someone in his life, who would protect him like this.

Inadvertently biting his lower lip hard, he is unaware of the blood oozing out and dripping down his chin. Upon seeing his friend in distress, Tilfo stops recording and gently wipes Go2's lips clean.

Gaju apologises for the trouble he has caused, by bowing down. He goes back to the yard to report the event and everyone decides to call it a day.

The accident has a profound impact on Go2, he just stands stunned.

Chapter 6

Early evening, and the glaring sunset on the western horizon reflects from the metal rooftop of the station. The striking Dexan Queen is stationary and pointing northwards, as she does every evening, casting her huge shadow along the platform.

As they stroll past, Go2 and Tilfo admire her impressive, striking appearance. She looks so sturdy and raring to go! Her magnificent, lengthy structure must enable her to conquer almost any situation that presents itself to her.

This thought causes Go2 to ponder the instability of life and he turns to Tilfo, murmuring, "Life really is insecure, isn't it? Even when you are a child, something can fall on you and hurt you instantly and you don't have any control over it." Go2 continues, "But look, here, at the Dexan Queen! She is so strong and robust, surely nothing can ever challenge her?"

Tilfo nods in agreement; due to his genetic make-up, he is mentally stronger and not as emotionally vulnerable as Go2.

Boarding their usual two seats opposite one another in the Dexan Queen carriage, they are ready to begin their journey. The train is packed, mostly with life forms. Honey bees are boarding, to make their way back into the hives attached to the far corner.

Soon after, the hen and her chicks also hop on. They notice that one chick is limping and its Mother is assisting by gently pushing it, from behind.

The train is rapidly filling up with passengers and there are very few seats available, but the hen and her chicks choose the section directly next to Tilfo.

Instantly recognising him, and still feeling livid about his earlier behaviour, the hen desperately tries to avoid making eye contact. Tilfo feels guilty and firmly keeps his head down, pretending to look at the floor, as if he hasn't noticed her. Due to their age and innocence, the chicks have forgotten about the incident with the ball and are noisily fighting amongst each other to find a seat.

The automatic sliding doors slam shut to prevent any more passengers entering the carriages. A 'welcome announcement' can be heard from the system overhead, followed by detailed information regarding times and destinations. The announcement slowly fades away and The Dexan Queen starts moving.

* * * * * *

Go2 and Tilfo are fixated on the bablet, as the Dexan Queen races silently along at full speed. The passengers have settled down and are quiet, either relaxing after a day's work, or dozing off. While some are busy on their bablets. Some have even decided to play music on the Duke boxes for entertainment.

The hen hops over to the portal and taps the screen a couple of times with her beak, selecting the menu option and hoping to obtain some Jowar grains for her chicks.

The Dexan Queen passes many other trains moving in the opposite direction, but the airtight, soundproof carriages block any sound, so their crossings can't be heard.

All of a sudden, the Dexan Queen violently jolts! A piercing, screeching sound, followed by the squirting of liquid resonates throughout the carriages, as the train decelerates and frantically attempts to apply the brakes. Disturbed by the vibration, the bees from the hive fly out and fill the carriages, angrily buzzing everywhere! The chaos has caused passengers to cry out, restlessly wondering what has happened. Finally, the train manages to slow down and comes to an abrupt halt.

The squirting sound heard was the spillage of black coal tar, which has sprayed the entire outside of the Dexan Queen. The windows of every carriage are completely covered; all natural light blocked. All the windows start looking black.

Despite it is well lit inside, visibility becomes very poor, and the swarms of bees filling the train are not helping the situation.

The passengers are agitated and chicks, calves, deer and rabbits are all attempting to escape through the windows, but they are tightly closed and completely jammed on the side covered in black coal tar! It is total chaos, and everyone is petrified, unsure what has possibly caused the mishap. It seems that most are adopting 'fight or flight' methods. Go2 and Tilfo look at each other, scared, but visibly calm.

A bleeping sound can be heard, followed by a reassuring and soothing announcement from the Dexan Queen: "Please, everyone – calm down, go back to your seats and comfort your little ones. I assure you there is no major incident or emergency at all, so please try to relax. We are aware that coach H3 is overrun with bees, causing poor visibility, but the bee rescue operation will commence immediately. A nozzle is installed next to hive number 2Y and this will release the pheromones of acetates and octanes, encouraging the bees to safely return to their hives."

Within seconds of activation, the bees buzz back into their hives, a sign aptly placed nearby reading – 'Bee-aware!' Their disappearance clears the carriage and everyone seems much calmer.

The authoritative, feminine voice of the Dexan Queen can be heard once again: "Please, everyone, if you could – take your seats. Parents please supervise your offspring – and robots, assist others if they need help. 4D images, if you could please gather in one corner and squeeze yourself in to make room for others."

The announcement also appears on the screens, for those who can't hear. Everyone patiently listens as the voice continues, "The Royal Institute of the Dexan Queen apologises for any inconvenience caused to our valued passengers. We will be investigating the incident, which is minor, type 01. We have never encountered an incident like this throughout our history and can only offer our sincere apologies."

The announcement goes on to say, "It appears the Dexan Queen has been deliberately targeted and sprayed with black coal tar while in motion. We currently do not know the reason why."

"That is so nasty!" Go2 mutters to himself, shocked that someone could be so deliberately spiteful.

The announcement continues, "Our emergency services were activated after 0.00003 decimal seconds. Please refrain from emergency emotion of panic. The Dexan Queen will move very soon and our journey will continue."

This reassurance enables passengers to relax after the nightmare they have just encountered. After around two decimal minutes, another bleep can be heard and everyone listens intently for further information.

The Dexan Queen announces, "The Royal Institution of Safety in Transport, in collaboration with the Royal institution of the Dexan Queen have conducted preliminary investigations and discovered that the Miss Mermaid train was passing at the time of the incident, at 7 decimal hours, 78 deci minutes and 89 deci seconds. Unconfirmed at the moment, but it seems that she might be responsible for the attack. A formal complaint and detailed incident report will be submitted to the Royal Robotic Institution of Justice, to find out why it happened. We believe that it could be a smear campaign in an attempt to discredit us. Evil really does exist."

Finally, the Dexan Queen starts moving and quickly gathers momentum.

A booming voice from an institution official fills the train. "The institution is here to support you. We apologise sincerely for the delay today and for any emotional trauma this journey may have caused you. If required, there is a counselling service available. If you'd like to consider counselling from our professional robots, please move now to coach number H5. Another option is to receive virtual counselling from the screens on the walls. In order to do this, you will need to pull down the earphones and insert them into your hearing orifices, located on both sides of your head. For those who understand and have the ability to see, particularly human life forms, you can receive counselling from the Duke boxes. Please just sit back, relax, and enjoy the rest of your journey with the reassurance of counselling. Thank you all for your co-operation."

After the announcement, there is a lot of movement in the carriage, as some animal life forms have decided to re-locate from where they are sitting and move into other carriages. Some pull down ear phones, as instructed, and a small number of human life forms put Duke boxes on their visibility balls. The eyes.

The tar on the Dexan now needs cleaning: luckily, there is a system already in place to do this. Above every window outside, there are several small square holes, usually closed and guarded by metallic flaps. Suddenly, the flaps fly open and cleaning -fluid starts spraying like a rainbow fountain! Once all the liquid has been released, huge wipers fall down from the panels above the windows, and the cleaning process begins. The black coal tar is sticky and very difficult to remove, so the cleaning process takes around three decimal minutes. Once completed, the Dexan Queen is as good as new.

Go2 and Tilfo are so engrossed in the situation, they do not realise when their station has arrived.

Go2 and Tilfo exit at their station and make their way towards the civilised residential unit.

* * * * * *

It is early evening. Go2 and Tilfo are seated at the virtual table for their evening meal. Go2 is finishing off a large plate of delicious, spiced tofu and washing it down with ginger flavoured soy milk from the portal. Tilfo has not eaten his pancake.

They are both fairly quiet, thinking about the earlier event on the Dexan Queen. In an attempt to break the awkward silence, Go2 teases Tilfo, "Oy, green revolution! If you don't like this food, why did you suggest me to order it?"

Tilfo turns his head to look at him, shrugging his shoulders. All he really wanted was to give Go2 some company tonight.

Go2 realises that his friend is in a serious mood and unlikely to appreciate his attempt at humour, but he still decides to have a go: "Look, Tilfo, I was thinking about the bees from this afternoon..."

Tilfo's eyes widen with curiosity, and he turns around to look at his friend, eager to hear what he has to say. The conversation is always one sided. However so, Go2 asks the questions and also gives the answers.

Go2 wants to lighten the mood and jokingly says, "And so, tonight, I'll enrich your life with poor jokes!"

Tilfo smiles and nods for him to continue. He knows the jokes will be complete rubbish, but he decides to humour his friend.

Go2 starts off: "There is a bee husband and wife. What does the bee husband say when he gets back from work?"

Tilfo shrugs his shoulders, so Go2 answers, "Hi, honey! I'm home!"

This poor attempt at a joke does the trick and Tilfo jumps out of his chair, grinning. Now, they are laughing hysterically and high-fiving each other, but the joke isn't over yet, as Go2 continues, "The bee husband then says to his wife, 'What did you do the whole day, darling?' and she replies to him 'Oh, I've been waxing my legs!'"

They are in raptures of laughter as Go2's narration of the joke continues, "The husband then says, oh darling you look bee-utiful!"

Tilfo chuckles to himself. Go2 carries on, because even he is enjoying his own lame jokes and more importantly, he is managing to make Tilfo laugh. "Wife says 'Yes baby, there must be a duty bee-fore any bee-uty." They both smile. He continues, "The wife adds, 'Look darling, never forget that there is a dutiful wife bee-hind any successful husband'."

Tilfo's body language has changed and he seems relaxed and at ease now. Suddenly, Go2 remembers that Tilfo recorded the football match with the robot elephant and says to him, "Tilfo, you were really active this morning! I'm sure you recorded me playing football. Have a look if you can find it on your bablet and we can watch it."

Tilfo remembers that he did and goes off to fetch his bablet.

Go2 asks him, "Can you project it, please, in a 4D format and we'll have a proper look at it?"

Tilfo obliges and plugs a wire in, to connect the bablet to the screen on the wall. He then changes the angle of all 3 projectors around the room, so that the high quality 4D images can be played on the floor. Go2 makes some space in the room and clears the chairs away. He then takes a remote control and starts pushing buttons to turn it on. They both stare at the floor, eagerly waiting for the images to appear – the floor of the dining area has been transformed into a stadium!

A few digits appear, followed by a screeching sound and then, very slowly, images begin to form. A miniature version of the football footage is shown: first the grass pitch can be seen, followed by a scaled-down version of Go2, who is enthusiastically running after the ball. They also see the robot elephant chasing after him.

Approving of the high-quality images, they sit back and enjoy reminiscing over the morning's events. When the part where the robot elephant kicks the ball, in with the chicks plays, Go2 says, "Tilfo, please zoom in on that and put it in slow motion!"

Tilfo reluctantly gets up from his comfortable chair and adjusts the settings on the bablet and remote control.

Zoomed in, to the size of a goat, the hen is much clearer and all her distinct features can be seen in precise detail. The scene begins from where the ball falls like a missile and the chicks are dispersed. The footage shows the ball hitting one of the chick's legs – and the chick falls to the ground and gets up immediately. The moment the hen sees the ball amongst her youngsters, she flies into action! She jumps over to the chicks and tries spreading her wings to protect them, but they are running away. In the midst of the chaos, she sees the ball and realises that this is responsible for the disaster.

Go2 widens his eyes and cranes his neck to see what happens next. Tilfo is also on the edge of his seat, eager to find out.

Confident that the chicks are not badly hurt, she goes over to the limping youngster, puts her beak on its injured leg and kisses it better. The chick then runs off limping, as if nothing has happened.

The zoomed-in footage shows, in great detail, exactly how the hen responded to the situation. Firstly, she slowly looks around in all directions to take stock of the situation. Her beady eyes widen and slowly redden with anger, her claws start curling and digging into the grass. The veins on her legs are pronounced and the small feathers on her neck are standing on end, like a lion's mane. Her large wings fan out and she bats them to launch herself, as she slowly lifts up towards the sky. A few loose feathers fly off as she takes flight. She spits with at Gaju, and squirts to evacuate her bowels, in anger.

"WCoocoooocoooo ddooooo!" is the horrifying sound she makes, felt with a reverberating echo.

Attempting to take a leap and fly down onto the ball, she falls short – she's a hen, not a falcon. The footage shows her slowly walking around the ball and looking at it from all angles. She uses one leg to steady her balance and the other to dig her claw into the ball, in an attempt to pierce it. When this is unsuccessful she tries a different approach and fiercely stabs at it with her beak. The force she uses is so strong that she manages to pierce the polymer on the very first attempt and punctures the ball, the air instantly gushing out of it. She continues to stab at the ball repeatedly, using her claws to angrily tear the polymer into little pieces. The hen is not happy until the ball is completely destroyed. All that remains is a few strands.

Feeling extremely proud of herself, a sense of victory is evident in her eyes. She wipes her beak clean on the damaged ball and proudly kicks the remnants of it as she walks towards Gaju.

Upon witnessing this outburst of rage, the footage shows Gaju becoming fearful of the hen and apologetic, trying to calm the situation down, by bowing in front of her many times, before it gets out of hand.

Go2 and Tilfo watch closely as it shows her flying onto Gaju's back and attacking him. She keeps on pecking Gaju with her fearsome beak, making a metallic sound. Her mother-love is fierce and frightening, and her revenge against someone who has hurt her child is awful. Her few attempts to puncture Gaju fail, before he manages to break free and runs off, back to the yard behind the civilised sports unit.

The hen takes flight and comes down back to her chicks. All the chicks cluster together, including the injured one. She takes all of them under her wings. They are evidently happy, cosy and in the comfort of her loving embrace.

Go2 and Tilfo are so engrossed in the scene that they don't even realise the video has come to an end, as they sit gobsmacked by what they have just witnessed.

Emotions are running high and Tilfo spots that Go2 has bitten his lower lip again. He quietly gets up and pushes some buttons on the wall to deactivate various screens and projectors. He comforts his friend, by his actions, definitely louder than words which he does not have. Going over to Go2, he reassuringly puts his hands on his shoulders.

Chapter 7

Lying in bed, Go2 is struggling to fall asleep. He glances over at Tilfo and sees him fast asleep, snoring contentedly. It's a very still, dark night, which is often a bad time for him and usually brings bad news. He has been turning over, trying to get comfortable for hours, but is restless and just can't settle. He has a lot on his mind and for some reason can't stop thinking about the hen from earlier.

He is feeling a little resentful of the chicks and thinking how fortunate they are to have the unconditional love of a mother. How beautiful it must feel to be under a mother's wing – so cosy and safe- knowing that someone is always looking out for you! He wonders where his mom is and whether she would care for him so well. He has so many questions about her – he doesn't know why she is not around, or if she loves him. He feels incredibly restless because there is no one to offer him any answers.

The following morning, Go2 and Tilfo are both fast asleep. A screen on the bedside table has been activated and is flashing every few moments, attempting to wake them up at a civilised time.

An attractive female human robot, gender type 1, is on the screen and enthusiastically saying, "Good morning, Go2. Wake up! I have good news!" Neither of them stirs, so she continues, "I said good morning, both of you! Did you not hear me? It's a beautiful morning outside and the sun is shining! Birds are chirping, bumblebees are buzzing and even the butterflies are awake. Why don't you get up and join them, instead of wasting the day sleeping?"

As the voice describes the picturesque morning scene outside, the screen shows pictures of it.

Go2 reluctantly opens his eyes and rubs them with the back of his right wrist, turning his head towards the screen. After such a restless night, he really does not want to get up, but the voice is pestering him too much.

She continues, "It is the ninth day of the tenth month, of the decimal calendar year. Wake up now, Mr Jones!"

Go2 finally sits up and looks at the screen.

"Hi, Go2, I hope you have had a good night's sleep? I am waking you up because I have good news for you! I am a representative from the Robocratic Institute of Social Justice and Welfare," she says.

Go2 impatiently asks, "Have you found my Mom?"

The voice responds, "Unfortunately, no. But we have found your Dad, your parental figure gender type 2! And believe me, it's definitely your birth father. He's willing to answer the many questions you have and will help to find your parental figure gender type 1, your Mom."

"Ohhhh, what good news," he sarcastically says, rolling his eyes. "Where did you spot that rare bird?" he taunts, knowing what his father is like.

"He was untraceable for seven decimal months, thirty-three days, nine decimal hours, seventy-three decimal minutes and eighty-eight decimal seconds, to be precise. He had disappeared in a place where satellite monitoring is prohibited by law. The place is known as 'Prost-ee-Glandin'. He had also removed his subcutaneous barcode tag."

"Then how did you ever manage to find him?" Go2 asks.

"Oh, he went to a different area to have his pleasure-seeking behaviour type r fulfilled."

Knowing how selfish his Father is, he replies, "That does not surprise me at all."

"Luckily, the programmes managed to identify him using the Anthropometric Optical Character Recognition technology.

Thankfully, the robocratic systems have the ability to do this," the voice explains.

"So, your systems can recognise characters? That's good to know," Go2 is impressed by this facility, continuing, less enthusiastically, "But why, exactly, did you find him?"

Realising that he is not impressed by the discovery of his dad, the voice attempts to calm him down, "Because he is your legal guardian and technically he is supposed to live here, with you! He receives child welfare benefits for you, to look after you – and the welfare systems do not allow small human subjects to live on their own."

Tilfo has somehow managed to sleep through the exchange between Go2 and the computer so far, but he is now stirring. He opens his eyes, sits up and starts to take an interest in the conversation.

The programme says, "We have been monitoring and keeping a very close eye on you, listening to your daily activities…"

"Listening?" Go2's curiosity is aroused. "How and why do you do that?"

"Look, Go2, let me try to explain. Every action has a sequence of sounds – for example, when you wake up, walk to the door, unbolt it and then open it; there are very specific sounds with each particular action. The programmes are able to identify what you are doing from the various sounds and their timings, without actually seeing you. The programmes do not allow any human –life- form to be watched continuously, for the reasons of privacy, confidentiality, and individual rights or privacy. But we also have responsibility of your security, so the systems have come up with this solution to look after your safety."

Feeling reassured that someone is always looking out for him Go2 says, "That is great, actually. So even when I am alone, you know that I'm safe?"

"Correct. However, we are unable to watch you at all times – due to the robocratic laws insist we adhere to."

She further says," But the programmes were not too worried about you, because you have Tilfo, a grown up, to look after you. The programmes and their systems are pretty confident in their creations."

Tilfo is flattered by this comment and feels proud that he has been given so much responsibility.

"However, we know that your PF2 is trying to cheat us by telling us that he lives with you," the programme chastises. "This behaviour is consistent with human -life -forms! The Royal Institute offers protection to parents, but he is enjoying the privilege of this a little too much!"

"What happens next?" Go2 curiously asks.

"We have advised him to meet with you as soon as possible, so you must wait for him. Unfortunately, the programmes are forbidden from disclosing confidential information to minors. Your Father will be able to answer your questions and we have made it mandatory for him to stay with you."

* * * * * *

Evening time, and its falling dark outside, with is an icy cold chill in the air. Go2 is chivvying Tilfo to hurry up and get ready. The PF2 has kindly agreed to see them in the waiting room of the train station, which is near Go2's residential unit.

Go2 goes over and presses some buttons on a remote control to activate the programme on the screen.

Suddenly, a cheerful male voice pipes up, "Welcome to the Royal Robocratic Institution of Welfare and Social Justice. What can we do for you two, today?"

Go2 says, "I am looking for my pocket money. In the last five months, I haven't spent any of it. Tilfo and I both decided to save it, but we would now like to receive it."

"Would you like all of your savings?"

"Yes, please, we both would," he replies.

The voice obliges his request. "No problem at all. Please go ahead and collect it now."

Their bablets are hanging like pendants around their necks. Go2 removes his bablet from around his neck and presses various points on the screen, until it shows a picture of a piggy bank. Go2 holds his bablet up high in front of the screen and the money starts to download, the piggy bank on the screen emptying as it does so.

"Go2, your money has successfully downloaded onto your bablet. Enjoy it, but always remember – penny wise, pound-foolish," the voice gives a little chuckle at the thought that he's offering parental advice.

Go2 is pleased that he now has his money and holds Tilfo's bablet in front of the screen to do the same for him.

They are in a hurry to catch Go2's Father.

* * * * * *

It is dark outside. Go2 and Tilfo are sitting in the waiting room, which is small, but has a high domed ceiling. There are no right angles in the structure and all the corners are rounded – even the polymer furniture is curvy. The table has a kidney-shaped top and they're sitting at the convex side of it, surrounded by numerous random chairs dotted around. But the room is otherwise completely empty, apart from the two of them.

The sound of a train halting outside can be heard. They both look at the door, their eyes fixated on it, in the hope of seeing Go2's Dad.

All of a sudden, the door bursts open and the eagerly awaited PF2 – Dad – appears!

The PF2 is a tall, thin, nervous, fumbling figure, who is apparently constantly mumbling to himself. He has a broken, high-pitched voice, and because he has his own language and a habit of rhyming things, it seems as if he is in his own world. He has various piercings in his right ear, right nostril and right eyebrow and is dressed all in black clothing that looks like it's made from shiny polymer. They also notice that he is wearing a black armband and wristband on his right side. His appearance is a little unkempt – he looks as if he needs some grooming.

Go2 stands up and walks around the other side of table to greet him, and Tilfo also gets up. The PF2 is extremely tall and towers above Go2, who only comes up to his waist.

Go2 says, "Hello Daddy," and instantly wraps his arms around him.

"Hello, Mr Go2," the PF2 awkwardly replies.

It is apparent that he's deliberately ignoring Tilfo for some reason and refuses to even look at him.

He pulls away from the embrace and says, "Move away, Mr Go2! I don't like hugging life forms of the same gender."

Go2' deflates, in disappointment.

The PF2 moves away from Go2 and sits in the chair opposite them. He seems a little agitated and demands to know, "Why have you called me? The Social Welfare State of Robocracy is looking after you just fine!"

Feeling deeply hurt by this comment and fighting back tears, Go2 says, "I called you because I feel lonely."

"Haha! Lonely? You have this animal form living with you, don't you? Why would you possibly be lonely? I'm happy with the arrangement and so are they. Loneliness can actually be a blessing. Solitude gives you independence and you can do whatever you want to, without having to answer to anyone! Take me, for example – I'm alone and I'm having so much fun hiding from the programmes!" The PF2 presses his right nostril closed and takes a deep breath through the other one, exhaling loudly from his mouth.

Go2 does not like his answer, or his attempt at justifying his neglectful behaviour, and Tilfo is also unconvinced.

Wanting to try to understand better, Go2 asks, "Well, what have you been doing?"

"I have been training to become a professor of horniculture," he replies.

Go2 and Tilfo have no idea what this means, as it's not a term they have heard before.

Go2 still doesn't understand why he has not been around, and asks, "So, where exactly do you live?"

Smugly his Father says, "I am seeking pleasure. Pleasure and I go hand in hand."

In a role reversal, it appears that Go2 is asking all the questions and enquiring about the PF2's welfare. He is growing frustrated now, and his Father's laid-back attitude angers him further.

Go2 persists, "Why don't you take responsibility for me, like you are supposed to?"

"Responsibility without any power is like being in a lower drawer," the PF2 says, mysteriously. "I need to hold the gold, because the gold gives me pleasure."

Still confused, Go2 asks, "Where do you find pleasure?"

The PF2 smirks, "There is a place called Prost-ee-glandin. I'm not a fan of the e-robotic e-girlfriend experience, because their beauty is only biofilm deep. There is no correct degree of temperature, shear stress, speed or humidity. I enjoy biology, not physics – and I love a real womaaaaan!" He chuckles to himself.

Go2 is annoyed because he does not understand anything that he is saying; all he understands is that the PF2 likes women. He can't hide his frustration and decides to give him some attitude back. Mocking his voice, he sarcastically asks, "And where do you find 'a real womaaaan'?"

"In bed!" Dad says.

Go2 is shocked. But he decides to be upfront and assertive because the PF2 has eluded him for so long and now he wants answers. He reluctantly asks, "Apart from that – what else do you do?"

Tilfo is a little surprised with Go2's behaviour, because he has never seen him so firm. He always finds him shy, polite and gullible.

"There are many ways to find liberation. Thee smack, thee scag, thee junk, thee dope, thee double-trouble. Wow!" The PF2 looks at the ceiling and continues, "Thank you for this biodiversity. I am a bio-materialist and biomaterial is always available."

Go2 is perplexed and looks at Tilfo to see if he can make any sense of what he's saying. Before he gets a chance to ask him to explain himself further, he hears a jingle coming from the PF2's pocket. The PF2 reaches and pulls out his bablet to receive the call.

Go2 can just about hear a faint voice on the other end of the call that it sounds like a female, perhaps the biological girlfriend. It sounds like she is saying, "Hi, honey. When are you coming back? I am mad for you, today."

PF2 laughs a little and answers, "You are mad, indeed! I am coming soon, baby, okay?"

The woman then says, "I am looking good, today. Please hurry back here. I am waiting for you!"

The PF2 smiles. "I will be with you very soon! In the meantime, you can see me on your bablet."

He cuts the call and mutters under his breath: "Oh, what a fun it is to ride, on a one-horse open sleigh!"

Clearly distracted by his call, he turns to Go2 and says, "Look, I am in a hurry. Can you please finish your interrogation soon?"

Go2 and Tilfo are astounded and look at each other. Go2 takes a deep breath and asks, "Where is my Mom?"

Starting to laugh at this PF2 replies, "Mom? Mom? Oh, that is very funny, indeed! I need some pennies from you – I'm suffering from beer pressure."

Go2 looks at Tilfo for help, and he appears to nod at him to go ahead.

Go2 reluctantly says, "Fine. Take out your bablet and you can download some money from mine." He then pushes some buttons to activate the transaction and holds his bablet in front of his PF2's.

The message on the screen says: 'You have 135 world dollars. The hundred world dollars are currently being transferred to PF2's account. Please select 'yes' if you are happy for this transaction to take place.'

Go2 says, "Yes."

A few seconds later a voice from the bablet says: "The transfer is complete. You now have 35 world dollars left in your account."

Go2 closes his bablet and looks at his Dad, not understanding exactly what he needs the money for.

"That's good, I can at least buy my girlfriend a drink, now. What do you need to know?" the PF2 asks.

"Why don't you stay with us tonight and we can all have dinner together?" Go2 decides this may be the best way of extracting more information from him. "What food do you like?"

"Oh, I eat herbi-hores and carni-hores."

Go2 and Tilfo don't quite understand what he just said but go along with it, anyway. Go2 says, "We can order those, along with my pancakes and Tilfo's fresh mint leaves."

PF2 is frustrated and angrily snaps, "I don't have time! I've said I need to leave soon!"

Feeling hurt by his outburst, Go2 says, "Okay, fine; but before you go please just tell me where my Mother, parental figure gender type one, is? I need to know!"

"Look, why do you need to know?" he impatiently says. "The past is in the past."

"I just need to know – for my own peace of mind!" Go2 pleads.

The PF2 does not want to stay and discuss it any further and snaps, "If you must know, you are a clone."

Tilfo understands what this means and is shocked at the answer, but Go2 is clueless and asks, "What is that?"

"You are a son of soiled soil."

Confusion sets in on Go2's face. Picking up on this, the PF2 continues, "I had heroin-induced nephropathy and my kidneys failed, so I was allowed to have a clone to provide a kidney transplant. Growing single organ is not allowed by the law. I had to clone the whole baby from my cells."

He continues, "Then I had to grow a baby from whom I was allowed to have one kidney. What a waste of resource. For a can of milk I had to have a full cow."

The PF2 continues,

"Anyway, I received a kidney from the first cloned baby, but sadly, the clone died during the operation. I felt I needed some extra security – after all, what if I need another organ? So, I decided to have another clone – you. One day, you will have to go, so I called you 'Go' and as you are second in line, I included the number 2. That's why you are called Go2. With the assistance of the Social Welfare Department, I have been able to provide you with shelter."

Go2 is extremely saddened by this revelation and asks, "Who looked after me when I was baby?"

"The foster care programme!" he responds. "When you were four years old, you came to live with me at the civilised unit. I wanted my tissue bank, and the child welfare benefits. Having children has its benefits, you know."

Go2 sits open-mouthed, astounded by his audacity.

PF2 gets up to leave, saying, "Hens lay golden eggs – and I love omelettes! The rescue guys gave me your animal friend, and along with that, I receive animal welfare benefits, in addition."

The PF2 has no regard whatsoever for Go2's feelings, adding, "I have two hens now – so that means double the number of omelettes for me!"

There's the sound of a train pulling up on the platform, and upon hearing this, the PF2 is now in a rush to leave. Tilfo has an understanding of the situation and feels sad for his friend.

Go2, however, still has many unanswered questions. "Please don't go," he pleads.

"You're pushing when I'm rushing!" The PF2 opens the door and steps out onto the platform, not in the mood to listen to any more. He mumbles to himself, "I must leave right now – it is prime time. Crime time!" He talks a lot of gibberish and can't help talking to himself. "I must go early. I don't want Jollypop to turn into a jellyfish!"

The doors of the train open and he is running towards a carriage and starts to climb on. In the distance, Go2 and Tilfo are running after him.

Go2 is shouting, "I don't understand what you are saying, but please – just tell me where my Mom is, before you go!"

The PF2 looks back and angrily snarls, "You moronic donkey! Why do you still not understand? You don't have a mother!"

The curved automatic door comes down, slamming shut, and the train starts moving. The lights from the windows of the train flash past Go2's face as the train gathers speed.

Within seconds, it disappears, leaving Go2 and Tilfo standing frozen in the darkness of the empty station, horrified by what they have just heard.

Chapter 8

It is a sunny morning of summer. Under the sunshine, various robots and life forms are busy going about their daily business. Trains are running smoothly and the roads are packed full of vehicles, with hustle and bustle everywhere. Parents are hurriedly walking along the footpaths with their children, eager to get them to school on time.

Go2 and Tilfo are not currently part of this busy morning, since they have not bothered to wake up yet and lie motionless in their beds. Still exhausted from the events of the previous night with Go2's Father, they are lazing a long lie-in. Tilfo is lying on his side sleeping peacefully, and Go2 is on his back, with a surgical dressing applied to his lower lip.

A screen on the wall beside the beds begins flashing and a light-hearted, sweet jingle can be heard. A human voice then says, "Please wake up, Go2 and Tilfo! It is past morning-time and your school, teachers, friends and programmes are missing you both."

Unperturbed, Go2 rolls over onto his other side and continues to sleep through the message. Tilfo is a little disorientated, but opens his eyes and looks around, realising they have overslept. He sits up to try and wake himself and eventually finds the energy to climb out of bed. He walks over to Go2 and starts pushing him, trying to stir him. Go2 reluctantly sits up and looks at Tilfo.

The voice and image on the screen have now changed and someone from the Royal Institute of Social Justice and Welfare says, "Good morning to both of you. I hope you slept well? I am here because I'd like to get a report on the meeting you had yesterday with your parental figure type 2."

Fully awake now, Go2 and Tilfo nod in agreement as the image adds, "I do hope your meeting went well and was a success. Could you update me please, if possible, so that I can provide some feedback to the office?"

"Yes." Due to his painful lip injury, Go2 is finding it difficult to speak, but he admits, "The meeting did not go well." He looks at Tilfo for reassurance and continues, "I have decided to dump my Daddy, once and for all!"

The image anticipated that he would say this and replies, "That does not surprise us, due to his disregard for others and failure to co-operate. We had attempted to contact and counsel him on numerous occasions, but he would not accept our calls and prefers to remain untraceable. Have you decided what you would like to do now?"

"I have decided to have a foster parent," he proudly reveals.

"That is perhaps the best decision for you – and is something we were going to suggest," the voice replies.

Deep in thought, Go2 says, "Instead of having a parental figure type 2, can I have type 1 instead, please?"

The image on the screen processes this for a moment and answers, "Yes. Why not? That could be a very good idea and hopefully will work much better for you."

Delighted with this, Go2 asks, "Am I allowed to choose my parental figure type 1?"

"Hmm... we usually select the parents, but I think we might just be able to make an exception for you."

Go2 asks, "Can I advertise in the media, for what I'm looking for?" it seems he has already given a thought to this.

"Yes, but we'll have to advertise on your behalf. Please know that there is a selection process, though, and we have to shortlist candidates. We'll advertise in the mass media for you and this will include I-casts, e-casts, radiofrequency transmissions, e-TV and e-newspapers. What kind of parental figure type one are you specifically looking for?"

Go2 and Tilfo look at each other gleefully before Go2 bursts out with excitement: "Somebody very active and fast, because we like to have fun! They must be dynamic, but also have an understanding and caring nature."

Approving fully of this, the image says, "Perfect, Go2! Exactly all of the characteristics we were going to suggest to you!"

"So, you'll sort it then, and help me find this PF1?"

"Yes! We will advertise for you and will hopefully receive lots of applications. From there, we will shortlist them and set up an interview process."

"So someone else will conduct interviews for me?" Go2 says with lot of scepticism.

"Yes we will interview. This is a standard practice."

"Can we take interviews on our own please?" Go2 asks because he wants to select his own mother.

The gender type 1 image on the screen thinks for a moment or two, and answers,

"Yes and No. You can take interviews. But, please be aware, though, that we will have to monitor the interviews, if you are an interviewer."

"How long will it take?" he asks with excitement.

"Something long, something strong, Go2! Sometimes these procedures can take their time, but as soon as we have made any progress, we will let you know."

Excited about it all, Go2 cries, "Thank you very much!"

"You're welcome! Now, get up, be happy and get yourself to school!" the image jokes.

The image slowly disappears – after words like 'thank you', 'goodbye' and 'god bless', they are programmed to vanish.

Go2 and Tilfo jump out of their beds and high-five each other. They realise they're in a rush now, because they have daily chores to complete before going to school.

* * * * * *

The Dexan Queen is in full momentum and charging through at her highest speed, running perfectly on time – not a millisecond out. She's full of the same commuters she usually has, and Go2 and Tilfo are on board the packed carriage, on their way to school. The bees are settled in their hives, not bothering anyone and Tilfo is busy entertaining himself on the Duke box.

Go2 is in a world of his own, enjoying watching the other passengers. All of a sudden, his eyes fixate on an advertisement flashing on the screen. He frantically shakes Tilfo's leg to try and get his attention, "Hey, Tilfo. Stop watching rubbish and look at the advertisement on the screen!"

Tilfo reluctantly stops what he's doing, frustrated that Go2 won't leave him in peace. He has to rely on conveying his emotions through facial expressions. He raises his eyebrow at Go2 who does know, this means, Tilfo is asking why he's bothering him. Go2 picks up on this and apologises, "Look Tilfo, I'm very sorry to interrupt you having fun, but there's something interesting on the screen that you just have to see!"

Go2 is speaking so loudly he draws attention to them both – and, now all the other passengers are looking at them. Go2 excitedly points to the screen and now everyone is fixated on it. Colours are flashing on the screen, followed by a short jingle. A professional-sounding voice, with an accompanying image, appears on the screen.

The image says: "Attention, please! This is an advertisement from the Royal Robocratic Institution of Social Justice and Welfare. A fantastic opportunity has arisen, due to absence. Our client is seeking an active, dynamic, caring and honourable parental figure type one – a Mother! Remuneration and perks are available, depending on experience and skills – and our client is willing to relocate, if required. We are an equal opportunities employer. A flexible and part time functioning can also be considered. If you'd like any further details, please contact our virtual office, any time."

The screen then shows contact addresses, numbers and codes.

Engrossed in the advertisement, they suddenly realise it is about them.

Chapter 9

It is midday and the sun is shining brightly in the sky. Tilfo and his companion, a deer life form, are happily enjoying grazing the luscious grass in the vast grounds of Den-twist. The grounds are truly picturesque – beautiful, colourful flowers, trees bursting with ripe fruit and a tranquil lake, set in the centre.

Various different life forms are enjoying the weather, either grazing or relaxing and taking a quiet moment in the sunshine. In the distance, a tall giraffe life form is attempting to reach some leaves high up in a tree, which is, ironically, somehow taller than he is!

Tilfo and the deer are so engrossed in grazing the delicious grass, they are oblivious to what is happening around them.

"Tilfo! Tilfo! Tilfo?..." a voice is shouting.

They both immediately look up and see Go2 in the distance, running towards them. As he gets nearer, they can tell that he seems happy about something. Tilfo hasn't seen him like this for a long time, so he grins in delight.

In Go2's right hand, he is waving his bablet in the air, like a flag. As he reaches them, panting, Tilfo starts staring at him. The deer carefully watches the exchange between Tilfo and Go2 with his beautiful, wide eyes.

Go2 exclaims, breathlessly, "Tilfo! Look at this! You won't believe it! I am so happy! I know I could have sent you a message on your bablet to tell you, but I had to come and see you in person. I left school early, to come and celebrate!"

Tilfo looks curiously at him, with no idea what he is talking about.

Go2 pleads, "Oh, Tilfo, please just look at the message on my bablet!" He touches the screen and hands it to him. "See, I told you!"

Tilfo takes the bablet, lowers his head and touches the screen. The following message can be heard: "I am sorry. You are not the legal owner of this bablet."

Go2 says, "Oh, sorry. Hang on a moment!" He takes the bablet back and gives it the command, "Open up, zim zim."

The bablet responds, "The correct voice frequency has been identified. Hello, Go2. Why, exactly, did you misplace your gadget? Someone else could have got hold of it. You must not be naïve – Tilfo has attempted to access your messages. We didn't allow him to do so, since it was not clear if you had given permission for this."

Apologetically, Go2 says, "I'm sorry, but yes, I did give him permission. Please open the message."

The message appears on the screen and he hands Tilfo the bablet.

A representative from the Royal Robocratic Institute of Social Welfare says, "Congratulations, Go2! We placed an advertisement for you and the response we had was overwhelming! There were fifty-three applications. We have carried out background checks including criminal records bureau checks. We have looked at health records, overall employability and have also allocated the necessary funds."

Tilfo looks at the grinning Go2 in amazement, while the voice on the bablet continues, "We have shortlisted three potential candidates. You are now required to schedule interviews at your convenience but please note that all the interviews will be telemonitored by us."

Tilfo is overjoyed for Go2 and jumps up and down. The deer life form shakes his head in disbelief.

The message continues, ". I trust this will be okay with you. And please, don't hesitate to contact us if you need any further assistance. Tilfo will assist you, but please be aware that all interviews will be telemonitored. Best wishes."

Tilfo cannot contain his joy. He raises his forelegs up high in the sky in glee, feeling truly honoured to have been assigned such an official role.

Go2 is ecstatic and so excited to get started, dancing and chanting, "Interesting, intriguing, and indulging interviews!"

He has the same trait as his parental figure type2, in not making complete sense when his emotions are strong.

* * * * * *

Go2 and Tilfo are sitting patiently at a patio table in the beautiful garden restaurant. Tables have deliberately been spread throughout the lush green gardens and are sheltered by tall conifer trees, ensuring that each table is secluded and private. The evening sun is setting on the horizon.

"Are we on time?" Go2 asks Tilfo.

Tilfo nods his head, and sighs. This is not the first time Go2 has asked him the same question this evening.

Shrugging his shoulders, Go2 replies, "Punctuality is a virtue, I suppose. We are all bound by time."

Tilfo nods and picks up his bablet to check the time again.

A robot waiter walks over to them and asks, "Excuse me, sir, would you like to order anything?"

Go2 replies, "Yes, please, but please could we have a couple of moments? We are waiting for a family friend to arrive."

"Right, sir, I will come back to you later. Meanwhile, I will provide you with some complimentary natural water. It is from St Serenity."

"Yes. Thank you!"

While they are talking to the waiter, they hear a voice ask, "Excuse me, are you Go2?"

A tall, thin female human –life- form stands there. She has long, black, curly hair. Go2's heart skips a beat. She is pushing a huge multi-functional pram that's carrying more than one baby – in several levels. She has another young child with her, who looks approximately two rotations old, holding onto her hand tightly.

"Yes, I am Go2 and this is my friend, Tilfo." They both stand up. Tilfo bows down and Go2 offers a handshake.

"Are you here for an interview for the post of foster mother, advertised by the Royal Robocratic Institute of Social Welfare and Justice?" Go2 asks politely.

"Yes, indeed. I am Cate," she replies.

"Thank you for coming. Please take a seat," Go2 instructs.

The child clutching her hand is a quiet gender type 2, who seems very well behaved and is curious and obedient.

Cate says to him, "Baby, please just sit quietly with me here and observe. I will talk to you once the interview is over, okay?"

He nods his head and takes the seat next to her. Cate moves her chair to the side of the table to make room for the pram, which is extremely sophisticated and is operated by her movements; without requiring manual pushing.

Cate immediately gabbles lots of details about herself, waving her hands in the air, in a very animated fashion. She seems extremely bubbly, perhaps leaning towards hyperactive. So much so, that they wonder if she perhaps has a learning disability, since she has no awareness of the fact that she might be overwhelming others.

She also has multiple breasts on her body and her shirt is cut with four pyramids, two on each side, to accommodate her four breasts. Two are on her chest and the other two are situated on her tummy. It becomes evident that she also has two more breasts on each thigh, poking out from two pouches in each leg of her trousers. Go2 and Tilfo have never seen such an anomaly before, so they are bit awkward and hesitant at first.

Once everyone is settled at the table the waiter returns and asks, "What would you like to have?"

Cate politely says, "Hello, I'd like a hot drink, please, and my son would like an iced mango punha."

Go2 says, "Good idea. We'd also like some iced mango punhas, too."

Tilfo does not know what he wants, so just nods his head in agreement, for easiness.

The waiter says, "Yes, sir, that's fine. It will take approximately five decimal minutes." He leaves.

Cate looks at them and boldly asks, "So, what do you want to ask me?" They are both cautious at first and feel slightly awkward interviewing someone much older than them.

Realising that they are perhaps a little intimidated, Cate begins, "Well, firstly, I have submitted all of the requested evidence to the Institute. I know you are looking for an active and charismatic Mother. I am an expert in manufacturing and raising children! I also feel I am a loving, caring Mom."

Impressed by this, Go2 adds, "Tell us more about your family and the daddy of your children."

Tilfo is intrigued to hear more about this, so is glad that Go2 asked the question.

"Well, I have a twin sister called 'Dupli-Cate' and I also have two twin brothers, 'Mark' and 'Re-Mark'. I have ten babies, and the children's daddies are spread all over the country!"

Tilfo is trying hard to hide his laughter but Go2 is a little puzzled because Cate already has so many children.

He asks her, "Why do you want to adopt more children, then?"

They are interrupted by the waiter, who comes over and places some glasses and straws on table. They thank him and he leaves. There is an awkward silence for a moment, while the older child takes a sip from his drink without using a straw. He tries to break the ice with his teeth, which produces a cracking sound, the loudness of which wakes the baby in the pram who starts crying. The cries of one baby then disturb another in the lower storey of the pram – and she also wakes and starts crying.

Cate places her drink down on the table and quickly gets up to tend to them, picking up one baby and trying to comfort him. She takes out a hammock from the pram and fastens it around her neck like a sling, then puts two of the babies in the hammock, says to Go2, "Excuse me, folks, but I need to feed my babies from my milk-feeding outlets. Natural milk is good for them."

Go2 and Tilfo stand up and Go2 says, "No problem at all. We will take the opportunity to pop to the toilet and will come back to you soon. Please look after your babies – they're more important."

They decide to go for a stroll afterwards, to give Cate a break.

Cate then pulls out a sarong, puts it over her chest, and starts breast-feeding her two babies under the cover of the sarong. There is another baby sitting at the lowest level of the pram, and she removes the flap to reveal it. The moment the light falls on it, its eyes immediately open, and it is apparent that it's a tiny, cute little puppy. She lifts the puppy up and stuffs his head under her sarong to feed him, too. She is feeding two human babies and one dog life form baby! She is hands-free. She is enjoying feeding her babies.

The accompanying child gets off the chair and walks over to his Mother. He pulls the zip down on her right trouser leg and puts his mouth against her to suck milk from the breast on her thigh; but he does not seem to like the drink very much.

Cate is now feeding four babies at the same time!

After a while, all the babies are all fed and ready to settle. She puts them back in the pram and the young child goes and sits back at the table.

Cate sits puzzled for a moment, then gives Go2 a call on her bablet because she is wondering where they are.

They haven't gone far, but Go2 has been telling Tilfo that he's impressed by how much of a natural mother Cate is and how she possesses all the basic maternal instincts they are looking for.

The waiter returns and Cate puts her bablet up to his, to complete the payment. He thanks her and leaves.

Go2 and Tilfo arrive back at the table and Cate shrugs, nodding at the sleeping children. "Sorry about this, but this is what motherhood is like."

"It's okay, you have to do it." Go2 smiled. "If anything, you have only proved that you are a dedicated mother." He continues with his previous question. "Why do you want to adopt me?"

"Because motherhood gives me happiness and I get great pleasure out of it. Besides, my bryan tells me to."

Tilfo stifles a giggle, but when she says 'bryan', Go2 knows she means to say 'brain'.

She continues, "I want to have hundreds of babies! Why shouldn't I? I have the capacity to!" She takes obvious pride in saying this and enthusiastically continues, "If you select me, you will receive guaranteed shared care. You will get lot of siblings for free. Buy one and get many more free!" She laughs at her own joke.

Go2 scratches his head. He doesn't know what more to ask her, so he opens his bablet – where he has prepared some questions for the interview in case he became stuck. Looking at his bablet, he spots a good question to ask and says, "Please tell us how you will move forward, if you are selected..."

"I can't leave my children!" she says quickly. "If you choose me, you will need to come and join my mothery!"

"Yes, we understand that. How about you, now tell us a bit about your strengths," he suggests.

"My children are most definitely my biggest strength," she replies.

He asks her to talk about what her weaknesses are and again she replies, "My children!"

He asks, "Do you have any personal development plans?"

"Yes, to produce as many children as I can – and then, to adopt as many as possible! My aim is to show to the world that I am the most productive parental figure type 1. This is my short-term goal."

By this stage, Go2 has as good as made his mind up, but he is just trying to be polite, asking some more questions to satisfy his curiosity. "How did you become mother to a puppy?"

"I was given the honour by the rescue services, because his mother sadly died just after his birth."

Feeling saddened, Go2 tells her he is sorry to hear he had such a cruel start in life.

Tilfo is a little restless, because he also has made up his mind.

Go2 asks Cate, "If there was one thing you could change about yourself, what would it be?"

"Actually, there are two changes I would make. Blood is thicker than milk, so I would like to produce as many babies as possible. I also would like God to give me more bryan," she replies.

Go2 is impressed by her ambition. "That's good to know. Let God fulfil all of your wishes. It has been really nice to meet you and some of your children. Thank you for your time. We will let you know the outcome."

"Please don't hesitate to call me if you'd like to know anything else."

Go2 and Tilfo both get up and shake hands with Cate.

Before she leaves, Go2 says, "I am a little curious about your pram. How does it move without you actually pushing it?"

"I don't quite know," she responds. "I was told that it's a bit like a pace-maker, it picks up on senses and is related to my body movements. Once I start walking behind it, it begins to move."

"What if you are walking on a downhill slope?" he asks. "Won't it run away from you?"

"No, it won't leave me, because it's tied to me by negative magnetic pressure – whatever that means…" she giggles.

They shake hands once again and she starts to leave. The pram moves on its own as she is walking behind it and the young child is clutching her finger tightly again.

As she is walking off, Tilfo suddenly lifts his leg up and gives Go2 a powerful kick! Before Go2 realises what is happening, he loses his balance and falls on to the ground with a shrill squeal, making a loud thumping sound as he hits the floor. Tilfo very cleverly does not offer to help his friend to get up.

Hearing the screech and the loud bang, Cate turns around to see what has happened. She spots that Go2 is in a heap on the ground, asking Tilfo for a hand to get up.

In the distance, Cate shouts over her shoulder, "Oh, just get up!" She continues walking off with her children and loudly adds, "Falling is good. It helps children to grow up faster if they fall over and jump straight back up again!"

She disappears behind a row of conifer trees.

Tilfo waits until she is completely out of sight and then gives Go2 a hand. He lowers his eyebrows, looking doubtfully at Go2.

Go2 says, "She is a compli-Cate! Let us shortlist her. I don't want to rusti-Cate her."

They both burst out laughing. Go2 loves to crack jokes and make Tilfo laugh.

"Imagine if she had another two twin-brothers! If the first one is Peter, what do reckon the second twin would be called?"

Tilfo shrugs his shoulders.

Go2 laughs, "Stupid! He'd be 'Re-Peter', of course!"

They both fall about laughing again and high-five each other.

Go2 is on a roll, "Tilfo, if she had another set of twin brothers and one is called Niall, what would be the name of the second twin?"

Tilfo does not know.

Trying to control his laughter he responds, "De-Niall, of course!"

They both crack up laughing!

* * * * * *

The following interview is to be held in a village community hall, where Go2 has hired a room for one decimal hour. To avoid any embarrassment, he has decided to download the questions in advance on his bablet.

He is dressed in something which looks like a school uniform and Tilfo is wearing a smart black suit, complete with a bow tie.

The bablet bleeps and tells them that the candidate has arrived.

Go2 jumps out of his chair and says, "Come in, please."

The door opens automatically and Cyto-Megano double AA confidently strolls in with an air of authority, giving the impression that she is an intelligent human looking-robot, which she is. However, she appears to be rather arrogant and does not care what anyone thinks of her. She is dressed from head to toe in white clothing, is of average height with short, blonde hair and her lips are painted a striking shade of red. Her facial expression is cold and looks as if she doesn't show much emotion. Once she approaches them, they bow and shake hands with her.

Go2 says, "Pleased to meet you! Welcome, I am..."

"I know who you both are," she interrupts him, a little rudely. "I am Cyto-Megano AA. Please be seated," she says.

Go2 is a little taken aback at how authoritative she is and tries to explain to her, "You are here to be interviewed..."

"Yes, I know I am. You are a clone, with the blood group O, rhesus negative, Kelly and Duffy, negative, Fy fy negative, HLA DR4, and negative for viruses HIV, CMV, EBV, Zika, Japanese B, and hep B, Zokodu 23 and simian CC. You consume 1600 kilo calories a day. Your body surface area is 1.1 meters squared, your IQ is 168 in old units and you complete around 25,000 steps a day."

Go2 and Tilfo both are astounded and look at each other in shock as she continues, "Please stop looking at each other with surprise emotion type YY7. I've revealed only a few of the facts, but I know a lot more about both of you. I am programmed to express facts with principles, ethics type 3."

They shake their heads because they can't quite believe how much information she knows.

Go2 tries to get the interview back on track and says, "Excuse me. Would you like a drink?"

Cyto-Megano AA declines the offer. "I energise myself in sunlight. Solar energy gives me B23 UV rays. Feel free to go ahead, please, if you need a drink; but from the lines on your face, you do not appear to be dehydrated by more than 0.3%. I don't believe you actually need a drink. You're just offering as a matter of human formality type 2b."

Tilfo's jaw drops at this, they have never met anyone quite like her!

Cyto-Megano AA continues, "So, go on, then – ask me questions. I am programmed to pre-empt questions and am highly skilled at mind reading, but I allow others to ask questions to put them at ease and show courtesy from my side."

Again, her answer has surprised them both. Go2 wants to find out more about her. "So, tell us a little bit about your family?"

"I was created from various small energy resources found on planet earth. My body was created from different metals from the junkyard and the polymers were from the refinery in space. My intelligence was programmed by the super genetic programmer and my core values derive from earth life forms. My outer appearance is designed by a specialist in biofilm cosmetology."

Go2 is impressed. "Oh, wow, that is just superb! Could you tell us a little bit about your experience, please?"

"Yes, I study the human -child -life form's mind interactions with non- life forms. I find it fascinating!"

"Why do you want to do this kind of work?" he asks.

"Go2, you are now getting a little too assertive! Your question started with, 'why'. It isn't very nice to interrogate people older than yourself in this way. Please speak more politely!" she orders.

Shocked by this, Go2 replies, "Oh I didn't realise. I'm sorry. Please tell us about your personal development plans for the future."

"That's much better," she answers. "In three revolutions of the earth, I will have finished my 16th doctoral degree. After this is complete, I will recruit several child life forms, in a multi-centred, randomised, placebo-controlled study to examine the inadequacies of humans."

Go2 and Tilfo do not fully understand what she is talking about, but they continue to be polite, and ask more questions.

Go2 asks, "I would be obliged if you could please tell us more about your strengths."

She snorts. "Well, I am better than bloody human -life -forms for a start – because I don't have blood!"

Go2 and Tilfo feel awkward at her response, but are careful not to show this, due to her ability to read thoughts and emotions so accurately. Go2 continues, "And your weaknesses... if there are any?"

"Yes. I don't fully understand how human -life -forms can emotionally blackmail one another. I find it to be pointless and irrelevant. It seems like they do it for their own selfish gain," she explains.

Go2 frowns then, responds, "Yes, that is interesting, actually. May we ask you what you hope to achieve by taking on the role of a mother?"

He does not feel she has demonstrated this, so far.

"There are two main reasons. In the not too distant future, I hope to apply for the post of Professor at the University, and I am required to have practical, hands-on experience in child-minding. Secondly, I am looking for a child subject to assist me with my psycho-social research."

"Oh, I see..." Go2 feels deflated.

Instantly picking up on his reaction, she says, accusingly, "You did not like my answer, did you? You said, 'I see', you see!"

THE DEXAN QUEEN OF SPEED

"No, no, nothing like that!" he declares, trying to hide it.

"Well, I hope you are being truthful. Anything else?" Her mind-reading skills have already revealed to her that Go2 is embarrassed and is hiding something.

Attempting to divert from the subject, he says, "Tell us about your concept of relocation."

"Typical human attachment! I am happy to stay anywhere, or relocate if necessary, as long as I get some sunlight every day!"

Go2 asks her, "Anyway, have you discussed your remuneration package with the office of social welfare and justice?"

"You said the word 'anyway' and I also notice that your eyelids dropped by 0.46 mm. To me, this suggests that you have already made up your mind. You don't want me, do you? You will instinctively look at Tilfo in a second, for guidance on what to do next."

Tilfo and Go2 did not anticipate that she'd be so astute and highly skilled in reading them.

Go2 tries to plead his case. He doesn't have much time for her any more, but decides to be polite and continue the interview. He asks, "Please do not read our body language. Listen to the words we are saying, instead. You must remember that we are not experts like you. We really do want to consider you for the role."

In an attempt to play her back at her own game, he adds, "Earlier, you used the term 'typical human attachment'. This gave us the impression that you do not like humans."

Cyto-Megano AA is angered and snaps, "Go2, this has no relevance whatsoever to the interview! But I will answer it, because I'd like my point of view to be heard. You are correct. No – I do not like human life forms."

Tilfo's jaw drops and he is horrified at how brazen she is in fearlessly expressing such a controversial opinion.

Go2 has essentially already made up his mind and decided not to select her for the position. As the interview is drawing to a close, he decides to have a little fun because he is starting to enjoy the interaction between a human -life -form and a non-human –life- form.

"Why do you not like them?" Go2 teases.

Without hesitation, she replies, "There are many reasons! Firstly, I believe that myself, and other life forms are far superior to human life forms. However, we do value some of the great humans, because they are the ones who created us. The majority of them, though, are worse than the scrap metal yard!"

"Why do you feel so strongly about human –life- forms?" he asks.

"There are many reasons," she explains. "Physical, emotional, spiritual, and financial; are the main ones. And I can elaborate on each of them, if you wish, although this is not part of the interview."

"Please – go ahead. We can have a more informal chat now," Go2 says.

She doesn't hold back in saying what she is thinking. "Human life forms are physically demanding. They get tired in the evenings; they soon become sick, old, frail, useless, and have a limited shelf life. They are always looking for time off at weekends and demanding holidays and recreation. In addition, they are biodegradable."

Go2 decides to get into a debate with her, since he doesn't have anything to lose and fancies some entertainment. "But non -life forms like yourself also have limited shelf life, don't they?"

Engaging in the argument, she replies, "Agreed, but other life forms are not egotistical, like humans. We degenerate, but there is no attachment – and we usually last much longer than the manufacturer's best-before date. We come in various sizes and shapes. Humans only come in two forms: pinched noses and punched noses. No variety! White trash and black scrap."

Go2 can hardly suppress a gasp. Her contempt for human life forms is so apparent.

"Humans are the victims of their own material aspirations," she goes on. "They always gratify their five senses and are slaves to pleasure through the eyes, nose, ears, tongue and skin. They conveniently forget to mention one more sense: reproduction. They call it human decency!" So far, she has referred to humans respectfully as 'human life forms', but in the heat of the moment she just says 'humans.'

Struggling to argue with her, Go2 sarcastically asks, "What about emotional superiority?"

"Humans are a junkyard of emotions! They are full of anger, jealousy, depression, apathy, sadness, arrogance and domination. Everything is a competition for them. They cheat, lie, disrespect, manipulate – and are so selfish! They use criminal activity as a way of fuelling their greed, and commit terrible crimes such as violence, bribery, corruption, murder and rape. Humans carry out infidelity, sectarianism and so, so much more! I have 87 negative emotions on my list. Oh, humanity has certainly lost its humility!"

Go2 and Tilfo's eyes are wide. They are amazed by this tirade.

She takes a deep breath and continues, "Unfortunately, every negative emotion has been institutionalised by humans. They love the body part called, the back. There are so many negative connotations with it you won't quite believe it! They are always backstabbing, backtracking, or backing off. They don't have any backbone and they always want to go back home. I don't really understand why they are so backwards!"

Cyto-Megano AA is enjoying getting it all off her chest and does not tire of criticising human -life -forms. She passionately argues, "Another thing they do is eat everything! They have left no stone unturned because they are so greedy! They go to the waters to catch marine -life -forms. They domesticate all sorts of life forms, so that they can eat them, and they captivate poor, innocent creatures like lambs and chickens. However, they don't have the courage to eat tigers."

Tilfo nods his head in agreement with what she is saying.

She continues, "They exploit all animal –life- forms for their own benefit, financial gain, food and amusement."

Go2 is intrigued by the conversation and wants to engage in more of a debate with her. "But we provide them with food, shelter and protection. There are millions of microbes living happily on our skin and in our guts. Sometimes, they want to cause us harm and deliberately attack us to cause infections and infestations."

Incensed by Go2's comment, she says, "If they cause infection, then it is because the humans have disturbed their balance and harmony! The exploitation of other life forms is just one thing they abuse, but they also destroy the planet and other poorer human forms. Greed breeds corruption. They don't only want their share, but they also want others' shares, too. They snatch milk from calves, eggs from hens, honey from bees and seeds from grains. There is so much snatching and looting going on, it's a disgrace!"

"They need to explore the earth to combat poverty perhaps," Go2 suggests.

She snaps, "That is a lie! Poverty and greed go hand in hand, poverty exists because of greed. If we are to eradicate poverty, then greed needs to be abolished first."

"But we have values of service, duty and sacrifice. Values that you have borrowed from us," Go2 insists.

"Yes, we borrowed some values from humans and therefore of course we appreciate them, but they are vanishing fast. Large empires have collapsed due to indulgence. Human -life -forms need to learn more about service, duty and the benefits of sacrifice from simple creatures like honey-bees. They are superior to humans," she explains.

Go2 is confused. "How?" he asks.

"Bees know that they are going to die, once they sting someone – and yet they still do it to help protect their species. Male bees know that they will die once they have mated with a queen, but they continue to do it to protect their species from becoming extinct. They are productive and you could learn from them, by seeing how brave they are. Do you understand what I'm saying?" she asks.

"Snakes, scorpions, stingrays and spiders sting or bite us to harm us, though," Go2 says.

"Yes, because you invade their space. You use animals and birds for experiments, when you could, in fact, learn a lot from them, instead. I can think of many lessons, but just off the top of my head, you should aspire to be more loyal, like dog -life -forms – and value hard work, like donkey -life -forms. You also degrade them by using their names as derogatory insults. For example, you might call someone a 'bitch', a 'dog' or a 'cow' if you want to offend them. These terms are used effortlessly in everyday conversations and we have decided to challenge this legally, because it is unacceptable."

Trying to prove her wrong, Go2 says, "We promote the growth of microbes."

"You use antibiotics," she replies, without hesitation.

He pauses for a second to think of which direction to take the debate next, and then says, "When you talk about negative emotions, I think you might be thinking more about the difference between good and bad. Good and bad are human values and we donated these to your world of robocracy."

"Yes. I appreciate that," she says. "Throughout history, Messiahs and Saints have taught humans the importance of the difference between good and evil."

Attempting to convince her that humans are good, he says, "So, at least you do appreciate how Messiahs have tried to change the world, then?"

"I do. However, it was only due to the injustice and immorality that they were required in the first place," she argues.

"Only humans follow spirituality. Non- life -forms don't," he says.

Cyto-Megano AA feels passionately about this and replies, "Yes, I agree to some extent, but humans use spirituality for two selfish reasons. The first is that they can hide their deficiencies under spirituality, and secondly, it enables them to hide the sins they commit. Spirituality has become a psychological refuge, for some."

"Anything else?" Go2 is enjoying teasing her because he can see how strongly she feels about this.

"Spirituality is also needed to combat the fear of death," she adds.

"Ohh, that's true, actually," he admits.

"Immortal concepts don't need spirituality," she finishes.

Suddenly, a loud voice booms from the screen on the wall: "Only two decimal minutes remain for the use of this room. Please organise yourself and prepare to leave."

Tilfo immediately stands up, fed up of the argument now. It has gone on too long.

Cyto-Megano AA says, "Before we finish...earlier you asked me about my strengths and weaknesses. My biggest strength is that I am not a human -life -form. My weakness is that I have to work with them." She is desperate to say everything she wants to and continues, "Planet earth would be much nicer without human -life -forms. We only tolerate them because we have to, due to our belief in the principles of equality and diversity." She can't help herself from having these angry outbursts and exclaims, "At the moment, they should be sent back to where they came from... caves!"

Unimpressed by this, Go2 rolls his eyes and sarcastically replies, "Ah, well, it's good of you to tolerate them. Aren't you just great? It's been nice meeting you. We will let you know our decision in the next couple of days or so..."

Picking up on his tone of voice, she says, "It seems that you have not selected me, but I will give you more time to take the opportunity to at least consider me. It's been nice meeting you both and I shall look forward to hearing from you."

She gets up, shakes hands with both of them and walks away.

Go2 and Tilfo stare blankly at each other, then stand up and gaze at the door. Out of nowhere, Tilfo lifts up his strong right leg and forcefully kicks out at Go2, who can't tolerate such a hard blow and instantly falls in a heap on the ground, making a thumping sound as he lands.

Upon hearing the terrible noise, the Cyto-Megano AA spins around and sees Go2 lying, helpless, on the floor. She unsympathetically says, "My insurance programme will not cover you, neither me to help you. Call the emergency helpline if needed." She continues on her way without a care in the world, unperturbed by the entire incident.

Go2 stands up and gives his leg a shake, and they look at each other and burst out laughing.

Go2 says, "She should be sent where she came from... to the junk yard!"

They both fall about laughing and high-five each other.

"It is a sin to laugh at your own jokes," Go2 says, but this comment only further encourages them, and they can't control their laughter.

* * * * * *

Midday at their residential civilised unit, and Go2 and Tilfo are rushing to get ready for the next important interview.

Go2 is standing outside the bathroom, shouting, "Who is in there?"

He knows full well it is Tilfo but is trying to prove a point. "Tilfo! Get out of there immediately! You take so long; I keep telling you to cut down on your portions of fruit and vegetables."

He continues shouting, but Tilfo just ignores him.

"Come on! It is already seven decimal hours past! It's your fault if we are late!"

He hears the sound of the toilet flushing and Tilfo walks out drying his hands.

Go2 cries, "Finally! Let's go now!" And they leave.

* * * * * *

Late afternoon, the sun is shining from the west, and the long platform is deserted, apart from a few security robots loitering around. The Dexan Queen is silently parked up on her track, parts of her metallic coverings reflecting in the blazing, golden sunshine. The front of the Dexan Queen is located at the north end and contains the automatic control room, artificial intelligence and the monitoring units. The two headlights at the front are carved and painted to look like eyes.

Go2 and Tilfo are sitting on two chairs on the platform, next to the front of the Dexan Queen, ready to conduct an interview with her. They are both bursting with excitement because it will be a brand-new experience for them: not something they've ever read about in bablets or seen in the media. Go2 is feeling slightly apprehensive because he is the one who is going to conduct the interview with this fast, powerful, dynamic and robust applicant.

The Dexan Queen says warmly, "Hello, babies! Welcome to this place, you who are stricken with mummy-poverty."

Go2 and Tilfo look at each other in amazement. They have never heard such a caring and soothing maternal voice before. She continues to reassure them and put them at ease, "I do hope you are comfortable. Don't worry about anything at all, Okay? Don't get stressed, because everything will be alright, I promise. All is well from my side."

Go2 is a little choked up and says, "Th...th... thank you for seeing us. We are really excited to be talking to you, because we have never been given the opportunity before."

"No, we have never had a conversation. I actually don't talk to anyone, apart from the announcements I make before I start my journey – but even then it's not me who does the talking, since the delegated systems do it for me. You are my most special guests and I am so pleased to be meeting you both," she says.

Go2 is slowly gaining the confidence to speak to her and says, "We did not know that you could talk. We travel with you almost every day."

Her comforting voice replies, "Yes, I see you two nearly every single day. You're the one that has a cute little dimple on your right cheek. I love it! No one else has one of those!"

Tilfo looks at Go2, having never noticed his dimple before. She continues. "I guess you must be living in a council civilised unit. I hope you are comfortable there?"

"Oh, yes, we are very happy there," Go2 replies.

Concerned, she says, "How about food? Do you eat well? I'm sure you look as if you have lost a little bit of weight in the past fifty days."

Go2 and Tilfo are surprised at this observation; it's not something either of them had noticed. Go2 says, "How do you know your passengers so well? We are amazed!" He continues, "I'm not sure if I have lost weight or not, but I feel absolutely fine. Thank you for your concern, though. I do appreciate it."

The Dexan Queen says, "It is my job to look after my passengers. I know all of them well."

Go2 and Tilfo again look at each other. Go2 has a burning question he can't wait to ask her and decides to just get straight to the point. "Don't you find it absurd that you are a biotrain and you want to become a foster mother? It's not something I've ever heard of before."

"Yes and no, darling," she says.

Go2 is perplexed. "I mean, how is it even possible? How would it work? How did they shortlist you? I have so many questions, I am at a loss!"

"Oh, baby, I am sorry to hear that. Ask me a simple question and I will try to answer for you. I am not as intelligent as you are, though – I do not have your IQ of 168."

Go2 and Tilfo look at each other in bewilderment, as she continues, "The Royal Robocratic Institute of Social Welfare and Justice have carried out checks on me. They assessed my functional suitability, applications and practical procedures and they gave me the green light to proceed."

Still confused, Go2 asks, "I mean, how it is possible that you could be someone's mother?"

"Tell me why not, cutie?" she replies.

"I'm sorry, but I thought you needed to be capable in all functions. I am not a doubting Tom, but I'm curious and want to know," he says. Tilfo nods in agreement with the question.

Her soft voice replies, "It is simple for me. Caring is second nature to me."

"Do you have eyes? Can you see us, or are you are just a voice?" he asks.

"Haha! Darling, can you see your own backside?"

Tilfo tries to twist his head to look behind him but cannot see anything of his own bottom.

Go2 replies, "No, of course not."

"Look here! I have thousands of small cameras fixed in my wall and trillions of pixels at my disposal to make up photographs. In addition, the whole platform is fitted with a similar number of cameras, which interact like tomography and give me a complete image from every angle at once. I see not only your front side, but the back of you, too."

Go2's eyes widen in surprise.

She continues, "There is an ant crawling up Tilfo's back right this moment – I can see."

Tilfo suddenly stands up and shakes himself to try and get rid of the ant.

"Are you alright, darling?" she asks him, and Tilfo nods his head.

Go2 says, "Oh, wow that is amazing! You are superb! But why would you need to see us like this?"

"You won't understand until one day, when you become a father. Mothers are always inclined to want to watch their babies, even when they are not with them. It is simply their maternal instinct to look after and protect them."

Go2 is impressed, but still needs some more convincing because he feels that his privacy could be compromised, due to this level of personal invasion. He asks, "How do you hear us?"

"Simple, darling – in the same way that I see you. Aww – bless you, you are so naïve, my little cutie! I know that you interviewed Cyto-Megano AA yesterday. To reassure you, I feel that I interact very well with human -life -forms," she says, confidently.

Go2 gets straight to the point: "How are you going to actually look after me, though?"

"The proof of the pudding is in the digesting," she laughs.

Thinking logistically and trying to understand how their relationship would physically work, he says, "I mean, you can't even walk, though; so I am confused."

Sounding dismayed, she says, "This is where you and the systems need to forgive me. It's like a mother who is paraplegic and confined to a wheelchair but is still a Mom. I hope you understand and accept this. Please forgive my disability."

Go2 hesitantly says, "Yes, but…"

Attempting to show that she is not disadvantaged, she excitedly says, "But I can carry you anywhere on my tracks! It will be as if you are on holiday all the time!"

"What will happen to all the other passengers?" he asks. Tilfo smiles at this productive question.

"I would take responsibility for you. Firstly, though, you'd have to come here and live in one of my coaches," she says.

Tilfo's jaw drops and Go2 is shocked at this proposal. He asks, "What? I am going to live with you?"

"Yes, baby. I wish I could come and live with you, but please forgive me. I will prepare a special coach for you behind my head unit and you will be the only one who will live there." She pauses and then continues, "When you are aboard and living with me, I will not make my routine trips – we will go on our own special journeys. Only when you go to school will I continue with my work." She explains, "You will be at school during the day and like most other mothers, I will take a part-time job. I will stop work in the evening to look after you when you finish school."

"What about weekends, vacations and holidays?" he asks.

"I will not be working, then, unless there was some kind of national emergency."

He looks at Tilfo and asks her, "Are visitors allowed?"

"Yes, sometimes – but that is another term the systems have imposed. I am only allowed visitors at the weekends."

Go2 and Tilfo look at each other, both having doubts about how this would work.

The Dexan Queen continues, "This is going to be a unique experiment in hybrid co-existence and the forming of a relationship between a life -form and a non -life -form."

"Why didn't the experiment start with a baby rabbit or a dog? Why have I been chosen?" Go2 asks.

The Dexan Queen chuckles and proudly tells him, "Well, they were looking for higher primates that had an excellent IQ – which you do. And you are also a sweet-looking substrate."

Feeling rather proud, he continues, "Are there any other terms?"

"Yes. My speed would have to be lowered at all times. I am the Queen and I am known for being the fastest, but for you, I will sacrifice this and become an average run-of-the-mill train," she says.

Feeling a little guilty, Go2 asks, "Does that bother you?"

Tilfo is intrigued to hear what her answer will be.

After a short pause, she answers, "The pleasure of motherhood is the greatest of all. Speed is just an advantage I have. Motherhood will provide happiness, whereas speed is purely pleasure."

"Yes, I see," Go2 agrees and continues, "Any other terms?"

"Yes. I can't hide anything from you."

"Go on," he encourages.

"We need energy for every single thing we do – and most like me take our energy from the electricity portals. Some of us have advanced solar panels embedded in our sides; only a small number of us take our energy from teleportation via satellites. I do have my own nuclear reactor in the end carriage, but I have been advised to lose this and go solar," she explains.

Tilfo looks sad at hearing this. Go2 asks her if she minds having to do this and she explains that she is okay with it.

"How do you dispose of nuclear waste?" he asks.

"That's classified information. Every now and then, when I gather nuclear waste, I go into hibernation. The place I go is underground, under the sea, and I go there for a long time. I dump the nuclear waste at a disposal site and return clean and clear."

Go2 and Tilfo nod slowly at one another, considering.

The Dexan Queen seems relieved that the questions appear to be coming to a close. She asks Go2, "So, big interviewer, do you have any more questions for me?"

He nods his head. "Yes. Do you have any experience of being a mother?"

Sounding a little deflated, she replies, "To be honest, no, I don't – and it *is* going to be an experiment. However, every mother has to do it for the first time at some point in their life."

"You have a good philosophy and attitude," Go2 says.

"Yes and mothers need that, if they are going to raise kids."

He asks," What motivates you? "

She thought he'd understood her explanation so far, but she appreciates that he might take a little more convincing. She pauses and says, "You know how machines do mechanical, repetitive jobs? And robots have artificial intelligence to enable them to perform? Well, this time, the Robocracy has decided to go one step further and has installed the emotions of life forms into robots. Some of us have even surpassed that and have ingrained instincts, as opposed to artificial intelligence and emotions. In short, I am robotic train which has been installed with the instincts."

Go2 and Tilfo are lost. She picks up on this and explains further, "Look – it's simple. It is just an upgrade from, jobs to activities, activities to emotions – and from emotions to instincts. Basically, I was just a biotrain before, but now I am fully equipped to become a mother."

Go2 tries to think of his next question and says, "What are your aspirations and personal development plans?"

The Dexan Queen gives a gentle laugh at the innocence of his question, realising that it must be one of the ones he has downloaded from a search engine in preparation for the interview. She says, "My progressive development plan is to become a mother and my main aspiration is to ensure I am the best mother on planet earth!"

He is satisfied with her answer.

She notices something about him and says, "Go2, you are not asking questions from your bablet?"

He decides to make a joke. "No, I'm not living in bablical times!" He continues, "What are your strengths and weaknesses?"

"Hmm, now that is a difficult question! My strength is that I want to serve the life forms in my own way. I think it's important to remember that sometimes your strengths are often your weaknesses." She pauses and then says, "Look Go2, darling, I can tell, by now, from your body language and your overall demeanour that you have selected me." She continues, "It gives me great pleasure to become your Mother and it's going to be a journey for us both. The representatives from the Royal Robocratic institution of social welfare and justice will have to come and check that all is well before you can come and live here, though."

Tilfo is sad, because the reality of this means he has to learn to live on his own, now.

Go2 is concerned and asks, "What about the inconvenience that will be caused to hundreds of passengers if you go part-time?"

"Flexibility of working is my choice! Yes, there would be some slight inconvenience caused to passengers, but they will put a replacement train on, when I am not working, so it will be fine," she explains.

Go2 feels guilty that he would be contributing to this and is a little sceptical. "Is this experiment really worth it?" he asks.

The Dexan Queen tries to reassure him. "In the long run, yes, I think it will be – because it will be the first experiment studying the emotional relationship between a human and a non -human -life form. If the experiment is successful, then this could mean there would be a new era of hybrid civilisations."

"Can I please ask you one final question? This one is not part of the interview," he says a little shyly.

Again, there is gentle laugh from the Dexan Queen and she agrees.

Go2 says cheekily, "How old are you?"

She giggles because he has asked this and replies, "Look, Go2 darling, it is cheeky to ask a lady her age! However, you are definitely old enough to be my son. I am not a granny. I'm just 28 revolutions old." She gives a comforting smile and says, "So, you now have a Mummy who is fast, dynamic, magnanimous and very active. Everything you were looking for!"

"Exactly. Thank you! That was my last question, I think, unless you have anything to ask me?" he says.

Hesitating for a moment, she then says, "No questions, but please let me know how many times a day you bite your lower lip. Your right upper incisor is much stronger than the left one."

Go2 is shocked that she knows this and feels embarrassed. "I don't know. I don't do it deliberately. I'm not even sure how it happens and most of the time I'm not even aware I'm doing it," he admits.

Picking up on his anxiety and attempting to put him at ease, she says, "No problem. That's something we can look into, in future. I hope we have a great future together! One more thing, your friend is very cute. Thanks Tilfo for everything you do, and you have been doing."

Tilfo bows down with appreciation by the giant structure.

"I thank you again," Go2 adds.

As Go2 and Tilfo get up to leave, she says, "I have some refreshments for you both for your evening meal. Make sure you collect them from the outside vending portal on your way out."

Appreciative of this, Go2 says, "That's a nice gesture. Thank you, you have been very kind."

"You're welcome, baby. See you both soon," she says as they leave.

They walk over to the external vending portal where Tilfo pushes the 'deliver' button on the touch screen, and within seconds, a big pack of snacks falls. Then another pack follows which contains two brand-new bablets. Then a third parcel is dropped which contains cloths for both Go2 and Tilfo. He picks the bags up and hands them to Go2.

As they are walking away, Tilfo decides to do his usual trick and gives Go2's right leg a good kicking. Although this always happens, it still takes Go2 by surprise and he falls down hard onto the platform floor, like a log. A metallic thud echoes around as he falls.

The Dexan Queen witnesses it happening and screams in horror, "Eeeeeeee!" There is anguish and concern in her voice. "Are you okay, darling? Tilfo, please help him get up and make sure he's okay."

Tilfo helps him and he gathers himself.

"Are you alright baby? Are you hurt?" Her caring nature is evident. "Please come in and stay with me for a while. There is a first aid box in the first coach."

"No, I am alright, thank you," Go2 says. And Tilfo agrees.

"What happened, baby?" the Dexan Queen persists, in concern. "Why did Tilfo kick you?"

"He gets involuntary tics." Luckily, Go2 had prepared a false answer for this question, in case someone asked, but until now, no one has ever questioned them. "It's kind of like a seizure in his legs. He is seeing a vet -neurologist about it and is taking the correct dose of disodium trivalproate, to try and help him."

Sympathetically, she replies, "Oh, sorry to hear this. Please come in, though, and both have some rest."

"No, we are really fine," Go2 insists. "We need to go, because I have some homework to finish and Tilfo has to eat his ketogenic diet."

"Darling, I'm afraid I'll only allow you to leave when I am fully convinced that you are both okay, because I'm worried," she says.

Insisting even more, Go2 adds, "Honestly, I promise – we are fine! My leg is okay and we can both walk perfectly, now."

With this, they both give her a live demonstration of them walking up and down the platform.

Unconvinced, but realising that she has to let them leave, she reluctantly says, "If you say so, then I will have to accept it, but please look after yourselves and get lots of rest. Make sure you are both eating well and get plenty of sleep. Don't stay awake until late at night – and apply a dressing if you can!"

"Yes. We will do," Go2 says, trying to reassure her. "But I'm not hurt – it's just a small scratch."

"Please forgive me for not running up to you and physically comforting you. I do hope you'll be able to accept a disabled Mother."

Go2 replies, "Yes, we're going to go and have a think. Thank you for interviewing with us and enjoy the rest of your day."

She adds, "Let me know if you don't feel well in the evening!"

Go2 rolls his eyes, "Yes, Mom. I mean yes, Ma'am!"

They leave and Go2 limps off.

* * * * * *

It is the middle of the night and The Dexan Queen is parked in a yard for the evening, since she does not operate overnight. She feels anxious and desolate, desperately longing to become a Mother, but she can't help feeling worried about how powerless she was when her potential son fell to the ground. She can't help thinking – is it even worth carrying out this kind of experiment? How will it make her feel?

She already knows the answers to her own questions but can't help momentarily doubting herself.

"There are plenty of disabled mothers on the planet – and they are all capable of offering love, care and affection, so why am I any different?" she thinks to herself. "All disabled mothers are victims of situations and they have no choice; but I do have a choice. Is there any point in me offering someone substandard care, knowing that it might not be enough? It's not just about me gaining pleasure from being a mother – it is a whole responsibility. There are only two options: to be or not to be, and either way, it will be a learning curve... It will work. It has to – and all I have to do from my side is give it my best! The system knows about my limitations and now Go2 does, too – so it will be their informed choice," she decides.

* * * * * *

Go2 is also having a restless night in his bed and going through similar thoughts.

"Will it work? Will it not work? How will it work? She has limited capacity and cannot run to me when I am fallen!"

He then sees the advantage of this – which is that he would have more freedom.

"She has exceptional talents that give her the edge over the other candidates. She is fast, mature, dynamic, active, and she is a protector and provider. In some ways, she could potentially be an ideal mother. And she is much better than the other two candidates!"

He is excited about the experiment and keen to see what will happen.

* * * * * *

Late afternoon, and The Dexan Queen has finished early today. There are no passengers waiting to be transported. She is tired and glad to be having a rest and lying idle on the track.

The sun is beginning to set on the western horizon and is reflecting on her left side.

Go2's parental figure type two, his so-called father is walking along the platform towards the front of The Dexan Queen. He is giving the impression that he is angry, stamping his feet on the ground as he walks along. He often wobbles while walking and is trying to regain his balance by putting his arms out.

He reaches her head unit and shouts, "Who do you think you are?!"

It takes her a moment to understand what is happening, but she soon realises that the man is talking to her. He repeats himself, "I said, who do you think you are?"

The Dexan Queen does not answer, having witnessed many irate passengers in her life – she does not entertain them. Apart from in her personal life, her policy is not to talk to anyone, ever.

Her silence even further annoys Go2's PF2, who removes the shoe from his left foot, takes it in his right hand and starts beating her with it! The Dexan Queen cannot do anything other than watch; but she's never been so offended in her life and eventually decides she has no choice other than to break her silence.

"Hey, Mister! STOP! What do you think you are doing? Stop it immediately, or I will call the robot guards!"

He angrily says, "Call them! I am not afraid of anyone, you bitchy scum!" He continues beating her with his shoe.

"Stop it!" she demands. "Otherwise I will activate the electrical protection systems and you will be electrocuted."

"I will not fall prey to your threats," he taunts. He stops beating her for a second and moves away, "You are a child snatcher, a child welfare snatcher and a child exploiter! Machines like you thrive on making innocent children your prey." He does not stop making offensive comments and allegations. "Systems and situations have lost their sanity!"

The Dexan Queen is now slowly realising who he is and asks, "Are you Mr Redmill? The so-called parental figure type 2 of Go2?"

"Yes. I am his Daddy and don't you dare try and snatch my son from me! You will pay for this, you wheelie bin!" he hisses.

Attempting to calm him down, she says, "Oh, now I realise. You are a famous human life form, gender type 2."

"Yes, I am famous! Are you jealous?" he snaps.

The Dexan Queen responds to him sarcastically, "Oh, I am very jealous. I am mainly jealous of your files in the records of the Department of Social and Child Welfare. Perhaps I am jealous of your record of constant movement and the fact that you can run faster than me. I am also jealous of your pleasure-seeking behaviour, I imagine, too." Without taking a breath she continues, "You are a great man. You enjoy child welfare money. You must be so proud of yourself! A real man of substance, you are!"

Mr Redmill doesn't pick up on her sarcasm, only pleased that he has at least got a reaction from her and is getting the attention he wanted. He replies, "Yes, yes – I am his father. You are trying to take him away from me because you want the benefits – and you just want to use him to show the world what a great machine you allegedly are!" He continues, "It is illegal child trading! You are taking a child away from his poor Father and you will sell him at a higher price when he has grown up. You will get a good price for all his organs. How yummy! You will get a big liver, two large kidneys, a mature heart, lots of joints and you will never lose your investment! You are a very crafty investor."

The Dexan Queen is shocked by the bizarre things he is accusing her of and is disappointed by how negatively he is thinking.

He continues, "You have skills in spills. When I am going through emotions, you'll benefit from promotions!"

The Dexan Queen is incensed and says sternly, "Stop this immediately, Mr Redmill! Firstly, it is all perfectly legal. Would you like to see a copy of the agreement?"

"Don't show me the crafty draft!" he says spitefully. "My little innocent angel has been lured by your glitter. You can't cheat me, because I am his legal guardian. No one has ever even consulted me about this to see if I am okay with it! Whatever document you might produce will be useless!"

The Dexan Queen is confused; she does not know why he is behaving this way. "What do you want, Mr Redmill?"

He is pleased to hear this because it gives him the opportunity to explain himself. "Yes, that is a good question." It looks as if he is about to cry as he attempts to show love for his son. "I want my baby back. I love him so much and I can't live without him! I am a single parent. You know how hard it is to become a single parent? I want him to be my support when I get old."

"Look here. We made an agreement with the legal authorities. You can't ask for him now because it's too late – and more importantly, Go2 doesn't want to stay with you."

"You shift the shit and blame me for it!" he says, through gritted teeth.

"Mr Redmill! You are talking to a lady who is referred to as 'the Queen', I hope you know. Please mind your language!" She decides she needs to be stern with him and says, "Do you know that we support, first – then we report, and then transport? We are transport specialists. Which of those do you want from me?"

He quietly says, "Support Ma'am, please." Mr Redmill has no option but to retract from his earlier behaviour and try a calmer approach.

Coolly, she replies, "Okay, and do you want that in cash, kindness or courtesy?"

"Kindness and courtesy are useful for rich vessels like yourself, but I am a poor man. I can only buy mash with cash," he replies.

Deciding that it's easier to give in to his demands to calm the situation down, she tells him, "You can collect two hundred world dollars from my external vending port."

He feels flattered that someone is taking notice of him and offering to give him something, but he is greedy. He decides to manipulate the situation further to try and get as much as possible.

"You are kidding!" He giggles and continues, "I love my child and he's my little treasure, but please, give me more pleasure." He looks to the skies and continues, "He is my next of kin. Don't show me an empty bin."

The Dexan Queen realises what he really wants and asks, "How much are you looking for?"

"Two hundred world dollars a month, indexed, which will be equal to his benefits. In addition, there will also be one-off counselling fees and relocation expenses – with VAT included."

The Dexan Queen agrees. Money is irrelevant to her, because she earns a lot of it. She also wants to ensure that Mr Redmill is happy with her adoption of Go2.

She says, "Okay, Mr Redmill. Squeaky wheel gets oil. Collect your money by scanning your bablet at my external vending portal every month. Do not ever show your face here again! Goodbye!"

Mr Redmill is ecstatic and his eyes widen with happiness. He will now have a decent income for the rest of his lifetime! However, his greed is relentless.

He adds, "It is my right to see him at least once a month and I want to give him chocolates every month, so I'll need those costs in addition to the payment."

Unimpressed by his attitude, The Dexan Queen replies, "Mr Redmill, I have been more than fair with you. Will you please leave now?"

He sheds some crocodile tears and wipes them away with his forearm, crying dramatically, "I am going to miss my cute little baby! Please look after him."

He goes to the external vending portal and scans his bablet to receive his money, grinning. Once he has the money, his other primitive desires are aroused and he mumbles to himself, "Oh, it is getting late! I must get there before Jollypop becomes a jelly fish."

He starts singing to himself, an expert in twisting words and rhymes: "Yankee Doodle went to town, riding on a penny..."

He puts his bablet in his side pocket and mumbles loudly, so that the Dexan Queen can hear: "They say if you try to rationalise the rationality of a gender type one, then you become irrational. It's a good job that I don't argue with them!"

He then starts walking away, although it is more of a wobble than a walk. He mutters to himself again, "Ah, I can't mingle well with the jungle of modern civilisation…"

Chapter 10

Late evening, and Go2 and Tilfo are walking along the platform towards The Dexan Queen; both pulling suitcases on wheels filled with a few items of clothes and shoes, toiletries, e-books and some game consoles. These are the only things Go2 owns, and they are taking them because he is being transferred permanently from the civilised unit to the Dexan Queen.

They are full of apprehension but also excited for what lies ahead. Go2 is in a talkative mood, his head buzzing with questions he doesn't know the answers to. All he can think to himself is: *What will it be like? Will I like it? Will I miss Tilfo? Will the experiment succeed?*

It's the uncertainty of these things that's making him feel nervous.

* * * * * *

The Dexan Queen is parked next to the furthest away platform, in the quietest spot without any disturbances. She has been elaborately decorated, both interiorly and exteriorly, and her colour has transformed to a beautiful shade of sea blue. Thousands of small colourful lights illuminate her and she looks simply breath-taking. Upon approaching her head unit, Go2 and Tilfo hear tunes of beautiful, uplifting music.

Seeing both of them, she says, "Welcome to my motherly home!"

In awe of how different she looks, Go2 says, "Wow! It's beautiful! We didn't realise how lovely it was! We are honoured and humbled."

"Yes, little cutie," she replies. "This is a very special occasion in our lives. Everything is organised for you and I have a little surprise prepared."

Go2 is excited. No one has ever given him a surprise before and he cannot thank her enough.

She continues, "Welcome aboard! The second unit has been especially designed for you and is where you will live. You'll have lots of fun in here!

Tilfo and Go2 both walk a few more paces further along, until they reach the door of the second coach. The automatic door that was originally there has gone, and it is now of a more traditional design, with two sliding doors that open sideways. Upon entering the carriage, they are sprayed with perfume from nebulisers installed in the door frame.

The Dexan Queen says, "Welcome, on this historic occasion. I hope you will enjoy this evening."

They enter the unit and walk towards a small landing area, where there is a robot- waiter sitting on a stool. He looks like a human –life- form, from the oriental sites. He is patiently waiting for them.

Upon seeing them, he jumps up and says, "Welcome aboard Sir." Bowing down, he introduces himself. "Good evening. I am Waitsharp. Madame Dexan Queen has appointed me to look after you. Please allow me to take your jackets, bags and belongings."

They hand him their belongings and he places them on a rack. Turning back to them, he says, "Please follow me inside and I will show you the arrangements and things that have been organised for you."

They follow him and he opens the door to another room.

Go2 and Tilfo are stunned and stare at each other, agog. The room is painted cream and there are luxurious curtains hanging from the windows. Party music is playing and the space is adorned with colourful balloons: so many, they don't even have room to walk around! Some are hanging from the ceiling. They've never seen a sight quite like this, before!

Tilfo stumbles on some balloons and falls to the floor amongst them, which Go2 finds hilarious! He then jumps forward and throws himself down on the balloons, too; both of them bouncing up and down and having the time of their lives.

Waitsharp is observing them from the doorway and appears to be overjoyed to see how happy and relaxed they are.

A table is placed in the middle of the room, with large and small cabinets on both sides of the wall. In the corner, Go2 spots his huge new comfortable bed.

Waitsharp says, "This is your dining and study table. Next to it you'll notice the large screen, which will enable you to communicate with anyone you like, at any time. You can also watch any programme or study any programme you wish."

An overwhelmed Go2 gasps, "Wow!"

Waitsharp says, "There is a vending portal on the opposite wall and from that, you can order food, or anything you fancy." He continues, "If you open the door in the far corner, you will see the washing and changing area, and I trust you will like it. Madame the Dexan Queen knows your taste well and has been preparing for your arrival for the past 23 days. I have helped to organise it for you, so please let me know if there is anything else you require. I will be waiting outside if you need anything."

"Okay," Go2 replies, "Thank you for everything."

Waitsharp returns to his stool and Go2 runs over and jumps onto the bed to test how comfortable it is. It immediately bounces him back.

He says, "It's very good, but it's not quite like the virtual one we had at the civilised unit."

Tilfo nods his head in agreement.

The voice of The Dexan Queen starts booming out from the screen on the wall, although she cannot be seen, as she says, "So, Go2, how do you like it?"

He gets off the bed, looks at a smiling Tilfo and says, "I like it very much! Thank you for everything! You have been so kind."

"No need to thank me," she replies. "In fact, I think I need to thank you for giving me the wonderful opportunity to be a mother to you. Many gender –type- one- life -forms crave being mothers – and not all are as fortunate as I have been, to get such a precious little gem like you."

Tilfo gazes at Go2, moved by her expression of genuine emotion.

She continues, "Today is a very special day for all of us because my little sweetie is going to get a new life. My own life is going to be very different and my priorities will change now. Go2, you are going to be so much more important than my career."

They watch the screen in disbelief at what she is saying, as she continues, "I know it's not your official birthday, but I have decided to assign you two birthdays every revolution of the earth – and today is one of those days."

"Thank you, Mom – I mean Ma'am!" he replies, feeling slightly embarrassed.

The Dexan Queen smiles to herself at his slip of the tongue, but in fact, she is pleased that he called her Mom, since this is what she has been waiting for. It's also the first time ever that someone has referred to a machine as 'Mom'.

"You can call me 'Mom'!" she laughs warmly, and proceeds to give them information on what she has planned. "So, today we will celebrate, and it will be telemonitored by the Royal Robocratic Institution of Child Welfare and Social Justice, just to assure them that the handover is going smoothly. They have sent us their greetings and best wishes," she informs them. "We will now cut the cake and have a delicious meal. Then, you can play until seven decimal hours and you will then walk Tilfo back to the station. Are you happy with the itinerary?" she asks.

Excitedly, they both jump on the balloons again in agreement. Although The Dexan Queen cannot be seen on the screen, she is proudly watching them have fun.

Every time Go2 jumps onto the balloons, she instinctively screams, "Watch out, Go2!" Her protective instincts have already kicked in.

Since Go2 and Tilfo insist on jumping on the balloons persistently, she realises that she needs to relax; they are just having fun and it can't hurt them. This does not stop her from still shouting the occasional expression like: 'be careful', 'steady on', or 'watch out'.

Go2 and Tilfo treat the balloons like a bouncy castle and energetically wear themselves out with leaping and bouncing until they are exhausted.

She orders them to stop bouncing. "Stop it now, boys! I can see you are tired. Let's cut the birthday cake, and then you can both eat cakes and some proper food, because you must be hungry."

They follow her orders and make their way through the balloons, wading over to the table in the centre of the room.

Tilfo pushes the bell attached to the side of the table. Waitsharp tries to come in by opening the door, although the balloons are now blocking the opening. But he manages to squash some and squeeze through. He has brought a tray in which candles and cake are placed. He puts the tray on the table, and lights the candles, and hands Go2 a knife and bows down, before standing back, out of the way.

The Dexan Queen insists, "Go ahead. I am watching you, but you need to make a wish as you blow out the candles."

He closes his eyes, makes a wish and blows, while they all excitedly clap and cheer him!

Waitsharp starts singing, "Happy birthday to you! Happy birthday to you! Happy birthday dear Go2! Happy birthday to you!" The Dexan Queen also joins in.

Tilfo picks up a huge piece of cake and feeds it to Go2; then Go2 offers Tilfo and Waitsharp a slice.

Waitsharp eats his before bowing down and says, "Would you like to order your other food now, Sir?"

They both nod, starving after all the playing they have done!

Waitsharp asks, "Would you like to order anything in particular? You can have absolutely anything at all!"

"Yes, please. Can we look at the menu?"

Waitsharp takes out his bablet, touches the screen and holds it up in front of Go2.

"Oh, no, Waitsharp, please hang on a moment!" The Dexan Queen interrupts. "I organised a very special menu, ages ago!"

Waitsharp puts his bablet back in his pocket and says, "Oh yes, indeed. My apologies Ma'am. It was an old habit which does not go."

The Dexan Queen continues, "It's Okay. To start with, they will have a coconut cream soup, with black cumin seeds and ground green coriander. For main course, Go2 will have a very special tofu koliwada and Tilfo has lemongrass cooked in soy sauce. They will both then enjoy a delicious course of cheese vada, followed by a sweet, thick rubdie for dessert. I hope that sounds okay to you boys?"

Their faces light up and they both nod their heads.

Go2 says, "Sounds fantastic, exotic food is my favourite! Tilfo will also be very pleased by what he's got coming."

Waitsharp says, "Yes Ma'am!" and leaves to go and process the order in the entrance area, ordering the food from the screen on the wall.

The vending portal immediately delivers the drinks in plastic bottles first, and says, "There will be a wait of three decimal minutes for the food. In the meantime, please enjoy your drinks. Thank you and please bear with us."

Waitsharp serves the drinks and later they enjoy all of their tasty five-course meals.

Throughout the meal, The Dexan Queen interrupts them, offering motherly advice, such as how to eat properly and the correct table manners. They manage to eat their puddings, but both of them are pretty full and start to feel a little tired.

After relaxing for a short while, they decide to have one last play – this time, less energetically bursting the balloons using their bablets – which emit a red coloured laser beam that they aim at the balloons. Tilfo, especially, thoroughly enjoys this.

They continue bursting the balloons until every single one on the floor, walls and ceiling is deflated.

It is starting to get very late and in an authoritative voice The Dexan Queen says, "We have gone off schedule now, and it is way past your bed time. Go2, please can you walk Tilfo out and then come back here to talk to me?"

Go2 obediently listens to her.

The Dexan Queen says to Tilfo in her soft voice, "Tilfo, darling, it is past midnight now and you need to go to sleep. Thank you so much for coming. You have been a great support to Go2 so far, and I cannot thank you enough. I appreciate everything you've done and I hope you've enjoyed yourself this evening."

Tilfo bows down to thank her.

The Dexan Queen continues, "I am so sorry, but the programmes have only allowed one person to come and live with me. Please don't feel that you are alone. You know you are welcome here at the weekend to come and visit Go2. Make sure you let us know if there is anything that we can do for you and we will be happy to help in any way we can."

Tears start streaming down Tilfo's cheeks; he has never experienced such affection and concern, ever before.

The Dexan Queen continues, "Please don't worry about Go2. I am his Mom now and I will look after him. Please look after yourself and good night."

Tilfo wipes his eyes dry and turns his head away from the screen.

Go2 places a reassuring hand on Tilfo's shoulder to comfort him and they both walk out. Waitsharp is quietly watching them and feels sad to see the temporary parting of two special friends.

As they walk out onto the platform, Go2 says, "Don't worry, I will see you every day at school and we can have loads of fun at the weekend!"

Tilfo is speechless, as usual. Go2 desperately wants to make him feel better about the situation. He says, "Come on, give me a hug."

They wrap their arms around each other, as more tears stream down Tilfo's face. They say goodbye in their own unique way, by crouching down and bending their knees forward to meet each other's. They both know this means 'see you soon'.

Tilfo reluctantly turns and slowly starts walking away, to go to the overbridge, and then come down on another platform to catch train. He walks away slowly with a heavy heart.

The civilised unit where Tilfo will remain is two stations away from the station; he will be staying here alone until the system assigns him a more permanent location. Go2 stands and watches him leave, before turning and walking back to his new home.

Go2 arrives back his new home to find Waitsharp eagerly waiting for him. The moment Waitsharp sees Go2, he says to The Dexan Queen, "Ma'am, Go2 is back home safely, now. Everything is completed for this evening and they have both eaten well and had a good time. May I ask your leave, please?"

"Yes, that is okay," The Dexan Queen replies. "Thank you so much for your assistance. Please keep in touch, as there will be many more occasions like this, in which you will be required. Please take yourself a generous tip and help yourself to your wages, using your bablet."

Appreciative of this, Waitsharp replies, "Nice of you, Ma'am." He then leaves, wishing Go2 well as he departs. "Well done, young Sir and best of luck to you. You have most definitely made the right choice. I must leave now, but I will see you again soon."

"Thank you and goodnight," Go2 replies and Waitsharp leaves.

Go2 walks to his new bedroom, makes his way towards the bed and sits down. "Hello, are you there? Can you talk to me?" he asks The Dexan Queen.

She instantly replies, "Of course I can talk to you, baby. Are you tired?"

"No, not very much. I just wanted to thank you so much for everything you are doing for me."

Feeling flattered by his appreciation, she replies, "You are very welcome, but it is my duty now. Are you enjoying yourself, so far?"

Nodding his head, he enthuses, "Yes, very much! Can I please ask you something, though?"

"Go ahead," she urges. "You don't ever have to ask permission to ask me anything."

He hesitatingly queries, "How long are you going to talk to me as if you are a ghost? Is there any way I can see you, at all?"

The Dexan Queen laughs warmly, "Of course. I kind of knew you were going to ask me this. As you know, there are certain restrictions that the programmes have put into action and I cannot take the shape of a physical robot and simply visit you. 4D image is no use to you and is forbidden, but you can see me in 2D picture format on the screen, if that would be of any use to you?"

"Wow! How?" Go2 exclaims. "That would be very interesting."

"I will show you a catalogue of various mothers of different ages and nationalities from different historical periods on the screen. You can select any form you wish to see me in. Okay?"

Go2 is amazed at how exciting technology is. "Brilliant! Please show me, when you are ready."

"Yes, darling. Here they are! Have a look and see what you think."

A menu of mothers appears. Go2 goes through the list and after careful consideration, chooses an attractive 20th Century Irish mother.

"I'd like to see you in this format," he says.

"Good choice, little one. Give it a moment and you'll see my image appear on the wall."

The entire wall of the coach is a sophisticated screen made up of trillions of digits and pixels.

A slight scratching sound can be heard and the screen turns black, before the faint image of the 20th Century Irish mother slowly starts appearing. Once the image has fully formed, Go2 cannot take his eyes off her. She is very good-looking, with blonde curly hair, green eyes, a sharp nose and a black mole on the right of her chin. It's the first time in his life he has actually seen a motherly figure, and it's like a dream come true, for him.

Go2 asks, "Are you my Mom?"

In a soft Irish accent, she replies, "Yes, darling, I am your Mom. Now, come a little bit closer to me."

Go2 goes right up to the image and places his left cheek close in front of her and she tries to kiss him.

"Aw, my little cutie," she says.

Go2 moves away and sits back on the bed, "How nice to see you! You are exactly what I wanted my Mom to be like."

Thrilled that he is impressed, she says, "I am happy for you, sweetie. Shall I keep this format?"

Fixated on her image, which occupies the entire wall, he is overwhelmed by her appearance and curiously asks, "How can you be so big? You are bigger than any human –life- form!"

She replies, "A mother's image is always larger than life. Well, it always is, in the books written by human –life- forms."

"What does that mean?" he asks, puzzled.

"Just watch. I will now adjust my size to that of a human -life -form." She then dramatically reduces in size before his eyes.

"Is this better for you?" she asks.

"Yes, perfect!" He smiles. "Please tell me – what would you prefer me to call you?"

"What do other children call their mothers?"

"Mom, Mummy, Mommy – lots of different expressions!"

"Yes, baby, you are right. Actions are way more important than words. Take the relationship between babies and their mothers, for example. How do they communicate with each other, when the baby can't speak? How does Mummy know that the baby is hungry? Through actions."

Go2 does not understand the philosophy much and tries to cut her short by saying, "Yes, I will call you Mom. Is that okay with you?"

"Any expression is fine with me, sweetie," she replies.

Go2 now wants to change the subject and get to know her a little better. He has a lot of questions to ask her and he has many things he'd like to share. He begins by asking, "Where did you gather so much wisdom?"

"Early train catches a brain," she jokes.

He laughs with her, happy that they are able to relax and joke together. Intrigued he asks, "Why are you called The Dexan Queen?"

She takes a deep breath and sighs, "Oh darling, you are curious! You want to know everything, today! Are you not tired?"

"Yes, a little bit, but I really want to know," he begs.

"Okay. If you stand looking towards the rising sun, the direction on your right side is known as the south, and on the left is the north. I am a southbound biotrain. The word Dexan comes from the old Sanskrit word for south, which is 'Daxin'. 'Dexterity' means 'the right side' and they call me the Dexan because I always go to the right. Besides, I usually choose the right path and I am very righteous. Do you understand, my little waxy potato?"

"I do. Please go on."

She continues, "The society gave me the nickname 'Queen' because of my outstanding performance and achievements in everything I do. In time, you will understand it better. Slowly, slowly, catchy monkey." Her head is tilted, facing left. She does not stop there. "Do you know, my little goaty, that queen ship is an achievement in itself? The title is not given to just anybody!" However, do you know what I like to be called best?"

"What?" he asks.

She sighs, "Mom, or Mummy. I would be so proud if I was known as Go2's Mom."

Go2 is touched by this sentiment. "Oh, Mom, do you really mean that?"

"I do," she replies. "You might not understand how much it means to me right now, but one day when you become a Dad, you will."

"Mo sss m," he says softly. He has never said it to anyone before, and his voice begins to crack. He feels emotional and so overwhelmed that gentle tears begin to run down his cheeks.

He gets up and walks up to the image to hug her and she spreads her arms out for him. Although she is only an image on a screen, it's an emotional moment between the two of them. The Dexan Queen's eyes are filled with tears and her nose becomes blocked. Through her sniffles, she says, "Oh, baby – control yourself. I will look after you for the rest of your life. I promise you; I'll never leave you."

"Yes, Mom," he answers.

After the emotional outburst, Go2 sits back on the bed and curiously asks her, "Why did you choose me, as your son?"

She wants him to go to sleep, now. "Darling, it's very late, you should get some rest."

"No, please – not yet. Tomorrow is a decimal weekend off. Please, please..."

Easily won over by him, she replies, "Okay, ten more digital minutes – because I know you have so many questions. But we have an entire life together ahead, and there is plenty of time for me to answer your questions."

"Please, can I ask just two more questions?"

"Okay – go ahead, but if you ask me a question, then I will ask you one, too."

"Deal! Why did you choose me as your son?" he asks again.

"It's a long story, Go2," she says. "First of all, you were my passenger. I get to know all of my passengers very well and I always noticed you. You have a sweet little dimple on your right cheek and it's so cute! I always wanted to kiss you every day and look after you." She continues, "A long time ago, I read that you were motherless and I have always waited for the perfect opportunity. One day, I spotted your advertisement, so I applied and they shortlisted me. Luckily, after interviewing me, you chose me and here I am! I hope this answers your question." She is proud of herself for achieving the role and continues, "I am not surprised that I was shortlisted, to be honest. I was fairly confident that I would be. Now, I'd like to ask you a question, if that's okay?"

"Okay, go on…"

"Why did you choose me?" she asks.

"We had only three choices. There was no doubt the first one was a good mother, but she lacked certain faculties. The second one was rather arrogant and did not have the nurturing side I was looking for. The third choice was most definitely the best one!" He grins.

Feeling flattered and a little embarrassed, she replies, "Oh, baby, you are such a little charmer! You will go a long way in life."

"It's my turn now" Go2 asks.

"Go on."

"What life forms you like?"

"All. Bu the human-life-forms like you, and the honey bees are my favourites. Okay, now it's my turn. What do you want to be, when you grow up?" Mom asks.

He rolls his eyes. "Well, I am grown up now."

She laughs at his innocence and says, "No, baby. I mean twenty revolutions later!"

"I want to build a castle," he proudly reveals.

"So you'd like to be a builder, or an architect? Am I correct?"

"Noooo! I want to own a castle."

In agreement, she says, "Oh, wow! That'll be fantastic! I hope it's like Connemara castle. Listen, you build a castle and I will get you lots of Irish fairies for it."

Go2 blushes at this. "It's my turn again, now. What do *you* want to do when you grow up?"

The Dexan Queen takes a deep breath, looks up towards the sky and slowly says, "Darling, growing up means growing old and I do not have a choice in this. If my major organs start to slow down, then I will be placed in a nursing yard where all my parts will slowly disintegrate and degenerate. The parts will then be moved to the junkyard and my memory chip will rust. Sadly, I will no longer be in anyone's memory." She chokes up as she continues, "That's one of the advantages of human- life- forms, when someone dies they are remembered, at least. That doesn't happen for us. We are disposable – just used and then thrown away."

Go2 sees how painful this is for her to admit, and says, "Don't worry, Mom, I will be here for you when you get old. I am your good son and it will be my duty to stay and look after you." He decides it's probably a good time to end the question and answer session, because she is getting upset. Go2 asks, "Can I please go to sleep, now? I'm really tired after my busy day, but I will ask some more questions at breakfast tomorrow, if that's okay?"

"Yes, that's fine, baby. Come here and give me a kiss," she says.

He then turns his cheek towards the image and she tries to kiss him through the screen. "Good night, honey – and sweet dreams! It might be a little strange for you, sleeping in a new place, but please give me a shout if you need anything."

"Okay, good night," he replies.

He then claps to switch off the lights, climbs into his big, new comfortable bed and pulls the duvet over his body. He has trouble dropping off to sleep, feeling overwhelmed so he can't stop thinking.

He dozes off occasionally, but wakes up several times, thinking about his new Mom. He wants to see her again but doesn't want to disturb her sleep. He can't wait for morning, so that he can see her again and talk to her some more.

* * * * * *

The sun has risen and a brand-new day is upon them.

Go2's new Mom appears on the wall again, seeming brighter and more energetic today. "Good morning, lovey!" she exclaims. "It's a glorious morning today – time to get up!"

Go2 is fast asleep and dreaming peacefully, a smile on his face. He is oblivious to what she is saying, so she repeats herself. Go2 mumbles and rolls over to change sides.

Again, she says, "Good morning, baby! Come on!"

He slowly opens his eyes and is a little disorientated at first, since he is in unfamiliar surroundings. He looks to both sides, for Tilfo, as he usually does; but realises that he is alone now, in his own home. He feels sad for a moment, but soon feels more warmth and reassurance when he looks over to the wall and sees his Mom.

A huge smile appears on his face. "Good morning, Mom! Did you sleep well?"

"Yes and no," she replies. "I spent a lot of time thinking about you and your future, which we need to talk about later. It is a two-day decimal weekend, so no school for you today and I have taken two days leave. We are going to stay parked up in the yard, where there is no traffic and we can spend some quality time together. Firstly, though, please tell me what you'd like for breakfast?"

"A modern, full, vegetarian Irish breakfast, please!"

She gives a little giggle and says, "Perfect! Good man yourself." She turns her back and continues, "Give me five decimal minutes while you visit the loo."

He goes to the bathroom while she then starts the cooking process, which can be seen on the screen. She fries vegetarian patties, a vegetarian sausage, tomatoes, mushrooms and cubes of cheese together. She then puts two slices of white bread in the toaster and boils the kettle. She moves to the vending portal where the milk pours from the tap, and she then pushes some more buttons to activate another tap for blackcurrant juice. She collects the milk in one glass and the juice in a glass jug.

She turns to Go2, and shouts, "Honey, breakfast is ready!"

Go2 comes out and sits on the table. But Feeling confused, he asks, "How are you going to bring it to me from your screen where you cooked the breakfast?"

"Easy peasy, my son! You can collect your breakfast from the internal vending portal," she says, proudly.

Taken aback, he says, "Oh, wow! That's great." He then walks over to the portal, where some processing sounds are heard before his breakfast drops down, in a pack. He lifts it up and puts in on the plate, then collects two glasses from the shelf and holds them under the tap in the portal to access the milk and juice. He carries everything over to the table and collects his cutlery from the drawer.

Admiring the delicious, colourful breakfast, he says, "Mmm, it looks yummy and smells so good! Are you not going to eat with me, Mom?"

"Yes darling, I will eat with you. Please go ahead," she replies.

Go2 carefully opens the pack, tips the items onto his plate and begins eating, while his Mom mirrors exactly what he is doing on the screen.

She asks him, "So... how is it?"

"Aye, Mammy. To be sure, it's grand!" he smirks.

They both laugh at his joke. "You don't have to tease your poor Irish mom like this."

"I am just trying to pick up some expressions to make you laugh. Grand, it is, to be sure!"

They both chuckle. Half way through eating his meal, he pauses and says, "I know you haven't cooked this, because you're just an image on a screen. The vending portal delivers whatever we order, and all you've really done is order and deliver it for me."

She agrees. "You are right, darling. This is called an 'e-breakfast'. I simply generate a picture of me cooking it, to give you a real breakfast experience."

"Oh right." He continues eating his breakfast.

He is still curious about everything. He starts looking around the structure of his room.

Go2 just tries to look on the wall on his back. Surprisingly, screen also appeared on the wall, on which mom is seen. He is astonished to see mom on the front and back wall.

He then turns his gaze on the side wall. Again a surprise! Mom is seen there as well.

Wherever he turned his head, mom appeared there.

Mom is watching him from all angles. He changes the subject, and asks, "Can I please ask you something that I couldn't, last night."

"Yes, go on…"

"How can you see my face, when I'm not always facing you, and how are you there wherever I see?"

"It's simple. The screens on the wall have millions of built-in cameras that take your picture in trillions of pixels. They see all the time and detect every movement you make. The cameras co-ordinate, like old CAT scanners, and they have the ability to see exactly what you are looking at. Your eye movements are sensed. I then just appear there; I am there for you all the time. Wherever you look, I will be there keeping you safe."

"Will you see me at all times, then?" he asks.

"No. I will give you privacy any time you want – and when you are sleeping, if you need me at all I will be next door."

Relieved to hear this, he replies, "That's good to know. How long do you plan on watching me for?"

"To be honest, all your life!" she laughs. "I want to see you grow. I want to see you with your first girlfriend, I want to watch you get married and I want to play with your children. Motherhood is the greatest accomplishment a life forms can have." She proudly continues, "I'll enjoy wiping bums and noses and rocking the cradle, while singing a lullaby. Giving birth is the creation of life and raising it is sustaining that life."

Go2 can see she is daydreaming and wants to tease her, he says, "But I've already been created and my bum has already been vacuum cleaned!"

They both laugh at his comment. He takes his breakfast plate to the washing portal and puts the packaging in the disposal portal.

"Mommmm! What are we going to do today?" he asks excitedly.

"There is a catalogue on the other wall, so we are going to go through it together and order some new clothes and shoes for you. Then we can eat, get some rest and probably do lots more talking! I have not chatted with anyone like this, ever. We have so much we need to share with each other."

"And then?" he asks, curiously.

She smiles. "Tomorrow, call your friend – because we are going to have a picnic!"

"Grand!" he replies.

* * * * * *

Chapter 11

The train-yard is always silent in the middle of the night. In the corner of the remote yard, both Belladonna and Miss Mermaid are parked parallel to each other, their heads facing one another. They are both unhappy with the progress the Dexan Queen is making on all fronts, and they feel they are getting left behind.

"Hi, Mermy!" Belladonna whispers to Miss Mermaid. "I hope you are well after the inquest assessment from the Royal Robocratic Institution of Justice?"

"Yeah, just about," she replies. "Thanks so much for seeing me at short notice – and at such an odd time."

"It's okay, Mermy," she replies. "Anything for you. Tell me how it really went, in court."

"To be honest with you, it went very well. My solicitor explained everything to the court and the jury. And even though most of them were human -life -forms, they were still fair."

"So, what exactly happened?" she asks.

Miss Mermaid takes a deep breath. "Well, I *pleaded* my innocence, and my solicitor told the court that it was an accident. He informed them that I always carried dark liquids and that there was a leak in the system. He then tried to explain to them that, due to the Venturi effect, the dark liquid I was carrying accidentally got squirted onto the honourable Dexan Queen."

"Did they ask anything else?"

"No. I think my solicitor pleaded my case well. They agreed that it was merely a sad coincidence that the acclaimed Dexan Queen happened to be passing in the opposite direction at the same time." She sneers, "Of course, I said, we all respect the Dexan Queen – and apologise for any inconvenience caused."

Belladonna is impressed by the solicitor's manipulation and laugh sarcastically.

Belladonna says, "Honourable? Ha! You apologise? Ha! Wow! Sounds like your solicitor did really well! What happened next?"

"Nothing," Miss Mermaid replies. "I gave an affidavit as an apology – and that was the end of it."

Impressed, Belladonna says, craftily, "Good! Well done. Your apology can be the first step towards revenge!"

"Yes, we need to do something!" Miss Mermaid insists. "She has become unstoppable, now! Have you heard about her latest fad?"

Enraged, Belladonna says, "I know. Apparently, she has now adopted that Redmill's son."

"She is a selfish daughter of a rabid canine!" her friend hisses. "Her best weapon is her sugary tongue, and her advances are never-ending. She's desperate for fame and will do anything! "

"You're right, baby! How about we call her the 'Desperate Queen?' instead?"

Miss Mermaid bursts out laughing. "Yes! Ha! I like that name. We could also refer to her as the 'Dextrose Queen', due to her sweet tongue."

"Yes, haha, that's a good one. But why should we call her a Queen at all? She doesn't deserve that respect from us!"

"Because she is a drama queen!"

They both laugh, enjoying mudslinging at The Dexan Queen.

Mermy says, "Rumour has it her so-called 'son' has gone to live with her!"

"Uh, I know," Belladonna replies. "But she doesn't know that shunting every wagon gives a jolt."

Miss Mermaid smirks, "Well, let her do the shunting and we'll take care of the jolts."

Bellodanna gives winning grin at this comment. Miss Mermaid continues, "It's just a relationship of convenience, to benefit her; but she'll soon realise just how inconvenient it's going to be. She has made two huge mistakes so far – the first was adopting that parasitic clone, and the second was taking me on, in court."

Belladonna continues, "Let her carry on doing little trials and we'll take care of the errors."

Miss Mermaid anxiously asks, "The question is, though, how do we get her back?"

"No worries, babe," she replies. "We'll simply follow the protocol of disruption and distraction, type 22, in our manuals."

"How can we do that?" Mermy whispers.

After a short pause, Belladonna quietly says, "The first step will be to disrupt her utilities functions; so we need to access the supply lines for her water, food, electricity, energy and raw materials."

Mermy loves the idea of this and excitedly says, "And after that...?"

"Then the second step will be to interfere with her memory chip, so she will become delirious, dejected and demented. Think how fast she'll be travelling! Instead of being south-bound, she will be burial ground-bound!" Belladonna reveals.

They are both excited by their plan and laugh.

"Oh, that sounds classic! You are great, my one and only Belladonna. I must admire you for your natural talent and genius plans. You really are my guru."

"Just wait, Mermy," Belladonna assures her. "The third step will be to defame her. I would love to see that."

"Yes, Belly. You open the slits, and I will fill them with sodium chloride. How will we get to our destinations on time, though?" Miss Mermaid asks.

"I'll explain it to you later, because it's now time for the KK4 east-bound train and we need to move, before she passes here. Remember, though, I have worked out a roadmap for the 'Queen', but we have to be careful, because she is supposed to have had human instincts installed in her." She pauses for a moment and snaps, "Her instincts inflict infringements on me and infest me, like a plague of ants! Goodbye."

* * * * * *

The sun is shining, the skies are blue and there isn't a cloud in sight. The Dexan Queen has parked herself on the top of a hill, because they have decided to have a picnic. She only has three coaches today: her head unit, Go2's room and the final coach, full of beehives.

The hill is in the middle of a spacious, green field surrounded with pine, mahogany, oak, cedar and giant conifer trees. At the bottom of the hill, there is a huge lake, with its water gently rippling and the vast expanse of clear water is still and calm.

Go2 and Tilfo are playing a game of football and are shouting at each other in excitement, as the ball moves.

An array of giant flowers surrounds The Dexan Queen, and suddenly, the automatic door of the third coach bursts open and a swarm of bees emerges.

The image of The Queen as a mom has appeared on the outside wall, and she looks more relaxed, today. Her blonde, curly hair is loose and flowing down her back and she is dressed in casual wear. She's busy preparing a barbeque and has just finished frying vegetarian sausages – the delicious cooking smell wafting from the external vending port, is making them all very hungry indeed! Everyone loves genetically modified corn on the cob, so she roasts three giant ones, gently turning them over, periodically. Her hair keeps falling forward, getting in her eyes, and although she tries to push it out of the way, her gloves are making it difficult.

Next to the track, there is a large picnic table set up, covered with plates, cups, mugs, plastic spoons, knives and forks – with a bin bag for the rubbish set up, already.

Go2 and Tilfo are still having an enjoyable game of football; Go2 is on the lower side of the slope, near to the lake. He kicks the ball high and far, and it lands exactly where Tilfo is waiting. He doesn't want to waste the opportunity, so he uses all the strength in his hind leg to kick the ball back to Go2. Unfortunately, his kick is so powerful that the ball flies up, high, into the sky. They both look up and their eyes track the movement of it. The ball slowly falls down and splashes into the lake, forming a huge wave of ripples as it lands.

Go2 shouts furiously, "You are so stupid! Did you forget that we were playing on a slope? Why do you always have to needlessly show how powerful you are?"

Tilfo is speechless, but gestures that he is apologetic.

Go2 realises that he perhaps responded a little irrationally, just now, and accepts Tilfo's apology by walking towards him and shaking hands. Tilfo lovingly puts his hand on Go2's shoulder and they start walking back to Go2's Mom. They've built up quite an appetite, after the football.

She sees them in the distance and shouts, "Come here, you big football players! The food balls are ready. You need to eat them before they get cold."

"Coming, Mom!" Go2 shouts back.

They pick up the pace and run to the table, but when they get there the food is not out yet. Go2 complains, "Mom, why did you call us when the food is not even ready?"

She laughs, "The food is ready, baby; just have patience." She then instructs, "Tilfo, darling, can you please collect the food from the external vending portal?"

Tilfo nods his head, before collecting some plates and walking over to the portal. He presses 'deliver' on the touch screen and within seconds, packets of food drop down. He collects them, puts them on the plates and returns to the table.

Go2 says, "I'm starving! Thanks, Mom!" He then opens various packs, the biggest ones containing the corn on the cobs. "I am going to try and eat as many sausages as possible! Tilfo, you try to eat the cobs."

Tilfo nods in agreement and they both tuck in.

"Mmm! It's lovely! Thanks again, Mom," he says, appreciatively.

"Enjoy, babies. I will try to keep you company." She also takes a small corn on the cob, adds a cube of butter, and starts nibbling.

Go2 is overwhelmed. "Mom, thanks again! I have never eaten such a tasty feast before, in all my life."

Tilfo agrees and it makes her feel contented, that she's made them so happy.

She says, "I bet you were both so hungry after playing such an energetic game!"

"Yes, Mom," Go2 replies.

Trying to be responsible, she says, "Most of today's calorie intake is in this meal, so you'll only have a small snack before you go to bed."

Unimpressed by this, Go2 moans, "Ah, but why, Mom? Don't be cruel! I love your food!"

She firmly states, "No. We need to monitor your calorie intake, carefully."

While they are busy talking and eating, the bees have finished collecting and, are pleased with their progress. They return to the hives in the last coach.

"Mom, why do you have only three coaches today?" Go2 asks.

"Darling, the first reason is that I am on leave – and I can't use the other coaches for my personal use. It would also be a huge inconvenience to the passengers if I took all the coaches! There's also fuel efficiency to consider. Do you understand?"

They appreciate her reasons. Go2 is still curious and asks, "Why do you need the third coach, and all of the bees?"

"Darling, bees need a change of weather and access to fresh organic nectar. Before you came into my life, they were the ones I kept as pets, and loved."

In awe of her wisdom, Go2 says, "Okay, Mom. Whatever you do, I know you're always right."

* * * * * *

The following morning, The Dexan Queen is proudly watching her son happily eat his breakfast. She is keen for him to eat more, to help him grow bigger, stronger and faster. She suggests he eats a little bit more, *at least in the morning*, but he is full.

He says, "Please stop insisting. I honestly can't eat another thing."

* * * * * *

"Okay. I don't have much time anyway, as I will be very busy today. I will drop you at Call Age, along with the other passengers, and you can return when school has finished. Please remember, that if you come back early, please go straight to your bedroom in carriage number two and wait for me to finish my shift. The other option, however, is to stay with Tilfo until I have finished. I'll contact you in the meantime, but I'll be careful not to disturb your studying or time with your friends. Is that okay?" she says.

"Okay, Mom," he agrees.

Sticking to her strict schedule, she says, "Now, go and get ready. I have to go and do the first south-bound trip."

Go2 and Tilfo are sitting on the stairs by the entrance of Call -Age, on their mid-morning break, and Go2 is chatting to his pals about his new Mom. His circle of friends is a mixture of robots, deer, ducks and children of human- life –forms, and most of them are innocent and eager to hear all about his experience.

One of the human- life -forms asks, "So, are you enjoying having a new Mom, then?"

"Yes, very much! I am so excited; you can't possibly understand."

His inquisitive friend asks, "But, how does she look after you properly, when you say she doesn't have legs or hands?"

"It's simple," Go2 replies. "She doesn't need legs, because she already has record speeds.

Still confused, he asks, "Is she paraplegic?"

"No!" Go2 replies.

"Do you have to catheterise her, then?"

"No, because she has drainage systems attached to the mains supply."

Most of the listeners do not fully understand his explanation, but they pretend they do, to avoid questioning him.

Go2 boasts, "Her intelligence and sophisticated programmes make up for other things she lacks."

Another student asks, "Does she cook breakfast for you?"

"The most delicious breakfast I have ever eaten!" he brags.

Still confused, his friend says, "I don't understand, though. How can she cook, when you say she doesn't have any hands?"

Go2 says, "It's simple – it's called e-cooking, and e-delivering."

"So, it's a bit like meals on wheels?" another friend jokes.

"Ha! Yes!" replies Go2.

"How does she buy you clothes, shoes and ice cream?" his original inquisitive friend asks.

"She orders everything I need online," he proudly says.

"It's really deals on wheels, then!" one of them jokes. "Does she take you on holiday?"

Go2 smiles. "Me and Tilfo had a picnic yesterday at the lakeside, and we are going on holiday to the Lake District in the summer."

"You're a lucky duck!" a different friend jokes.

The duck friend listening to Go2 is confused by this and wonders why he isn't lucky.

* * * * * *

It's teatime and Go2's Mom is visible on the screen in Go2's room. She's just finishing cooking in her kitchen, removes her plastic apron and hangs it on a peg on the wall. Go2 is sitting at the dining table in his studio bedroom and has just finished his homework.

Mom asks, "Darling, tell me – how was your day?"

Before Go2 answers her question, she says,

"The stew from the vending portal is ready now for you to go and collect. Be careful, though, because it's hot. I hope you like it!"

"Oh, I love the Irish vegetable stew, Mamma," he says excitedly, his mouth watering. Then he answers her first question.

"I've had a good day, and my pals gave me a bit of an interview!"

"What was the interview for?" she asks curiously, as she puts the plates and dishes in the sink and starts washing up.

Go2 replies, "Everybody wanted to know about you. Nobody wanted to hear anything about me."

Mom laughs and says, "It's because they know you and see you every day. They don't know anything about me. Come on, what did you tell them?"

A little embarrassed, he replies, "I said I'm very, very happy for the first time in my life." She smiles warmly at his answer. "I also made sure to tell them that my Mom is a famous, fantastic and a figure of respect."

Go2 collects his stew from the portal and sits at the table to start enjoying it. Her actions within the screen are mirroring his, and she, too, sits at a table, giving the impression that she is sitting opposite him.

Watching him tuck in, she asks, "How do you like the stew?"

Not wanting to put the spoon down for a second, he replies, "Mmm! It's yummy! Why don't you cook this every day? It's my favourite!"

"Good. I'm glad. I can cook it every day, but I need to look after your health, by making sure that you have a balanced diet." She is also taking delicate bites of a stew, as her way of spending time with him and giving him company. "How about you tell me what you'd like to eat in advance? And then, I can design a menu for the upcoming decimal weeks."

"You are such a good Mamma." Suddenly remembering something he needed to ask her, he says, "Mom, did you inform the school authorities about my official parental figure change?"

"Yes, I did inform them. The legal department and social security departments know about us, anyway."

"Oh, so that was the reason all the teachers were congratulating me, today! It's okay the school knowing, but why did you have to inform the legal department? The social security department would have done this, wouldn't they?"

Feeling as if she has perhaps done something wrong, she says, "I just thought it'd be better to inform them; just to be on the safe side."

"But why?" he persists.

She gives a slight smile and says, "Because, my little soldier, you are my legal heir, now."

"What does that mean?" he asks, before swallowing a huge spoonful of stew.

"It means… if anything happens to me, then you will get all of my earnings, belongings and assets."

"Don't worry!" he reassures her. "Nothing is going to happen to you, because you are a very strong woman and I have nothing to worry about. However, I am intrigued to learn that you have earnings. I didn't know about that."

"Yes, all the bio trains keep a certain percentage of their earnings from the fares and freight charges. The other share goes on taxes, expenses and the train board's share."

"Wow, all of this is new to me." Shocked at this revelation, Go2 jokes, "I didn't know you receive a private income, too. It's a good job I've become your son."

Mom laughs at his cheeky comment. "Thankfully, my earnings and the percentage of the share, I receive are the highest of all the bio trains. I think this is one reason, there is so much jealousy and animosity amongst us."

"I am proud of you," he admits. He is curious to find out more. "What do you do with your earnings?"

"I spend it on charity for all life- forms, because I don't need it. All my needs are met, and there is nothing I want. The definition of economy is: 'the process of matching unlimited wants and limited resources'. I don't believe in this. *I have proved the definition of economics wrong because I do not have unlimited wants."*

"Wow, Mom, I think I'm starting to understand, now, what you mean when you say how leadership is achieved."

"Yes, baby," she replies. "Leadership always comes with sacrifices. Anyway, is there anything you'd like me to buy for you?"

Go2 thinks for a moment. Then, his eyes light up and he replies, "I'd like lots of 4D games consoles! I'd love to collect hundreds, so I can take part in live games. Some holidays would be nice – and also, lots of sweet drinks!"

His Mom looks at him and says, "Of course, baby. I can buy you all of those things; but you must remember – it's not real life."

Go2 is slightly disappointed with this. She notices his sadness and tries to make him feel better.

"Look, we can go on holiday, but you know – it's as if I am disabled. I can do so much, like getting you close to the holiday spot, but then you and Tilfo have to take over and I will join you on your bablet. It's difficult, but please try to understand – this is what life is like for us."

"No problem mom. We have done one picnic, and I know what it is going to be. That's good enough for me!" he answers. "What about games?"

"You can have lots of games, but they must be physical and you can only play for a limited time each day. You must also remember the importance of your studies."

"Deal! How about the sweet drinks?" he asks, while grinning.

Firmly, she says, "You can drink as much milk and organic water as you like; but the sweet drinks will be for a decimal weekend treat only."

Go2 is excited to have all these things, but he isn't best pleased with the restrictions that come with the pleasures. He jokes, "Oh, here comes the momocracy."

She giggles at his cheeky comment and says, "I want to know more about your likes and dislikes; so that when I want to buy you something, I'll have an idea if you'll like it. Let's start with... what is your favourite colour?"

Go2 thinks for a moment and then says, "It changes according to the weather. For example, in the Summer, I like green and blue and in the Winter I love canary yellow. How about you?"

She replies, "I like every colour that is bright and positive."

Go2 is also keen to learn more about his Mother, so he thinks of a few questions to ask her. As usual with him, it becomes more like a question and answer session. "So, what's your favourite animal?"

"You have asked me this before. I love all animal forms, particularly their babies. She says softly. "I like the babies of honey bees the most. They are innocent and pure. What animals do you like?"

Go2 proudly says, "I love hares."

"Why?"

"Because they are spotlessly white; they have long ears, big red eyes and they are beautiful, clean and harmless," he answers.

"Very good choice, honey bunny!"

"Can I please ask you a question that I've wanted to ask for a long time?" he says.

"You can..."

"Why did you want to become a mother?"

"You have asked me this before, but I'm happy to explain again. When you become successful and peak in your life and career, things become difficult. It gets very windy and precarious at the top, and you then seem to think you are above everyone. You don't have any real friends or relatives because people will either just praise or criticise you. There is a great deal of isolation at the top. I wanted a close relationship, to be dependable to someone, and to care for them as if they were mine." She takes a pause and then continues, "I hope you understand a little better. Right, next question is – what three things do you like the most?"

Without hesitation he replies, "Easy – you, Tilfo and my bablet! How about your three favourite things?"

She knew he'd ask this and she has the perfect answer prepared. She counts on her fingers and gently says, "You, you and you."

Chapter 12

It has been a few decimal weeks since Go2 moved in with his new Mom, and things are going extremely well for them. They are starting to understand each other and most importantly, there is genuine love between them. She has worked hard to try to transform Go2's disjointed life into one with structure and schedule. She has changed his quirky eating habits and makes him follow a strict routine for meal, sleep and waking up times. They are both happy, although Go2 does occasionally complain about his regimented lifestyle, since it's not something he has been previously exposed to.

His day typically begins with a light jingle from his bablet and his Mom will say something like, "Good morning, lovey. Please wake up, because it's a beautiful morning outside and your friends are waiting for you."

He always cheekily tries to pretend he hasn't heard her and changes sides, pulling his blanket up over his head and trying to sleep some more. His Mom is, of course, persistent in attempting to wake him up and usually says, with good humour, "Look! The birds are chirping and calves are walking around! Everyone has responded to sunrise, except my cuddly little ball of gold!"

Go2 always reluctantly sits up, rubs his eyes with the back of his bent wrists and will cheekily joke, "Mom, you are horrible! It's a sin to wake up a sleeping baby. Just because *you* are punctual, that doesn't mean everyone else on the planet has to be like you!"

He then climbs out of bed and uses the toilet, while his Mom cooks him a healthy breakfast. After collecting it from the portal, he sits and eats it, while she enjoys a cup of coffee and a chat with him.

After breakfast, Mom works as the Dexan Queen, taking off from the parking yard with Go2 on board and she drops him off at the junction or Call-Age. She is usually busy all day, working hard transporting thousands of passengers from their stations and delivering them to their destinations far and wide. Occasionally, she will find a spare minute during the day, to give Go2 a quick call on his bablet to check he's okay.

In the evening, she always collects Go2, Tilfo and a host of other passengers. Tilfo is dropped off first and then she continues back to the parking yard, where she terminates and retires for the day with Go2. He also travels on other coaches to get to school, on his Mom's orders. She likes Go2 to socialise with other life –forms, and it gives him the opportunity to meet up with Tilfo. When the Dexan Queen arrives at the parking yard, Go2 goes straight to his room in the second carriage. He opens the door with his bablet – no one else, apart from him and his Mom, can open this door.

They then spend the evening relaxing together. She does not work very long hours because she is now gone part-time. If the weather is nice, she allows Go2 to go and play with his friends. When he gets home, she's always cooked him something nice and they usually sit and eat together *Go2 on his table, and mom on screen.* Go2 always has lots of homework to do, so after dinner, she helps him to complete it and then they usually play chess or cards, or sometimes she will tell him a story. Bedtime is always very strict and Go2 is not allowed to stay up late on weekdays, because of school the next day.

During decimal weekends, Tilfo often spends the day with them, when they like to go for picnics and walks and spend hours playing outside, weather permitting. For the first time ever, life is good for all three of them.

The following morning, Go2 has finished his breakfast. Mom is frantically rushing him to go and get ready, because they are both running behind schedule. Go2 has an important exam today and Mom has to make an additional trip, due to one of her colleagues cancelling at the last minute.

Go2 is struggling to get his shoes on and is pushing down hard to get his left foot into the shoe. It's his own fault, because he never bothers untying the laces, and usually just pulls the shoe off, so he can easily just slip his feet in next time, but for some reason, today this is not the case. It's causing him to get stressed out and seeing him struggle is causing, and Mom to panic, because she has to get to work on time. She is known for her punctuality to the decimal millisecond and has to drop Go2 off before he can catch the correct train to school.

For the first time ever, they are both slightly annoyed with each other. She is nagging at him to hurry and he feels that he's trying his best and going as fast as he can.

"How many times have I told you to untie your laces when you take your shoes off?"

"I just think this way is quicker," Go2 tries to explain.

"But this way, you spend even more time putting them on."

"Don't pester me, Mom. I will do it!" Go2 snaps.

She has noticed that he has started to become argumentative lately and wonders if it's due to him having to follow such a strict timetable. Trying to offer him some motherly advice, she wisely says, "You can't dig a well when you are thirsty."

Go2 cheekily replies, "Mom, I'm not thirsty! I just had a drink and more importantly, I am not digging a well – I am digging into my shoes."

His sarcasm annoys her and she advises, "Look, Sonny, there is no beauty without discipline."

He doesn't appreciate her attempt at offering pearls of wisdom when he is rushing, and replies, "I am already beautiful. I don't need any discipline, thank you."

She does not like to his subtle arrogance. "You know, lovey, you are getting bolder and bolder every day!"

"Yeah, I kissed the Blarney stone!"

* * * * * *

Apart from the distant howls of dog -life -forms, the pitch-black parking yard is always completely silent in the middle of the night. Mom is worried because she can still see light coming from beneath Go2's bedroom door and she doesn't know why.

The door knocks, and she appears on the screen, asking, "Can I please come in?"

Go2 is surprised, because it's not the first time he has broken her bedtime curfew. He stays awake most evenings to read stories or watch programmes on his bablet.

"Yes Mom? Sorry for still being awake, but I couldn't sleep, so I was studying," he craftily answers back.

Suspecting that he might not be telling the truth, she says, "Oh, okay. But I will find out from the server what kind of study takes place at this time of night, after you have spent the whole day studying!"

"No, Mom, I was really studying!" he insists.

"Okay, but good boys don't stay up late, you know..."

"Well, good mothers don't keep a constant watch over their children and intrude on their privacy!"

Since moving in with the new Mom, Go2 has started to feel emotionally secure and comfortable. He loves her, but like any typical relationship between a mother and child, they do have arguments when he gets annoyed about things. They know each other well, and he has acquired the confidence to answer her back.

Mom is hurt and becomes defensive at this statement, replying, "Babe, I don't keep watch. I didn't come into your room without permission, did I? I saw the light on and wanted to check you were okay, because it's my duty to keep you safe. That's all."

He doesn't like being over-mothered, and replies sarcastically, rolling his eyes. "Yes, your majesty. You're the spy who loves me."

She can see he is in a bad mood and does not want to argue any more with him. "Goodnight, Sonny."

* * * * * *

Mid-morning of the decimal weekend, Tilfo and Go2 are enjoying relaxing in a meadow at Den-Twist. Any life form is permitted to spend time here grazing, wandering around, socialising or playing. Today, there are quadruped –life- forms, birds, deer, rabbits, turtles, frogs, goats, dogs, cows, cats, bees, and butterflies! They are all busy completing their daily chores, or socialising.

Go2 has a paper cone in his hand, picking out salted peanuts one by one and munching them, while Tilfo is eating a carrot. They have just finished taking a long stroll around the meadow and decide to have a sit down on a large rock to rest for a moment. When he reaches the bottom of the cone, Go2 pops the last peanut in his mouth before crumpling the cone up in his hand.

While he's looking around for a rubbish bin, a black and white cow standing still under a fig tree catches his attention. She looks as though she is waiting for someone. Go2 watches her as she then makes her way over to an isolated corner, as though she doesn't want anyone to see her. Her big, bright eyes look full of love and compassion. She waits there for a while, before becoming impatient and as a last resort she starts loudly mooing for her missing baby calf. She looks around in desperation but no one appears, so she moos again, loudly. The passion in her cries reminds him of his mother, The Dexan Queen, calling him.

This arouses Go2's interest and to get his attention, he elbows Tilfo, who is busy eating his carrot. They both sit and silently observe the cow as she moos for the third time.

All of a sudden, her calf comes running out of nowhere, taking huge strides as he excitedly bounds towards his mother. The calf is adorably cute and instantly runs underneath the cow, restless with hunger, straight to her udder, to start suckling. He hits her teats with his head a couple of times.

The cow keeps looking back towards the calf while he is busy suckling, unable to keep her eyes off him. The calf is starving and tries to get every single drop of milk from her, so that some of the milk spills out of his mouth and drips down onto the ground. It's a heart-warming scene to witness, and it's evident in the cow's eyes that she is appreciative of the calf, for completing her as a mother.

Go2 is so touched by the scene that he does not realise that he has bitten his lower lip and caused it to bleed. He was so engrossed in watching real motherhood in action that he got distracted. He decides to suggest that Tilfo should record this, but Tilfo is smarter than Go2 assumes, and Tilfo is already shooting the scene on his bablet.

Tilfo stops recording when he spots Go2 bleeding; takes out a posy from his pocket and presses it on Go2's lower lip.

* * * * * *

Tilfo wisely decides not to leave Go2 alone in this state, so he stays with him and they catch a train to take them to the yard where his the Dexan Queen is parked. They cross over the bridge and walk to the corner where she is waiting and then both enter his room using Go2's bablet.

Mom has the ability to sense human movement, and she comes alive on the screen as soon as, they walk in.

Her first reaction upon seeing Go2 is a scream. She asks anxiously, "Oh dear, honey! What happened, Tilfo?"

Go2 is very casual about his sore lip because it's not the first time he has done this. "Nothing serious, Mamma. It's just normal," he tries to reassure her.

Trying to remain calm, she says, "Please take a plaster from the portal. I am sending it to you now."

Tilfo goes over to the portal, collects it and starts carefully applying it to Go2's lip. Go2 can be hard and could quite easily be thinking about other things. However, he complies with his Mom's order to put her mind at rest and accepts Tilfo's kind efforts to help.

"Will someone please just tell me what has happened?" she asks, in concern.

"Mom, why are you so worried? It's fine. I just tripped and fell over, that's all."

Tilfo is surprised to hear this, because Go2 hardly lies to anyone.

"How did you fall?" she asks.

"Accidents do happen, Mamma." He turns his head away from the screen because he is embarrassed.

But she instantly appears again in front of him, on the wall. "I know, baby, but we can prevent accidents by being careful. Look at me! I carry thousands of passengers safely and do everything I can to prevent even the slightest of accidents from happening."

"It's okay for you, Mom, because you are programmed. I am just a human. To err is human"

"Anyway, enough philosophy," she orders.

"You started it!"

"Just stop, please!"

All of a sudden, she looks sad and her eyes start to fill with tears. A lump appears in her throat and she starts to sniffle. "I wish I were human. Sometimes, things like this make me realise just how disabled I actually am."

Go2 and Tilfo swap guilty looks.

She wipes her eyes and nose and continues, "I'll be okay, boys. Just give me some time." She orders, "Go2, have a wash and I will cook something quick. Tilfo please have tea with us this evening and then you can go back home."

Tilfo can't say no to her.

"The food will be ready soon." She puts on her apron and starts cooking.

Go2 goes to the bathroom, while Tilfo entertains himself on his bablet.

They sit and eat a delicious three-course meal, but Go2 struggles to eat properly, owing to the large plaster on his lip.

After the meal, they say goodnight to Tilfo and he leaves. Go2 finishes his homework on his bablet and before bed, he plays a quick game of chess with Mom.

Go2 is sitting at the table with the chessboard in front of him; on the screen, Mom is seated opposite him. Go2 makes the first move by moving his pawn. Mom orders Go2 to move pieces for her.

"BXe4," she says.

Go2 places her piece and then, makes his own move. As he does this, she is closely watching him. She knows there is something wrong with him but can't quite put her finger on it. What is he hiding? How did he fall? She suspects he is not telling her the truth, because, by now, she has the ability to read his body language well.

"QXheR," she tells him.

Go2 is frustrated by her intelligent moves, but still ends up winning the game, which pleases him. He is oblivious to the fact that she deliberately made incorrect moves to allow him to win. Usually she always wins, since she is the one with artificial intelligence. Fortunately, she has emotional intelligence, too.

* * * * * *

It is late at night and Go2 can't sleep. He can't stop thinking about the cow and calf he witnessed today, which was unforgettable! He can't get over how she called for him by mooing, and he responded – and then, the look of pure love in her eyes! He noticed that all her emotion was shown in her eyes, as if they were the mirror of her inner turmoil, and then, immense love.

The thought of the cow is troubling Go2, because the scene he witnessed was one of maternal instinct in the so-called lower life- forms. He is supposed to represent the higher primate -life -forms, but he actually feels inferior to the calf, because he doesn't experience that sort of warmth and pleasure. Yes, he has a mother, but she is almost dysfunctional and devoid of comforting warmth in the sensation of loving touch and the direct, intimate look of love in her eyes. She was grateful to her child for making her a mother. He knows his mom is intellectual, but at the end of the day, she is just cold metal. There is no blood, sweat or warm tears flowing through her. He will never feel her warm embrace, the throb of her living heartbeat, or nestle in her familiar human smell.

Despite having a Mother, Go2 still feels he is missing something. Although she is the highly respected 'Dexan Queen', and despite her caring, she cannot properly look after the basic emotional needs of a child, and he still feels like an orphan.

* * * * * *

The following day, after tea, Go2's onscreen Mom is busy putting pots and pans away in the kitchen. He's just finished his pudding and is watching her closely.

"How was your day?" she asks him.

He shrugs his shoulders. "Same as usual. Water under a bridge."

"Wow, my son is now using expressions. Great!" She frowns, worried, realising that something is wrong with him. She gently asks, "How is your lip? It looks a little better than yesterday. Does it still hurt?"

"Yeah, it's much better today. I changed the plaster at school, as per your *instructions*." He emphasises the word 'instructions'.

"You're a good boy, Go2. Please tell me how you fell yesterday? I'm worried about you," she admits.

"Mom! Please don't nag me!"

She is astonished by this answer because she expects to know the whole truth and hates him keeping secrets from her. Attempting to change the subject, she asks him, "Do you have any homework to do? If not, we can play a game, maybe?"

"I don't have any homework today." He adds, "But what can *you* play with me anyway?" His inner thoughts have indirectly surfaced. "It's not like you can actually come out of the screen!"

Feeling sad, she says, "I know, baby; but maybe we can play cards or chess, here?"

"No, I'm bored with those."

She's annoyed by his attitude but is experienced and intelligent enough not to show it. She suggests, "How about *hide* and seek?" She says the word hide a little louder, to encourage him.

"No, I'd rather just talk," he mutters. "Or maybe I'll go out for a walk."

"Fine, we'll talk here." She takes a seat at the table on the screen.

"I have a question," Go2 admits. She gestures for him to go ahead, so he continues: "What is the role of a mother in anybody's life?"

She is taken aback by this philosophical question, which he should have asked during the interview. She becomes defensive, suspecting that he is perhaps looking for something more in a mother, after all.

"Well, a Mom is not exactly a superhero, like you read about in stories. She can only ever try her best and do whatever she can, according to her capacity and remit," she says.

"Her capacity," he repeats, picking up on her insecurities.

"Well, her main duty is to protect and provide."

"And how does she provide?" he asks.

"By looking after the needs of her children."

"How does she understand their needs?"

"By using her maternal instincts – she knows when her baby needs feeding, even though babies do not speak," she explains.

Go2 doesn't understand this concept. "But how does it happen, without the use of language?"

She tries her best to explain it to him. "Language is just a means of communication. Bonds, understanding, nonverbal communication and needs all come way before language. Look at Tilfo – he doesn't speak, but we all understand him."

"Oh, right," says Go2. "Good to know."

"Why are you asking me this?" she asks, exasperated. "What more do you want from me? Do you think I am failing or something?"

"You said that a Mom protects and provides, but I still don't understand exactly how she does this."

Worried, she says, "Let me know what else you want from me. And please let me know if I am falling short of your expectations."

"I am fine," he assures her, to smooth things over. "I'm just trying to learn more about the dynamics of the relationship." He is not deliberately trying to hurt her, but at the same time, he feels that he is missing something. He continues, "How and what does she provide, exactly?"

"Well, when babies are small, she provides food - EM EYE EL KAY."

"What dairy does she buy it from?" he asks, although he already knows how a mother's milk is produced.

She gives a little laugh and replies, "My darling, it is produced in the body, from blood."

"How does red blood produces white EM EYE EL KAY?"

"Exactly the same way that we produce tears, sweat and saliva."

"Do bio trains have blood?" he asks.

Trying to understand what he is getting at; she is starting to think he is over thinking. She doesn't have an exact answer for this, but knows she has to tell him something.

"Blood is just a vehicle – and bio trains are a vehicle in themselves. They do not need an alternative fuel."

"So, they cannot produce milk?" he asks again.

"Blood, milk, tears and sweat are liquids that life -forms need. We are above this."

"So, high and dry?"

Mom is left speechless by this sudden attack of questions.

* * * * * *

Nowadays, Go2 is more withdrawn; he's quieter and is trying to live more independently. He doesn't talk to his

Mom or Tilfo much and they are both starting to notice subtle changes in him. He's not explicit in saying why he is like this. There's a possibility that Tilfo knows, but he cannot speak.

Go2 has also changed his eating and drinking habits and has replaced every other drink with milk – drinking milk before and after every meal, during school breaks and whenever he is thirsty. His Mom is happy with this, because she knows how good it is for his health, helping his growth and strength.

It's teatime and Go2 is enjoying a meal of pasta and melted cheese, with two full glasses of milk on the table. Onscreen Mom is also eating her food. All of a sudden, he bites down on something hard, like a bone, which produces a cracking sound. He stops biting, jumps up and rushes over to the sink.

Concerned, she asks, "What happened, babe?"

Speaking with his mouth full of pasta, he says, "I don't know! How did a bone end up in the pasta?"

He then bends over the sink and spits it out, with a metallic clink when it falls.

Hearing the sound, his mother immediately identifies it. "Oh, baby – it's nothing to worry about. It's just your tooth that has fallen out – in fact, congratulations!"

Go2 turns the tap on and cleans the tooth. It's a second lower incisor from the right side.

He washes it and shows it to his Mom. "Look! It's been wobbling for the last few days, and it's finally reached its last station."

"Good! You will get a new bigger and brighter one, soon. Drinking lots of milk is doing you good!"

"What shall I do with it?" he asks, peering at the tooth.

"You should leave it under your pillow tonight, make a wish and go to sleep. A tooth fairy will pay you a visit in the night."

Go2 is sceptical about this. "How will she come here? She doesn't have the code on her bablet to open the door… and what will she come for, anyway?"

"Well the fairies are friends of children and they come during the night. They bring pocket-money, gifts, sweets and lots of good luck with them!"

"How will she get here? What will she bring for me?"

"She will come as a spirit and she only needs a small slit to come in, so she can use the vending portal to do this. All you have to do is move your bed, to beside the portal."

"What does she look like?"

She smiles. "Fairies are the most beautiful creatures! When you are older, I will find a very special one for you."

Go2 is excited and can't stop feeling the gap in his mouth with his finger, and a toothpick. "Mom, when will I lose all of my other teeth?"

She gives a little laugh and reassures him, "There is a time for everything and it will happen gradually. Every time you lose a tooth, a fairy will come – that is guaranteed."

"Will I be able to see her if I stay awake all night?"

"No, darling, they are like dreams – they will only come to you when you are asleep."

Eager to have a fairy visiting him, he says, "Okay, Mom, I've finished my homework, so can I go to bed now?"

She laughs to herself at his sudden enthusiasm to go to sleep.

"At least I have one less tooth to brush, now!" he jokes. He closes his eyes and bows his head. "Please can I say goodnight, now? I am very, very sleepy."

"Go on," his mother laughs.

He goes and brushes his teeth as fast as he can and comes back again to wish her goodnight.

He pulls the top of the bed close to the portal.

Mom turns off the lights, and her image disappears from the screen.

Go2 turns his bablet on and places it on the table next to his bed. He strategically puts it facing the vending portal and sets it onto a video recording mode. He closes his eyes, makes a wish and drifts off to sleep.

* * * * * *

He wakes up suddenly the following morning, to the sound of his Mom saying, "Good morning, baby! Please wake up! The sun has risen and it's time to get up."

He reluctantly opens his eyes and tries to go back to sleep when he suddenly remembers that he was awaiting a visit from the tooth fairy last night.

Eagerly he asks, "Mom, did the tooth fairy come? What did she leave for me?"

She smiles. "I'm sure she visited you. Why don't you get up and see what she has left you?"

He leaps out of bed and races over to the portal. He is thrilled to find two coins, a bag of toffees and a note written on yellow and green paper, waiting for him. He picks them up and reads the note to Mom.

It says: 'Congratulations, Go2! It's the Tooth Fairy here and I must say, you are growing. Well done for looking after your teeth so well – and I look forward to the next one falling out, so I can visit you again, soon. I have given some money to your Mom, so she can buy whatever she thinks you might like. Remember to always love your Mom. We like children who do this and you and mom are very special. Goodbye!'

He opens the toffees and starts eating them, one after another.

"Go2, darling," Mom says, "have you brushed your teeth?"

"No, I don't want to brush them because, then, I might have to keep them and I want them to fall out soon, so the Tooth fairy can come back again."

Mom bursts out laughing at this. "If you want your teeth to fall out early, then you must look after them."

"Hmm," he says. "That seems counter-intuitive. But... anyway... Mom, what are you going to do with the money she gave you?"

She pauses for a second before revealing, "We will buy you some new games consoles, lots of clothes and shoes and perhaps a new bablet for you and Tilfo!"

"And what else?"

"What else? What else?" she exclaims. "A big weekend break!"

"Yesssssssssssss!"

* * * * * *

Chapter 13

The Dexan Queen is racing through valleys, mountains and countryside on a typical sunny day. Go2 and Tilfo are sitting in Go2's room, admiring the beautiful scenery flash by, outside.

She enters a mountain pass section, with a steep cliff on one side and a huge mountain on the other. Upon spotting the cliff, Go2 and Tilfo gasp; they're so close to the edge, they feel as if they are going to fall.

Go2 proudly says to Tilfo, "My Mom is so great. She's organised this trip to the Lake District, especially for us."

Tilfo nods his head in agreement. They are astonished by how picturesque it is, as she thunders past beautiful cedar, conifer and oak trees. There is also a genetically modified gulmohar – or flame tree – which creates a canopy of red petals overhead. Acacia trees are blooming with yellow flowers and both sides of the track are lined with colourful daffodils, tulips and the occasional cherry blossom. It's like a festival of colours - red, green, blue, white, yellow, pink and purple. Go2 and Tilfo have never seen so many flowers before.

The Dexan Queen's journey then takes them to the land of the lakes, and she is passing vast, serene lakes on both sides. The blue sky is reflecting down onto the water, making it glisten crystal blue, and it's as if her appearance has disturbed the tranquillity of lakes.

She finds a quiet place to stop and slows down near some flat, bluebell-covered land, with a lake on her right. There are not any human -life forms, robots or 4D images here. All that can be seen are a few bird life-forms flying high in the sky.

Mom appears on the screen in his room. "Boys, we have arrived at our destination! We will stay here for tonight and

I will be with you all day. You can bring your luggage out now and go and set up the tent."

They grin excitedly, and she continues, "I have to go to the parking track at night time, but I'll be back with you in the morning."

"Okay, Mom," Go2 replies.

They collect their bablets, the packed tent, tins, bottles, milk bottles and ball, and get off.

Mom reminds him, "Don't forget your sticky plaster, either! Tilfo, please keep a close watch on him, because he is such a sensitive boy."

Tilfo nods; he already knows this. Go2 looks at him and rolls his eyes; he always gets frustrated when he thinks she's nagging him.

They place their luggage down outside and Mom appears on the external screen of the wall on her head unit.

"I will cook some light food for us now, and you can go and have a quick play. But before you go, I'd like to show you something I have bought for both of you."

"What is it?" Go2 asks.

"Just a little something to celebrate your tooth falling out."

"Oh wow, thank you. What have you got for us?" he asks, eagerly.

"Please open the box inside my head unit and you will see."

They go to the head unit and retrieve two boxes, which they frantically tear open. Inside one, they find yellow shirts, trousers, caps, socks and shoes. In another box, they find two shiny, new bablets.

Go2 hands Tilfo one and says, "One for you, and one for me."

They are both overjoyed at this wonderful surprise.

"Thank you, Mom! Can I wear this now?" Go2 excitedly asks.

"Of course, you can! Go to your room and get changed. Awww..." she sighs, fondly. "My yellow son will look so good on a green background!"

Go2 goes to his room to get changed and comes back outside. Tilfo meanwhile, is playing with his new bablet and has no interest in putting on his new attire.

Go2 feels very smart in his new outfit and asks, "How do I look?"

"You look like a little prince," she replies, proudly.

"Can we play now?"

"Yes, of course you can, but before it gets dark you need to set up your tent," she reminds him.

They move their luggage into a corner, out of the way, and Go2 takes a big swig of milk from the bottle. They then start playing football.

While they are busy playing, Mom puts on her apron in the kitchen, and starts cooking: grilling carrots, parsnips and corn on the cobs. She flicks the kettle on to boil and opens a pack of dry soup.

After a short while, she calls out, "Boys, come here! The food is ready!"

They race over and lay the table with knives, forks, plates and glasses; both starving! In the frantic rush of laying the table, Go2 knocks over a bottle of ketchup and it falls on the table and spills everywhere.

"Why are you always in such a hurry?" Mom asks.

Go2 is not afraid of answering her back, these days. "I learnt it from you! You're the one who's always running around."

"It's my job, though, I need to be efficient."

"Yes, but it's easy for you to be efficient because you are automatic, programmed and mechanical. I, on the other hand, am just a poor, useless human."

Trying to divert an argument, she says, "Stop talking now, and go and get your food. Tilfo, please help yourself."

They walk over to the external portal, collect their hot meals and lay them out on the table. They both tuck in, while Mom eats a corn on the cob. It's a nice opportunity for them all to relax and unwind, away from the hassle and bustle of everyday modern life. They decide to play again after their food.

They don't realise how late it's getting, until they hear, "Boys, it's getting dark, now! You should go and sort your tent out. There is plenty of food on the table and hot drinks in the thermos, so you can eat and drink whenever you like. Please remember, I am only half a kilometre away in the parking track and I'll be able to see you on the telemonitors. Be good boys – and Tilfo, please look after yourself and Go2. This is a very safe place but call me on your bablets if you need to. Okay?"

Go2 asks, "Why do you have to go?"

"Babe, I really don't want to. But they might need this track in case of an emergency, and I can't be obstructing it. Bye, boys."

"Okay, I understand. Goodbye Mom," Go2 says, and she leaves.

Go2 and Tilfo instantly feel more relaxed. After a struggle, they manage to set up the tent, make two neat beds inside and sit down.

Go2 confesses, "Tilfo, I have something I want to share with you." Tilfo gestures for him to continue. "I *am* happy with Mom, but it's not the same," he admits. "I miss that human-to-human close contact, where you can feel their presence and one another's heartbeats."

Tilfo is confused, and doesn't know how to respond, so he places a hand on Go2's shoulder to try to convey to him that he knows things are difficult for both Go2 and his Mom, but everything will be alright.

Go2 says, "Anyway, I am not here today to moan and be miserable. Let's play a game! I have an idea for one I'd really like to play!"

Tilfo nods, since he loves playing games.

"I saw a kangaroo not long ago, and the relationship between the mother and child is my ideal. So, let's play kangaroos, today!"

Tilfo likes the idea of this, and they both clamber out of the tent. Tilfo ties a sheet around his waist to create a pouch, and then lifts Go2 up, placing him into the small pouch, so that he's the Mother and Go2 is the baby. Go2 is squashed but tolerates it.

"Ready, steady, go...!" Go2 excitedly shouts, before Tilfo takes a big leap and starts hopping and jumping around.

After a couple of hops, Go2 slips down and his neck gets stuck in the sheet. "Stop, Tilfo! It's too tight! I'm choking!"

Tilfo stops, but finds it funny, and can't control his laughter. Go2 clambers off him and goes back to the tent to collect another sheet.

Tilfo ties the second sheet to the one attached to his waist and tucks it between his thighs, to be tucked again, at his back, so that the whole pouch resembles a giant loin cloth. He lifts Go2 up again into the new pouch, this time facing each other.

They hop around a few times, but their noses end up rubbing against one another's, so they are uncomfortable and it's clearly not working. Tilfo bends down to let Go2 climb out, and they decide to see if it's more successful if Tilfo lifts him up and places him backwards. It seems to work, and Tilfo stuffs him into the loincloth. The only problem is that Go2's legs are hanging down so far they are touching the ground, but he bends his knees a little and they begin to hop.

They hop around until Tilfo is exhausted, without realising how late it actually is. Using the artificial light from Go2's bablet, they sneakily eat the leftover food from earlier and then each takes a glass of hot milk from the thermos, while they sit cross-legged on the ground, watching the stars.

Go2 says, "When a parent dies, their child always looks at the stars in the hope of seeing them."

Tilfo agrees with him.

"I can't even do that, because I was produced without a real mother. She is not up in the sky, so there's no point even looking there," he says, sadly.

He starts biting his lower lip again and the blood starts to drip down, but no one can see what is doing, due to the darkness of the night.

He looks up at the starry sky and continues, "I am just a black hole in the universe."

Tilfo is sad, having similar thoughts.

Go2 admits, "My Mom says I am star, in her eyes, but it all just seems so mechanical."

Tilfo agrees, Go2 keeps on chatting for a long time before they both eventually fall asleep in the tent. They have a peaceful rest and the night is silent, apart from the distant howl of foxes.

* * * * * *

Bright and early the following morning, Mom appears on the screen, and cooks breakfast. She gives shout to both sleeping in the tent. They wake up and join for breakfast.

She looks at the plaster on Go2's lip, worried about him, but she doesn't say anything because she knows he will be moody and it will end up in a foolish argument.

They enjoy a tasty breakfast outdoors, before The Dexan Queen takes them on an exciting trip, racing through the valleys to show them the true beauty of nature.

In the evening, she returns to the parking yard and says to Go2, "Boys, there is still food left over. You can heat it up in the mega-wave if you're hungry."

"Yes, Mom."

Go2 heats up some food for them, and they tuck in. Not long after finishing, she says, "Go2, can you walk Tilfo out of the yard?"

He agrees. Tilfo is sad to leave, but they do their usual goodbye ritual – bending their knees forward until they meet. Tilfo strolls into the distance and Go2 returns to his room.

Mom is waiting for him to come back, because she wants to have a chat with him to try to find out why she's seen such a change in him, recently. He has become argumentative and more detached, and she has noticed that he's quiet and doesn't express any warmth of emotion any more.

"What's wrong with you, Sonny? Did I do something wrong? Is there anything you'd like me to do differently?" she gently asks.

Go2 is not in the mood to talk and replies, "No, Mom. You are a perfect bio -mother. I am just tired, after such a busy two days of being outdoors on holiday."

She remains silent, not knowing what to do; but she knows that something is going on with him.

* * * * * *

After finishing a busy day at school, Go2 boards The Dexan Queen at Call-Age. He usually always goes straight to his room on the second coach, but today, he boards the fourth coach, which is open to all life- and non-life forms. He does this, because he's waiting to join Tilfo who boards at Den-Twist. It is evident that Go2 is not himself, due to the doubts he's having about his mother. Tilfo knows and understands this.

Go2 is travelling northwards, with various characters, and the blazing sun outside, is shining on the left side of his face, lighting it up with a golden yellow hue. The passengers are quiet and all look tired after their busy day.

Bored, Go2 starts messing with a flap in the wall. Inside the flap there is a Duke-box, which he takes out and puts on his eyes and ears.

An advertisement from the Department of Health Sciences for Life Forms appears on the Duke-box. After an initial jingle, two characters appear on the screen: one is a human -life -form, gender type one and the other is a pig, gender type one.

The human -life form character is a good-looking person who says, "Attention, attention! Please, everyone, watch this advert. It will change your and your children's lives for good. You do not need to purchase anything."

There is another jingle and the ad continues: "God Nature has blessed many animal l-life -forms with special glands, called the mammary glands, and you should be proud of having them. Some animal-life-forms are even referred to as 'mammals' because of these."

The pig -form type 1 takes over the announcement, saying, "Research shows that if you don't use it, you lose it. If life forms lost their mammary glands, then their health might suffer, as a consequence."

The voiceover returns to the human -life -form type one. Go2 is interested in what the advert is saying and tries to fix the Duke-box snugly to his head.

The advert continues, "Sustain life, and feed your babies naturally! The milk is warm, germ-free and has immunoglobulins, which will help to protect your vulnerable children from the attack of pathogenic germs. It also helps babies to feel secure, as they receive physical touch that is necessary for their healthy growth, as well as the right temperature, and pressure. Babies will be able to hear your heartbeat and this will establish the bond between a mother and child."

The pig -life -form adds, "I am blessed that I am a mom and am very proud of it. I'm not ashamed of feeding my babies, anywhere. I am the best mom because of my children, and I make them healthier by providing them with a natural source of energy. Sustain life and feed your babies!"

Go2 is appreciative of this advert, since it has helped him to understand the benefits of natural milk.

While he is daydreaming, an announcement from the Dexan Queen can be heard, sounding formal and official. "We will soon be approaching the next station – Den-Twist, in approximately three decimal seconds."

The Dexan Queen slowly comes to a halt and some passengers get off while others climb aboard.

Tilfo knows exactly where Go2 is sitting, because he's always in the same place, so he boards the fourth coach and they greet each other as usual, with a high five. Tilfo is carrying a bag containing a bottle and some other equipment, which he hands over to Go2. Then the Dexan Queen slowly starts to build up her speed again.

Go2 thanks Tilfo for bringing what he asked for, and Tilfo nods at him. Go2 hands the Duke-box to him and tells him to watch the advert he's just seen.

After watching it, Tilfo realises why Go2 recommended it and looks back at him, helplessly.

Go2 is sitting at the table in his room, enjoying his evening tea, with two large glasses of milk on the table that he's sipping between mouthfuls of food. Mom is sitting with him, via the screen, to give him some company, tucking into a plate of biscuits.

After some light-hearted chit chat about his day, Mom takes the plunge and boldly asks, "What was in your bag today?"

"Just a paint brush and some colourful paints, Mom, that's all."

"Oh, so, now my son is taking an interest in art? You could have ordered them on a portal here. Why did you trouble Tilfo? Anyway, What are you planning on painting?"

Go2 doesn't have much choice – and it's going to be a whopper. He says, "No, Mom, Tilfo knows which leaves need to be crushed to get the exact colour I'm looking for. Anyway, I'd like to draw a picture of you first, to kick-start my career in painting."

Mom laughs, "Wonderful! So, you want to make me even more colourful?"

"Mom, can I ask you something?" Go2 is trying to appease.

"You don't have to ask for permission, you know that," she says.

"Why are mothers so great?"

"What makes you say that?" she asks, suspiciously. "Do you think I am failing in any way?"

"No, Mom. I'm just wondering," he reassures her.

She smiles, "This is a third time you are asking this question. Well anyway, yes, mothers really are great; as are fathers. However, a mother is the one who carries a baby for a certain period of time, and sometimes it can be risky, or even life-threatening for her."

"Is that the only reason?" he asks.

"No, the next function she has is to protect and to provide for her children."

Go2 is becoming repetitive deliberately, and asking,

"What does she provide, exactly?"

"Well, we have discussed this before. But when babies are small, they can't communicate and need nourishment to help them grow, and mothers produce milk for them."

"Yes, I saw an interesting advert earlier today, promoting breastfeeding. They said that it can help to cut down allergies in children and how important it is for mental wellbeing."

"Yes, that's all true."

"It also promotes a special bond between them," Go2 adds.

"That is absolutely right!"

"Can I ask you something related to this, please?"

"Sure..."

"If you were my birth mother, would you have nursed me?"

Without hesitation, she replies, "Of course I would have done, babe."

Go2 is a little apprehensive, but says, "I need to tell you that... sometimes... I do feel as if I've missed that bonding."

"I know you do, but it's important to remember that we don't always get everything we want in life, every time, everywhere."

Go2 looks glum. "What can you do for me?"

"How do you mean? I can do anything for you, lovey. You know that."

"If that's the case, then I am looking for that exact experience that babies have. I want to feel close to you.

Can you give me that nursing experience? I want to become your real son, because I feel like something is missing, otherwise."

Mom is shocked speechless by his demand. After a short pause, she manages to gather herself and says, "Go2, I can't believe you are demanding this! It's absurd and strange!"

He remains silent. He half expected her to react in this way.

She continues, pained, "Even if I wanted to, it's not possible. You are almost seven – quite grown up, and I am not your biological mother. I am a biotrain installed with human instincts. I'm not even permitted to appear in 3D robot format. And, most importantly, I don't want to do it."

Go2 blinks. With a lump in her throat, she adds, "I love you so much! There is already a perfect bond between us, so you don't need breastfeeding to establish this. There are millions of mothers who cannot breastfeed, due to disabilities. Your gratitude and loyalty are enough to me."

Go2 is embarrassed and doesn't react; he just looks down at the floor. Mom continues,

"You've made me feel very small, by saying what you have just said. And it's hurt me, because you've reminded me of my limitations."

Finding it tough to control her emotions, she bursts into tears. Through her sobbing she says, "You are growing now, but perhaps you need to do some more growing up. I did not realise, when I took on the role as your Mother, that I would be expected to complete this function! You can't expect to get juice out of dried fruits."

Shocked by her extreme reaction, Go2 feels guilty for his bluntness towards her, but he feels that by not saying anything that he would be suppressing his primitive desires. He feels relieved that he's got it off his chest, at least, and is not hiding it from her, now.

Trying to compose herself, she wipes her eyes and says, "Those adverts have sent you crazy! I am going to complain to the advertising standards agencies, to get them to remove those types of adverts from the public domain. Go to bed now, I'm tired. Goodnight."

She immediately disappears from the screen. She is never so abrupt, usually – she's always been more than happy to stay until late, talking to Go2.

* * * * * *

Later that evening, the Dexan Queen is parked in her usual spot, in the corner of the parking yard. A light can still be seen in Go2's room, because he's having trouble dropping off to sleep. He is restless and feels guilty for unnecessarily hurting Mom, and also feels torn by what he wants from life.

He climbs out of bed and goes over to the dining table, where he finds a full bottle of milk that he puts on the table next to his bed. He bends down and reaches under the bed to find the bag that Tilfo gave him, earlier. He takes it out, puts it on the bed and opens the zip.

The bag contains a nappy, an empty bottle and a square packet with a rubber teat in it, which he rips open. Opening the bottle of milk, he pours it into the clear, empty baby bottle, then screws the teat tightly over the top of the bottle.

Holding the nappy against himself, over the top of his pyjamas, he sticks the two ends of the nappy around his waist. He is now ready to 'play baby'.

He places the bottle on his pillow in a slanting position and curls up in his bed, like a baby.

Folding his hands into fists, he clutches the bottle tightly, his fingers bent up like little claws, using both hands to grip the bottle. Before drinking from the bottle, he sucks air in, to practise, confirming that his cheeks work efficiently. Holding the bottle in his lips, he starts sucking. He doesn't like the rubber and plastic smell or taste from the bottle, but he carries on drinking. Some of the milk accidentally spills onto his pillow when it drips from the corner of mouth, which reminds him of the scene he saw, between the cow and the calf.

Suddenly, the screen on the wall activates and a door can be seen onscreen, with the thudding sound of it being knocked at, from outside.

Taken by surprise, Go2 guiltily pulls the duvet over his bottle to hide it and looks towards the screen, reluctantly asking, "Who is it?"

"It's Mom," is the reply.

"Come in," he says, sheepishly.

On the screen, Mom opens the door, and it's clear that she is stressed and has not slept.

"I just wanted check that you were all right! I saw your light on and was worried that you might not be sleeping. Are you okay?"

"I'm fine, Mom," he lies. "I couldn't sleep, so I was reading some stories on my bablet."

He wants to convince her to believe that he is telling the truth, so he leaps out and runs over to the screen to show her the bablet. However, he somehow accidentally knocks the bottle of milk onto the floor, when he does this.

He has also totally forgotten about the nappy he's wearing over his pyjama trousers. Seeing him standing there like that, and the baby bottle of milk on the floor, a look of horror appears on Mom's face. She turns pale.

In a choked voice, she says, "Baby, I don't think you *are* okay. I think you perhaps need some medication rather than milk. It's perhaps time we got you some help."

Chapter 14

The psychiatrist's consultation room is painted white, with matching white furniture. The handles, doors, wash-basin, walls, sofas, chairs, lampshades and desk accessories – everything is white, except for the bright blue bablet.

The psychiatrist, Dr Smith, is a human -life -form: an old man with white hair, beard and moustache. He seems sociable and philosophical, and is smartly dressed in a white shirt, coat, trousers, hat and tie.

Go2 and Tilfo sit anxiously across the table from Dr Smith in his white revolving chair. Go2's Mom is also present, appearing onscreen on the wall in her natural human size. She looks stressed; it's the first time ever in her life that she has appeared on a public screen in the outside world.

Dr Smith smiles. "Thank you very much for coming to see me. I'd like to talk to Go2 alone, if you could both please excuse us."

"Thank you for seeing us at such short notice," Mom says. "I will close myself down, but please call me when you have finished with Go2." She disappears from the screen, which turns white.

Tilfo also gets up and bows to the Doctor before walking out of the room.

Closing the door behind him, Tilfo sits down on a black sofa in the corridor outside. He notices a clock on the wall in front of him with the numbers one to ten on the dial, representing the decimal hours. It is at number four on the decimal clock, he continues to stare at it, watching the decimal seconds pass...

* * * * * *

It gets to five on the decimal clock and Go2's counselling session is still going on, inside the room. Meanwhile, outside, Tilfo has dozed off to sleep on the sofa.

The Doctor finally finishes talking to Go2, having taken note of his history and his problems, and he says to him, "Could you please go and wait outside? I just need to talk to your legal Mother."

"Yes, I will do. Thank you for seeing me." Go2 shakes hands with Dr
Smith and leaves, closing the door behind him.

Back in the room, the Doctor is pressing some buttons on his bablet to try to connect with Go2's Mom. A few digits appear on the screen and then, suddenly she can be seen.

"Thank you, Doctor," the Irish mother wrings her hands in concern, her face even paler than usual. "What do you think is wrong with him?"

Dr Smith pauses, his lips pressed together. Then he says, "Thank you, Ma'am, for giving me the opportunity to have a look at Master Go2. His case is very complex, intriguing and most atypical." He scratches his white beard, thoughtfully. "I will start from the beginning." He continues, "Go2 was a knock-out baby."

"What does that mean, Dr Smith?" Worry-lines appear on her forehead, as she frowns.

"I will try to simplify this for you," he answers. "His biological father had him cloned as an organ bank. His father is a drug addict – and studies have shown that a few genes are responsible for drug addiction. So, when Go2 was created, they removed the substance-abuse genes from his primitive cells to prevent him from becoming a drug addict, like his father. So, now he will grow into a normal adult, without inheriting the drug addiction."

"Well, that's great news!" says Mom. "Thank you for giving me this information." She still looks a little puzzled and concerned.

"There is something else," the Doctor adds. "As children grow from infancy into childhood, they normally lose their primitive reflexes and instead, grow in their cognitive and metacognitive domains."

"What does that mean?"

"Well, for example, we lose the new-born's instinctive grasp and suckling reflexes, as we grow into adulthood." He spreads his hands open and closed, to demonstrate a gripping motion. "Go2 is a highly intelligent boy, with an IQ of 168 – in old units. In certain respects, yes – he has progressed very well. Exceptionally advanced. However, I'm afraid in other respects, he has actually gone backwards. This is referred to as 'regression', or 'infantilism'."

"Oh, no!" Increasingly anxious, Mom's hands fly to her open mouth. "That sounds…Well, what? What is it?"

"Regression is a state whereby children start to behave like infants. They have a desire to do things they did early on, in life."

"Why does this happen?"

"It is a complex area of research in psychiatry and many mental illnesses can cause regression to occur…"

Mom gives an audible gasp. "Mental illness!"

"Some children just want to revert to the level of comfort and attention they experienced as infants."

"I am happy to give him all the comforts he seeks, as far as I can," Mom's says, sadly. "But unfortunately, I am just a biotrain and not a life- form. I have my limitations."

"Thank you, Ma'am. Well, this might be the reason for his behaviour. It's possible that he wouldn't have developed these symptoms if he had chosen a life –form- mother."

His words sting, and her eyes fill with tears. After this comment, she can't control her emotions any longer. Taking a tissue out of her purse, she gently wipes the corners of her eyes. The realisation that she is helpless in resolving this has hit her, and she asks, "What can we do? I will do anything to make him better."

"Ma'am, you don't need do anything. You have been a brilliant mother, but it's our turn now," the Doctor reassures her, his voice soft. "Regression can occur after any psychological stress or traumatic event in life – and Go2 has been stressed and traumatised for his entire life. Although he now has security and comfort, his subconscious mind is playing up," he explains.

"What is the plan of action, Dr. Smith? What can I...?"

"Hold on!" he gently raises his hand to stop her. "There are other problems we need to address, such as his attention deficit and anxiety. His treatment will be part of a long-term plan since he's going to need sessions of counselling, behavioural therapy, cognitive therapy, psychotherapy and also some desensitisation."

"Whatever it takes Doctor, please do it!"

"If it's any comfort," he explains, "the good news is that his regression is harmless and, hopefully, he won't require pharmacotherapy."

"No drugs?" she says. "Yes, Doctor, that's reassuring."

"What is interesting," Dr. Smith goes on, "is that regression usually happens because of the past experience of comfort and caring babies have received. However, in Go2's case, he never received any comfort or caring and therefore has no subconscious recollection of such experiences."

Mom looks blankly at him as he continues, "Go2's case proves the theory that regression has a genetic basis. Because he is a knockout baby, there is a possibility that some of the genes have been deleted – this could be aggravating his regression."

Mom is struggling to understand; only interested in getting him better. In desperation she asks, "Will he have a speedy recovery?"

Dr. Smith gives a slightly sarcastic laugh. "Speed is your domain, Ma'am. But psychology is a slow passenger train and it will take many stations and passengers, for him to get there."

She understands exactly what he is saying. Her tone of voice changes and she says firmly, "We'll do whatever it takes and I will bring him to you for as many sessions as he needs."

"Is there anything else you want to ask me?" Dr Smith is now trying to wrap up the consultation.

Mom pauses for a moment. "Yes – there are two things, in fact. Go2 is starting to become very erratic, argumentative and at times, withdrawn. I've also noticed that he bites his lower lip when he's stressed."

He nods. "Anything else?"

"Doctor, if I may – why is he regressing to breastfeeding and not any other experiences?"

"That is an interesting question," Dr. Smith considers, stroking his beard. "It could be because, even in manhood, males equate breastfeeding with their original survival, in their subconscious minds. The primitive survival and subconscious mind are linked. Therefore growing into manhood and manhood itself, are preoccupied and obsessed with two survival objects, birth canal and milk outlets."

She only half-understands what he is saying but it doesn't sound like a conversation she wants to get into. Trying to hide this, she gives a forced smile and changes the subject. "I know this is irrelevant, but can I please ask you why your room is entirely white?"

Dr. Smith gives a little wry smile – just a twist of the corner of his mouth – and says, "To show contrast in life and to help us see things more clearly. Most of our patients are suffering from dark lives, black experiences and shadowy subconscious minds. I built my career on exploring the dark side of the mind. My colleagues used to jokingly call me Dr. Black-smith, once upon a time. The colour white is to try and project some positivity – it's all part of chromatotherapy."

"That's amazing!" exclaimed Mom. "How complex the mind can be! I thought a network of train tracks was the most complicated thing! And – even your hair is white – that's fortuitous!"

"You'd be surprised to know, Ma'am," Dr. Smith leaned forward, confidentially. "That my hair, moustache and beard are actually black, but I dye them white!"

"Good for you, Dr. Smith!" she jokes. "It suits your bright personality!" She reaches the junction called 'flattery'.

"Thanks, Ma'am." He changes track. "Go2's treatment will start tomorrow." He closes his bablet and puts it away in the drawer, adding, with a smile, "Please don't forget the white plaster for his lip."

* * * * * *

It is the weekend, and the Dexan Queen has the day off. She has stopped going to work at the weekend, ever since Go2 joined her and is parked up in the yard.

It's early morning and the sun has just finishing rising. Bright rays of sunlight shine into Go2's room through the big window he's standing next to, with his arms folded firmly across his chest. He has a plaster fixed to his lower lip to prevent bleeding, following the Doctor's advice.

Mom is on the screen and they are clearly in the middle of a confrontation. Things have got so bad that he's not even saying good morning to her any more. And by now, she has learnt to read his body language well, and can tell that he's angry from the way he's standing.

"Don't get annoyed, darling. The Doctor is going to start your treatment sessions and you'll soon start feeling better."

"That's the whole point!" he spits. "I don't want to go and see that brilliant-white Doctor."

"Why don't you want to go there, babe?"

"Why *should* I go?" He doesn't look at her, continuing to glare out of the window.

"When we get a fever, we go to the Doctor, don't we? The mind is the same – if it has a fever, we also have to go and see a Doctor."

"There you go, again!" Go2 snaps. "You never stop! You have a habit of running away with things. I don't have any fever or psychiatric illness."

He just feels that his natural urges have never been fulfilled, and that she's making a big fuss over nothing.

"You're trying to say I am mad! Why?"

"Who is saying you're mad?" Mom soothes. "You just need a little counselling, that's all."

"You're trying to prove I'm a psycho!" Go2 argues, pointing his finger at her. "Anyway, why should I believe you? You're a cheat and a liar!"

"What did you say? Liar? Cheat?" Mom raises her voice, her eyebrows furrow, asks "Why do you think that? How dare you! Never forget – you are talking to a Queen!"

"Your Highness said the Tooth Fairy comes at night, through the vending portal! But for your information, I kept my bablet on recording mode, and no one came! The only thing that happened was that some parcels were delivered through the portal. Isn't that a lie? Isn't it cheating?"

He'd had great expectations of his Mother that aren't being met – and his freedom has also reduced since he came to live with her. His resentment has bubbled up and is now erupting.

Mom is sad and helpless, as Go2 continues, "Not only a cheat and a liar, but you are a huge control freak as well!"

"How Go2? How?" About to cry, she takes a tissue from her purse.

"You control when I eat and sleep – what I do, and even what I wear! You don't let me go anywhere alone and you control what I study!"

"Yes, Go2," she says steadily. "But this is not controlling, my darling, it is being a parent. I also have a responsibility – to make you a good citizen."

"Well, you're not very successful," he says. "All you're looking for is status and recognition. My life was much better and happier before I came here! This place is worse than an open prison!"

She cannot control herself, and tears gently roll down her cheeks. She never imagined that the one person she loves more than anything would make such allegations! She changes her tone, not wanting to respond to his irrational outburst. Instead, she decides to support him.

"These are just teething problems; but things will be alright. You just need to be patient and to try and learn how to become a good son. Good sons do not disrespect their parents."

"You should maybe learn how to become a good mother first and try not to control others!" he snarls, sarcastically. "What teething problems are you talking about? You lied to me about the Tooth Fairy! That was enough teething trouble for me." He pauses, then attacks further, "Now, you talk about giving respect to parents! Gender type two keeps absconding. He isn't worthy of anyone's respect at all! And the gender type one parent is just a machine who lies. So, is any parent really worthy of respect?"

Mom does not have an answer and instead, sighs in surrender. "Go2, darling, we will do things your way. Will that be better? All I've ever wanted to do is look after you."

He gives a sarcastic smile and says, "Look after me? Do you even know how to look after me? All you say when I'm bleeding is, 'Sonny, please put a plaster on your lip'."

"What else can I do when your lip is bleeding?" she asks.

"The whole time you nag me to put a plaster on my lip, but – my honourable Mom – you should know that a plaster on the outside doesn't cure a wound on the inside."

In a fit of fury, he rips the plaster off and throws it away in protest, while all she can do is watch.

"Please... just let me know what your problems are on the inside, darling."

"You're my Mother! You should know! Why should I even tell you?"

Mom decides it might be best to keep quiet now and let him have his own way, but Go2 responds to her silence by continuing to express his anger: "Look, your Majesty the Queen, I'm not sure this will work anymore."

She is shocked to hear this, but he doesn't give her a chance to say anything and dumps his decision on her. "I've decided to take a break. There's a summer holiday camp and most of my schoolmates are going, so I'm going to go away for 25 days. Maybe when I come back we can see if we can work it out."

"If you want to go to the summer camp, then go," she says, softly. "I have never said no. Please don't make untrue allegations and then leave, though. We need to sort this out."

"I'm going anyway!" Go2 stamps his feet. "It will give you some peace, because you won't have anyone to keep a constant watch over."

He storms off to the wash area in the corner of the room. Mom is devastated.

* * * * * *

Dr. Smith is in a hurry, as though he has somewhere to be; busy closing drawers, cabinets, and trying to organise his table. He takes up a remote control to turn off some gadgets when, all of a sudden, his bablet starts vibrating and says, "Madam the Dexan Queen is online. She wants to talk to you for a few moments if she can, please."

He frowns, not quite understanding what the call could be about, but says to the bablet, "Yes, she can join me on the wall screen in my office."

Immediately after this, a few digits appear on the screen, a low screeching sound is heard and Mom appears on the screen – distressed, by the look on her face. It seems as though she has not slept overnight. "Good morning, Dr. Smith."

"Good morning to you, too. I hope all is well."

"I am fine, thanks, I'm sorry to bother you without notice, but if you could please spare me a few moments…" Her voice is slightly husky and he wonders if it is perhaps because she spent last night sobbing.

"No problem, Madam. Please go ahead."

"It is about Go2."

"I imagined it might be. Please go ahead. I am alone in my office and everything you say is confidential."

"Go2 fought with me last night. He says he wants a break and is going to a camp for 25 days," she says, her voice wavering.

"Why are you worrying, Madam? He is temperamental, but he will be okay; so please, forgive him and allow him this. In fact, I think it might even help him."

"But I don't know anything about this camp. Will he be safe there?"

Dr. Smith scratches his beard and says, "He will be absolutely fine. After all, his birth was a 'recorded delivery'. He's not going to get lost."

"I know, but what happens if he falls sick there, or something?"

Dr. Smith reassures her: "There will always be some basic medical service. Don't worry too much. It is affecting you. One thing certain though. This summer camp will be both diagnostic and therapeutic for Go2."

* * * * * *

Chapter 15

The campsite is located in a valley far away, surrounded by mountains, woods, gullies, streams and life -forms that have not yet been genetically modified. Small civilised units have been built between the top of the mountain and the bottom, and they look like ancient huts from past centuries. A small playground sits between the units, at the far end of which there is a community hall and a public urinal.

The attendees of the camp are various types of moving characters: some are human –life- forms of various ages, but the majority are younger boys and girls. There are also robots and non-human -life forms. In total, there are 88 different characters.

There is a variety of sleeping arrangements. Some have communal dormitory rooms and others have special rooms in the civilised units. Go2 and Tilfo are lucky enough to get a room with twin beds in one of the civilised units. The dining area is also a large communal hall, full of long tables and lots of chairs. It is a buffet-style self-service system and is called the 'Officers' Mess'.

The days are pretty busy at the campsite and typically start with an alarm bell, although it is not compulsory to get up at that time. There is no fixed schedule for a day. When the alarm sounds, some get out of bed and begin their daily schedule, but others linger in bed and have a lie-in.

After getting up, they gather in the community hall, where there is an experienced humanoid robot teacher who usually conducts classes on meditation. When one of these classes is going on, the tranquil sound of a sitar can be heard in the background. In one of the typical classes someone would start with a question.

"What's meditation?" an enthusiastic young delegate asks the teacher.

The teacher holds his jaw in his right hand and in a low-pitched, slow voice says, "My dear, it is an easy way, to earn all the worldly pleasures in one go, without going anywhere."

"How is that possible?"

The teacher takes philosophical approach and asks, "My child, what do you like to play?"

"I love soccer!"

"Why do you play soccer?"

"I like it because I feel happy after scoring goals."

"After creating one goal, you are happy? Imagine what it'd be like if you scored 100 goals a day! How much happiness do you think that would give you?"

"Is this a game on a console, or bablet?" the young student asks. Some laughter can be heard in the audience when he asks this.

"Yes. Played on the screen background of our clean minds."

The enthusiastic delegate is puzzled.

"Imagine you are alone," the teacher continues, addressing the whole class. "What would you do? "

No one knows who the teacher is directing this question at, and they shuffle uncomfortably, gazing at one another.

He realises this and continues, "Who can answer this question?"

A delegate raises his hand and the teacher encourages him to speak.

"When I am alone, I look into Daddy's pocket," she says. There is a burst of laughter at this answer.

A different student raises his hand and says, "When I'm on my own. I take a shower and walk around without a towel." There is another burst of laughter in the hall.

A third delegate says, "When I'm alone, I watch a programme on my bablet that Mummy doesn't ever allow me to watch. I know the code for the parental controls because one night Daddy was using the code. I was pretending to be asleep, but I saw it. Since then, it has been a lot of fun during the day – and at night!" A few giggles amongst the audience can be heard after this answer.

The teacher then asks, "Go2, my child, what do you do, when you are on your own?"

Go2 looks at Tilfo and hesitantly says, "Teacher, most of the time now, I am on my own. I just do the things I need to do to live."

There is silence after Go2's answer; the teacher recognises this and tries to improve the mood of the room again. "So, when we are our own, we do the things that are necessary to live. Good answer! Well done, Go2. When we are alone, we are in our own little world." He then sweeps back his long, white hair with his hand and continues, "Our sole goal is to have pleasure – a positive emotion that we always want to have. Once we get bored of physical pleasure, we then start thinking, and go into a world of fantasy. Even then, the sky is not the limit."

"Is space a limit, then?" one cheeky girl delegate asks.

"No, my child! Space is an endless medium, one in which stars and planets survive, grow and reproduce. There are no limitations."

Go2 and Tilfo are quite amazed to be receiving this kind of wisdom and experience.

The question has distracted him a little, but the teacher soon remembers what he wants to say next. "So, when we think, and go into our own fantasy worlds, we imagine a lot – and it's always happy emotions. Our minds go wild and our imagination allows us to think of any pleasures we like."

Go2 nods his head with approval as the teacher continues, "All our happy imaginings at one end of the mind, we call wild imagination dream therapy." He goes on, "My children, in this camp we will be carrying out wild imagination dream therapy sessions every evening!"

"How will we do it? Will it be played on the ground, or on the bablets?" Go2 asks.

"No! We will all gather here in this hall and will sit on the floor with our legs crossed. We will then close our eyes and begin to imagine all the things that give us pleasure. There will not be any limits, boundaries of morality, censorship, or protocol – we will just keep on imagining. Any wild imagining is allowed and you will be the masters of it. Create your own worlds and be happy there, because there is no one to watch you."

"Wow! How wonderful it sounds!" an excitable delegate says. "So, will we be doing this tonight?"

"Yes, every evening. There will be no tickets, entry-fees, or taxes to pay. Play and never pay – it's all fun," the teacher replies.

He looks at the students, who all seem excited at the prospect of this and continues, "Everybody will be happy with this kind of play. Dream therapy will be carried out during the evenings."

"What are we going to do now?" the third delegate asks.

"Imagine that, at one end of the mind, we are picturing pleasure."

The teacher looks at the bewildered students, scanning their faces, before putting a twist on this explanation.

"Now, imagine the exact opposite from your imagination. Try to reach a state of mind where you do not imagine anything at all. Think of nothing."

Most students have closed their eyes and are trying to do what he has asked them to do.

"When we don't imagine anything, our minds are empty. It's a blank mind that does not contain any thoughts, dreams or imagination."

Some students are struggling to not imagine anything, as the teacher continues, "Achieving an empty state of mind is known as meditation. Or concentration exercises."

The teacher sees a response from the delegates, who are now starting to understand what meditation is. The teacher says, "So, every morning we will gather here, to sit and think of nothing. Initially, it will be difficult to concentrate, because a lot of thoughts will come to mind. But it will practise, and then you will all become masters of it."

"But why do we have to meditate?" someone asks.

"You do not have to if you don't want to – it is optional. However, psychology has proved that we get more pleasure from meditation than we do from dream therapy. The ultimate goal is to have lasting pleasure, without damaging the earth. Meditation brings health."

Go2 asks, "What about physical fitness?"

"That is a good question, Go2. Meditation is an exercise for the mind and is not an alternative to physical exercise, at all. You should do physical activity every day, during the day."

Go2 and the others take it all in, some nodding.

The teacher explains the daily schedule: "Every morning, there will be a meditation class and every evening, we will study dreams. I hope this is okay with everyone."

Most of the delegates are happy with the schedule. After morning meditation, they gather in the community hall for a buffet breakfast. And after eating, they go outside to play various traditional sports such as fencing, football, baseball, bungee jumping, rafting, or swimming in the deep stream. Some prefer to play games on the screens on the walls.

The most popular attraction that everyone wants to play is cricket on the Moon and Mars. The special larger civilised unit has been converted into a playground where delegates are given a space suit to play cricket in an environment that has the same gravity as the Moon. Most of the students play this, bouncing slowly. Even Go2 and Tilfo have a go, and stumble, many times. Every time someone falls over, the spectators behind the glass partition burst into laughter.

For the first time in a while, Go2 laughs and has fun. He finds it even funnier, because laughter doesn't come easily in reduced gravity.

Another popular, funny game is playing the colour festival, 'A Holi'. Holi is played in a large hall in one of the civilised units; an artificial space that does not have gravity. They squirt colours at each other, but the colours never really reach the other person, and instead get stuck somewhere in the middle, hanging in the air. Going through it is the only way to break up the squirt of colour. All the fun can be witnessed by onlookers through the big glass partition.

* * * * * *

After playing football on the ground in the middle of the camp, Go2 and Tilfo visit the communal urinal. Tilfo always takes much longer in the toilet than Go2, because it takes him a while to get his trousers down, with his tiger paws. After all, he is an animal life form wearing human clothes.

Go2 is amused by the flyer stuck on the wall above the sink. It reads:

"Bablets are blue,
Duke boxes are red.
The reader has got
a donkey's head."

Go2 starts laughing and calls Tilfo over to share it with him, "Hey, Celtic tiger! Come here quickly and read this!"

Tilfo runs out in such a hurry, his trousers are stained with few drops of pee, but he ignores the fact and pays more attention to the flyer. They both laugh loudly and high-five each other.

After this, Go2 and Tilfo find every excuse to go to the communal urinal at the far end of the camp. The following day there is another flyer:

"Duke boxes are red,
bablets are blue.
I'm a donkey's head,
you're monkeys' poo."

The day after, the next one reads:

"Duke boxes are red,
bablets are blue.
I'm monkeys' poo
to be eaten by you."

Go2 and Tilfo are always helpless with laughter, not wanting to miss the opportunity to read the free messages; so they continue to visit every day.

The next day the note is:

"Duke boxes are red,
bablets are blue.
I liked your poo,
I puked it up,
On your plate too."

Tilfo and Go2 are crying with laughter. These questions and responses go on for days, until after a few days, the flyers change. Perhaps new sets of enthusiasts are coming into the picture. The next flyer says:

"Duke boxes are red,
bablets are blue.
On a loo,
without a poo.
What shall I do?"

The sequence of toilet humour continues and the next day, the response to this is:

"Duke boxes are red,
bablets are blue.
Take milk of magnesia
for a day or two."

This response is more like a medical consultation! Go2 and Tilfo are addicted to going to the toilet to read the messages every day.

* * * * * *

At midday, they always gather in the hall for lunch. After which, they are free to go to their units or to go and play again. During the evening, dinner is served slightly earlier than usual, before the dream therapy session takes place. Following the session, there is always some entertainment in the theatre – usually a play, film, live show, or an illusionist show.

This evening, the entertainment is a film, and the theme is 'Films of the Twentieth Century', which turns out to be more like a documentary than a film.

Go2 and Tilfo are sitting on the third row and Tilfo has worn a necktie today. The show starts with an MGM film.

In the opening seconds, 'Leo' the MGM lion appears, moves his head to the left, and starts roaring.

Go2 is in the mood to tease Tilfo and playfully says, "Tilfo, look – that's your lost step grand-father."

Tilfo laughs and gives Go2 a big swat with his elbow.

* * * * * *

The next day, Tilfo spends a lot of time playing and Go2 spends most of the day lazing in bed. As usual, there is an entertainment programme going on in the community theatre. Tonight, the theme is old, short films based on folk stories and there are several being showed on the big screen in the theatre. They have erected a traditional, old-style white screen on the stage and the film is projected from one corner behind the audience. The archaeology department has kindly provided the screen and projector to the camp.

Go2 and Tilfo have sat and watched ten films and are now getting bored. They are about to leave when a film entitled 'Mother Loves You' catches their attention.

Old lines appear on the screen throughout, and a subtitle at the start of the first scene says: '12th Century England'.

The opening scene is a bright sunny day and a character called Henry is holding Johanna's hand. They are sitting on a steep rock – almost a small cliff – beside a lake.

Henry is a brave soldier, and his horse is tied to a tree beside the rock. Johanna is a noble lady who comes from a rich, aristocratic family. She is well-dressed and confident. Her cart and driver are parked a short distance away.

Johanna says, "Well, should I say congratulations?"

"For what?"

"For receiving the honour conferred by the King – the gallantry award."

"I did it for you."

"Why?" she asks, batting her eyelashes.

"You are my constant and endless inspiration. Every time I fight with enemy, I think of you. I imagine you are watching me and I know I should never let you down."

"That's nice of you! You got an award to add to your collection of many gallantry awards. What do I get?"

Go2 whispers to Tilfo, "I bet she is always looking for something."

"Well, lady," Henry says. "The award is yours. And more, besides, I have something for you; something I got from a merchant from Venice."

"What is it? Tell me, tell me! Show it to me." Johanna can't control her excitement. "It must be something nice!"

"No, darling, not like this. Please close your beautiful little lotus-shaped eyes for a moment or two."

Tilfo bursts out laughing, and muffles his giggles, while Go2 grins.

Go2 leans over to Tilfo and mutters, "They are in love, but are both slightly shallow and superficial in their emotions, which is apparent in the way they talk to each other."

"Here you go! Closed!" she says as she shuts them and pushes her lips forwards, towards Henry.

"Now, turn around," he says, steering her by the shoulders, her eyes still shut.

Johanna turns around so she is facing the lake with her back to Henry. He takes out a beautiful necklace made of black pearls, emeralds, ruby and golden beads, with a red silky tuft at the end to fasten it. He gently puts the necklace around her neck and pulls the tuft upwards, so that it fits around her neck.

"Hmm..." Go2 mutters, bored. "If it carries on like this, I might just –"

Suddenly, Henry feels the ground underneath him start to shake. In a fraction of a second, before either of them realises what is happening, Johanna slips down the slope, screaming for help and he frantically tries to stop her falling, by grabbing her hand. The necklace has fallen off and the cuff of her sleeve is silky and slippery, so her hand somehow slips from his grasp!

She continues to slide away. Her distressed screaming can be heard, followed by the sound of her falling into the lake. It all happens so fast that Henry is bewildered for a moment and does not know what to do. He rips off his shirt, tearing at the front laces, and immediately jumps into the water.

Go2 and Tilfo are watching intently, their jaws dropped open.

The next scene depicts exactly how Henry saves her. He somehow manages to lift her up, and swims , dragging her out of the lake. She is stunned, only half-conscious, lying in his big, strong arms. The necklace is nowhere to be seen and must be lost somewhere in the lake. Water is dripping from the bare-chested Henry.

A few days have passed, and she is still recovering from the incident, resting in her soft bed. Henry is sitting beside her, holding her hand. She looks pale, listless and sad.

In a weak voice, she asks, "What is true love?"

"The feeling I have for you," he replies, without hesitation.

"What feeling do you have?"

"I think of you every moment, and I cannot live without you. I want to spend the rest of my life with you and start a family, with lots and lots of children!"

Go2 bites his lip, and winces, staring at the screen.

"Is that what love is?" she asks, softly.

"Yes, darling."

"How much do you love me?"

"Much greater than you imagine. My love knows no boundaries of skies, or oceans. I love you more than I love myself."

"So, how exactly do you measure your love? How would you categorise it – large, small or medium?"

Go2 gasps, "She is testing him to see how much he cares about her."

With this question, Henry is stumbling, because he doesn't have an answer and is struggling to find the words. "Whatever I feel for you is definitely the biggest." He continues, "My love, please take some rest. You need it. We can talk again later, once you have recovered properly."

"No, don't worry. I'm fine. I can talk. I think this is the right time, because I need to ask you something."

Henry cannot escape her questioning.

"What is most important and precious thing in life?"

"You, my love."

"If that is the case, why did you take a while before jumping into the lake when I fell? I mean, why did you not jump in straight away?"

Henry is shocked at this question and does not understand where she is coming from. "No, darling, I jumped in immediately!"

"No. you must have been too busy looking for the jewelled necklace, on the rock."

"I did not, darling. That was not important to me."

"Then why did you hesitate about jumping in?"

From the look on his face, Henry has never been questioned by his love like this before. "No, that was not the case.

Johanna, please take some rest and I will fetch you some hot soup."

"Thank you, but I do not need soup at the moment. The only thing I need is answers."

Henry gives up. Johanna asks, "When you rescued me, you weren't wearing your shirt."

Go2 nudges Tilfo, and mutters, "Ah! I wondered about that, too."

"No, darling," Henry says, puzzled. "I removed it before I jumped in."

"That proves my point, then," she says. "So, your shirt is more important to you than my life? Is that what you're saying?"

"No, darling!" he exclaims. "I was bewildered – caught in the moment. I didn't know what I was doing. The shirt would have impeded my swimming anyway!"

"Well, if the same thing ever happened to you I would jump in straight away!" she scoffs. "I wouldn't stand around, feeling bewildered."

"So what exactly are you trying to prove, my Johanna?"

"I don't want to prove anything! Your actions spoke louder than your words."

"I hope to clear your mind of the misunderstanding," he replies, weakly. Henry is losing the argument, but still feeling confused

"He did what he thought was best in that moment," whispers Go2. "And he saved her life. But – the shirt!"

Johanna and Henry remain silent.

She has some more questions and is determined to get all the answers she needs, and move on with her life, so she then asks, "Henry, you were wrong in saying how you measure love. Love is measured by sacrifice."

"Go on."

"If you don't know what I mean, Henry, then let me clarify. Love is measured by sacrifice, and the bigger the sacrifice the more love there is."

"Point well-made and noted, my lady."

"So what sacrifices can you make for me?" she asks.

"Anything you like. My life is all and only for you. I would die for you."

"Yes, I know – as long as you save your shirt first," Johanna sarcastically says. "Anyway, moving on... I don't want to throw all my toys out. You don't have to die."

"You just ask anything of me and you will see," Henry says, in a wheedling, but comforting tone.

"Do you want me to look even more beautiful?"

"Johanna, you are already the prettiest woman on this earth, but in all honesty – yes, I would like to see you even more beautiful."

"It's good that you said that." She cunningly asks, "What is the most precious thing in your life, to you?"

"Why are you asking me all this today?"

"Today is judgement day. I have decided," she replies.

Henry repeats, "The most precious thing to me on this earth is you, Johanna."

"I know that; how about apart from me? Your shirt?"

Henry thinks for a moment and then says, "After you, it is my mother."

Go2 gulps. After hearing this answer, he looks at Tilfo, who is too busy watching what happens next. Go2 starts feeling upset about everything that is happening with him and his mother, at the moment.

Johanna continues, "There is a new, special type of eyeliner and most of the noble ladies apply it to their eyes."

Henry frowns. He is lost because he doesn't understand where Johanna is coming from. He says, "Go on."

"I asked one of the ladies in the ballroom, and she told me the eyeliner is made from the blood of a woman's heart. The blood is then mixed up with various pigments, dyes and herbs, to get the exact shade."

"Yes, darling, if you want it, we will get the eye liner for you. Now, relax – you should definitely get some rest."

"No. Let me continue," she insists. "So – to summarise, you love me more than anything else in the world. You would do anything for me. You would die for me, right?"

"Yes, my love, you are absolutely right."

She fixes him with a stare. "Would you do anything to prove your love to me?"

"Yes, my love. Yes."

"Can you do one thing for me? Take your time before you answer – and you can get back to me later, if you wish. You will need to think it over. I am not rushing you. However, until I have an answer, I do not want to see you. "

"Yes, I am sure I'll do anything. I don't even need to think." Henry is determined to prove his love to her, especially when she is so unwell. "I will do anything it takes."

Johanna pauses and in a gentle voice, with an eerie smile on face, says, "I want the very best eyeliner there is. You need to get human blood for me."

"Yes, darling. No trouble. There are so many criminals beheaded every week, I can easily get some for you."

She sneers, "No, darling, that is not what I consider to be proving your love. I am not looking for a love of convenience, I am looking for exclusive love."

She lifts her head up from the bed, and craning her neck, brings her face close and presses her nose against his. "I want you to bring me your mother's heart, so that I can squeeze the blood out with my own gentle fist."

Henry is horrified, and for a moment he just looks at her in shock. After a horrible pause, he gathers himself and squeals, "This... this is just absurd! No way! I cannot do it!"

"It is over then," she snaps. "Go home to your mother and live in her lap for the rest of your life." She turns her head away from him, to avoid looking at him.

Go2 and Tilfo stare at each other in alarm. They are developing a strong sense of hatred for this character, Johanna.

In anguish and pain, Henry is desperately trying to persuade her: "Johanna, darling, don't you think your demand is somewhat exorbitant? It's hardly a legitimate request!"

"No, Mr Gallantry-award-winner. All's fair in love and war, and you are clearly only capable of showing fairness during wars. You are completely lost in love, Henry. Go home."

"No, darling! But my mother is the one who has raised me single-handedly after the death of my Father! I don't even remember him…" Henry cries, trying to dissuade her.

"Do you love me, or not?" she demands.

"I love you," he answers, in distress. "But what you are asking me to do is a sin."

"Since when did soldiers worry about sins? You kill humans every day, in war."

"Yes. You are right, but that's in war. Killing someone vulnerable is not gallant and is certainly not the within the moral code of a warrior. That is an act of cowardice."

"You are fast losing the opportunity to prove your love. Go!" she orders.

Henry decides to ask, "You are asking so much of me. But what have you ever actually done for me?"

Outraged by him asserting his authority and attacking her with this question, she bangs her head against the headboard and yells, "Who do you think you are? You're nothing but a cheap soldier! I come from a noble family! My Father is Lord of Lyndon Colognia! We don't even talk to folk like you, you commoner of commoners. I have proved *my* mettle, soldier."

Shocked by this attack, Henry tries to retract and says, "Look, Johanna, thank you very much. I will see what I can do. Please don't be troubled."

She rages, "If you ever want to see me again, I want to see the heart of your mother in your dirty hands. Otherwise, it will be goodbye for good – and you will never show your face again."

She flings off the bedclothes, gets up and walks away from him.

Go2 and Tilfo are enjoying this weird film, because they have never seen anything like this before.

In the next scene, vultures are flying high in the sky, chasing Henry, who is running through a wood. There are hundreds of hungry vultures staring down at Henry running, his hands and clothes heavily stained with blood and he is holding a sandalwood box in his hand, also daubed with blood.

The paths in the wood are crooked and bumpy, not straight or smooth – and it's windy. Henry has to run fast to get to Johanna and he is exhausted from running away from the King's guards, the vultures – and his own guilt.

Droplets of sweat have gathered on his forehead and are dripping down the back of his neck. He is trying to be careful with the box in his hands and is trembling, trying to avoid dropping it. He is excited because in the next hour or so, he will please Johanna and she will be happy. He will have proved his love to her and they will marry and live happily ever after.

All of a sudden, he stumbles on a small stone on the ground. His hands have lost their grip on the box and it goes flying! He falls down, hitting his forehead, which starts bleeding.

The box flies a few feet away from him and flips open, while the bloody heart inside is thrown out into the wood. Henry is dazed but gathers himself together when he realises he has lost the heart and his chance of a happy future with Johanna.

He stands up and frantically looks around for the box, spotting it lying at the base of a large oak tree; but the heart is not in it. He runs around – here, there and everywhere, trying to find it. Henry is upset for the first time in his life and screams out, "Oh, God above, please help me!"

There is no one above, in the sky, except the hungry vultures. He doesn't realise that the vultures have spotted the heart on the ground and are swooping down fast.

The heart, lying still in the shrubs, hears his despair. It suddenly bounces over to him and asks, with gentle concern, "Are you alright, my son?"

Go2 gasps. Suddenly, the italicised letters saying 'The End' appear and the film has finished. The whole hall is silent and Go2's face is full of tears.

Tilfo, for the first time in his life, is also weeping. The girls on the row behind them are wiping their eyes dry, too; sniffling through sobs.

* * * * * *

It is now late afternoon, the following day, at the camp. The golden yellow sunshine is still shining brightly, making the trees look sharp and crisp. In the big, main hall, everyone has gathered for the 'Art of Living' class, where the teacher is standing in the middle of the room and the students are gathered around him. Go2 and Tilfo are sitting in the third row and Tilfo is excited to see what the class will be about. Go2, however, is still distracted by the film they watched yesterday.

The teacher starts, "The purpose of life is to live – and to live happily. Some of the biggest factors that determine our daily pain and pleasure are our relations. Our relations give us happiness, but at the same time, they can also be the main thing that makes us most miserable."

With the teacher's comment about relations, Go2's attention is aroused. He quickly looks at Tilfo, then turns his head back to the teacher. He is interested in this topic because this is what is wrong in his life.

The teacher continues, "So, today, we will discuss one of the most important relationships in our lives and that is the relationship with our parental figures type 2: our fathers. We will discuss this topic today, and then, in our next session, we will focus on the relationship with our parental figures type 1: our mothers."

The students are alert to this announcement and listen carefully to the teacher. Go2 begins to bite his lip, his eyes wide.

The teacher continues, "We all have a father. We cannot be born without one."

"Excuse me, sir. How about clones that are born from gender type ones?" an intelligent-looking robot student asks. "I'm talking about clones from females only."

Go2 is alerted by this question, and recoils with feelings of embarrassment and guilt.

"Well, you are right, Mr GF4 – and that is true with asexual reproduction. However, today, we will restrict ourselves to the products that have a parental figure type two, and the importance of them in their lives."

The teacher turns around to look at the other students and says, "Today, the topic we have is: 'My Daddy is my Hero'. It is optional, but you are free to share your own experiences with the audience if you wish."

Go2 lets out a big sigh. The teacher looks into the audience and asks a gullible student, whom he thinks will be reasonably willing, and unlikely to deny his request: "Kiran7, can you say a few words on this topic, please?"

Kiran7 stands up, and in his childlike language says, "My Daddy is very hard-working. He goes to work early, when I am still in bed and comes home very late. He works really hard because he has the responsibility of putting food on the table – and, even, of providing the table!"

Everyone applauds this comment. Except for Go2, who is unsure whether he should or not.

The teacher says, "Well done, Kiran7! Please take a seat. Does anybody else want to share their stories?" A few hands are raised and the teacher says, "Wow! I am glad to see such a huge response; you must all have things to say about your dads. Yes, Miss Zow Q?"

Miss Zow Q starts off, "My Daddy is a hero because he is a fire fighter. He saves lives and properties." The audience claps as she sits down.

The teacher calls, "Next, please!"

A boy stands up and courageously says, "My Daddy is a brave hero and I am proud of him for many reasons. He is a scavenger – he cleans clogged drains, blocked toilets and picks up litter, pee, poo and puke. Tell me why, in modern times like these – when everything is done by machines, robots and cyborgs – is a human gender type 2 life -form doing such a job?"

The audience are curious. The boy continues to provide a response to his own question, "The answer is simple. When things are done by hand, it is a symbol of status. We like handpicked fruit, handmade crafts, organic and home-cooked food. In a similar way, some rich life forms want their cleaning done traditionally, and organically – so they appoint people like my Daddy. This type of cleaning is called 'organic handmade cleaning' and when everyone else refuses to do a job, my Daddy happily accepts it. He helps to keep us clean and prevents cities from smelling bad and inhabitants getting diseases. I am proud of him because he does the job that no other intellectual wants to do. He does not earn much money, but he is a happy man and so are we. I am proud to be his son – and that's why my Daddy is my hero."

For this lengthy speech, the applause is louder and even the teacher starts clapping. "Yes, Miss Queensland?" he goes on, when the applause subsides.

Miss Queensland starts, "I love my Daddy. He is undoubtedly a hero. He loves everyone, both life forms and non-life -forms, and the earth, too. He loves me loads. He also loves my Mom very much; so much so, that he is always in the bedroom with her."

The audience starts laughing at this, but she continues, "I was born because he made love to my mom properly and I am thankful to him. He had the option of using contraception, but he said no because he wanted to have babies. He has a lot to offer; he is a messiah of love and peace and is my ultimate hero." She sits back in her chair.

The applause is growing and the teacher is happy because it looks as if he has chosen the right topic and the response from the students is brilliant. He can't control himself any longer and says, "I am a Daddy, too."

They all laugh and clap. Once the clapping tapers off he turns to Go2 who is sitting quietly still, and says, "Go2, why don't you share your experience with us? Remember the theme and tell us why your Daddy is your hero."

Go2 swallows hard and hesitantly gets up because there is no way he can say no to the teacher. He has always been sceptical of his Dad's role in life, and in his eyes, he has the worst dad ever; but now he has been cornered and has to say something. He looks over at Tilfo, who understands the pain and suffering that Go2 is experiencing.

"My Daddy is a hero..." He starts slowly and the audience is silent because they can see he is serious. He is searching to find the right words to say. And then, they come out in a rush: "I am proud of him for many things. He loves me a lot and tries to spend all his time with me. When my Mom passed away, he could not marry again, because he was so attached to me and wanted to give me every little bit of his time. He spends all of his earnings on me and buys me expensive clothes, shoes, food and entertainment. He also takes me on very expensive holidays. When I fall sick, he looks after me and takes on the role of Mummy as well as Daddy. Mr Mahatma Gandhi once said that if a man acquires a mother's virtues then he has acquired humanity and godliness. I believe my Daddy has earned this status."

The audience is in complete silence. Tilfo is the only one who is smiling, out of the corner of his mouth.

Go2 continues, "A couple of years ago, I fell sick and both of my kidneys were not working. The doctors said I needed a kidney transplant and without even thinking about it for a moment, my Daddy came forward to offer me his kidney. I am alive today because he is not only a donor – he is a donor hero!"

With the last sentence, it's all too much and Go2 can't control himself, so tears start to fall from his eyes and his voice becomes choked. He knows his Daddy has not done anything he has said has, but he is upset because this is how he would have wanted his Dad to be, with him. Tilfo stands up, goes over to Go2 and starts patting his back.

The audience stand up and start clapping. The teacher is overwhelmed by what he has just witnessed. The applause goes on for a long time and can be heard outside the hall.

* * * * * *

Mid-morning, the sun is shining, and there is a lot of hustle and bustle around the camp. Most of the delegates are enjoying either archery or fencing. But Go2 and Tilfo are not part of this and are absent from the crowd; in a separate room, busy playing their own game of being in a court of law.

In the centre of the hall, they have created an elevated platform, with a long table with a red tablecloth spread on it. Behind the table, there is a black mahogany chair where the honourable judge, Mr Tilfo, is sitting, wearing a court wig – and like a typical judge, his face is expressionless.

Below the platform, on the floor at the right-hand side, they have created a witness box by erecting wooden bars and joining them together. No one else is in the makeshift courtroom: only Go2 and Tilfo are playing. Go2 is standing in the makeshift witness box, hanging his head in shame.

He mutters, "Your honour, thank you very much for giving me the opportunity to present my case. I swear, by the holy scriptures written for all life forms, that I will be speaking the truth and nothing but the truth."

The Judge, Mr Tilfo, nods his head, acknowledging the oath.

Go2 continues, "Your honour, I understand the two allegations for which I am being held responsible. These two allegations have dragged me here and I will discuss each one individually."

Judge Mr Tilfo lifts his head to tell him to proceed. Go2 starts,

"My lord. Allegation number one is that I lied, cheated and misled the audience when I spoke during the discussion 'My Daddy is my Hero'. The judge nods.

"Yes, I am guilty, your honour. However, before passing any judgement upon me I request you look at the circumstances in which I was cornered to commit such a sin." The judge's eyes are widened at hearing this.

"My lord, the main reason was peer pressure. Everybody's Daddy is something great and mine is nothing. If I hadn't lied then I would have looked like a fool and everyone would have laughed at me. I didn't want to be seen as a fool; I was only fooling around! Fooling is not cheating, lying, manipulating, or misleading!

Judge Tilfo nods his head in agreement as Go2 continues,

"My lord, reason number two is our mediocre value system. The teacher, who suggested the discussion topic assumed that everyone's Father is someone special and that everyone must be proud of their Daddy. This is not the case and was unacceptable of him, I was cornered into fooling them to try and maintain my dignity and self-respect."

Judge Tilfo is happy so far with his argument.

"Your honour, I therefore request you consider all of the circumstances. Please take into account the young age of the offender and the fact that it his first offence and exonerate him. That is all, my lord."

The judge twiddles the pen between the claws of his right paw distractedly, thinking about what to do.

"My Lord," Go2 goes on. "I will now talk about the second allegation against me. This one is very complex but should provide answers."

He frowns, becoming more serious and the jolly mood they both had when they first started building the court for the game has completely disappeared.

"The allegation is that I was not nice to my Mom. Apparently, I have been horrible and made impractical demands that have hurt her."

THE DEXAN QUEEN OF SPEED

Judge Tilfo nods his head in agreement. Go2 says, "Your honour, an opportunity should be given to me, to correct my wrongdoings."

Judge Tilfo's eyebrows shoot up in wonder; he is intrigued to see what the solution could be.

"My Lord, let us ensure that two negatives make a positive. The first negative thing I did was to lie about my Daddy. Please let me speak, so that I can try to make things positive again."

Judge Tilfo gives him permission, by dropping his finger in the air.

"Your honour, I am now going to say some false and incorrect things. It is part of my reflection and repentance, please note that every sentence is untrue."

Judge Tilfo nods for him to continue.

"My Mom is no better than my Daddy."

The judge is puzzled initially, but then starts to understand the allusion, as Go2 explains.

"My Mom is not a nice person. I have been here at camp for a long time. She doesn't call me twice a day to check I am okay, like the other kids' parents, and she does not ever enquire about my wellbeing. She doesn't worry about me, or truly care about my welfare. She does not check that I have eaten or if I am being nurtured and cared for. In fact, she is actually the worst Mother anyone could have! I am a nice boy, I'm reasonable and rational and I never cause her any trouble."

Tears begin to stream down his cheeks and his voice is starting to choke up. He slowly slumps down in the witness box as he continues, "I am not proud of my Mom and I... I'm afraid I will..." his voice broke into a sob. "I'll always trouble her."

He falls to his knees, bows his body down in front and holds his face in his hands. Overcome, he can't control himself, and gives free rein to heart-breaking cries.

Judge Tilfo is taken aback and desperately tries to sympathise with Go2.

Go2 shouts aloud, his voice wracked with agony, "My Mom is the worst Mom in the whole wide world!" He continues crying heavily and repeats the same line, "My Mom is the worst Mom... in the whole... wide..." He cannot continue any further, dissolving into loud weeping.

He pushes the bars of the witness box and they fall down. The entire witness box collapses, just as Go2 has done. He is still on his knees, doubled over again.

Judge Tilfo is entirely in agreement with him, but he has nothing to say to Go2 even if he could speak), because he has now heard his side of the story and wants to exonerate him with full dignity and honour.

"But... it's not true!" weeps Go2, his face wet with tears; distraught. "I still love her!"

The judge starts weeping, too, and stands up and walks over to Go2. He removes his wig and black robe and becomes Tilfo again; bending down, he puts his hands on Go2's shoulders to help him get up off the floor.

Go2's voice has become high-pitched with trying to control his emotion. "Take me out of this camp, please! We need to leave tomorrow. I want to apologise to my Mom. She is the best."

Outside their courtroom, the fencing and archery are still in full swing, the sound of striking swords can be heard.

* * * * * *

Chapter 16

The valley is full of yellow flowers; mainly linseed, rapeseed and mustard, and they line both sides of the track. Go2 and Tilfo are travelling back home on an ordinary train through the fields and valleys; going back home, ten days before the summer camp is due to end.

Go2 is feeling happy for the first time in a long time, and so is Tilfo, although his own happiness depends entirely on Go2's mood. They are leaving early because Go2 has realised his mistakes and wants to be with his Mom, knowing that they have issues to resolve – and it got to the point where he was not enjoying the camp anymore. Go2 is in a cheerful mood but is also reflecting on everything that has happened over the last fifty days.

Initially, Go2 thought he was simply missing having the presence of a mother in his life, for all those early years. However, once he actually had one, he realised that it was not just the physical presence of a mother that was important. There needed to be bonding, too, between a mother and child – and in his mind, bonding came from a real, maternal experience such as nursing a baby. He now realises how stupid he was in thinking this – that this was essential and punishing his Mom for her perceived failings. He realises that he has troubled her unnecessarily, especially when she was trying her best, considering her disabilities and natural limitations.

Half of the day is spent travelling, but Go2 and Tilfo's cheerful moods and the scenery outside help to make the long journey much more pleasant. Usually when they get bored, they use their bablets for entertainment, but this is not the case today. Go2 chatters animatedly about the camp, and all they have done – and what he has learnt.

When they reach their station, Go2 gets up and takes his bag from the rack, while an announcement is made about the station. Tilfo also gets up and they give each other a high five, then bend their knees forward to meet each other, like they always do when they part.

Go2 says, "Hey, Mr Whisker, I will call you, once I am settled at home. I will see you again tomorrow, but now, I have to go and apologise to my Mom."

Tilfo agrees with him. Go2 climbs down from the train with his trolley case and walks to the main platform, where there is a small shop, which is manned by a brown coloured robot. He does not go inside the shop, but instead goes over to the vending portal on the wall outside. He holds his bablet up to the screen and pushes some buttons to order a bouquet of flowers.

The screen shows the message: 'Don't pick the flowers: save them! Save the bees, save the earth and save ecology.'

Go2 has heard this slogan many times before. It continues: 'Flowers always blossom well, on human emotions. We can supply the most natural-looking flowers with a beautiful scent, colour and aura. Just choose whatever you like."

Go2 chooses what he would like and then orders verbally, "I'd like ten yellow tulips, ten white tulips and five blue roses, please. Can I also sample the smell before purchasing?"

'Yes, certainly! Press button 'S',' is the reply.

Go2 then presses 'S'. A beautiful smell then starts emanating from the nozzle in the corner of the screen. Go2 bends down to put his nose next to the nozzle, and, once he is satisfied with the scent, he says, "Okay, please execute an order."

'Please wait a few decimal seconds while the goods are downloaded.'

Go2 waits for a while, until the screen says, 'Please collect your order now. Be happy and make others happy!'

Go2 collects a bouquet of natural looking and smelling flowers that are wrapped in transparent paper. He smells the beautiful smell again and then makes the payment by swiping his bablet.

He starts walking to the parking yard, pulling his suitcase along in one hand with the bouquet of flowers in the other.

There is still a little bit of daylight spread on the parking yard. The Dexan Queen has parked herself in a corner, since she does not work evenings anymore, because of Go2.

He walks to his coach, which is the second unit in line, puts his case down on the platform to get his bablet out and swipes it, to open the door. Going into his room, he puts the bouquet down in the corner.

Mom senses his movement, appearing on the screen, and the moment she sees him, her face lights up and she puts her arms out as if she is hugging him.

Go2 sees her and runs straight towards the screen. He tries to hug her by placing his hands on the screen and she bends down to kiss him. She appears to hug him and kiss his shoulders, head, cheeks and eyes through the screen. Go2 closes his eyes and uses his imagination to feel a warm, motherly embrace.

They hug for a while, then he takes a step away and looks back at the screen. He notices that his Mom appears to be unwell: it looks like she has neglected herself. She is almost grey and colourless and her hair hasn't been combed for many days.

Go2 is very happy to see her again but is sad to see her in this state. He says, "Hi Mom! I missed you too much. I love you so much!"

She replies, "I love you too, my baby, and I missed you." Her voice sounds broken, possibly because she has spent the last few days crying.

She continues, "You must be very hungry after your long journey. I bet the food at camp wasn't that good, so I'll cook something for you very quickly. Just give me a moment."

Mom leaves to start cooking and Go2 goes to the bathroom.

* * * * * *

Go2 is sitting at the dining table and eating a dish of vegetable pasta. Mom is sitting on a comfortable chair on the screen.

She asks, "So, how was the camp? Did you enjoy it?"

"It was great! I did enjoy many things, but there were a few things that made me sad."

Curious to know more, she asks, "Why? What made you sad? No one goes to a summer camp and feels sad."

"I know, Mom. But I was there for business *and* pleasure."

"Oh? And since when did my son start doing business?" Mom laughs.

"You know, Mom, it made me think. I was a fool before I went to camp, and it was a huge learning experience for me."

She agrees and says, "Yes, Go2. The difference between a fool and a wise person is experience – or experimentation."

Go2 gets straight to the point and says, "Mom, please forgive me. I was unreasonable, childish and stupid."

"Don't worry, baby. At least you have realised your mistakes and that is okay with me."

Once he realises that she has forgiven his previous behaviour, he decides to enquire more about her, "Mom, what have you done to yourself?"

She tries to hide her face and says, "Nothing, Sonny." She doesn't want to give him an account of the painful days she has had and instead, diverts his attention by asking, "How is Tilfo? Did he eat well? Did you both have fun? Tell me, tell me!" She is asking too many questions.

"Slow down, Mom, you are not on your track now," he advises her, before answering her questions. "Tilfo is fine and yes, we both ate well and had lots of fun!"

"I don't think you have eaten well," she adds, her eyes scanning down his body. "You look as if you have lost weight."

"No, Mom! I think you've been the one who hasn't been eating well."

"I am fine, babe," she replies, before changing the subject again. "I tried to call you on your bablet every single day and you did not answer."

"I know, and I'm sorry for that. I was spending time reflecting and trying to manage myself independently."

"Well, you managed pretty well, it seems," she answers, although she is sceptical.

"No, Mom," he continues, "I want to talk to you about something."

"I want to talk to you, too."

"Hmm. Okay. You first," Go2 says.

"No, you first! Age before beauty," his mother says, jokingly.

Go2 tries to smile. "Mom, please forgive me. I was stupid and now I have had time to think, I know that I was unreasonably demanding and I hurt you a lot."

"It's okay, baby."

"It isn't, really. I was a selfish monster and I never thought about your feelings." His voice wobbles. "Please forgive me!"

She has tears in her eyes again and shifts uncomfortably, changing her position in the chair. "My silly little son, just hold on there. Forgiving and giving are at the forefront of every mother's nature, so of course, you are forgiven!"

"Thanks, Mom. I promise I will never leave you again and I will be a good mummy's boy."

She smiles at this and says, "You are already a good boy."

"Mom, I have realised that I am happy and content *now*," he explains, tears shining his eyes. "I was mad to look for small stupid, momentary pleasures. I know that I was wrong, and I am truly happy now, just because I am with you."

Mom smiles and says, "I was waiting for you to come back, because I knew you would return earlier than planned. I have good news for you, but you must finish your tea first."

"Tell me, tell me, tell me!" Go2 is impatient and drops his knife and fork down onto the plate and crosses them. "I have finished my tea."

His Mom gets up from her chair quickly: the emotional reunion with Go2 has energised her. As she walks around the kitchen she says, "I have five surprises for you. Number one.

You like white hares, so you will see one every time you want to."

"Have you got some pets for me, then?" Go2 says, excitedly, clapping his hands and looking around, as if expecting some to come bouncing out of a portal.

"No, darling," Mom explains, "Because no other life- form is permitted here, while you are in this place. You know that."

"Where are they, then?" he asks. "I want to see one, and you just said I can, whenever I like!"

"Hold on! Patience is a virtue." She adds, "I knew you were going to return home early, so I thought I'd plan you a few surprises."

"Go on," he encourages.

"Ready... Steady... But first... keep your eyes closed!"

Go2 closes his eyes and says, "Yes! Yes!"

"Hold on. I have to leave for a moment or two, but I will carry on talking to you."

A moment passes and Go2's eyes are still closed.

"Won't be long," his mother says. "Just be patient."

The anticipation is almost too much for Go2 to bear, and he is sorely tempted to open his eyes, but doesn't want to disobey his mother, especially not now, when he has only just made up with her.

"I'll be back in a few seconds."

He screws his eyes even tighter shut.

Then, Mom orders, "Okay! Now, you can open your eyes."

Go2 opens his eyes and sees that she has disappeared from the screen. A window has now appeared there instead: a real, life-sized window, with the curtains drawn closed.

Mom says, "Now, Go2, just say 'open'."

"Open!"

The moment he speaks, the curtains fly open and a large glass window can be seen. Go2 takes a step closer to the screen and has a surprise! A wide grin breaks out on his face, in delight. He sees a huge lawn, with lots of white hares hopping, running, and playing around. They are all a bright white colour, with long ears and big red eyes, and one of them is busy eating a carrot. It's a beautiful sight!

Go2 is so happy! "This is amazing! Thank you so much!"

He watches them for ages – absorbed in their every movement, wondering at their beauty and brilliance. He can't stop smiling; his eyes wide.

Mom asks, "Are you happy now?"

"Yes, Mom. I'm very happy indeed."

"Now, close your eyes again," she tells him, and he closes his eyes for a few moments, used to the routine by now, but more patient this time; until she says, "You can open them."

The window on the screen has disappeared and the visual of his Mom has returned. He asks, "Mom, when can I see them again?"

"You can see them at any time. Just adjust the programme with your bablet, whenever you like."

"How about at night time?"

"You can see them at night time, but they are life -forms like you, and therefore, they also need their rest. It would be unfair to disturb their sleep just for your entertainment."

"Yes, Mom," Go2 considers. "That's true."

"Now, get ready for the second lot of good news," she says.

Go2 can't wait; but, as if to change the subject, she says, "You got me some flowers but forgot to give them to me."

He realises his mistake. "I'm sorry. I was just so happy to see you that I forgot everything else. I'll get them now." He stands up and picks up the bouquet from the table in the corner of the room. But, eager to find out more about her next surprise, he says, "Please tell me what the next good news is!"

"Bring the bouquet close to me, please." He returns to the screen where his Mom is waiting, and she says, "Now, try and pass me the bouquet."

He is bewildered and does not understand how he can possibly try to pass the bouquet to a 2-D image on a screen. "Mom, what are you talking about? You are on a screen; you are virtual, and I'm the only real one, here. How can I deliver the flowers to you?"

"Just give them to me."

He goes up to the screen and extends his two hands out, as if he is offering a bouquet to a real person. The flowers touch the screen and at the very moment this happens, the bouquet starts appearing in Mom's hands, on the screen!

"Thank you so much for the flowers, babe." She holds them in front of her nose and sniffs in a deep breath through her nostrils. "They are beautiful; but please remember – you don't have to buy anything for me."

He is still confused, because although he knows he is still holding the bouquet in his hands, it can be seen in Mom's hands onscreen. And incredibly, although he can feel it, he can't actually see the bunch of flowers he's holding, on his side of the screen. He exclaims, "How did you do that, Mom?"

"It's simple! You know there are thousands of cameras all around this room? They act like tomographic scanners and form the 4D image of the bouquet. The next step is to simply internalise and integrate that image with the image of me that you see on the screen."

"Wow! You are so clever. But what happened to the flowers in my hand?" he innocently asks. He can feel the stems in his fingers, but he can't see them – except for on the screen, in his mother's hands. He stares down, and his hands, although clenched, look empty. Amazed with modern technology, he asks, "How did you do that?"

"That is, again, very simple and the answer is 'camouflaging'.

Basically, the image behind the bouquet is superimposed onto the bouquet. So the bouquet is not seen even when it does not go anywhere."

He stares at his bent fingers and moves the apparently invisible bouquet with a swishing motion. If he looks closely, he gets a glimpse of the flowers in reality, as the camouflaging image is a fraction of a decimal second behind real time, if he moves fast. "But... the bouquet doesn't go anywhere?"

"No, it does not go anywhere. It is a very simple technique, but I thought this surprise would make you happy."

This is my surprise? he wonders, trying to hide his disappointment. It's amazing, but now he knows it's a trick... Well, he had been hoping for something more. But he conceals his disappointed expression with a smile. "Oh, I am very, very happy!"

She smiles with real happiness, "Similarly, we will take this technique further. Please come here to me. Now it's time for the third surprise."

Go2 goes closer to the screen. All of a sudden, he cannot see himself in the room, but instead, he can see himself on the screen, hugging his Mom. He gasps. He looks down at where his feet and body should be, but there's just floor and wall.

Impressed by this, he cries, "Mom, you are the best illusionist ever! Where am I?"

"You are here with me, baby," she laughs.

"But I am standing here in the room – I can feel the floor under my feet." With this, he stamps his foot, and although he can hear it, he can't see it. "And yet, I'm only seeing myself with you on the screen."

"Yes, Babdoo."

They both start laughing.

"Similarly, you can feed your hares as many carrots as you like, day or night!" she tells him.

"Especially if I'm invisible!" They both laugh again, and mom removes the camouflaging, so he has a visible body again in reality.

Go2 takes a pause, thinks over and asks, "Mom, I can come to your world, but when will you come into my world?"

Mom, as usual becomes philosophical, looks blank, and says expressionlessly, "We are working on it. The trans-world journeys are operated by supernatural powers."

"What does that mean?"

"You will know more about it when you are older."

Go2 changes the subject. "So, what is the next lot of good news you have?"

"We are going to celebrate your birthday!"

"Yesssssss!" he says, and he starts jumping around. "Can we invite Tilfo?"

"Of course yes, you can invite as many friends as you like!"

"No, Mom, I only want Tilfo there, because he's the only one who knows about my birth story..." as he says this, he looks distracted, thinking. "Mom, but what date should we have for my birthday party? Because Daddy has never celebrated one before and I have never been told what my date of birth is."

"The date does not matter, Go2."

Go2 nods, accepting this easily. "What other news do you have?"

"The president and ministry are going to honour me with a knighthood at a ceremony."

"Whoa! A knighthood?" he grins. "Hey Mom, hey Mom!" He starts dancing around again. "Long live my Mom!"

"Stop it. Don't be crazy!" she laughs.

"You deserve it. You are in a class of your own. When is it going to happen?"

"Soon. We will celebrate your birthday first, though."

"Mom, you are so very thoughtful. What is the next bit of good news you have?"

"How many do you need? Greedy! You wait," she smiles. "Now, that *is* going to be a big surprise!"

"Oh, Mom, I am the happiest boy of my size today."

She laughs at his comment. He goes up close to her, to enter the screen and hug her again.

* * * * * *

It is a dark evening in the yard where the Dexan Queen is parked. A light can be seen from the window of the second coach, which is Go2's room, and giggling can be heard, even outside.

Inside the room, Go2, Tilfo and Mom are having fun, chatting and laughing, celebrating Go2's birthday. Balloons are everywhere! Some are lying on the floor and others are floating up in the air. Party music is playing in the background and Go2 and Tilfo are cracking jokes, and organising things for the celebration. Their movements have become rhythmical as they dance to the music.

Mom is seen on the screen, dressed up for the occasion and is sitting on a chair in her kitchen, watching and enjoying the celebrations. She does not forget to give them instructions while she watches them. Although she is sitting on a chair, her legs are moving to the rhythm of the music. Go2 and Tilfo are dressed similarly: the right halves of their shirts are green and the left yellow, and their trousers are the same colours, but with the left and right legs reversed. Tilfo is wearing a navy cap and Go2 has dyed his hair red for the occasion.

Go2 opens a bag and pulls a cake box out of it. Placing it on the table, he teases Mom, "Why are you so beautiful?"

She laughs, the dimple on her left cheek looking more pronounced. "Because my son wants me to look beautiful," she replies.

"Why don't I have a classy dimple like you?"

"Do not worry, baby. Tomorrow I will call the road diggers to ask them to make a pot-hole on your cheek," she laughs.

"You are cheeky, Mom," he smiles.

"Open the cake and put it out on the table." She can't stop herself from giving them instructions.

Go2 opens the box, and inside it, there is a huge birthday cake – one half of it yellow and the other half, green. Tilfo is listening to the conversation between Go2 and his Mom and is enjoying hearing them joking with one another. He opens a box of candles and places eight candles on the cake, lighting them with a lighter on his bablet. Go2 goes and fetches a shiny silver knife to cut the cake and puts it down on the table.

Mom instructs them, "Go2 and Tilfo, stand on one side."

They stand so the cake is in the middle, between them all. But she can't stop ordering them around, telling them what to do. "Okay, now it's time to cut the cake."

Tilfo hands the knife over to Go2, who closes his eyes, makes a wish and blows the candles out.

Tilfo and Mom clap, and Mom starts singing, "Happy birthday to you! Happy birthday to you. Happy birthday, dear Go2, happy birthday to you!"

Go2 then cuts the cake into six large chunks. Tilfo picks one up and puts it into Go2's mouth, and as Go2 takes a bite, he says, "Thank you."

Go2 then picks up a slice and feeds it to Tilfo, then does the same for his Mom, holding the cake up to the screen to let it touch it.

She bends forward, takes a big bite, and as she eats it, she says, "Thank you, baby – and many happy, happy returns of the day. May my son live forever!"

Go2 takes another bite and chews it appreciatively, saying, "Oh, the cake is lovely. Where did you get it from, Tilfo?"

Tilfo takes out his bablet and tries to explain to Go2 in gestures that he ordered it through this.

Tilfo then goes into the corner of the room and gets a small box that he was hiding. He opens the wrapping: it is his gift to Go2 and Mom. This is the first of his two gifts, since he plans on giving the other one after the meal. He hands the box over to Go2.

Eager to know what is inside, Mom asks, "What have you got?"

Go2 opens it and replies, "It's a kind of chip, Mom."

He can't wait to see what it is and puts it straight into his bablet. As it starts, he sees that it is the video recording Tilfo made when they were playing football. It shows scenes they have already watched, for example, he sees the hen tearing the football apart.

"Thanks Tilfo, but you didn't need to bring me a gift. You make me happy every day – and that is way more important than a gift."

Mom agrees with him and says, "Yes Tilfo, you're family. You don't need to be formal with us."

Go2 says to Mom, "You will enjoy this, though, and you can watch it later. I'll swipe my bablet on your portal now, to transfer it over."

She is more interested in feeding them, however, and says, "Okay, come on boys! It is meal time now, and I need you to get the table organised. I have cooked something really special for you, so I hope you are ready."

Go2 asks Tilfo if he's hungry, and he nods his head to say he is. Go2 teases, "The tiger doesn't eat grass, even when he is very, very hungry!"

Tilfo smiles and raises his fist to make a playful knock on Go2's head, and he slowly and gently hits him.

Mom tries to join in with the fun and says, "Come on, boys, start grazing!"

They eat a delicious seven-course meal, with Mom delivering all the food via the portal; spending time chatting and laughing while eating. Tilfo is thoroughly enjoying being a part of the celebrations.

After the meal, there is a programme of dance and music, and Tilfo is the sole organiser of this. He has invited a professional dancer to attend – which is, in fact, his other gift to Go2 and Mom. He shows Go2 the details on his bablet.

Excitedly, Go2 says, "Mom, Mom! Tilfo has got us a surprise, he has invited a professional dancer, tonight."

Surprised, she asks, "Wow! Where are they? Because it's getting late... why don't you give them a call?"

"Tilfo, Oh tiger of my eyes, please call the dancer ASAP. Who have you invited?" he asks.

Tilfo gestures with his finger for him to wait and pulls his bablet out; he swipes it against another screen, opposite to the one that Mom is on, so they can all see it. As soon as it connects, all his activity can be seen and the screen shows the following message:

'Welcome to the age prediction tool. Please upload a photo of the life -form whose age profile you wish to predict."

Tilfo then uploads Go2's photo.

The message back is: 'Thanks. This is Go2. What age would you like to see him at?'

Tilfo selects the age range of between 170 and 180. Go2 soon realises what is happening: Tilfo is trying to see how Go2 will look at an ancient age. Mom starts smiling at the idea of this, but Go2 has a slight complaint.

"Tilfo, you are mad! I want to live to at least 200 years old, which will be 200 of the earth's revolutions. You are grossly underestimating my potential!"

Tilfo again lifts his finger to tell him to wait. The age prediction tool says:

'The answer is: yes, Go2's genes can match with this longevity. However, he will need to have a kidney and lung transplant, two new knees, two cochlear implants and two hip replacements. He will also need his ankles replacing, a shoulder implant, a new retina and a heart transplant to achieve it. There is also the option of having half a liver transplant, if required. Here you go. Enjoy Go2, without any trichology or dermatology interventions."

Everybody laughs at these suggestions. Tilfo then chooses the option to see the image, and after a few moments, the screen shows an image of Go2 at the age of 180. Everyone starts laughing, including Go2, but he soon starts playfully hitting Tilfo's back with his fist to get him to stop it.

But Tilfo does not stop. The image shows that Go2 has a shiny bald head, with only a few hairs left on his temples. He is wearing a thick pair of glasses and has a hearing aid. His skin has wrinkled and is sagging and there are two big folds of skin hanging down on his neck. The image of Go2 attempts to give a smile, but as he opens his mouth, only gums are seen as all teeth are lost.

Go2 continues to hit Tilfo's back, but Tilfo is too busy getting the image right. He chooses from the options to select a voice, and chooses a full image, followed by a 4D and then a responsive image. Tilfo then switches off all of the main lights and turns on two spotlights on the ceiling, to give the illusion of a dance floor. Go2 isn't enjoying being teased and is now almost trying to throttle Tilfo! Without paying him much attention, Tilfo carries on trying to get the image correct, and Mom can't stop laughing.

In the centre on the floor, there is a large beam of light, kind of like a spotlight. Slowly appearing in the spotlight is a 4D image of a 180-year-old Go2, with a stick in his hand to help him balance.

Tilfo starts the music and orders the image to dance, by pressing few buttons on his bablet.

Tilfo, Mom and Go2 are bursting into laughter as Tilfo gets up, walks into the spotlight and begins dancing with old Go2. Old Go2 cannot dance very well and is losing his balance; he is swaying like a drunk and making bizarre, random body movements. It looks funny and they are all in fits of laughter. It appears that old Go2 is the professional dancer, Tilfo had invited tonight.

Go2 does not know what to do initially, but soon realises that it is fun, so gets up and starts dancing with both of them. Mom is watching and laughing from her chair, her legs are jiggling in time to the tunes. All three of them are dancing well. Tilfo tries to tease the image and pokes his finger at it.

Go2 decides to take the joke further and says, in an old, croaky voice, "Ouch! Please don't hurt the old me! I may fall." He then jokes to Tilfo, "Don't trouble old me, or you will be sued for causing grievous harm to a senior citizen!"

Again, they all laugh at this. Tilfo is feeling euphoric from the dancing, so he takes his cap off and throws it up to the ceiling. The cap falls down and lands right onto the head of dancing old Go2, piercing through the image, causing it to distort for a while, before the cap lands on the floor.

Go2 is annoyed because he does not want his image made a mockery of.

He says to Tilfo, "Hey, buddy Tiger! Stop this now or I will sue you, in 180 years' time."

Mom puts her hands over her mouth to try and hide her laughter. They carry on dancing for a long time, while Mom has fun watching them.

The celebrations continue for a decimal more hour, and music can be heard for a long time.

The light from inside, stands out in the darkness of the parking yard.

It is now the middle of the night and Mom is trying to hide her yawning. "Boys, it's very late now. If you could, please stop now…"

Tilfo reluctantly stops the music and old Go2 gradually fades away, digit by digit. The main lights are switched back on, and they are both sweating and laughing.

"It was great fun, Tilfo! Thank you so much for inviting a professional dancer," Go2 says, and they giggle.

Mom asks, "Boys, do you need a drink? You must be thirsty after all that dancing."

"Yes, please, Mom! We both need a drink," Go2 replies.

She then pours two glasses of water and adds a few cubes of ice from the fridge. "Go2, please go and collect your drinks from the portal."

He fetches them and they both drink them, thirstily.

"Go2, please walk Tilfo out to his train. Hurry up, because we have a big day tomorrow."

"What do you mean, Mom?"

"Silly boy! Have you forgotten about the ceremony?"

"Oh, yes. I remember! I had forgotten all about it." He asks, "Mom, what do they call it? Is it going to be your honouring, felicitation, or coronation?"

Mom shakes her head, smiling. "Wait until tomorrow and you will see."

"Yes, Mom."

"Fine then. Tilfo, have a good night and go safely. I must retire now; I am so tired." Mom slowly disappears from the screen.

Go2 and Tilfo exit the coach and start walking along the platform, from the quiet section of the platform into the centre and climb the bridge, which spans over many tracks. Down on another platform, they sit on a bench, while they wait for Tilfo's train. They are both tired from dancing, so they are not speaking much.

Then, Go2 remembers something and starts the conversation: "Tilfo, I am cross with you."

Tilfo raises his eyebrows to ask him what he's talking about.

"I want to live to at least 200 years old and because you are thick, you want me to finish me off at only 180 years old."

Tilfo smiles at this. He takes out his bablet from his pocket, messes with the screen and shows it to Go2.

The bablet reads: 'The programme says that you will live for at least two centuries. You are not going to die before that, so you will be troubling me for a long time, yet."

This brings a smile to Go2's face. "I am still sad because I don't look good when I am old."

Tilfo again scratches his bablet to show Go2 his reply, which reads: 'Don't worry. We will do a biofilm implant using the best material available, with a top robotic plastic surgeon. Technology will have evolved more by then, anyway."

"Tilfo, you have made me very happy!"

They high-five and Tilfo laughs.

A few decimal minutes later, the train arrives: an ordinary southbound train. They both get up and bend their knees forward to meet each other's.

Go2 says, "Thanks for coming and for organising everything. Goodnight."

Tilfo starts walking towards the automatic doors, which open and the light falls on his face.

Go2 remembers something and shouts, "Tilfo, don't forget! Tomorrow is a big day, so please be early."

Tilfo nods his head, boards the train and waves goodbye to Go2.

* * * * * *

Dr. Smith has just finished with his first patient of the morning and is in a hurry to catch up with the other patients on the ward. He closes the drawer and puts on his white coat, which is hanging up on the back of his white chair. As he gets up to walk out, he hears a bleep on his bablet, so he puts his hand into his pocket to get it out.

The bablet says loudly, "The Dexan Queen would like to talk to you. Please confirm if this is okay by saying 'yes'. She wants to come onto your screen."

Dr. Smith agrees and after a few scratchy digits, Mom appears on the screen. Her long, curly hair is flowing and she is wearing a long tunic made from green tweed, with several speckled colours intermingled. The tunic has a lace collar and she is wearing a coat over the tunic.

"Good morning, Doc. I am sorry to take up your time unscheduled but thank you so much for seeing me without notice."

"It is okay. I have a few decimal minutes to spare. What can I do for you, Ma'am?"

"I just have a quick question to ask."

"No problem; please go ahead. By the way, I must say – you are looking gorgeous today!"

The Dexan Queen smiles because she is glad someone has noticed how different she looks. "I am expressing my roots in Munster through my attire today. Thank you very much." Changing the subject, she says, "I'd like to invite you to my felicitation today. Along with Go2 and Tilfo, you will be my special guest."

Dr. Smith is flattered by the invitation and humbly says, "Thank you, Ma'am." He then suddenly remembers, "Yes, I heard the news about it on my bablet. I am privileged. I will definitely come and join in with the celebrations."

"Thanks, Doc!"

"On the track of life, you are capably speeding through. You have done so well; despite all of the difficulties you have faced."

"Yes Dr. Smith, motherhood has helped me to reach a day like today, and I am feeling very happy."

"I can see that."

The Dexan Queen smiles at this and changes the subject again. "By the way, I wanted to ask your opinion on a small matter."

"Go on."

"Firstly, I must thank you for looking after Go2. He is doing very well. And also, I'd like to have some information about the bond between a mother and a child."

Dr. Smith becomes wary and says, "Thank you. Good to know that he is doing well. Yes, go on. But the bond of motherhood is not a simple or a small subject."

The Dexan Queen smiles at this and asks, "What makes the bond so strong?"

Dr. Smith wants to try and summarise the answer in a nutshell. "There are many things. And they depend on the psychological substrate, impressions, the upbringing of both, the mother and child, and also their values, instincts, genes, aspirations and desires."

"Doctor, please can you make it slightly simpler for someone like me?"

He smiles. "There are many things. The first thing, in the psycho-bio evolution, is breast-feeding. In the earlier, formative years, breast-feeding helps to strengthen the bond between mother and child."

Feeling assured she says, "Thanks, Doc. That is very helpful."

"I hope so."

"Please don't forget to come to the big occasion tonight!"

"I will definitely be there."

"Thanks again."

The Dexan Queen disappears from the screen and Dr. Smith uses his bablet to close down the screen.

He mutters to himself, "You need to mind the gap, lady."

Chapter 17

Balloons and bunting are flying everywhere at the ceremony and a huge crowd has gathered. There is not enough space to accommodate everyone, so they are sitting in any space they can find; some robots and children are even sitting on the rooftops of some of the parked trains. All the train tracks have converged to form the shape of a wheel, with the spokes joining up in the centre. There are more than 80 trains parked up, on the radiant tracks.

Thousands of chairs are laid out between the tracks for the public to sit on and enjoy the ceremony, and every single chair is occupied. There are all kinds of life forms and robots there, but the majority are human -life -forms. Many of the human and monkey –life- forms are carrying their youngsters on their shoulders. Energy and enthusiasm are everywhere! Children are excited, and some are even waving flags with pictures of The Dexan Queen on them; others are holding up flyers that say, 'Long live The Dexan Queen'.

Go2 and Tilfo are also excited and they are properly suited and booted today – their black bow ties making them the centre of attention – and they are almost like celebrities. They are sitting on the front row beside the Dexan Queen, on a special two-seater sofa that has been specially arranged for them. For the first time in their lives, they are feeling incredibly proud.

Some children are asking Go2 and Tilfo for their autographs, and in the times between scribbling their signatures, they are eating Jowar pops. Dr. Smith occupies the special guest chair next to them, where he is enjoying the ceremony preparations, while talking to fellow spectators and shaking hands with them, feeling honoured to be there.

A huge stage facing the crowd has been set up especially for the occasion, although it is not open yet and a curtain is hanging in front of it. An arrangement has been put in place to record the event on thousands of cameras and the recordings are displayed on huge screens erected in all four corners.

The President has not yet arrived and there are some robot technicians in front of the stage, checking that everything is working.

The biotrain, The Dexan Queen, is standing quietly on her track, spending time reflecting on everything. Hundreds of small, lit bulbs, looking like pretty Christmas lights, have been placed all over her coaches. Parallel to, and on either side of her head unit, are two giant cranes, arching over her; at the very top of the crane arch, there is a huge closed box suspended in the air, but hidden behind a curtain.

At the far end of the tracks are two other biotrains, Miss Mermaid and Belladonna, who are also thinking and reflecting on this occasion.

All of a sudden, there is an announcement and everyone stops talking, and listens. "Please observe silence! The President of Robocracy for the province is arriving very soon."

The lights on the audience go off and everyone looks towards the stage, in anticipation. The curtains slide apart to reveal the stage, lit up with spotlights; although no one is on it, yet. A few decimal seconds later, the floor of the stage slides apart and chairs slowly start to rise from below, with characters seated on them. The President and his ministers have arrived.

Everyone stands up and there is huge round of applause as everyone claps and cheers them. Go2 and Tilfo stand up too quickly, and Tilfo accidentally spills his drink all over his expensive trouser.

The applause continues until an announcement is made: "Ladies, gentlemen, children of all life forms, 4D images, and robots – please, be seated. Our honourable President of Robocracy appreciates your applause."

The President, a human life-form, is sitting in the middle of the other ministers, smiling and waving at the crowd.

A further announcement can be heard: "Now, we request our beloved and respected President, Mr Walsh, the pioneer of the robocratic movement, the messiah of peace and integration between life and non-life forms, to guide us in the felicitation of a new experiment: the pioneering breeding of biotrains. Today, we are honouring The Dexan Queen!"

Again, there is huge applause and the crowds sit back down in their seats. Go2 and Tilfo look proudly at each other. The President stands up slowly and gracefully before stepping forward to address the crowd, while everyone claps again.

In a very low-pitched voice, Mr Walsh slowly says, "Dear brothers and sisters of all life and non-life-forms, and my robot comrades!"

When the crowd hear his voice, there is more cheering, and he waits, smiling, for the applause to subside.

"I know and understand the love you have for our robocratic processes. The fact that you are here – and in large numbers – shows only one thing: that you love robocracy, and you love The Dexan Queen."

"She is simply great!" A voice from the crowd shouts, and more cheering erupts.

"We are here to felicitate and honour this special lady who has broken track records." The audience starts clapping again, but the President continues: "I will start with some historical facts…" The crowd now falls silent, eager to hear what the President has to say. "If we look at the history of civilisation, there has always been a process of evolution in all life forms." Mr Walsh raises his right index finger and states, "The basis of civilisation was supported by one technology, in particular – and that was the invention of the wheel. Of course, like everything else, there were plenty of movements that criticised the role of the wheel. They argued that the wheel was a curse; but we do not have to dwell on those thoughts now."

There is such silence that you could hear a pin drop.

"When the wheel was invented, human life forms used to move it manually, and some thought this was a curse because they believed it was exploiting human -life -forms."

The President takes a deep breath and continues, "Then came the horses, bullocks, elephants, donkeys, monkeys and parrot life forms that pulled the wheels. Our non-human-life forms, our brothers and sisters, worked hard to keep the wheel running. In fact, many of them lived a life of slavery and bore the burden of vehicles on their shoulders, for millennia."

The horses and monkey-life-forms in the crowd look at the President proudly and respectfully as he continues, "The invention of bicycles and automobiles helped to stop the exploitation of animal-life-forms, to some extent."

A peacock in the crowd gives a loud sigh of relief.

"However, these wheels still needed human-life-form riders or drivers; so, they too, were exploited. Machinery was both a blessing and a curse. Many died in accidents and wars and they would work long hours without food and water. Technology then went one step further and a new breed of vehicles was invented: auto-piloted. This only happened in the last century – but since machines and programmes have taken over from human -life -forms, this has helped to stop the exploitation."

Dr. Smith nods his head in agreement, as he sips a soft drink through a straw.

Mr Walsh continues, "The introduction of auto-piloting removed the need for drivers – and trains, planes and drones transported people and products without them. The advancement of this technology helped to save lives."

Go2 is so busy listening to the President, he has stopped eating his Jowar pop.

"Now, with the intention of making life better, we have gone one step further and have given total autonomy to robotic vehicles. By giving them autonomy, we have now entered a new historical time and have even promoted some biotrains to do this. They are able to choose their own path and the tracks they use; no one tells them where to go and they are their own masters."

The president has to take a pause, as there is yelling in the crowd, "Long live robocracy! Long live robocracy!"

"There are a few models of this experiment in practice. We have moved away from the old era of auto-piloting and on to more modern times of autonomous vehicles. We've gone from automatic to autonomous – and from slavery, to freedom." The crowd claps again. "We have continued to take technology further and have installed instincts into machines. A huge step has been taken in transforming some of the autonomous trains to biotrains."

Belladonna and Miss Mermaid are listening to the speech in alarm, as they are also autonomous biotrains.

He continues, "Our principles and values have made this change possible. We have some biotrains in practical use that can act with love and respect and can even look after other lives. Our respected lady, The Dexan Queen, is one of them!"

Huge applause can be heard.

Go2 looks around and for the first time in his life, he is feeling proud of his mother.

"The fact that you are all here shows that you love her and want to be a part of her felicitation."

Belladonna's wheels are rattling.

The President intones, "Let me tell you a little bit about her activities – the activities that have helped to contribute towards building nations and societies." Go2 leans forward to listen. "We had policies, procedures and ideologies planned. Our administration took 28 years and 36 days to decide if we would be allowed to create a biotrain that would carry and look after all life forms." Tilfo's ears prick up as he hears this. "This is how The Dexan Queen was born. We created her to use instinct."

The yelling can be heard in the crowd.

"Let me share some facts about her. The way she lives, operates, runs, cares and nurtures, is inspirational. I'm going to talk a little bit about her daily schedule." The President takes a breath and continues, "While she is parked up at night, she gets her own water and minerals by attaching herself to the mains supply."

Go2 is bewildered; he did not know this about his Mom.

"The honourable Dexan Queen is programmed to self-generate and is a unique example of self-sufficiency. She does not need outside programmes to repair her when she requires it and, in fact, manufactures her own spare parts and integrates them into her system. Her manufacturing units are located in the last two coaches, and any parts are carried through channels and ducts built into her walls. She has systems in place, she hardly ever needs any repair work doing. She is a tough masterpiece, in a class of her own."

Go2 and Tilfo look at each other with amazement.

"She is independent, in regard to her energy needs and her final coach is a small nuclear reactor, which generates energy. She not only uses her own energy, but she attaches herself to the grid, to provide energy to other trains in need."

The President has to stop for a moment or two because the clapping and cheering is so loud.

Belladonna is listening to him with great scepticism.

"To take in nuclear raw materials and to dump waste, she hibernates, like a reptile-life-form."

Go2 is wondering how his Mom hibernates, but soon hears.

"Every now and then, she takes time off from work and goes to the underground track, under the sea. She stays there for a few days and dumps her nuclear waste. She then gets the raw materials she needs and returns to work."

Go2 is now getting worried about what will happen to him when she goes into hibernation.

Mr Walsh says, "So far, I have spoken simply about how she works; so, now, I will talk about her virtues and values."

Go2 and Tilfo again look at each other in surprise. They are hearing facts about Mom's life that they did not know.

"She carries all life -forms, punctually, to the nanosecond and has never had an accident. When she was very young, she would run day and night without having a rest period. She is a role model for providing a service to society."

Another huge round of applause starts, and amidst it all, Dr. Smith is nodding his head in agreement.

"She has not built gambling dens, swimming pools or 9-star hotels inside her."

Miss Mermaid is flapping her windows subtly at this comment.

"Instead, she has set an example of charity and duty, and has even built a hospital within herself: the fourth from last coach is, in fact, a hospital. She has always been the first and fastest one running in if any life-form is endangered, and she would always reach out to help them."

The audience shuffles in amazement, and yelling can be heard.

The President orders them, "Please observe silence. I have not finished. I can go on and on praising her for a long time, yet."

Go2 is trying to understand everything he has learnt about his Mom.

"Our great Megano Constitution allows her to generate an income and dispose it off according to her fee will. She is the only biotrain allowed to do this. She is an icon of success and earns a high income from carrying her passengers. Everyone wants to travel with her and because of this, she generates the highest income out of all the trains in existence."

Go2 says, "Wow!"

Miss Mermaid steams, even though she is not a steam train; seething in annoyance.

"You will be very happy to hear that she donates all of her money to the welfare of orphaned tiger cubs."

Tears have gathered in Tilfo's eyes and he tries to wipe them with the back of his wrist. Go2 spots him and offers him a tissue from his pocket.

"She has even gone a step further and has accomplished uniqueness! This will surprise you all."

The crowd fall silent to hear what he is going to say next.

"Only recently, she became a mother and adopted a son! And, we must say, he is the most fortunate boy in all of humanity."

Go2 is overwhelmed by this comment.

"It is the first time in history that this kind of experiment has been carried out – and generations to come will remember The Dexan Queen."

The public are excited now, and some have raised their arms and are shouting, "Dexan! Dexan! Dexan!"

The President has smile on his face as he continues, "Please wait and let me finish. I won't take much more of your time. To become a mother, she has had to sacrifice her speed, her nuclear reactor and has even invited enmity from a certain sector."

Belladonna and Miss Mermaid are listening carefully.

"Madame Dexan Queen is a prime example of service, duty, sacrifice – all values that are eroding in modern and materialistic societies. She goes wherever she is needed and does whatever she has to, in order to protect and preserve lives."

There is more audience clapping at this comment.

"So, to summarise: she is the one and only. She is a historical figure, a symbol of integration and a model of love and respect. She is in a class of her own and a beacon of the future, for all life and non-life-forms."

The crowd can't control themselves any longer and they all stand up and start clapping and cheering.

"Members of the public already call her a Queen, and today, on this historic occasion, I will crown her, officially."

The entire crowd is now shouting, "Dexan! Dexan! Dexan!"

Mr Walsh, the President, pulls out a remote control from his pocket, holds it up in the direction of the big box held up the two cranes and pushes the button. The curtains covering the box slide open and a huge golden crown embedded with coloured precious jewels can be seen inside. The audience are cheering even more, at the sight of this.

"I will now crown her, on behalf of all the governments, societies and moving characters that wish to honour her."

The President pushes another button and one crane drops down its claws to lift the crown up slowly and carries it forwards, towards the head unit of Her Majesty, The Dexan Queen. They gently place the crown down on her head unit, the base of the crown is sloping down, so that it fits snuggly on her head unit.

"I officially hereby declare the Madame Dexan Queen as the Queen of all our hearts, -from this moment onwards. She will always be remembered as, 'Her Majesty, the Queen!'"

The moment this happens, the cranes release golden glitter from their sacks and her head is covered with it. Go2 is standing beside her, and he, Tilfo and everyone near to her is also showered with glitter.

Everyone is clapping, cheering and shouting, and a five-gun salute can also be heard in the distance. The happy chaos lasts for a few decimal minutes, while even the President and his ministers are clapping.

The President says, "We now request Her Majesty, the Queen to speak and guide us."

The audience members have been waiting for this moment and loudly cheer, again. All the lights are switched off and the crowd quietens down to listen to her, as huge screens appear along all of the coaches on both sides and slowly, digit-by-digit, she starts to appear in her Irish woman image on each one. It is the first time she has ever appeared in public in a human- form.

Go2 and Tilfo turn their heads towards the screens and everyone gets into a position where they can get a good view of her. The image on the screen is wearing the same crown on her head and her long, flowing, blonde, curly hair gives her the appearance of a queen. The glitter has fallen on her face and she looks both bashful and excited. Go2 has never seen her look so happy. She is waving with her right hand whilst holding a microphone in her left hand, saluting in all directions.

The crowd is shouting again, "Dexan! Dexan! Dexan!"

She holds the microphone up to her mouth and says, "Brothers, sisters, and children of all life -forms – not forgetting my robot brothers and sisters…"

The crowd are going so crazy for her, that she has to raise her voice.

"Thank you so much. Thank you; thank you. If you could, please stay silent just for a moment, so that I can speak."

The crowd obediently falls silent and she continues, "Thank you all very much. I am humbled by the love you have showered me with, today."

The crowd cheers loudly, with cries of, "Yeeeeeeeeee!"

"I am honoured today, and I cannot thank you enough for the motherly instincts I have acquired from all life forms. We are merely machines that have borrowed our values from humanity. We owe generations of human civilisations for this. With the help of technology, we have been able to implement these values and I cannot sufficiently thank humanity and the robocratic processes that have helped to make this day a reality."

The robots in the crowd start dancing at this comment.

She continues, "Two sources in particular have inspired me. Around two hundred years ago, there was a lady called Mother Teresa, who she was a great source of inspiration to the future world. The second lady who inspired me is called Cate. Cate was my competitor when I was trying to adopt my son, and we were both in direct competition for the motherhood we cherished. If all gender type ones on earth were like Cate, then the world would be very beautiful. Thank you so much, Cate, if you are watching. Cate is truly inspirational in wanting to feed and raise as many children as possible."

Cate is watching at home, on the big screen on her wall, while she is feeding her babies. All of a sudden, she jolts when she hears her name and tears spring in her eyes.

She says to her other children, "Thank you – you made me mother, famous, today. God bless The Dexan Queen."

Back on the screen, The Dexan Queen says, "My biggest aspiration is to raise as many children as possible, of all life forms. I don't just want to be an artificial intelligence covered by a biofilm; I wish to make a journey from the virtual to the visual and real. I want to be able to touch my children and for them to touch me."

Go2 is starting to understand now why his Mom is known as the Queen. He looks at her, unblinking.

She continues, "Nature has given me plenty and I am saying this with great humility: I wish to donate this crown. It can be auctioned and I would like the proceeds to be donated to the welfare of all children in the world."

A huge cheer comes from the crowd, as they shout, "Long live Dexan!"

"Please give me your blessing to continue with this kind of work – and keep me in your hearts."

The crowd is shouting, "Don't go, Queen! Don't go! We love you! We love you!"

"I love you, too," she replies. "I thank you all again and I thank my son for allowing me to be a mother."

Go2 continues to gaze at his Mom. All the ministers and the President on the stage are clapping, in appreciation.

Chapter 18

It's getting dark. The public have gone and the music has stopped – everywhere is quiet. The Dexan Queen is still on the track where she has been just recently felicitated. All the small lights are switched off but she can still be seen on the big screen on her head unit.

Her track where she is parked, are surrounded by news reporters, sitting on chairs near her head unit: most of them robots, but some are human -life -forms, too.

On the screen, she is seen sitting down on a train track, answering every question intelligently.

One of the reporters is fidgety and asks, "Ma'am, why are you sitting on the ground? Is it not dirty?"

The Dexan Queen nods her head twice, agreeing, "Yes, there may be a little bit of dirt here..." and disagreeing, "but it is good for your health." Her eyelids are lowered to answer,

"This is my real place, firmly grounded, in your hearts, and lower than yours."

Some reporters cannot stop themselves from clapping. A gender type 1 reporter raises her hand to ask permission to speak. The Dexan Queens says, "Please go ahead."

"Is money not important to you? We learnt that you donated your crown to the orphan cub welfare programme, but aren't you at all insecure about your future?"

The Dexan Queen gives a gentle smile and answers, "Too many questions! Money is important, but really, it's just a vehicle and shouldn't be your destination. No, I am not insecure about anything, because insecurity is part of an inferiority complex. Besides, my son will look after me, in my old age."

An old human-life-form reporter nods his head in agreement, saying, "Mr President touched upon your capacity for auto-manufacturing. Can you please tell us more?"

She answers confidently, "In the past, it was called 3D printing. All the programmes help me to make whatever I need to. I draw down the raw materials from the ducts; then the parts are printed and are transferred to the site using the channels built in me. It's like circulation in a body, where oxygen is carried from the lungs to the liver via blood, through blood vessels. All of this happens while I am resting at the parking yard. It is good to be self-sufficient."

One inquisitive reporter asks, "We heard that you've been punished for adopting your son – by having your nuclear reactor removed and your speed slowed down. Is that true?"

"No, that's not true – it is not a punishment. It's just a safety measure, because I want young lives kept safe."

"If I remember correctly you were attacked once," one reporter reminds her of the incident when she had black tar sprayed on her by the Belladonna. "Are you attracting enmity because you're egotistical?"

The Dexan Queen thinks over this question for a few moments, before replying in a serious tone, "God bless all. I do not envy anything, anywhere. Sometimes, others envy you because of your success – but you should rejoice in it."

A robot reporter is agitated by this answer, "You must have worked very hard to achieve all your success. You have name, fame and money! You're rich and famous!"

The Dexan Queen is happy to answer and she leans forward on the rail track. "I just work. Others consider it hard. Fame and money are not my destinations – they're simply stations I go through."

The reporters giggle at this answer. A flashy gender type 1 reporter asks, "So, you've adopted a son. Are you going to adopt a husband to play around with, now?"

There is an eruption of laughter amongst the reporters at this question. The Dexan Queen frowns slightly. "No. I have become a mother, not a wife. If I can become a mother without having a husband, why should I get one?"

Most gender type 1 reporters acknowledge this answer.

"What are you looking forward to?" a robot reporter asks. "What are your aspirations and future plans?"

The Dexan Queen takes a deep breath and replies, "I want to adopt as many chicks, cubs, calves and children as possible and I want to be the greatest mother ever. I also want to come into your world."

Some reporters clap at this answer, as another one asks, "What has been the happiest moment of your life?"

"The first moment was when I adopted my son. The next happiest moment will be happening soon. I will let you know when it happens."

One of them says, "Well, best wishes for your future ventures. You mark the beginning of a new era."

She is delighted with this comment.

"By the way, where is your son?"

"He has gone to drop off his friend."

The question and answer session has dragged on for a long time and The Dexan Queen suddenly remembers that Go2 might be hungry, because it is his teatime.

"Please forgive me, ladies and gentlemen, but I have to leave. My son will be getting hungry now and will be waiting for me."

The reporters all stand up and clap. Some of them say, "Best of luck!" and "Best wishes."

The screen slowly fades away and she disappears.

* * * * * *

The Dexan Queen arrives at the parking yard. After a while, Go2 also arrives and goes to his room. His Mom is waiting on the screen for him and has changed her attire, wearing a white top and bluebell-coloured bell-bottomed trousers. The moment she sees Go2, she shouts with joy, "Hey, Sonny! I was waiting for you."

"Yes, sorry, Mom. I got a bit delayed."

"It's okay, I have only just arrived."

"You must be very happy, Mom!"

"I am very, very happy."

Go2 takes a seat on the sofa and says, "Mom, I now realise why the public call you the Queen."

Mom smiles at this comment. "I am waiting for two more moments of happiness."

"Wow that would be lovely. What are they?"

"You might have forgotten; but do you remember your surprises? It's now time for your fifth and final surprise."

Go2's eyes widen in excitement. "What is that, Mom?"

"If I tell you, then it won't be a surprise, will it?"

"Okay, Mom," Go2 says, rolling his eyes. "Tell me when you're ready."

"I am ready now, I think. Yesterday was your birthday; but today, it's my birthday."

"Wow! Happy birthday, Mom!" Go2 exclaims, with joy. "Why didn't you tell me before?"

"I want to celebrate it with just you, in an untraditional manner!"

"Okay, Mom, I'll order food for us or we'll go out tonight. Or sometime later, over the holidays, if you're tired."

Mom laughs at her son's innocence. "Hold on, babe. I want to give you the biggest surprise of your life, right now."

Go2's eyes widen and he cannot control himself, jumping up and down, he cries, "Yes, Mom! Go ahead and surprise me, then!"

"Hold on. Close your eyes."

"Okay, I'll close my eyes. But what have you got for me?"

The Dexan Queen laughs, shaking her head. "Well – shut your eyes first and wait until I ask you to open them! It will take a few digital minutes."

He screws his eyes tightly shut and waits to see what he's going to get. She extends her arms towards him and stays there for a few moments, then orders the programmes: "Auto manufacturing mode, please."

She then disappears from the screen, which starts showing zigzag lines. The programmes go through a sequence, and the words describing the sequence appear in a box in the corner of the screen, starting with: 'The screen is going into auto manufacturing mode.'

The rest of the screen is evolving, without any sound. The box onscreen shows the messages: 'A 3D image has now been identified.'

A voice states, 'A picture will appear on the screen.'

Go2 is almost tempted to open his eyes to see the picture but thinks better of it.

'All the appropriate biomaterials are being uploaded.'

Then, the auto manufacturing of the image begins, with the declaration: 'Please wait. It will take 11 decimal seconds.'

'Please get ready.'

Go2 keep his eyes squeezed closed as he waits.

The screen has started printing a 4D image of Mom. The digits start disappearing and solid dots begin to replace them; the dots gathering to form outgrowing buds and then, forming into contours. The contours start to grow out of the screen and begin to take the shape of human organs. The outstretched realistic, solid fingers start to pop out of the screen: long, slender, soft and representing a beautiful woman.

The hands follow the fingers and they slowly emerge, followed by the forearms and the arms. It all happens in a designated sequence, with the chest, neck and nose forming, next. Finally, she is fully formed, is wearing the same clothes, and the whole body comes out of the screen. She has come to this side of the world intact, in body, mind and material! She curiously starts looking around, everywhere. She stands there for a moment and looks at Go2, who still has his eyes closed.

She is overwhelmed by being part of the material world and tries to see how everything works, wanting to touch her screen, but she decides not to.

She looks at Go2 again as she stands in front of him and says, "Go2, darling, open your eyes now."

Her voice is less mechanical and more human-sounding now.

Go2 opens his eyes, but can't believe that his Mom, whom he has only ever seen in pictures is alive and in front of him!

He screams, "Mom, I can't believe this!" and jumps up instantly, moving forward to hug her. She bends down to hug him and starts kissing him all over, on his head, forehead, eyes, cheeks and shoulders, she can't stop kissing and hugging him. She wonders at the strange sensations of feeling his physical body at last, with its warmth and pressure, its softness and textures and the boniness of his head. So much to hug and experience, in all its variety.

Go2 is become speechless in happiness, and surprise. Mom is similar, can't speak a word and they both have tears of joy in their eyes. Sitting on the sofa, with Go2 on her lap, encircling her neck with his arm, feeling her cool skin with his hand. She embraces him, her hands on his back, and says, "So, do you like your surprise?"

Go2 looks up at her, in wonder. "Yes, Mom. It's been the biggest and greatest one so far."

"Yes, babe, it has been for me, too."

"I am the happiest life form on earth now! I must share this with Tilfo."

"Hold on, Babbo! Let me enjoy these moments, as real mother, first. I've waited for this for so long, I just want to stay like this for a while. We'll discuss this... with other people later, okay?"

"Okay. Mom, why are you so smart?" He hugs her tighter, pressing his face against her chest, thrilled at the feel of her arms around him and the beating of her heart against his ear.

She smiles at him and they continue to talk for a long time. They don't realise how much time has passed or notice that it's getting very late night.

The hundreds of small light bulbs on the Dexan Queen in her train-form are still lit up outside.

"Mom, I am a bit cross with you," Go2 says, after some thought.

"Why, Sonny?"

"Why didn't you come to my world sooner?" He frowns. "If you could do this, now…"

"You mean why didn't it happen yesterday? What a question, babe!" She turns to one side, gazing wistfully into the air, and continues, "It wasn't easy for me. It is never going to be easy. You know how many legalities and barriers I've had to break, to do this?" Mom is serious, since she is not allowed to become a 3D image and enter the world. The law has prohibited her from becoming a living image, as it compromises her basic duties and functions as a train.

"What are you talking about, Mom?"

"This must be kept a secret – just between us. Only you and I can know – even Tilfo can't know about this. I'm not publicly allowed to be a 4D image – adopting a son by a biotrain was just an experiment, and the authorities don't want to have any conflicts of interest. There are certain procedures and rules I must abide by."

"Okay, but why can't they just change the procedures?"

"We will try and do this in future, but my journey has not been easy. I've gone from a picture to a prototype, from copyright to patent, and from a crowd to a crown!"

"I don't understand what you are saying," Go2 says.

"This incarnation was done in my personal capacity. I've had to break many signals, barriers and go off track. It's all for you. I would do anything for you."

"I'd do anything for you too, Mom." She smiles again at his innocence as he continues, "Mom, I don't want to go to school tomorrow."

Mom is surprised. "And may I ask why?"

"I want to spend all my time with you."

She gazes at him fondly and smiles again. "That is not possible right now, because – apart from evenings – I have to work. Don't worry. We have all our lives to spend together and we'll stay together… until you get bored, which you doubtlessly will. You will hate me in my old age!"

"No, Mom! Never. Let me stay off school and stay with you. Please, please, please…"

"As I said, we have our lives together. When you grow up and get a girlfriend, you won't want to spend any time with me."

"No, Mom that will never happen! I will take you with me on my dates."

Mom chuckles at this. "Listen – it's getting late. Aren't you hungry?"

"Yes. And no."

"I have something to offer you, over on the table."

"What is it?" Go2 spins round.

"Yesterday was your birthday, yes?"

"Yes… and?"

"Today, it is mine."

"I am sorry, Mom. I forgot. Anyway, happy birthday to you!"

"Thank you."

"Mom, let's celebrate on a grand scale!"

She smiles. "My grand scale is different to yours, though," she replies.

"You know, Mom, sometimes you are philosophically unnecessary."

"I want to be a real mother. That would be my grand scale."

"You *are* a real Mom! You shouldn't have a complex about it – you are far better than any biological mom."

"No, I mean I want to develop a real mother's bond with you." She looks at him meaningfully.

Go2's eyebrows dance, quizzically. "You already have done, because you're a mother to many."

"Not in that way," she clasps his hand, and pats it, gazing into his eyes. "I mean… in the way you've always wished a mother to be. My wish is to become a real nursing mother to you."

Go2 laughs and exclaims, "Oh, Mom, you're going crazy!" He gets up and goes to the vending portal, shaking his head in disbelief.

"No, I have really thought about this," she says, standing up from her seat. "The only bond that makes the mother-child relationship grow is through nursing a baby. I have asked this to an expert!"

He swings back around, and says, assertively, "Mom, I was a stupid fool, and a psychiatric patient. Now, you shouldn't act like one."

She lifts her hands, imploringly. "It is my wish. I want to see you regress to infancy again, just for a few moments… please?"

Go2 gasps, a look of distaste on his face. "What a weird Mom! What a weird wish!"

She sent me away for weeks! he thinks. *She called me weird, took me to a psychiatrist and sent me away to be cured!* He doesn't want to go there.

"You said you would do anything for me," she whines. Go2 just turns his head, in denial, as she continues, "Try to understand me. My journey through life has been difficult. It started at a junk yard full of scrap metal, where pieces were then assembled into my train-form and artificial intelligence installed."

"What has any of that got to do with your weird wish, now?"

"I started doing service and charity work and society started recognising me," she explains, her face lined with worry. "Then I became a mother, which gave me some dignity as a human. I went from scrap metal to dignitary."

"You should be happy with that," grumpy Go2 says.

"Yes. It is good to be a human and to live and grow like one. I am addicted to becoming more human, now."

"But you're already a human."

"Not really. Without you, I am not a mother, let alone a Queen. I need to be your real mother."

Go2 pulls a face and waves his hand dismissively. "Mom, go to sleep. I'm tired." He's lost his appetite and just wants to get away.

Her voice starts choking and tears are falling down her cheeks. Sniffling through her sobs, she cries, "If my wish remains unfulfilled, I will be an incomplete mother. It is you who can make me complete." She wipes her eyes with her hands and continues, "I have made a long journey. You only need to take a few steps."

"What has made you mad like this, Mom?" Go2 is questioning her now, feeling a little sick.

"Remember when you had that phase of regression to infantilism? That was when I started thinking about this."

"Oh," Go2 murmurs. He is unwillingly losing ground now and can't see a way out.

"Go2, please! I beg you. Just give me the opportunity for a few seconds and I will prove myself to the world and proudly say I am a biological mother."

He lowers his head and reluctantly considers what she said. He is losing the argument and receding from his definite, defiant stance. In fact, a little stirring of desire flickers within him, as he remembers that time… those feelings.

"Yes, Mom. Whatever." He agrees to regress and become her baby for a few moments. "I will be your baby just once, just to give you the feel of it."

"Yes, my bubdie!" She beams in delight and spreads her arms to hug him; he steps into her embrace and she leads him back to the sofa. Her eyelids lower slowly as she looks at him, adoringly. The moment has come for her to finally become a real mother! It is going to be a historic moment, one that has never happened before, the re-enactment of a moment that is natural, and yet one that has implications for the future of humankind – that changes the way kids grow up. A moment that will bring glory to the integration of human life and machines. It's going to be a moment of change for civilisation and privately, one that will be unforgettable for the two of them.

Go2 slowly clambers onto her lap, and she pulls him close – she cannot wait to hug him and offer him the cosiest place on earth. She pulls a sarong over her shoulder, and covers her chest, opening her top. Go2 stuffs his head underneath, when suddenly, out of nowhere, a bulge rapidly appears in the wall of the room and explodes within a fraction of second. Before anyone realises what is happening, Go2's room completely explodes!

The sound of the explosion is like thousands of firecrackers bursting at once, and it can be heard all over the town. Birds, sleeping in the trees, wake up, screeching and squawking and flying out from the branches. The vibrations are heard and felt everywhere, and the shock waves resonate for a while.

Back at the Dexan Queen, it is dark and silent, since all the lights in Go2's room have been destroyed by the explosion. A small lamp post standing in the far corner of the parking yard is the only source of dim light. Fumes, smoke and dust are everywhere.

The whole room has burst outwards, and there are big holes on both sides. The wrecked room is tilted to one side, but the rest of the coaches are still on the track. Wreckage is all over the room and the platform outside, and lots of holes, cracks, and shattering of glass and metal have occurred.

The edges of the holes are bent outwards in all directions and numerous flaps of half-burnt walls are hanging down, swinging slowly. A big hole, with ripped metal dragged upwards in the roof, has formed a chimney, emitting smoke.

Even the floor is destroyed – the track can be seen through the holes. The remaining floor, which Go2 and his mom are buried under, is full of rubble. Heaps of splintered glass, wood, plastic and biomaterials have fallen through the gaping floor and onto the track.

Blood and flesh are splattered all over the remaining dilapidated walls. Both sides of the platform are covered with splashes of blood, and the smell of burnt flesh is drifting through the station.

Chapter 19

It is dark, gloomy and cloudy, and the rain has only just stopped lashing down a few decimal minutes ago. The coloured roads have become shiny and the wheels of the vehicles are reflecting in the rain. Tilfo is walking slowly along the pavement, dragging himself up the road, as if he has lost all his strength.

He gets to the hospital reception area, removes his rain suit and hat and hangs them on the hanger in the corner, leaving the rain suit to start dripping on the floor. He walks glumly along the corridor, his wellington boots dripping wet on the shiny hospital floor.

He gets to a side room in the 'Paediatric Surgical Intensive Care Unit for Traumatology' and walks in. There are already four senior members of staff waiting for him: the robot Intensivist, in hospital scrubs, is sitting in the corner of the sofa, with Dr. Smith beside him. On the other sofa, at a right angle to it, is Go2's dad, Mr Redmill, who stinks of drugs, and Dr. Smith, who is trying to shuffle away from him, wrinkling his nose with distaste. Junior doctors and nurses are standing in the corner. Mom is on the screen on the wall, with a bandage on her head and her right arm is in a sling. There are many black and red bruises all over her face and she has put a scarf around her neck; the beautiful woman is almost unrecognisable. They are all waiting for Tilfo to join the conversation.

The meeting has been called by the Intensivist, to update Go2's relatives on his state. As Tilfo walks in, the Intensivist gets up, touches his shoulders and shows him where to sit.

He then opens the conversation by saying, "Thank you all for coming here to discuss the condition of Go2. I trust that most of us know each other, but still, it will not be inappropriate to introduce each other, regardless. I am Dr. CIBIS - X32 and I am an Intensivist here, who is looking after Go2." He then points at his team and says, "This is our team involved in Go2's care."

"Well," Dr Smith begins, "I am Dr. Smith and I have looked after Go2 in the past. I am here, now, in my capacity as a family friend."

All of them now look at Go2's father, who is angry and frustrated. He is known to be stubborn and often rude. "I am Mr Redmill, the unfortunate father of Go2. Even though I am the legal father of my son, I am the one whose role has been taken over by systems and greedy... 'relatives'." He shows a flash of anger in looking at The Dexan Queen.

Mom, The Dexan Queen, is on the screen on the wall, looking sad and depressed. Her eyes are swollen and it looks as if she has been crying for a long time: her eye-sockets are sunken and she has black shadows around them. Her nose is also swollen and she has wrinkles on her concerned brow. Her voice breaks: "My name is Dexan and I am the mother of Go2."

With this comment, Redmill shakes his head and tuts in denial.

They then look at Tilfo, questioningly. Dr. Smith realises the difficulty he'll have speaking <u>and</u> comes to the rescue: "He is Tilfo, a close friend of Go2."

The Intensivist starts again, "Well, thank you all. I must start with an update on Go2." Everyone turns their attention to listen to him as he continues, "As you know, Go2 was admitted to us fourteen days ago in a very desperate situation after a blast in his living room on the biotrain." Redmill squirms, restless, but the doctor continues: "When he was brought in, we found that he was unidentifiable."

Mom gives a sob and wipes her eyes with a white handkerchief as the Intensivist continues, "When he was brought in, his blood pressure was not recordable, and even his lungs and muscles were burnt. The breaking down of his muscles had released proteins, which had blocked the kidneys, meaning that they were in a state of failure. We maintained his blood pressure, using gadgets in his blood vessels and we have been administering oxygen using outside circulation. His failed kidneys have been dialysed. Although this is only half the problem…"

The intensivist deliberately stops for a moment to avoid giving too much information to the relatives all at once; Dr. Smith is holding Tilfo's hand.

He continues: "When he was brought in by the paramedics, half of his head was blown off and more than half of his brain was lost." Mom cannot stop crying, but the doctor persists, raising his voice above her loud sobs. "This was in addition to the multiple fractures in his long bones, pelvis and rib cage."

Dr. Smith asks, "So, Doctor, what is the prognosis and the future line of management?"

"Thanks for asking." The Intensivist has been waiting for this kind of question, and leaps to answer. "With hardly any brain tissue left and with multiple organ failure, there has never been a documented case to suggest that such a patient could survive."

Redmill shouts, "What do you mean, Doctor?"

"This means that he is not going to make it, I'm afraid, and we are just prolonging his misery. It's in his best interests that we withdraw his life support," he says, emotionlessly.

Mom wails loudly.

"In whose best interests, Doctor? There are other people to consider!" Redmill is angry. "Go2 is my tissue bank! I want him to live as long as I am alive!"

Mom stops wailing in shock, and even the professionals look horrified by this human's selfishness.

Redmill continues: "It's only in *your* best interests, because you're trying to save your skin more than his life."

Although the Intensivist is a robot, he has never seen such a reaction from a parent before, so is surprised. "That is not the case, Mr Redmill. We have tried our level best to keep Go2 alive. We have gone out of our way, and beyond the protocols, to try and support his life."

"I don't know about anything else, but you're a doctor and you've taken an oath to keep everyone alive until the end," Redmill growls. "That includes me! I reckon I have about a hundred years to go, and I might need some tissues or organs in that time! So, I want what's left of him kept alive for at least another hundred years. That's my right – and your duty!"

"Calm down, Mr Redmill. We understand the various emotions you are going through."

"No. You don't. I want you to keep his organs alive at any cost!" Redmill does not recede.

"Anyway, our responsibility is to inform you, rather than to involve you, because it is a medical decision. We cannot recommend further intervention because it won't have any benefit."

"Benefit? Benefit? Benefit to who, Doctor? You are the ones who benefit whether patients live or die, while hard working single parents like me are left with nothing! I don't care. I want him alive!"

Dr. Smith and Tilfo have become visibly uncomfortable, feeling awkward, hearing this argument. Go2's Mom is inarticulate with grief, not in a position to say anything, so she just watches with her eyes tearful.

The Intensivist responds to this by saying, "Please. We do take an oath to save lives, but we are dealing with a different scenario, here. By continuing life support, we are harming him and we also take an oath not to harm anyone."

Redmill is now furious and he gets up and starts shouting, "How dare you! You are…!"

"Anyway," the intensivist interrupts him, "It is our duty to inform you. Especially, his legal next of kin, who is the Madame Dexan Queen. I assume she endorses our views and our expertise."

"That is absolutely unfair!" Mr Redmill shouts back. "He is my most loved one and he has a whole lifetime left! How can you allow a full lifespan to vanish, just like that? I want him keeping alive!"

Dr. Smith has understood the situation fully and knows that Go2 is at the point of no return. "Yes, we can keep Go2 alive, but he will be in a vegetative state...." He tries to mediate between the family and medical staff and uses a different tactic to calm Redmill down. "He will need organs – such as the liver, heart, lungs and a kidney."

With this comment, Redmill becomes alert and crosses his arms, becoming defensive.

Dr. Smith continues, "Mr Redmill, Go2 is your clone and his tissues are identical to yours. Would you be happy to consider donating your organs to keep him alive?"

Redmill gives a choked cry and points his finger at Dr. Smith. "Don't turn this around and throw that back at me, Dr. Smith! You have no authority in family matters! Besides, you're not thinking like a doctor. You sound more like a game player."

"Will you donate your organs, or not?" Dr. Smith is now firing at him, point blank.

"No, I won't. I created him. He didn't create me. It's my welfare that matters."

The Intensivist gets up and says, "I'm afraid we won't be able to do much more, here. Please forgive us, but we have many more sick patients to see."

With Redmill still protesting, the Intensivist then starts walking out with his team, but as he leaves, he says to Mom, "Ma'am, if you wish to discuss anything, please get in touch with us."

Dr. Smith thanks him and the medical team walks out of the door. Mom has her eyes closed, possibly muttering a prayer. Dr. Smith, Tilfo and Redmill are the only three people left in the room.

Redmill goes over to the screen and points his finger at Mom. "This all happened because of you! Because you wanted to get a name, fame, and glory. You were the one who wanted to be part of this historical experiment. It was all due to your greed." Mom just looks at him while he carries on blaming her, "You should have the slogan, 'speed with greed!"

Tilfo and Dr. Smith are both annoyed at this comment and hate watching him humiliate her. "Now, look, here," Dr. Smith says, standing up.

But Redmill does not stop. "You cannot use my son for your own selfish motives! My tissue bank cannot become your tissue paper."

Mom, in a broken voice, tries to say something. "Mr Redmill, you are talking about my son and I love him."

He laughs sarcastically. "Yeah. You love him. Yeah.

Dr. Smith tries to intervene. "Mr Redmill, please calm down. I know Ma'am, The Dexan Queen, very well and she is doing her best. That's all any mother can do."

Redmill doesn't pay any heed to Dr. Smith and lashes out at her again: "She cannot have her own children but she is good at grabbing others'. Madame, you are just a rusty grab-rail."

Dr. Smith says, "Look Mr Redmill, you cannot use this kind of language. Madame legally adopted her son."

"My foot! Legal adoption! It was the great train robbery."

"Mr Redmill, please leave. My client is already disturbed."

"Disturbed? You can disturb others and still live an honourable life. Who looks after me when I am disturbed?" he asks.

"Well, you are entitled to see your own counsellor."

"How does counselling solve the issue of child trafficking?"

"It was a legal adoption!"

Mr Redmill walks towards the screen, points his hand at Mom and shouts, "Miss Munster, you are a big spinster!"

Dr. Smith cannot bear to hear these uncivilised words and starts ushering Redmill out, but he's still yelling, "I will not sit quietly! I will make her run from pillar to post; from platform to court! I will see you in court!" he threatens. He does not stop. "You wanted me to report and transport. Well, it's my turn, now. I will show you how to report and then transport you to jail."

He then stamps his feet and walks away angrily, slamming the door as he leaves, to sit on the couch in the corridor. He is desperate, frustrated and restless because his organ bank is in serious trouble. He gazes into infinity and mutters to himself, "Go2 is really going. Go2 – you, too!"

The robot nurse walking along the corridor looks at him and shrugs her shoulders. Redmill is not bothered who is looking at him and again says to himself, "My loyalty card is expiring. I must do something."

But he does not know what to do, so gets up and starts walking out of the hospital.

It is raining. He goes to a parking area and takes out a small, flat bottle from his pocket and puts it to his mouth. He looks at the bottle and says, "To win a war one has to lose a bottle. How many bottles am I supposed to lose?"

* * * * * *

In the middle of a day, Mr Redmill is sitting with the human looking robot-intensivist, in the side room, arguing, and trying to convince the intensivist.

This is my 14th day since I have given written application to the hospital authorities, to keep Go2 on life support machines indefinitely. It seems no one is listening to me. I have to come here every day. This is compromising my quality of life. I have not even serviced my protruding organs in a long time."

The intensivist knows is not much interested in Mr Redmill.

"I know Mr Redmill. I know that you want Go2 to be kept alive, which we have been doing for last 29 days."

"Continue doing good work Doctor."

"After your application, we put forward your application to the legal department of the hospital, and they appointed a retired judge to look into this."

"Why a retired judge? Retired? They do not have enough hormones. They do not understand."

"Please Mr Redmill, try to understand, it's is hospital policy. Besides he is highly experienced."

"Anyway, what did he say?"

"The final verdict will be declared tomorrow. It seems that all the life support will be switched off." The intensivist says this without showing any emotion on his face.

This comment infuriates Mr Redmill. He shouts,

"Why did you not involve me in those discussions? I do not expect all the decisions to be taken by you only."

"I understand that you are angry. But the legal parent was involved."

With this information his frustration grows bigger.

"This is all illegal. I will see you, and her in court."

"Please do not threaten us. We work very hard."

The intensivist then stands up and wants to leave.

"You work hard for yourself. Not for us."

"Look, I don't have time. I need to go."

"You don't have time for me. But you have time for that Irish woman. You give her a lot of time, just because she has two succulent lips, left and right?

"Excuse me Mr Redmill. I am not obliged to see you. This is just our courtesy."

In a fit of anger, Mr Redmill threatens him further,

"Look I want a second opinion."

The intensivist blinks his eyes, looks at him, and gives some advice,

"Look, second opinion is a double-edged weapon. If the second opinion is different than the first one then we are lost, then we have to take the third one. Besides, we have taken a 'second opinion' from a first, and the legal parent who is, Ma'am the Dexan. And now, if you don't leave, we will take second opinion from the Robocratic guards."

With this answer Mr Redmill become defensive, as he is losing his ground. He now changes his tactic and tries to lure the doctor.

"Look Doctor, I am going to sue that woman. I will get lot of compensationitis. Cure me if you can. I will give you ten per cent. Please keep Go2 alive."

"Mr Redmill, you are crossing your limits. Typical human solutions! He looks up, and continues,

The intensivist is angry now. "You are trying to commit an act of bribery"

Mr Redmill tries to convince him,

"It is bribery in your eyes. It is a survival instinct for us."

"Look I need to go." the intensivist now restless, want to make move out of the room.

"Look Doctor. I don't mind whether Go2 is alive or dead. Life and death are like, shuttling trains. They come. They go. All I want is his organs. Can you preserve those for me?"

"We cannot. We do not have legal or ethical permission to preserve the organs without appropriate legal permissions. Anyway, I am leaving now." he starts taking steps towards the door. On his way, he gives some advice to Mr Redmill.

"Mr Redmill, you must see into your behaviour, and do a critical reflective practice."

Mr Redmill becomes defensive again,

"Doctor you are not my counsellor. I am not the one who has started all this business of child trafficking. If you really want to give any advice, then go ask your beautiful woman to run in the reverse gear, fast."

"Mr Redmill, I am going." He comes to the door.

Mr Redmill stands up and asks.

"Last question Doctor. What will you do to his body?"

The intensivist turns his head to Mr Redmill and assertively says,

"We had given the options of incineration, burial or a pyre, to Madame the Dexan Queen. She has decided the burial site. She believes in life."

Mr Redmill is gobsmacked with this information. All the decisions are taken.

The intensivist continues,

"I can quote her, 'Thank you doctor for setting his departure time, up bound. Dust to dust, ash to ashes, and life to lives. Bury him, so that some microbes will live on, using his biomaterial'."

* * * * * *

Chapter 20

It is winter, and the sky is cast. Dr Smith is watching the withered tree. He is standing at the window, in his bright office. The curtains are pulled apart after a long time.

He is busy watching through the window. T

The screen on the wall starts bleeping and reminding him of his appointment with the Dexan Queen.

The only person the Dexan Queen sees regularly is Dr. Smith, with whom she has daily counselling sessions.

She appears on the screen.

Dr. Smith, realises this, and takes his bablet out of his pocket. He blows out at it. The curtains take this order, and they slide in to close the window.

He then keeps his bablet on the table and takes seat on the revolving chair. He then says,

"Good morning. And sorry to keep you waiting."

"Yes, Thanks. Don't worry."

Mom still has some bandages over her forehead. Her hair is half cut and burnt and she looks unkempt. Her voice is become husky. Her subconscious mind knows that something terrible has happened.

In all the counselling sessions, Dr Smith tries to speak less, and listens more. He does the same thing today but starts open the conversation.

"Yes, Ma'am, how are you today?"

"I do not know how I am today, Doctor. But, why is everything dark these days?" she murmurs. "The sun doesn't seem to give enough light. I feel I am running in a dark tunnel all the time."

Dr Smith says,

"Yes Ma'am, I am listening. Go on."

"Why do I feel cold all the time? Sometimes, I feel I am a cold metal, and Go2 is cold meat."

Dr Smith tries to give a superficial but rational answer, "Yes Ma'am, it is winter but keep yourself wrapped up."

"Doctor, Go2 says, 'please do not prescribe an external ointment for an internal disease'."

Dr Smith is surprised by her intelligence, insight and communication. He tries to dwell on this comment, before trying to explore more, "What would the internal disease be, and who has it?"

"Since Go2 went, I am feeling cold. I do not want to see anyone. All the faces appear foggy to me. "

Dr. Smith wants to pursue this further and plays the innocent, knowing that she has been in denial. "Where do you think Go2 has gone?"

"He fought with me over a silly little thing," she sighs. "He always does that to me. One day, a fortnight ago, we had a heated argument and he walked away. He and Tilfo left for the summer camp. He always does this to me – whenever we fight, he goes to get refreshed at camp."

Dr Smith goes with the flow: "The summer camps are good for children. I'm sure he will be very happy when he comes back."

"Yes, Doctor, I agree with you. Last time he came home from camp, he was more attached to me."

"Good for you."

"Since Go2 is gone for the camp, I do not feel like going to work. For the first time in my life, I have taken sick leave."

"Humm. Don't worry about it, I can certify for the leave."

Mom is really not worried for the certificate. She changes the subject, "Shall I share a secret with you, Doctor?"

"You know I am your friend; you can tell me anything and it will remain in these four walls."

"I want him to go to lots of the camps, so that every time he comes back he is more attached to me than before."

"Good for you! Many parents send their children to camps."

With this comment, her mood is now changing and she starts saying the exact opposite, "But Doctor, I don't want him to go to camp because I miss him very much," she weeps.

Dr. Smith doesn't know what to say. She continues, "Doctor, please call him on his bablet because he listens to you. He won't answer my calls. Will you do that for me?"

"Yes, I will ring him as soon as our meeting is over," he soothes.

"Doctor, I have one more question for you."

"Go on."

"Can you fast-forward the ageing process?"

Dr. Smith is taken aback with this question. "Why do you want to fast-forward time?"

"That's just another little secret about a woman. I want to see him as a medical doctor, just like you, and see his girlfriend, see who he loves after me – and then I want to see them get married."

"And then?" Dr. Smith is intrigued.

"And then, I want to take his children for a picnic and let them sit on my back. I want to be their play-horse."

"Wow, you have some dreams!" Dr. Smith says, supporting her. "And then?"

"And then, once I grow old, I want to live next to all of them, in a granny flat. I want my Go2 to become my walking-stick in my old age."

"Yes Ma'am, you have it all. Tell me how you will manage in a granny flat?" Dr Smith is just trying to go with the flow. Mom goes further,

"It will be easy. I'll do some work. My family will help me and I will also have a home help. Look, don't you worry – my old age is going to be happy."

"You have thought ahead," he replies.

"Yes, when my urine is blocked, I'll let my Son or Daughter-in-law put a catheter in me."

The doctor suppresses a smile. "Well, I hope you won't need that!"

"And then once I am gone, I want my Go2 to drop a fistful of soil on my grave."

"Ma'am, you want all the pleasure now only? Patience is virtue. Live this moment."

"Yes, I will. And I will tell you now, what is bothering me at this moment. What is bothering me, are the weird sensations I am having."

"Well, I'd like to know, if you are happy to share them with me." Dr. Smith says, aware of her feelings.

She had never thought about her own welfare since adopting Go2 and had always put him before her.

She admits aloud, "When I sleep, I have nightmares."

Dr. Smith is alerted by this symptom and wants to know more. "What kind of nightmares do you have, Ma'am?"

She takes a moment, as if she is trying to find the right words to describe it. "When I sleep, I dream that I am making a trip to the mountains. The mountains have sharp tops, like pointy, tall spikes and at the bottom, there is a river, with a bridge. I run on my track over the bridge, but when I get to the middle of it, all of a sudden, it collapses."

Dr. Smith thinks for a moment and says, "Any other bad dream?"

"Yes, one more, that I see."

Dr Smith nods his head to tell him more, Mom

"I am running slowly, in a remote forest. I then enter into a dark tunnel. The tunnel does not have the light at the other end. It's only darkness, and darkness reining me. My track or wheels do not make any sound. And I hear a call from Go2, lost in the darkness somewhere, and in distress. He keeps on calling, Mom, Mom...... I know from his voice that he is troubled, hungry, and missing me. The voice keeps on echoing"

Dr Smith looks worried with these nightmares.

How often do you have these dreams?"

"Almost, every night."

"Then, what do you do?"

"I wake up and go into Go2's room," she says, sadly. "Then, I realise he isn't there. I forget he is at summer camp… and then I find it impossible to get back to sleep."

"Okay, we will do something about this," the doctor reassures her. "Do you have any other problems?"

"Yes. Food."

"What happens with food?"

"Firstly, I have no appetite and I don't feel like even looking at food. Every time I try to eat something, I get the smell of burnt flesh."

The doctor shifts in his seat, uncomfortably. "Oh, so you are not eating, or sleeping?" Dr. Smith tries to summarise her symptoms.

"Yes, and yet, my cheeky little sod must be eating, sleeping and enjoying camp!"

"Yes, he should be. Anything else? "

"There are other problems too. I sweat a lot. I am constipated. I have a dry mouth, sore throat, backache and many other aches and pains."

Dr. Smith is trying to interpret all of her problems, as he notes them down. "We will get there. There are medications and counselling sessions that will help you."

"When Doctor, when?"

Dr. Smith is becoming slightly defensive. "Well Ma'am, we will start some counselling today."

"Okay, then, let's start."

Dr. Smith scratches his head. "Well, the first thing, is that you need to do is, to support yourself."

"How?"

"Imagine that Go2 is always around somewhere, with you."

She realises the worthlessness of this suggestion. "Doctor, you are asking me to live in an illusion."

Dr. Smith becomes cautious. "Yes, and no. If the so-called illusion is making you feel better, then, why not?"

Mom does not like this idea and wants to finish the counselling session for today. "Doctor, I just remembered something. I need to go."

"What's happened? Where do you want to go?"

"I suddenly realised that I need to go home," she says, standing up onscreen.

"What for?"

"See, Doctor, please don't mind me going, but Go2 has a habit of coming back from camp suddenly without giving me any notice. I have to go."

"But he can wait. Why do you have to rush?"

"No, Doctor, you don't understand. You'd need to be a Mother to understand."

"What do you mean?"

"He may be hungry; he doesn't eat well away from home. Every time he comes home, he loves my cooking and says, 'Mom, you are the best cook'."

"It's good to know that you are a good cook," smiles the doctor. "Invite me over some time."

"Yes, I will, when he comes back, but let me go now. I need to go and cook something, fast. I don't want my son to come home hungry and for there not to be any food."

"Yes, you can go, but will you come and see me again tomorrow, at the same time?" the doctor asks. "What does he like to eat, by the way?"

"All of my cooking, but my vegetable and corn sausages are his favourite."

"Will you be cooking them today?"

"Yes."

"Bring me a sample tomorrow."

"Yes Doctor, bye for now. See you tomorrow."

Mom disappears from the screen. Dr. Smith understands her problems and takes out his bablet to ask it a question. "So, Mr Diagnostician, what do you think?"

The bablet starts talking in a mechanical, robotic voice: "Thank you, Dr. Smith, for being my colleague today. I have been watching and listening to your conversation with Madame, The Dexan Queen, the virtual patient number - BB54.4. She is traumatised due to the loss of a real son. The diagnosis is delusional depressive psychosis, type NU23. The plan will be virtual chemical therapy, electrical therapy and behavioural therapy."

Dr Smith says, "Thank you Mr Diagnostician, you have been a great source of help to me, today. Thank you for your second opinion. I agree. I also think this is what she has. Thanks again."

He then closes his bablet, looks at the empty white screen on the wall and mutters to himself, "Denial is the best weapon."

Chapter 21

Dr Smith is sitting in his room, exhausted. The window is open, and curtains are drawn sideways. He has kept the bablet on his table and narrating the conclusion of all the case. He starts his long text, while looking outside through the window.

"Motion is a rule of all creatures and everyone has to reach somewhere, be it a life form, or non-life form. Disasters happen in our personal lives, and the world keeps on going.

The motion of the world has not stopped after Go2's death. The colourful trains are running as busily and fast as usual, and the roads are still full of vehicles and busy with traffic. Nothing has really stopped since Go2's departure, and everyone is still going at full speed. Speed is endless and timeless, as if speed is the only reality of life and death.

My client, cum family friend, the Dexan Queen, has gone through the various emotional stations of grief. She initially was in denial, which then turned into anger, guilt, bargaining, acceptance and depression. She has reached the final junction of acceptance of the truth and reality."

Dr. Smith looks again down at the busy street and continues to talk to his bablet.

"I have worked hard, day and night. My job was difficult, because I wanted to be there for Mom as a friend, but also as a professional counsellor to treat her: it is a dual responsibility. Mom is still not working and prefers to remain detached from the world.

The systems have been busy trying to discover the cause of the fatal explosion and it has taken 193 days for them to do a root cause analysis. The matter is taken to the criminal court of the Robocratic Institution of Justice."

Dr Smith then looks up at the blue vast sky, and says,

"We think we control our lives. But in real life, the life is controlled by the physical systems, and the supra-non – physical systems."

* * * * * *

Chapter 22

On one side of the courtroom wall there is a screen, where Mom can be seen, standing up. She has wrapped her neck and head with a black scarf, since she feels cold all the time.

"All be seated," says the presiding judge.

She hears the order, grabs a chair behind her and sits down. The frame of her screen slowly disappears, giving the impression that Mom is not on the screen, but is sitting in the court, where a court wall can be seen behind her.

Everyone in the crowd in the courtroom sits down. In one corner is Redmill, who does not usually attend court proceedings. He is there, today, standing and waiting on the final judgment day, because he is hopeful of winning compensation. Sitting on the front row, on the right side, are members of the prosecution council, and on the left are members of the defence council. The second row is full of members of the jury.

In the other corner are Dr. Smith and Tilfo, who are sitting waiting for justice. All Go2's school friends have also come to the court. In the last few rows there are the media, both life forms and robots, who are gathered to capture the news. They all are silently waiting to hear what will happen next.

The robot -human -looking-bailiff shouts, "This is a premier court of the Robocratic Institution of Justice for major criminal offences. The robot judge, Mr XIBL 8 will be presiding over the proceedings."

The robot human looking-judge then takes a bablet in his hand. He does not have to, as he knows all the case by a process of e-internalisation. He is holding bablet just to give natural humanoid look to the process of justice.

Everyone is silent, waiting to hear what he has to say, and they all look up at him. The judge tries to clear his throat before he starts reading slowly, "Today is the final day for two, long drawn-out cases. We are here today for the conclusion of these two cases. The first one is a simple case: a petition from Mr Redmill against the defendant, Ms Dexan Queen. The second case is related to the death of a boy, Master Go2, and there is a prosecution council against the defendant. It seems that this is going to be a historical case, for many reasons, Firstly, it has taken more than 180 days to hear both sides, and yet, in modern times, case hearings do not take more than 17 days, on average. Secondly, the first case is by a life-form against a non-life-form and the second is a case of systems against non-life-forms. Because both cases are interrelated, we have decided to conclude them in one day."

Everyone is eager to hear what the judge is going to say next.

"Let us start with the first – the simple case. In this case, Mr Redmill has asked for compensation because he thinks that he has lost his son because of Ms Dexan Queen. He believes that her adopting his son violated the law, and that she did not look after him properly, which resulted in his death. In his petition, he also says that Ms Dexan Queen is greedy, showy, shallow and flashy and according to his petition, and I quote, 'the defendant likes to be in the news for cheap popularity'."

Mom is listening to the allegations, knowing that she is not guilty. The only thing she did to Go2 was shower him with love. The judge continues, "The proceedings so far have presented both sides and we have seen various statements, affidavits, and depositions. There are also many witnesses."

The judge pushes another button on his bablet and continues to read, "Myself, as judge and members of the jury have reached a conclusion. All the evidence to date supports the postulation of a violation of law in adopting Go2."

A low whispering is heard in the court as the judge continues, but Mom is still listening impassively. It does not bother her much, now, because she has lost the most precious thing in her life. She is now just curious to see the systems' justice.

The judge reads further, "So, there is evidence to support that there were violations in the adoption of Go2. We have compared all the other biotrains, and analysed their behaviour, and no other biotrain has ever adopted a child before. So, there is truth in Mr Redmill's allegation that the Ms Dexan Queen is hungry for fame."

There is a gasp from the audience. Dr. Smith and Tilfo are surprised at this comment.

"The defendant has given a statement that the adoption was made on an experimental basis and to give a boost to the integration of human life -forms -and machines."

Mom nods in agreement.

"The proceedings did not find any permission from the ethical committee. If this was an experiment, then why was permission from the ethical committee not sought? The court wants to ask: why were the legal institutions and statutory systems bypassed?"

There is low muttering again in the audience and the judge bangs his hammer to silence them. "The court also has taken into account some of the reports from forensic scientists."

Dr. Smith is alarmed by this and sits up, alert, wanting to know what is going to be said.

"At the site of blast, splintered pieces of a biomaterial were found splattered all over."

Mom is waiting to hear more, too.

The judge continues: "There is evidence to show that the biomaterial was the product of teleportation technology and a self-manufacturing programme that Ms Dexan Queen uses." The judge's face is expressionless. "This proves that Ms Dexan Queen trespassed beyond her limits. She was not allowed to appear in 3D, nor 4D, formats in front of Go2, for safety reasons. And she transgressed the law by trying to appear in 4D format. This is clearly a violation, under the rule of MINy, *bye*-law, ONH76. Ms Dexan Queen breached the trust that the systems gave her."

Mom, Tilfo and Dr. Smith are, again, surprised.

"The defence states that it was act of an extreme love and motherhood. She wanted to be with him in person and did what her motherly instincts wanted her to do."

Mom nods her head in agreement.

"But, all members of society must understand that, the law of nations is above all, and above anyone's instincts."

The judge pushes a third button on his bablet and reads, "The defence solicitors also state that Ms Dexan Queen is a famous, popular and a generous charity worker. There is evidence to support this, but fame can be cheap and sensational. Politicians, for their own cheap populism, can often exaggerate and blow simple acts out of proportion. Ms Dexan Queen did achieve a certain position." The judge looks at her on the wall. "But, people who are in a position like this are often liable to misuse their position – and she did violate the law on at least two occasions." The courtroom held its breath. "Therefore, the court upholds the petition, and finds Ms Dexan Queen GUILTY!"

There is crying and shouting, but the judge expected some noise in the court after this statement, so starts banging his hammer. "The court advises Ms Dexan Queen to provide the lump sum of three million world dollars in compensation to Mr Redmill."

All of a sudden, Mr Redmill stands straight up, after hearing this and his eyes and lips widen with happiness. Redmill, possibly for the first time ever, is truly happy. He never imagined that he would see this much money in his life. The clone he created has, at last, turned out to be profitable.

The judge persists: "The court knows that Ms Dexan Queen has her own earnings and she donated her crown to charity. She should give this compensation from her earnings and if it is not paid in 100 days, she is liable for a further penalty. In addition, the court orders Ms Dexan, the so-called Queen, to remain off the track, in the confinement of her choice, for one full earth's revolution. The date will start from tomorrow."

The judge bangs his hammer again, this time to assert his statement. Mom does not cry, as she has lost her most valuable possession, everything else is valueless to her.

"The court orders Mr Redmill to use this money to get a new clone. Mr Redmill can name him as Go3, if he wishes. A new clone will be his new tissue bank."

Redmill is slightly taken aback by this condition, but quickly calculates that he can probably get a clone more cheaply, and pocket the rest of the money. He cannot thank the court enough and keeps muttering, thank you, ..thank you....

"The court will take a recess of five decimal minutes, before it announces the judgement of the second case."

* * * * * *

The court restarts after a short recess. The judge, again in a very cold and calculating voice, starts reading from his bablet: "Now, we come to the next and most important case. This case relates to the death of Master Go2, and it is the prosecution council, versus the defendants: Ms Belladonna and Miss Mermaid. This case is a complex one, and it took a long time to get witness statements from all parties involved. The witnesses were Ms Dexan Queen, forensic scientists and doctors, pathologists, police officers, detectives, ambulance crew, treating robots, Dr. Smith... and the defendants. In this case, the defendants are two other biotrains: Ms Belladonna and Miss Mermaid."

There is booing in the court, and again, the judge bangs his hammer and says, "Silence!"

He continues, "We have established the facts based on the evidence gathered during the proceedings. Delivering justice means finding out the truth."

Many in the audience nod their heads in agreement.

"Let us start with a simple statement made by the prosecution council that 'a precious little boy, Master Go2 was killed'."

Mom is happy to hear that the prosecution council considered her son as precious.

"From the evidence gathered so far, the court can say that Master Go2 was not a precious boy!"

"No!" Mom screams. She cannot control herself. "How can you say that? Your honour, you need to ask other mothers whether their babies are precious or not!"

The judge, otherwise expressionless, is annoyed by this and frowns. "You need to control your emotions. This is not a stage play. If you cannot hold them back, you will be held in contempt and will be excluded from the court. The choice is yours."

Mom starts weeping in silence. She does not want to be kicked out of court. She wants to hear the judgement and get justice.

"There is no evidence to suggest that Master Go2 was precious and if he was considered so, why was he not insured? The court does not find any evidence of his value."

Mom, on-screen, bites her lower lip, to stop her crying out.

"Moreover, it takes just a man and a woman to come together to make a new life form – and, one act of vulgar sex, which may last a few decimal seconds to make a new life," the robot judge says, judgementally. "Where is the preciousness in that? There are billions and billions coming and going, in life and death, and the court does not believe that any human -life-form is precious. They are a cheap labour force. The precious ones are the machines that keep the systems running - and they take time and effort to make."

Dr. Smith is horrified with this comment; his life is spent looking after lives that he always considers precious.

"Our next step was to find out the truth about his death. After going through the details, we have found that the defendants were responsible for the event. Let us look at the details of the act first, and then we will get to the motive."

The crowd mutters in low voices before settling in to hear the story.

"That night, when Ms Dexan Queen was parked in the yard and was busy entertaining her so-called son, there is evidence to prove that Miss Mermaid was parked in the darkness, parallel to The Dexan Queen. The systems in the Dexan Queen could not sense her presence, as they were either locked, or were busy – entertaining her son."

Mom's throat is now choking with this information as she remembers that she had shut down her sensing systems that night because she wanted to give Go2 her full attention. Guilt flushes her onscreen face.

"Miss Mermaid offered her an alibi and was on standby to cover her friend, Ms Belladonna. At the moment of the explosion, Ms Belladonna rapidly ran onto another track, parallel to Miss Mermaid, so that Miss Mermaid could shield the Belladonna from view."

Tilfo's mouth is open with surprise on hearing this information, as he was not aware of this.

"So, when Ms Belladonna passed through, she fired a camouflaged missile at Ms Dexan Queen through the gaps between Miss Mermaid's wagons."

There is boo in the audience and Mom's eyes are wide, her face ugly with anger.

"So, the court has come to the conclusion that Ms Belladonna fired a missile and her friend, Miss Mermaid assisted and allowed this to happen."

Recognising that justice must be served, Mom smiles bitterly.

"Now, let us get to the motive of the act." The judge continues. "There is evidence to suggest that it was an act of jealousy. Biotrains like Ms Belladonna and Miss Mermaid are programmed for simple basic instincts and they can respond with anger, jealousy, retaliation and revenge after provocation, like any animal -life -form. A more sophisticated biotrain like Ms Dexan Queen is installed with kindness, compassion, empathy, generosity and charity. Machines are more methodical and mathematical and therefore, more precise."

Mom gets some solace from her description and relaxes a little.

"It is all due to the intelligence of programmes and the act or behaviour has nothing to do with crime. Ms Dexan Queen cannot be praised for her virtues and similarly, Ms Belladonna cannot be blamed for what she did because she only does what she is programmed to do. There are no motives here, other than the programmed instincts."

Mom opens her mouth in shock. Many members of the audience look at each other in disbelief.

"Now, let us see whether it was murder, or not. The prosecution council pleads the death of Master Go2 was an act of a murder."

Members of the prosecution council sitting in the front row start listening to the judgement carefully.

"There is no evidence to suggest that it was a murder, since there was no intention, motive or plan. This court dismisses the charges of murder."

The crowd protests, but the judge calls for silence, hammering his gavel. There is some movement in the members of the defence council and they are pleased to hear this. Their body language changes and many of them try to relax by leaning back into the backrests.

"As the prosecution council arguably states, it is not even an act of manslaughter." The judge continues, "The modern courts do not like the term, 'manslaughter'. It gives an undue importance to only the life of men, when in fact all life is important."

The members of the prosecution council sitting on the front row are bewildered by the words, and glance uneasily at one another.

"There is no evidence to suggest that it was manslaughter either."

The crowd cries out, but both the bailiff and the judge call for order.

"Ms Belladonna only wanted to fire at the coach. She did not want to harm Go2 in any way. Master Go2 got killed – but he was merely collateral damage, because of an accident due to programmed instincts. Ms Dexan Queen had detached some of her back coaches that night and that, most fortunately, at least saved any damage to the bees, which were based in the fourth coach."

Onscreen, weeping, Mom stands up and starts walking away, realising that she is not going to get justice here.

The judge ignores her and continues reading his judgement. "Some of the biotrains were initially programmed as weapons to fight wars and a few of them have retired to civil life now, but they still are active within the programmes. Ms Belladonna and Miss Mermaid are two examples of this – retired war veterans, now. This time, however, they misused their programmes. Ms Belladonna, although not guilty of manslaughter, is guilty of machine slaughter – because they have damaged a highly precious and programmed coach that was used by Master Go2 as his living room."

There is a loud outcry in the audience, and the judge bangs his hammer a couple of times to order them to remain silent.

"Justice is not equal to punishment, but it is an opportunity for the systems and parties to reflect. The court finds Ms Belladonna and her partner, Miss Mermaid, guilty of machine slaughter and we sentence both of them to come off the tracks for one full earth's revolution. They will stay confined to the parking yard – and the date starts from today. In addition, they are advised to undergo and install programmes of meditation, mindfulness and self-realisation. They should also download programmes of peace and reconciliation."

Again, the whispering audience starts whispering louder, their protests audible.

"The court is now adjourned!" The judge bangs the hammer hard.

Chapter 23

It is evening and Tilfo and Dr. Smith are sitting in the doctor's consulting room, both of them feeling sad, helpless and unsure what to do, waiting for Mom to call them on the screen. All of a sudden, their attention is caught by a screeching sound from the screen on the wall.

A few more scratching sounds are heard before Mom appears, blank and emotionless, but also assertive in her speech. The scarf on her head is scruffy and has stains on it: she has not been looking after herself.

She starts the conversation without any salutation or greeting: "I hope you are both well. I am."

Dr. Smith had wanted to welcome her and give her some support, but she does not allow him to say anything. Instead, she is a bit rude and interrupts him with: "I am here today to say couple of things. I am not here for a dose of counselling. Thank you."

"Please go ahead, Ma'am," Dr. Smith says, not wanting to upset her any more.

"Firstly, I must thank you, Dr. Smith. You have been a great soul and I cannot thank you enough. You were there in the difficult times, for both me and my son."

Dr. Smith tries to assuage her. "Anytime, Ma'am, anytime."

Mom is determined and says, "Dr. Smith, thank you for your continued support, but there will be no need for it in the future."

Dr. Smith is astonished. "Why? What has happened?"

Mom gathers her thoughts and says, "I am a machine. Go2 wanted to see me in human form, so he did. My purpose for incarnation as a human image is over, now."

Dr. Smith is a philosophical man and says, "Humans need images to worship, though."

"There should be no image of me, hereafter."

Dr. Smith understands that she does not want to be a human image any more, but tries to persuade her to reconsider. "Think of his friend, Tilfo! Please don't go away, just like that!"

"It's okay. I have made provisions for Tilfo."

Tilfo looks at her gratefully, but he does not want her to go.

Dr. Smith again tries to reassure her. "We will be very sad to lose your image."

"You are sad to lose just my image. Imagine how I feel! I have lost my son, in flesh and blood." Mom is drained and does not show any expression.

Dr. Smith then tries to open a less painful subject. "What are your future plans?"

"Well, the judge has asked me to pay Mr Redmill and I have transferred the compensation money to him. At least, amongst all of us, my son's Dad is happy." Mom continues, "The judge also asked me to reflect, which I am spending time doing."

Dr. Smith, using his psychologist side, asks, "And what has come of this?"

"What did I get? I tried to be righteous and to be a good mother, but it did not work well. The happiest moments of my life were with Go2 and I always felt enormous pride when you all called me Mom, or Mother."

"Yes, I know."

Mom continues, "I now know what most other machines don't know, and what they are missing in their lives."

"Yes, motherhood is great."

"Good. I have infected you with my enthusiasm. Tomorrow my confinement starts, so I'm going to be incognito and will be in hibernation. I will self-manufacture to become stronger and will soon be back on track."

"Good. We will wait for you."

"There is no point in waiting, because I won't be seen in human form again."

"Okay. Actually, it's not okay," the doctor corrected himself. "But you are your own master. We will see you running on your track again soon. Do you want us to do anything for you?"

"Yes. Tomorrow I have to detach a coach full of beehives and I would like to see the bees, genetically modified. Please take them to the gene laboratory and I will give them a plan. Then take them to the hill beside Lakemore station. They will make new hives there and will live a peaceful life."

Tilfo cannot control his emotions and starts crying, listening to Mom and hearing what she is asking them to do.

Dr. Smith says, "No problem; we will do as you wish." He is not happy she is going but cannot control her.

Mom asks, "Lastly, please tell me about an emotion called 'R'."

Dr. Smith is surprised to hear this question and replies, "Please don't go there. Don't use the R word." Understanding the gravity of the question, he tries to dissuade her.

Mom says with great conviction, "I'll tell you. R is an emotion that has two components. Firstly, you destroy others and then you take pleasure from it. When all the pleasures are gone from my life, only the R will provide some."

Dr. Smith is wise enough to understand where her emotions are going and hints, "There is a third component: getting destroyed."

"Who cares? Rabid machines only understand big bites."

Dr. Smith is worried now. "Please don't do anything that is inappropriate to your honour and ideology."

"Oh, yes. I will behave appropriately, like a machine, and I will think like a mother. I have been watching the video clip of the hen that Tilfo recorded."

Tilfo is now trying to remember the clip.

Mom continues, "R is rejoicing when you are cold and the other party is hot."

"Ma'am, please don't go there." Dr. Smith is still trying to convince her against this.

"What choice am I left with?"

"Two wrongs don't make a right."

"Right. But if you are not right, then the only option left is left, Doc." In a very convincing and loving voice she then says, "Dr. Smith, I am looking for peace, not rationality." She continues, "I was supposed to provide and protect and I couldn't do it." She then starts to become cold and calculating, with something on her mind. She continues, "There is no fun in an attack when the other party is sleeping and meditating."

"Ma'am, please don't!"

Mom continues, "R happens when it is planned or provoked and I have both of these on my side!" She is not in the mood to listen to anyone and is determined. "I would love to be remembered as a mother. Today is the thirty-fourth day of the eighth decimal month of the year, 178. I will come back on exactly the same date next year. I will go incognito. Only military programmes will know my whereabouts. I used to go there to dump the nuclear waste. I have I will come back a year later. Wait for me and then you will see what a natural beauty of natural justice is."

Tilfo now understands that Mom really is going to go. He gets up and tries to touch the screen and she kisses him from within it.

She looks out, towards eternity and says, "I will do or die. Goodbye!"

Mom disappears slowly, digit by digit from the screen. Her image as a human -life -form will never be seen again, because, as she says, her role of incarnation is now over.

* * * * * *

The small, ordinary train comes to a halt slowly, without making much noise. It is early morning. The fog is dense, and it is difficult to spot the train. Only one door opens. The square light falls on the fog. Tilfo gets down, with a bouquet of the naturally looking flowers, holding In hand. He is the only one getting down here. The door closes and the light goes away.

Tilfo turns around himself to walk. The train starts and goes away slowly. Tilfo keeps on walking on the platform, in the direction opposite to the train.

After a while, the platform comes to end, and the gritty path starts. Tilfo keeps on walking for about two hundred meters. Then he turns right, to come to a big land. The grass underneath has gathered dew drops and crystals of frost. This produces a cracking sound with his feet falling on it.

He comes to his favourite place. He looks at the headstone which reads,

'Go2 lays here. A hero who sacrificed his life for the integration of the humans and machines. Born: 02.02.171 - Died: 03.02.178.'

Tilfo looks at it with a pride in his eyes.

He goes over to the gravestone and lays down a bouquet. There are hundreds of such bouquets lying all over, withered. He visits this place every day!

He kneels, closes his eyes and settles down; then opens his eyes and touches the gravestone.

Tilfo just sits there, pondering on their friendship. He cannot forget the night of celebration they had for Go2's birthday.

Go2 had walked him to the station, and had said, "I won't look good when I am old."

Tilfo sits there till the sun has risen, and the fog is cleared. The trains continue passing through the tracks nearby the memorial. Tilfo is not distracted by the sound, sight, or speed of them.

Before he leaves, he bends his knees forwards, like they used to do when they left each other – to say goodbye to his friend.

He turns and looks at the train station. It is named to Keep, his friend's memories alive. He reads the yellow letters on the board. The train station is named as, 'Come 2'.

Tilfo again feels proud of his friend's achievements.

* * * * * *

Chapter 24

One year has passed and the world is carrying on at speed, as usual. No one is interested in counting the days, except for Tilfo, Dr. Smith and the Dexan Queen.

The day that everyone has been waiting for has arrived: the ban on all three biotrains is being lifted today. Belladonna and Miss Mermaid are determined to go back to work, wanting to prove to the world that they are good workers now.

Belladonna has a new look and now appears plump, nourished, rested and energetic. She is in good humour today; after all it is the first day of shining. She has parked herself at the station, 'Fly Force' and is alone at the filling station. There are four other tracks beside her, parallel to her. She only has tanks today and is just finishing filling them.

Her friend, Miss Mermaid, has parked at a different station, away from the town, amidst farmland. It is a filling station and is called 'Dairy Maid'. She also has finished her confinement today and is like a newly dressed bride, with a new avatar. She has changed her outside colour to a spotless white and is feeling energetic, due to starting work today.

The station is quiet because there is no hustle and bustle like there is in a passenger station. There are three tracks on her left side and one on the right side. The station is filling milk, cream, clarified butter and other dairy produce into her twenty tanks. There are also some wagons, filled with farm junk. Automatic hoses carry out the filling and they run parallel to the entire track, which is north bound. The filling is almost complete and she is about to start her journey northwards to offload the goods at the subsequent stations.

All of a sudden, out of nowhere, the Dexan Queen quietly appears on the track on the right side of Miss Mermaid. The Dexan Queen is slow, confident and determined as she waits patiently on the track. She has also changed her looks and has grown bigger, her coaches are now strong, sturdy and wide. The number of coaches has increased to twenty-seven and the last two coaches are now service coaches and not for bees anymore.

Her outside colour has changed to black and the surfaces of the coaches have been replaced with granular, coarse coatings; very different from the old, shiny surface she had, once upon a time. She is standing with a powerful stance, and this time she had been waiting for the right time and place.

Miss Mermaid senses the presence of the Dexan Queen beside her, so she is cautious, and senses that something is going to happen. She becomes restless and doesn't know what to do. Her guilt does not allow her to greet the Dexan Queen and she realises that it may be the calm before a storm. She thinks it may be better to run away from an awkward situation.

She finishes her filling in a hurry and starts moving ahead. The Dexan Queen does not want to do anything at the moment. Instead, she decides to observe, watching the movements of Miss Mermaid.

Miss Mermaid sneaks away slowly and gradually starts to gather a high speed. She goes far ahead, leaving the Dexan Queen behind.

The Dexan Queen wants to play a game of a cat and mouse and lets Miss Mermaid run away a little. She then waits for a couple of decimal seconds more, before taking a slow start, deliberately letting Miss Mermaid run ahead of her on a parallel track.

Both the biotrains are now running, with one slightly ahead of the other. Miss Mermaid is more cautious and speeds up to get away from the chasing Dexan Queen.

Miss Mermaid looks around to see whether she can go onto the tracks on her left, to run away in a different direction, but there is no connection between her track and the others.

She decides to keep running faster ahead because this is the only way to leave the Dexan Queen behind.

It really is becoming a game of a cat and mouse, with Miss Mermaid racing ahead and the Dexan Queen chasing behind her. They both go a distance of forty kilometres, and pass through a couple of small stations where they are not expected or programmed to stop.

After a while, they both end up in a hilly, mountainous area where there are no stations nearby. The Dexan Queen has been waiting for them to arrive here.

Miss Mermaid now has no doubt that the Dexan Queen is chasing her and realises there must be a purpose. She thinks that if the Dexan Queen was going to attack her, why has she not done this in the first place, since attack is the best form of defence? She looks for an opportunity to attack the Dexan Queen, deciding that this is the right place and time.

Miss Mermaid decides to open fire at the Dexan Queen. Many of her wagons and tanks have side ports, covered with square flaps. She orders all of the flaps to open in one go, and instantly they all flip open upwards, and thick, wide-bore gun barrels protrude from the portals.

The Dexan Queen is running behind Miss Mermaid. She speeds and tries to catch up with her to see what she is capable of. She comes parallel to Miss Mermaid and they are both now running side by side, the Dexan Queen deliberately lagging slightly behind.

Miss Mermaid wants to do a test shot, just to see the response from the Dexan Queen and fires a ball of explosives from the last firing port. It makes a crazy echoing firing sound, because it is in between two running trains. The ball hits the wall of the black, sturdy Dexan Queen and produces a loud thudding sound. Nothing happens to damage her. Not even a scratch!

The Dexan Queen wanted this to happen. She wanted Miss Mermaid to fire at her first, so that she could make a strong case of defence for her retaliation. The Dexan Queen is well equipped with systems and also has two rows of firing ports, all guarded by invisible, camouflaged flaps. She opens the flaps of all the ports along the bottom row and gun barrels come out of the ports. She aims at the wheels of Miss Mermaid and decides the first right wheel is a good target.

For the first time in her life, the Dexan Queen fires a large, fat bullet at the wheel of Miss Mermaid. The bullet passes through an empty space in between the spokes, and nothing happens, since it only pierces the earth between the tracks. Miss Mermaid gets angry with this and starts firing through all of her ports. A series of explosive balls hit the Dexan Queen.

The Dexan Queen is prepared for the attack and has made herself stronger by fireproofing herself. A series of 'dub' sounds of is all that happens.

The trains are both running fast now. Miss Mermaid is trying to run away, while the Dexan Queen is chasing her, with determination.

* * * * * *

Meanwhile, in the central trains control room, everyone is panicking. Operators, coordinators, supervisors and managers have all become frantic.

A human -life -form operator says, "The satellite pictures show that they are both on line number BT3. Look, they are firing at each other, now! Please stop them!"

The humanoid robot supervisor replies, "Firstly, they are unstoppable and secondly, let the Dexan Queen take her revenge. We have witnessed the injustice."

A robot technician says, "And they are autonomous. They can choose their path. If we try to stop them, there will be a lot of destruction and collateral damage!"

"Yes," the human -life -form manager says. "Look, this is an opportunity for all of us to stand behind the Dexan Queen. Let us reverse the wheels of injustice."

The human -life -form operator seems convinced. "Yes, we are all behind her. She is a righteous queen and cannot do anything wrong."

Everyone in the control room now seems excited and determined. They all raise their hands in the air and shout, "Long live the Dexan Queen!"

The manager is a bit cautious and politically correct and says, "Please don't show any emotions here. We need to act."

The operator says, "Yes."

The manager orders, "Close all other lines and keep only three lines open for them. One is for Miss Mermaid to run for her life, and the other one is for our Queen. Keep the third line open for service."

"Yes, Sir."

The manager continues, "Close all the crossings on their lines and on the BT3 line. Stop all the trains on this route. Evacuate the other trains and stations along the line – and the crossings."

"Is this not bit drastic?" a sceptical robot clerk, gender type 1 asks.

"I will declare an emergency level 4 at spectrum red – and this will entitle us to do what we want to do."

Everyone again raises their hands to shout, "Long live the Dexan Queen!"

The clerk is not happy with what is happening.

* * * * * *

Back on the BT3 line, both biotrains are running speedily. They cross a bridge over a river. Miss Mermaid is running fast for her life and the Dexan Queen is still chasing her!

Miss Mermaid is now firing from all of her ports and the Dexan Queen has also opened her two rows of ports and is retaliating. The metallic sounds of bullets hitting is masked by the sound and the speed at which they are travelling. The Dexan Queen tries to use larger bullets to fire at the wheels of Miss Mermaid, but it doesn't work, because the wheels are all bullet proof.

They now pass through an empty train station. The Dexan Queen, realising that it is not easy to disable Miss Mermaid, decides to use a different tactic. She starts firing at the head unit of Miss Mermaid. Again, a metallic bang is heard. Apart from small scratches on the surface, all of the bullets fired fall like marbles.

The speed and firing of bullets are in full swing from both sides. They cross the evacuated trains standing on the lines, which are parallel to theirs.

The Dexan Queen needs to change her strategy and decides to disable Miss Mermaid by destroying her tanks and wagons. This time, she uses a rocket launcher and a big explosive, and opens the large port behind her head unit. She aims at one of the tanks and fires. The explosive hits the tank and it explodes! A huge mushroom of white milk can be seen above Miss Mermaid.

The milk is splattered everywhere and all the wagons and tanks behind the exploded tank are smeared with splashes of milk. A big trail of white is left behind on the track. The Dexan Queen, for the first time, gets pleasure from this. She remembers the hen taking revenge against the ball, in the video clip made by Tilfo.

Miss Mermaid now doubles the speed of firing at the Dexan Queen, but the Queen is clever enough to understand the strengths and weaknesses on both sides. She now targets all of the wagons and tanks one by one, by using her large bore explosive device. To do this properly, though, she has to run behind Miss Mermaid.

Many of the tanks and wagons are empty, so when they explode, they don't spill too much. Only a few tanks are filled with dairy produce and after the explosion, they leave another white trail of spilt cream and clarified butter. However, many of the tanks and the head unit are still intact.

They arrive at another empty junction, nut Miss Mermaid has been waiting for this junction, and to lead the Dexan Queen here. She has been contacting her friend and partner, Belladonna, throughout all of her endeavours.

The Belladonna is a superpower amongst biotrains; she is a war veteran, and has experience fighting wars with rebel robots. Belladonna is parked at this junction; Miss Mermaid was clever enough to lead the Dexan Queen here, at the expense of some of her losses.

Belladonna joins the speeding two trains and enters the track on the right side of the Dexan Queen, the track that was supposed to be reserved for emergency services only.

Now, the Dexan Queen realises that she is surrounded by two giants with one on each side, Miss Mermaid on her left and Belladonna on her right.

The shooting continues between the Dexan Queen and Miss Mermaid. Miss Mermaid wants to run away now as her giant friend has arrived, and because she wants to leave it to her to destroy the Dexan Queen. She speeds up again to leave, but the Dexan Queen also speeds up to match her speed. Belladonna is also chasing the Dexan Queen, and all three are travelling at a speed they have never achieved during their careers.

Belladonna is not firing anything at the moment; she is thinking and choosing her strategy. Once she makes her mind up, she decides to only open one big row of portals, on every tank. She starts firing explosives one by one.

The Dexan Queen is having explosives fired at her from both sides and, is fighting on two fronts. She continues firing explosives at Miss Mermaid, although she is not causing much harm to her. After hundred and eighty kilometres, the Dexan Queen does not have much damage, so Belladonna changes her plans and opens up her top row of portals. Barrels pop out of the portals and suddenly start squirting jets of fire at her.

On the other side, the Dexan Queen is using her reflex reactions to respond to the bombardment of jets of fire from Belladonna. She opens the row of portals on that side and starts emitting fire retardant foam, water and gas. The fumes, gases and vapours end up making the space between them invisible. The fire retardation helps to limit some of the damage and extinguishes some of the jets. However, Belladonna keeps on firing the jets, which eventually do some damage to the shunting cables between the coaches of the Dexan Queen.

The Dexan Queen continues firing retardant foam from her right side and she quickly learns Belladonna's tactics. She uses this on Miss Mermaid's side and squirts liquid petroleum at her. The Dexan Queen deliberately slows down a bit, so that the squirting covers the entire length of Miss Mermaid. She then fires a huge fireball at Miss Mermaid, which sets the entire biotrain on fire!

Miss Mermaid is a classic build and does not surrender easily. She carries on running and firing explosives, despite the fact that she is on fire. Most of her wagons and tanks are destroyed now, and her remaining parts are burning amongst the blaze.

The other side of the Dexan Queen is not very strong and her firing of guns and rockets is not touching Belladonna. The fire retardants are not working well, due to them being more of a defence than attack, and Belladonna has a thick enough structure to not allow any penetration by rockets or guns. The Dexan Queen then tries to target the wheels of Belladonna, but her wheels are fire and shockproof.

It seems that the Dexan Queen is losing, on her right side, to a very strong giant! The Dexan Queen decides to use the same trick of covering her enemy with petrol, again. She squirts a large dose of petroleum solvent at Belladonna and then fires a huge ball of fire. However, it does not do any damage to Belladonna because her entire build is made from fireproof material.

Despite this, the Dexan Queen keeps on firing explosives in the hope that at least one or two tanks can be weakened. Belladonna, however, is also using the same trick, and the Dexan Queen has to squirt the fire-retardant foam, in between. The exchange between them goes on for a long time.

The three biotrains are still running parallel to each other; although one is on fire, she is still racing along and firing, while the Dexan Queen is still doing her best to the attack from both sides. They are crossing river bridges, road bridges, crossings and stations. They arrive at the deep hilly area where the Dexan Queen used to have picnics with her son.

Belladonna has never come across a force as strong as the Dexan Queen before, so she has to change her strategy again and stops firing the explosives. The Dexan Queen is bewildered and does not understand what is going on. Has Belladonna run out of ammunition or, is it just another trick?

She soon finds out the answer to her questions. The rooftop of the second tank of the Belladonna slides down, wide open, and exposes what is hidden inside. The tank contains a heli- flyer.

The heli flyer resembles the old helicopter that was in use many centuries before but is much sleeker in size and fits easily into a tank or coach. The heli flyers are programmed now; pilots and operators are something from the past.

The heli flyer slowly takes off and rises to lift out of the tank. It hovers above the rooftop and then flies towards the Dexan Queen. All three biotrains are speeding along.

In the next couple of moments, every rooftop of the tanks of Belladonna slides down, each one harbouring a heli flyer. The heli flyers start their engines on Belladonna's order and rise above the rooftops. They hover around for a few seconds before flying towards the Dexan Queen.

There is now a row of heli flyers above the Dexan Queen, one above every coach, and they start firing fireballs downwards on the roofs of the coaches of the Dexan Queen. She is now fighting on every front, from the left and right she is getting explosives fired at her and from the top, she is receiving fire balls.

The Dexan Queen is equipped to deal this kind of attack and opens the portals on each roof. She then starts firing jets of water, retardant foam and gas, high up into the sky, which makes visibility poor for a short while.

So far, there is only really damage to Miss Mermaid, who is still running, but on fire. The Dexan Queen has incurred some damage to her connecting cables, but Belladonna is still intact and unhurt. After running for a few decimal minutes, the stock of fire retardants runs out, and there is now full visibility.

The heli flyers start firing explosives again, in an attempt to bore holes on the roof tops of the Dexan Queen's coaches, but they have not been successful so far and haven't caused her any significant damage. The last two of the Dexan Queen's coaches are only service coaches and are not equipped for fighting, or defence.

The heli flyers adopt a new technique and stop firing explosives. Instead, they throw laser beams onto the tops of the last two coaches. This manages to cause some damage to the Dexan Queen and the laser beams drill holes into the rooftop of the last two coaches. This experiment has been a success to them.

The heli flyers then send pipes into the holes and fill them with liquid petroleum to fill the coaches from the inside. They use liquid petroleum instead of gas, due to gravity and the fuel needing to travel downwards. The Dexan Queen realises what is happening and increases her speed, but it does not help, because the trains and heli flyers also increase their speed.

The Dexan Queen does not want to go further ahead to run away, since she is not bothered about her destruction. She knows there are no life -forms in her coaches, and she knows that Go2 is not there anymore, so it's a 'do or die' situation for her. She is not bothered whether she lives or dies, but she has to teach them a lesson. Speedy manoeuvres are not helping her and now they have filled the last two coaches with fuel. She is shooting in all three directions and they are all retaliating.

The last two heli flyers move backwards, fire one final fireball and fly away for good. The fireball ignites the last two coaches and they explode with a big bang! It is a massive setback for the Dexan Queen. The explosion of the last two coaches was initially just a dry run for the heli flyers. They now want to do the same thing to all of the coaches.

The Dexan Queen knows she has to do something and increases her speed, going further ahead of the two chasing trains while they are trying to catch her up. All of a sudden, she opens up the roof of her second unit, and a big pole emerges and extends upwards, towards the sky.

The pole grows about half a kilometre tall in a fraction of a decimal millisecond, and is made from a strong metal, prepared to resist any pressure or temperature. The other two biotrains do not understand what is happening. At the top end of the pole are two strong metallic nets that start to emerge sideways, similar to football nets.

The Dexan Queen suddenly slows down and within a fraction of a decimal second, the heli flyers entangle like mosquitoes in the net! They all crash down or into each other; some even collapse on the ground. The debris falls on the rooftops of both Belladonna and the Dexan Queen, and some falls onto Miss Mermaid. The falling debris on the burning Miss Mermaid then catches fire on her remaining rooftops and some of the heli flyers collapse down on the tracks behind.

Most of Miss Mermaid's tanks and wagons are burnt now and her shooting frequency has also gone down, so she slows down and slumps to a halt on the track – completely spent and immobile. This means at least one victory for the Dexan Queen!

There are now only the two biotrains left running and shooting at each other. Belladonna has lost her major armaments in the heli flyers and decides to bring something else out of some different portals. She now attacks the Dexan Queen with laser beams coming from the portals, since she has learnt how well that laser beams work.

After firing for few decimal minutes, Belladonna realises that the Dexan Queen is stronger than she thinks, since the metal and material of the sides of her coaches are not melting, despite the onslaught.

Belladonna is fully aware of the ethics and logistics of war because she has fought in wars before. She knows that a biotrain is not allowed to directly attack the tracks of any other vehicle, even on the battlefield: a principle agreed by all biotrains and the railway authorities, as part of their ethics in war and peace.

Belladonna is a different breed, however, and it would be insulting to the animals to call her animalistic. She forgot about ethics a long time ago, and does not believe in norms, regulations, religion or laws, considering herself above any law.

She tries a dirty game now, and speeds up, further along the track, firing explosives and lasers onto the tracks of the Dexan Queen. One side of the track is damaged by the blast, getting bent and buried in the ground. The Dexan Queen never expected this to happen but applies her e-brakes, coming to a halt with a screeching sound and the friction of her wheels against the track produces sparks.

Some of her wheels on the right side come off the track and get half buried in the ground, still running. The firing of shots and lasers from the Belladonna continues, relentlessly. The Dexan Queen does not have much choice now; her ammunition supply is coming to an end and she only has a few explosives left. As she always says: do or die.

She decides to run until she gets to Lakemore station. Her speed has decreased since her wheels on one side are on the track, while the other side is on the ground, churning up soil. She keeps on running slowly, almost as if she is limping to the station. Belladonna has slowed down to match the speed of the Dexan Queen, so that she can shoot at her.

Belladonna is having fun, watching the Dexan Queen crippled in pain and she gleefully continues her on-going attack. The Dexan Queen has now stopped firing anything at the Belladonna: her main aim is to remain alive, until she reaches Lakemore hills. Belladonna is getting pleasure from destroying the Dexan Queen, while the Dexan Queen is powerless.

After a few decimal minutes, they both pass behind the 'Come 2' station on the right, where Go2's memorial is on their left. The Dexan Queen has reached her destination, the Lakemore mountain range.

A flashing red light can be seen on one of the screens in the Dexan Queen's head unit, showing a warning: 'There are only two explosives available now. Change the strategy'.

The Dexan Queen now decides to play the same game Belladonna has played, and fires one of the explosives at the track Belladonna has just passed, behind her enemy. The track is destroyed, ensuring that Belladonna cannot go backwards now.

The Dexan Queen stops here, exhausted and almost destroyed. Her wheels are not rotating properly and she is tilting to the side, towards Belladonna. She has to withdraw the pole because she doesn't want it to fall on the innocent trees around them, so she uses the little bit of energy she has left to retract the mast and pole, bringing it down. The right-hand net falls on Belladonna and when released from the pole, the left side falls on the Dexan Queen beside her. The nets fall with some entangled heli -flyers, and some burning debris. The trees are far away from the tracks, so they are saved.

Belladonna also stops, for two reasons. Firstly, she has the burden of the net over her rooftop, and secondly, she wants to take pleasure in seeing the Dexan Queen hurt, destroyed and ready to surrender.

The Dexan Queen has only one explosive left now, which she fires straight at the track ahead of the Belladonna, and with a bang, it successfully destroys the track! Belladonna now reverses backwards only to realise that the track behind her is destroyed. In a fit of fury, she fires a load of explosives at the Dexan Queen, which weakens the Dexan Queen further, and she becomes motionless, quiet and wrecked.

Belladonna feels victorious, despite the fact that there is a heavy load on her roof and she has nowhere to go. She is still confident that she will receive technical help to get the weight off her, and have the track repaired, so that she can return to pavilion with pride. She keeps thinking about how she can get away, even when the tracks are damaged in both directions.

She busies herself making enquiries with the authorities about repairing the track.

The Dexan Queen is lying motionless, while Belladonna is absorbed in contacting technicians to repair the track.

The purpose of the Dexan Queen in bringing Belladonna to this spot has been served. Lakemore hill is a hilly area on the right side of her and the forest is where the Dexan Queen had released the trained, genetically modified bees. The bees are now living a peaceful life in their newly formed hives. But they come out of their hives when they sense the presence of the Dexan Queen – since she is their queen too.

They see that the Dexan Queen is there and is in a moribund state, and they know what they have to do next.

* * * * * *

One bee comes out of her hive and flies over to Belladonna, who is waiting patiently for the technicians to arrive. The bee goes to the wall of her wagon, and sits on it, trying to inject her proboscis into Belladonna's wall. The material of the wagon wall is tough, but the bee's proboscis can squirt enzymes that can biodegrade any synthetic material, which is what they are genetically modified to do. The bee secretes her lytic enzymes onto the wall and it rapidly degrades and damages the material, until a hole is created.

Belladonna is aware of what is going on and fully understands biological warfare, although she brushes the idea off, thinking that a single bee and one tiny hole will not make any difference. But gradually, other bees start flying towards the Belladonna and sit on her walls, secreting enzymes through their proboscises to make holes. The enzymes also damage her network of sensing probes and terminals, numbing her in a similar way to receiving an injection of local anaesthetic.

The process of creating holes continues, unbeknown to her. All the Belladonna sees is that a swarm of bees surround her and she isn't even aware that they settle on her. Neither does she sense that she is getting billions of holes drilled into her walls.

Meanwhile, the Dexan Queen stands, broken and still, as if slumbering.

A couple of decimal hours pass by and Belladonna is still surrounded by the bees, busy using their biomaterial and making a humming sound. Belladonna keeps thinking that she is sweet like nectar, which must be why she is attracting bees. For the first time ever, someone is cheating her and this time it is a small creature life-form. Millions of bees cling onto her walls, wagons, head unit and shunting cables. It is only much later that Belladonna realises that she has been destroyed by one hole after another. She tries to move away, to get off the track, but she has become so brittle – a lacework of barely connected threads of metal and synthetic material – that most of her structure starts to fracture and collapse.

The bees knew that to kill a snake, they needed to destroy the head first – so, the head unit, initially surrounded by millions of bees, falls first. They then move onto the remaining structure and destroy it all. Belladonna, a strong, evil force in modern civilisation, dies a painless death, without even knowing that she was dying. It takes time, because it a precise and slow process, but millions of bees work hard to break down the gigantic structure. When they have finished, all that is left is, sludge of plastic and biomaterial, slowly flowing around the track.

The bees go back to their hives.

The Dexan Queen remains wounded, dilapidated, destroyed and wrecked, but her programmes' spirit cannot be dampened. A spark of life remains, flickering into a flame of victory. It was do or die. And she did.

She may have to undergo a criminal trial, for which she is fully prepared. What is important is that Go2's death has been avenged, and since she was attacked on numerous fronts, she hopes to be vindicated, this time. For the future, she needs to be rejuvenated, recharged, recycled, redesigned, restructured, refurbished, refined, rewheeled and refreshed, to lead a new life. She wants to cater to civilisation again and to get back on the track of values, service, duty and sacrifice.

About the Author

Dr Fy is a pen name taken by a senior medical consultant working in the National Health Service in the UK.

Dr Fy deals with physical and emotional agony every day, as a part of his work and see how modern science utilises gadgets and equipment to relieve human suffering. The interaction of humans and gadgets is very intriguing and Dr Fy tries to capture this concept in this title.

Dr Fy is an author of many medical textbooks but has put his heart and mind in penning this fiction.